The Last Song of Manuel Sendero

ALSO BY THE AUTHOR

NONFICTION

How to Read Donald Duck

The Empire's Old Clothes

FICTION

Widows

The Last Song of Manuel Sendero

Ariel Dorfman

TRANSLATED BY GEORGE R. SHIVERS
WITH THE AUTHOR

Viking

VIKING
Viking Penguin Inc., 40 West 23rd Street,
New York, New York 10010, U.S.A.
Penguin Books Ltd, Harmondsworth,
Middlesex, England
Penguin Books Australia Ltd, Ringwood,
Victoria, Australia
Penguin Books Canada Limited, 2801 John Street,
Markham, Ontario, Canada L3R 1B4
Penguin Books (N.Z.) Ltd, 182–190 Wairau Road,
Auckland 10, New Zealand

First published in 1987 by Viking Penguin Inc.
Published simultaneously in Canada

Originally published in Spanish as *La Ultima Canción de Manuel Sendero* by Siglo XXI Editores, Mexico.

LIBRARY OF CONGRESS CATALOGING IN PUBLICATION DATA
Dorfman, Ariel.
The last song of Manuel Sendero.
Translation of: La última canción de Manuel Sendero.
I. Title.
PQ8098.14.07U413 1987 863 86-40266
ISBN 0-670-80214-X

Printed in the United States of America by
The Book Press, Brattleboro, Vermont
Set in Bodoni Book
Designed by Amy Hill

This book is
for the children of Rodrigo and Joaquín,
for the grandchildren of María Angélica,
for the remote descendants of my parents.

I wish to express my appreciation to the Wilson Center, an affiliate of the Smithsonian Institution, for the opportunity to spend a year in Washington, D.C. During that stay, I was offered the calm and the resources to write a considerable portion of this novel. The rest I owe to my friends and family, who helped me to carry it forward and to finish it under less favorable circumstances.

This book is about frontiers and how to pass through them without being destroyed. My thanks, therefore, to my editor at Viking Penguin, Nan Graham, who thought it possible for my words and my characters, all of them foreign to English-language readers, to reach an audience that needs to know about Manuel and the babies, about the Davids and the Felipes, of this world. She worked loyally and with great imagination to bring our message to other countries.

Well, as a result
of pain, there are some
who are born, others grow, still others die,
and there are others who are born and do not die, and others
who are not born nor do they die (they are the majority)

—CÉSAR VALLEJO

He who would be born must break a world.

—HERMANN HESSE

CONTENTS

PART I

Incarnations

INSIDE

And now, as if we were all dead, as if we could do nothing anymore to make people believe us, they've started to deny the whole story, they've already started.

Grown-ups like their prologues nice and tidy.

Begin at the beginning, they say. Hold it, children. Not so fast, they say. When did all this begin?

It began with Grandfather, if you have to begin with somebody. But now that they seem to have forgotten it may be better to begin with Grandfather's undeniable and very own father, Manuel Sendero, the day they released him from the concentration camp. It's true that even that may not satisfy them. The idea is spreading that Manuel Sendero never sang that last song, that nobody ever heard it, a time may come when they'll be murmuring that Sendero himself never existed. Grown-ups need proof of everything, sad to say.

Manuel Sendero himself may be partly to blame for these doubts. He was an adult too, after all. And if his mother had told him that his son had not yet been born, he wouldn't have believed it either. Who could have believed that a year and a half after the child had been conceived by him in the warm and devouring inner alleys of Doralisa, the kid had still not made its appearance into this world, was still waiting there, inside, refusing to come out? . . . So Manuel's mother didn't say a word to him, that day when he stepped into the supposed freedom of the warm spring air, just as she hadn't told him about it on the day three months before when the military allowed a first visit by relatives.

But there were things she couldn't keep from him. She had come with the firmest intentions of hiding everything, her brain bursting with convoluted explanations that would justify Doralisa's absence on this day of all days, when all the other prisoners were watching their own spouses filing eagerly in. Manuel Sendero couldn't speak a word, and he certainly couldn't sing a solitary note at that stage of the story, but he had saved enough urgency in the fingertips of his eyes to press his mother, to corner her look by look until she finally had to confess what had happened to Doralisa. She didn't say a word about the baby, in other words, about me, said Grandfather, but she couldn't very well ignore the fact that Manuel's wife had not come to see him, nor would she be there on the day of his release, across the street with the other women. It may have been the clumsy way in which the old woman broached the matter, or it may have been because even if her son had lost his voice, he had increased, by way of compensation, the quota of stubbornness that had always been in his character—whatever the reason, the fact is that Manuel Sendero refused to believe his own mother.

He couldn't question the other prisoners directly, but when his friend Skinny—that's what they called him in those days—was also arrested, he forced him to find out about Doralisa, to go round asking the others about her. Yes, Doralisa, a tall woman, sparkling eyes, a fiery woman, she always wore her clothes tight, clinging to her the way robes cling to images of saints, she always looked like she was naked, impossible not to recognize her. Doralisa? No, they would shake their heads, no one of that description. They'd remember someone like that.

So Papa thought they had killed her. Doralisa was such a hothead, he thought, she had probably gone out the night of the military takeover, knife in hand, to cut a few policemen's throats, to throw stones at the trucks brimming with soldiers, to spit insults at the officers. When she heard that he had been arrested, she would have done that—Manuel was sure. He needed proof, however, adult that he was, and when Skinny swore that he was going to escape from that concentration camp, Manuel Sendero made him promise to get news back to him about the whereabouts of Doralisa. An obviously senseless promise, because even if he were to succeed in getting out of the place, it would then be impossible, as well as stupid, for him to try to get back in. He had dug a tunnel under the walls—such a narrow tunnel that only he, who in high school had been called Toothpick, could fit in it—swallowing and digesting bits of earth, piece by piece. The guards never suspected anyone could be planning such a harebrained adventure. In fact, Skinny's bouts of indigestion were an integral part of his scheme, in view of the fact that the medical assistants who attended the prisoners certified that indeed something very strange was going on in his digestive tract, especially in his small intestine, which because of the extreme gauntness of the detainee in question was so small as to be almost nonexistent, and it was that which gave him a ten-hour advantage over his pursuers. They thought he was ill and taking aspirin, the universal remedy and the only one prescribed for any illness, when in fact his squalid silhouette was already appearing out of the tiny hole on the other side of the nocturnal wall.

Skinny kept part of his promise. He went to see the old woman. "Manuel thinks Doralisa's dead," he confided to her in that first conversation, and was astounded when she told him the same thing she would tell Manuel some months later, when the authorities, having decided to recognize that all those people had been captured and were in custody, finally permitted visitors.

"My daughter-in-law is not dead," the old woman said to Skinny. I listened to her, Grandfather told us, through the walls of Mama's belly, even though she was in the other room. "She's just . . . indisposed."

Skinny was immediately able to go and verify for himself if this was true. But Manuel Sendero, months later, couldn't even touch his own mother to ascertain if she was feeding him a pious lie. A guard made sure that prisoners and their visitors maintained a meter's distance on each side of the barbed-wire barrier, so their most intimate concerns had to be discussed in a loud voice, as if they were haggling over the price of fish. The different voices darted through the air like worn, bedraggled birds. Grandmother could read the disbelief in his face.

"She's not even hurt," the old woman continued, unwillingly. "Not even a scratch," and quickly added: "And the baby too." Which—take my word for it—was more true than she imagined. And eluding the clean demand in those still musical eyes that were pleading for information, a photo, some anecdote about his firstborn, she deflected Manuel's disquiet by telling him about his brother's death. They had come to do him in right there, at the door of the house. They had ordered him to lie facedown, but his legs wouldn't obey such an infamous order and refused to bend. On your knees, you son of a bitch. Uncle looked down in surprise; his legs were still as straight as a pair of poplar trees in a storm. They threatened him with their revolvers, but Uncle made no response. Since they were going to kill him anyway, he preferred to die standing up, thank you. The lieutenant in charge of the operation acceded and right there in the doorway, knocking over a pot of geraniums in the process, they shot him in the neck.

And what about Doralisa? Far from running out brandishing a butcher knife, Doralisa had not even hurled the petal of a biting or contemptuous word at them. The only thing she did was go out to pick up the flowerpot. They had come for her husband's older brother, the immortal uncle, the one who had consoled Manuel during the nights of his fatherless childhood, swearing to him that death didn't exist, that if it dared to show up here, we'd give it a good scare, kid, and Doralisa managed to do nothing more than straighten the damn flowerpot and only a couple of hours later she had gone off to—

"She was afraid," the old woman would explain months later, as they made their way home along dusty and abandoned avenues, taking his arm and pinching it from time to time to remind him that at least she was there at his side, perhaps to remind him that he was alive. For the first time his wife had known what fear was, son, and she just went dry—and the old woman raised a hand as if to emphasize her opinion.

The guard had interrupted her explanations that first day. "Let's go, lady," he had said, and before that: "It's time," unwisely laying a palm and five fingers on the old woman's shoulder. Although his voice wasn't all that rough. "Let's go, lady," the man insisted, and there was the old woman, her hand extended in the air like the extremity of a wrinkled statue. Her voice came out small, half sigh and half imprecation, a low voice, zigzagging and arrowlike, which the soldier could never have heard even if he had been closer to her than Manuel. It was like a bee buzzing in his ear. And then she told Manuel what had happened, adding in a whisper, "It's not her fault, poor thing."

The buzzing stopped, the swarm of light and age that was Grandmother went off with the soldier, Papa's fingers, our Manuel Sendero's fingers, pressed hard against the wire that was as cold and distant as a star.

How do we know all this?

Very simple. I found it out, we all did, largely from the mouth of my grandfather, our old granddaddy himself, and he was unquestionably present in the veritable middle of the story from beginning to end. It's true that he hadn't been born yet, but undoubtedly nobody was closer to the events than he was, there was no one who was more involved and paid more attention. After all, we're talking about his own birth, a unique and rather decisive event in anyone's life and especially in my grandfather's case—if you'll pardon our self-centeredness—because the old man had been waiting too many months beyond the conventional nine and, in view of the fact that all the predictions suggested that the possibilities of his receiving a real, genuine birth were close to zero, and that—to top it all—in those days the first infant rebellion was launched and about to fail, the baby traversed those years with his heart inclined toward what was happening in the outside world, pushing with all the strength his half-soul could muster—his soul wasn't finished yet—trying, from that grotto of miracles that was Doralisa, from beyond the savory rumba walls of his mother, to be granted the gift, which he also considered his natural right, to be finally born. A better witness is unlikely. It's evident that his perspective—since you insist on interrupting me so punctiliously, so exactingly—was somewhat blocked by the discomfort of his position and that the fetus perceived things with a certain twisted abandon and fragile distance, but neither can it be ignored that the hysteria of his confinement sharpened some of his faculties and exaggerated others, and that, in addition, he succeeded in setting up a vast and buzzing information network in his own defense, a secret service that was so secret and so efficient that no one ever knew it existed. Besides, he was able to investigate, after the fact, the strange circumstances surrounding his desire for seeing the light, even managing to reconstruct some of the least known details of the life of his father, my great-grandfather, our Manuel, something of a father, grandfather, great-great-greatest-grandfather to all who dare to keep on having children in times like these.

Ah, yes, Grandfather returned decades later. Some would object that *return* is not the proper word, since he had never before set foot on this soil, but let's leave that kind of quibbling to the dictionary lovers. If there ever was a return, that was one. And no one ever had to wait so long. It wasn't enough that he had spent his whole existence dreaming about that land into which his parents had barely been born—he had to camp for six more weeks in a neighboring state, so near the border that he could almost touch the sky of that country, he could almost reach out and touch that familiar, even friendly sky, with the tips of his fingers, like a blind man, because its soft, blue interlude was like the color of the world observed from the maternal refuge of Doralisa. It had been six weeks since the second rebellion, the definitive one, had begun, and still those irresponsible fools, those other babies, kept him there without giving him the go-ahead, still unable to agree on the suitability of that implausible mission or even on whether he was the best person to carry it out, when it was perfectly clear that he was the only one on earth who could do it; they wouldn't let him cross that mountain range that he knew about only from hearsay. When he finally did cross it, he thought it would be as friendly and as intimate as the sea-sky, because for decades he had heard mothers murmur to their children to put mountains in all their schoolchild drawings, but the crossing turned out to be narrow and threatening, the mountains, as high as a woman, as long as the extended thighs of a woman in heat, but narrow and suffocating, totally different from what he had imagined based on the watercolor landscapes. It was only the relief of that abundant fresh air, of smelling for the first time the odors that had come to him before through an intermediary womb and person, which restored his self-confidence. This was the land he had been exiled from, and he was so happy to inhabit it and so sure that everyone would help him that he asked the first man that he met on the street if this wasn't the most beautiful country in the world, if he didn't like it, as if that man were a tourist, newly arrived from the airport, and as if the son of Manuel Sendero were a taxi driver or the owner of the whole thing, and the man smiled at him, as if it were unimportant that they both were slightly crazy, and said, of course, the best in the universe, someday we'll have government officials as clean as our fruit and our sea. From that answer, Grandfather deduced that the speaker was an ally from whom he could coax instructions to orient himself, how to get to a street named—but the man went on, anger in his voice, a government as good as the women who are the apples of our eye, for that matter as good as the apples we eat, yes, sir, a really fine government. And if he wanted to see, come to the protest march.

"Protest?" Grandfather demanded, already interested. "What kind of protest?"

"Don't you know that not one baby has been born in this country in six weeks?" the man answered in disbelief. "Don't you know that?"

Faithful ambassador and representative of the unborn that he was, how could Grandfather not know? How could it fail to satisfy him that at last—in contrast to the first rebellion thirty years before, which no one had paid any attention to—the alarm and dismay of the populace would facilitate his mission?

He hurried on because he was sure that the adult he was looking for would not miss a march, any march, but especially a protest march. In that, at least, he was right. After following the directions—go eight blocks, climb three flights—he found himself face to face with Manuel Sendero's best friend, Skinny in person, ready to slip away downtown to give voice to a rage that was no less vehement for the meager frame of the man. Grandfather thought: I'll go with him, great. In that, however, he was wrong. Each of them would leave, kids, but they left separately. They were never to see each other again.

OK. We admit it. They quarreled. Let's put it this way: their versions of the past didn't entirely coincide. This was Grandfather's first journey, and, like a woman in her first love affair, he insisted on unconditional commitment. But those of you who are frivolous and meticulous should beware of attempting to sabotage our tale by exhibiting these disagreements. Eduardo may declare that the song attributed to Manuel Sendero is only one among many splendid legends that the people have woven on the shores of their memory, an indemnity for an eternity of frustrations. But Skinny would never have said anything like that. Never. That same afternoon he spoke of Manuel Sendero's last song, confirmed that he had heard it. It makes no difference that there aren't any proofs or traces left, he said, for a moment we felt it was our own youth-voice speaking through him. The things you do out of love for your fellowmen aren't done for a place in a history book or so someone can put up a statue in your honor. The only page my buddy Sendero wanted was a page in the hearts of his people. Sentimental bastard, Skinny was.

But we quarreled anyway. Skinny was an adult, and so, like any ordinary adult, he demanded that I begin at the beginning. And later—playing his role to the hilt—he became skeptical. What are your sources? he asked. Where did you find all this out? Who told you?

In the years to come, you kids, children, grandchildren, and great-grandchildren, you kids sitting here openmouthed and umbilically at my feet, every time I start at the beginning, like I am asked to—every time I try to tell what happened to Manuel Sendero on his way home that day (which according to know-nothing meteorologists was the first day of spring)—I am accused of raving. At my age, they actually dare to imply that I am lying. As if it were a lie, the business of the Caballero, the elevator, my meeting the blind woman again, the nights when our immortal uncle came to see us—all of it. They have their reasons, they must have, Eduardo certainly has his, for doubting so many amazing events. It's not enough to explain that those were different times, that back then, in the days of the first rebellion, things happened differently. They laugh at that sort of explanation. And I also realize that it's not enough to present the testimony of my companions who, from the watchtowers and nests of other wombs, from behind the transparent curtains of maternity fashions, observed and reported everything without anyone even noticing it. We had an information network, captained by the twins, that today would be the envy of any intelligence agency.

But I have got a witness, a bona fide one, as they say. You know, the kind who can go into a court, raise a hand, and swear to tell everything so help him God. I met him half an hour after speaking with Skinny, kids, I let my unhappy feet carry me to that street corner toward which my father and his mother had been walking so many years before. Papa pecked the author of his days fleetingly on the cheek, as if she hadn't been waiting for him patiently since dawn, and they set out for home. His plan—if you could call it one—was absurd. He thought that it would be enough to face Doralisa, talk to her tenderly, like lovers do, and everything would be fine, back to normal again. Absurd because, to spell it out clearly, Papa couldn't even whisper one of those words. He had become a mute.

He may have forgotten the desolate climate in his throat because the sun was too gentle on his body, making the air dizzy with pleasure, making the country for a moment like the one all of you would like to cover from stem to stern with your jumping toes—dear children of my freedom—even though you don't really understand what freedom costs, what we have to pay in order to be free. He may have thought, intoxicated by the air, that there could be a way into Doralisa's dreams through the back door, through the mattress where for years—and I insist on this, even if the censors refuse to allow such words to reach an audience so young and innocent—they had pushed their mutual exploration beyond the limits of the sacramental to the very frontiers of what human veins can endure, yes, Manuel Sendero probably thought he could wake her up.

Poor, my poor mama. You wouldn't have awakened then, even if Papa had come in with a drunken serenade, a tango, an orchestra behind him. You would open your eyes only once every twenty-four hours, like clockwork, at six o'clock in the evening, to take those pills, swallowing them without water, and then you'd snuggle up in the pillow again, sunken in the innocence of your twentieth month of pregnancy, falling more and more into your bedclothes, barely breathing, a kind of sweetness still apparent in your expression, only the whites of your eyes showing when Manuel raised your eyelid—as if some dark frog from the fairy tales you never told me, the ones you might still tell me someday, had stolen the pupil and the iris and maybe even the eyeball itself—never eating, never drinking, not even dreaming, or so your mother-in-law supposed, though how she could know that is anybody's guess, Mama, with the mountain range inside you completely empty except, of course, for the baby, crater without a comet, empty if it hadn't been for the baby crouching there and conspiring and smiling.

"Completely, absolutely asleep," the old woman had whispered that day before the soldier pushed her aside. And now, on the way home, added: "It was that man," she said. "The Caballero, that devil."

Absorbed as he was in his mother's monologue, Manuel Sendero picked up the noise of the vehicle buzzing along the street behind him. It was an army jeep. My witness, decades later, when I went to that street corner and asked him to describe the scene, told me that he had noticed it, and also Papa and Grandmother walking along. You may object, children, throw out objections from your perversely rational minds, mesmerized by algebra and other Eduardian stupidities that sterilize the thought processes, but that man, whose newsstand had been on that corner for ages, also saw what the old woman saw. And, if many years later he didn't confirm my version entirely, there's an explanation for that too.

My witness did see the army jeep. As for Manuel, he didn't need eyes in the back of his head to know what it was, what model, why it was there. He had had ample opportunity, all of the prisoners had, to have that sound indelibly stamped in his and their memory from the nights when those jeeps could be heard from far off first and then passing by the cell, coming from far away and then braking in front of the barbed wire. Now, in the outside world, where too many horizons were piling up—I know what that phobia is, that fear of an open and pale sky—Papa understood what that roar might mean. Rumors had been circulating about the fate that awaited some political prisoners, once they were freed, according to the defense lawyers. Outside, a friendly automobile with a driver awaited them, and an occupant in the backseat who offered them cigarettes, a good brand. The prisoners would never be seen again. To those who came for information, the authorities showed smiling documents, signatures, seals, everything as it should be, everything in order. The prisoners had been granted conditional freedom. They told wives and mothers to check at home—in their homes—and to come back again next week. Papa's body got tenser and tenser as the jeep drew nearer. After so many months of being locked up, you don't need to tell me about how every noise was like a slap in the face to him, even the playful breeze a threat. He could hardly resist the need to turn around. He kept trying to focus his attention somewhere else, up the street, on a woman of opulent breasts who was watching the whole scene from her balcony in the next block; he recorded that face with its sunken eyes and cheeks and went on walking as though nothing was wrong and then he heard the brakes.

"Hey, you," a voice hissed.

Slowly, as if he were climbing a hill, as if he were pressing the hump out of a back, he turned his head, and contemplated that voice that had assumed the body of a sergeant.

"Child, child," moaned the old woman that night to a sleeping Doralisa, and I shivered inside listening to her, "he had a machine gun in his hand, a huge dog with him, and there were other soldiers."

"I'm not talking to you," the sergeant explained to Manuel almost calmly. "I mean him . . ."

It was only then that Manuel Sendero's gaze could sweep every nook and cranny of the street and he realized that, besides the wide-eyed woman with the melon breasts, they were not alone there. A little farther up the street a bakery delivery man was pedaling his bicycle. And still farther up, on the opposite corner, a newspaper vendor was watching the encounter out of the corner of his eye. That was me, sir. Of course I can describe what happened. I saw the whole thing. This is the first I knew about its being Manuel Sendero, I didn't identify him at the time, but if you say so.

The sergeant raised and leveled the aim of his vocal cords.

"Hey, you son of a bitch. You there, baker-boy, I'm talking to you."

But listen to me, children of my grandchildren, that fellow paid no attention. Deaf, irresponsible, carefree, he just kept on pedaling. The wind was with him, the bicycle was a jewel, and he was anxious to put distance between himself and the scent of jeep, bullet grease, and sergeants, to cast off with his little boat laden with bread fresh from the oven and to sail, his shirt unfurled whitely behind him, down the street. Like the first kick of a game, a ball dribbled Houdinilike through the defense line, like a winning goal, a ball solidly placed in the net—yeah, that's right, our newspaper vendor was a soccer fan and had a mania for sportscasting every event, even this cycling one, in terms of his favorite sport—that's the way it was, the bicycle grew wings, so to speak, whistled, and took flight.

According to persons worthy of confidence, it was then that Manuel heard or thought he heard voices nearby, something like a crowd whispering something, like before, just a few years before, when there were so many songs in his throat and it was just a question of turning on the tap and the music flowed like water.

The water, the voices of children.

"Voices?" the news vendor asked dubiously. "Children?" He came out of his kiosk, the same one he had occupied for forty years, and looked down the street. Begging your pardon, but I really don't remember any voice except the soldier-boy's. It made you feel like shouting for joy, cheering the goal on, you might say, that bicycle was coming along so beautifully. But nobody would have dared do that—cheer, I mean. You know how fear is.

I changed the subject. His fear had made him forget those voices which I knew warmed Papa's throat like a band of angels. "So the bike was coming real fast?" I asked him, just to say something.

"Down center field," he whispered solemnly.

The soldiers didn't wait. The sergeant released the safety on his gun. He wasn't going to give the cyclist another chance to disobey, kids of my flesh, my little heart-readers. He fired point-blank.

For one interminable instant the voices of the slumbering children, now totally shocked, froze over. I myself, who knows how many blocks from there, was shaken in my sanctuary and must have given a kick in protest, because Doralisa groaned. There was no place to run, no place to take refuge. The noise of the motor, the screech of the tires, the explosion of bullets, the barking of the dog, filled every corner of that abused and icy space. Even the scent of spring in the air was canceled out. And they wanted me to come out, man, to be directly penetrated by that explosion, without Mama in between. For that you want to go out, Croupy? I whispered, as soon as I could make myself heard, to one of the children who, according to the twins, was showing signs of weakening, who had argued in a raspy and musty voice, hence his nickname—Croupy—that it was time to make the crossing, to follow Eduardo, to be born. For that? In another fifteen years or so, Croupy, you or I could be the one delivering the bread and this sergeant or his nephew could be waiting for me, will be waiting for you, to ambush us in the street. In fact—and the idea came to me like a black placenta from the twins, I didn't think of it myself—someday we could end up growing up and becoming the sergeant himself, pulling the trigger against one of our own. Is that what you want, Croupy? Is that the set of alternatives you want to be left with—pull the trigger or get the bullet? Is that what you want?

"A tremendous uproar," the newspaper vendor said.

Manuel felt corralled, backed against an invisible display window, and hung up to dry like an Instamatic photo. The bicycle, on the other hand, kept on advancing jubilantly. An animal; it was just like an animal. It swayed first toward the curb, then incredibly it righted itself and, swinging, its wheels spinning and dancing, its pedals chasing the shadow of the shoes, it was an animal that took its rider in tow in the middle of the desert, as if nothing serious had happened, and the distributor of bread was only resting for a few minutes, his head and chest bent confidently over the handlebars. While the rebellious machine followed its reckless course farther, farther, farther, and nobody could stop it.

The sergeant took aim, this time at the bicycle itself.

"Stop, damn you," the newspaper vendor says he shouted.

Before the sergeant could fire a second time, the young man started to come apart; like a small avalanche he slid from the seat. His hands still clutched metal, but one of his feet was halfway tangled in the spokes of a wheel. We heard something that sounded more like a dry farewell hymn than a cracking of bones and flesh, but the fact is that the bicycle slipped to one side, hesitated, finally fell over, scattering the bread over the pavement as if it were a corpse.

In a moment Manuel Sendero caught his breath. The colors of the world came back, along with the stirring of the breeze and the perfume of the spring buds. Once again he had the sensation that someone was telling the end of a tale, that some voice was spelling out a story, although the exact syllables were incomprehensible, just babble, something that hangs in the air. He couldn't attribute much importance to such a fleeting idea, and he shoved it to the back of his mind. He took his mother's arm and they crossed to the other side of the street. He didn't want to cast even a second glance at the scene. Now the soldiers were getting out of the jeep, they were tearing the bread to pieces, first with their feet, then with their bayonets, finally with their hands. The only one who was paying any attention to the dead man was the dog, who was sniffing at him with a certain annoyed tenderness.

"Don't look, son," the old woman said. "Don't get involved."

They continued walking toward the corner as if they were on a Sunday afternoon stroll. That's the way the newspaper vendor describes it. But the truth is I didn't recognize Manuel Sendero. Begging your pardon, sir, I don't doubt your word. But the person who walked by that day doesn't look anything like the picture of Sendero that's on the cover of my record album. No, I don't have the record anymore, nor the cover. All that was lost. They destroyed it, sir. Of course, if you say that's who it was, who am I to contradict you?

"I'm not going to look," the old woman wisely announced. "I'm going to keep on as if nothing had happened."

But Manuel couldn't contain himself. As if Doralisa were the one who had been dumped out on the street or in a mirror, with the same sick curiosity with which he would have attended his own funeral, he turned his head and viewed the scene.

There are no longer any witnesses to what he saw. The old woman kept on going. The newspaper vendor closed his eyes to deceive his own fear. And the woman? What about that opulent, magnificent, and very pregnant woman on her balcony? They murdered her a year later, we don't know where. Of course her daughter is still around, the one who observed everything that happened, who then purred it all to us from out of the depths of her mother there on the balcony, the daughter that woman gave birth to, sent forth into light and touch and scent and sound, with great fortune, just a few months or days before her own death. I spoke to her, if I didn't speak to her afterward, to that beloved child with the sunken cheeks, to that future Pamela of mine, I told her everything just as she had described it to us twenty or thirty years earlier, just as I describe it to you now, and even though she had forgotten it, as all those who are born forget, she did not deny it. If you say so, she answered calmly, touching my lips with her hand. She believed me, not because it was she who had witnessed it or remembered it, but because I was the one telling it.

Skinny, on the other hand, was not going to have such unilateral consideration, when it came to me. I stopped him before he went downstairs on his way to the demonstration. I had been able to identify him immediately: his sad, unmistakable figure, his voice as soft as a baby's bottom, his flutelike strides, how I would've loved to see him spread out his arms in welcome. But I held myself in, and I only introduced myself as one of Doralisa's long-lost nephews, I was here on her behalf, which wasn't exactly a lie, a distant relative, interested in finding out some facts about Manuel Sendero for a definitive biography, taking advantage of the fact that the babies' strike was a bit of news which was worthy of attention from the international magazine for which I supposedly worked. That was the story that, to my sorrow, circumstances would force me to go on using in the days ahead. I can trust Skinny, I'd told the Supreme Council of the Unborn before I left. He's so skinny his backbone is shaking hands with his navel, can you believe it?

He's become almost invisible just to trick all the hunger and the repression. He'll be the key to having our demands heard by the authorities. But in spite of that prediction, my experience was that people never believe anything from a newcomer, so, to cover myself, I refused to reveal my true and clandestine identity to him right away.

And I had no monopoly on suspicion.

"How can we confirm your relationship with Doralisa?" Skinny inquired, nevertheless ushering me into a room that was hardly bigger than a closet. As small as it was, he fitted into it with room to spare.

If my ears had been prepared before by the hesitations of the doubting newspaper vendor, at that point I wouldn't have told Skinny my version of Papa's first day of freedom as proof of my genealogy. But what better demonstration was there that I was a member of the family? Could anyone else repeat the legend the way I could? I began to unravel the tale, while I gauged his belief or disbelief by his expression and his gestures, waiting for the moment when he would offer me the welcoming handshake, when he would realize who I was. He shook his head affirmatively a few times at first, he stiffened when I mentioned the bicycle, and he was as tense as a fiddle string when I insisted that Manuel had thought he heard voices that day; he cleared his throat, obviously upset, when I came to the part where Papa turned around.

"And what was it my old friend Manuel saw exactly?"

Where the bread had fallen, crumbs were bouncing in all directions, blue crumbs, red ones, some yellow ones, like lemon drops; the crumbs were like the shining eyes of the dolls and teddy bears that keep us company in the dark when our parents turn out the lights, green and violet crumbs, bouncing and rolling among the soldiers' boots, trying to fall far beyond the reach of the sergeant, who held them up at eye level like someone examining a manuscript. I didn't tell Skinny, much less the newspaper vendor, what the twins had said on hearing that faithful account from the pregnant balcony: whoever eats one of those crumbs, they expounded in their most evangelizing and once-upon-a-time tone, will never forget his childhood. That is, he will always carry within him the child that he was. That is, it will be hard for him to lie or to kill. Or to put it another way: he'll always be a rebel.

"Crumbs?" the newspaper vendor asked in the same perplexed tone he had used in reacting to the matter of the voices. Voices? Crumbs? You must mean loaves, the loaves of bread were everywhere, a real cascade of bread. Poor kid. He must have been hard of hearing.

So the newspaper vendor had not seen it or he had forgotten it. That can be explained. In those days it was better to see nothing. Just like Papa. He shook his head and without looking up at the balcony where one who would be progenitor of his grandchildren impatiently awaited permission and her turn to emerge with dignity, without even a final glance of farewell and welcome, he tried to catch up with the old woman, who by now was a good block away, scurrying home to Doralisa and the child. He completely erased the scene he had just witnessed from his memory; he succeeded in blocking out those voices of ours, which were whispering a promise of streamlets of water running among the stones of urinals and cemeteries. With time, if it hadn't been for the pressure of his son and our grandfather, Manuel Sendero would have convinced himself, just as the newspaper vendor had done, that in fact he hadn't seen anything out of the ordinary, that he hadn't foreseen anything out of the future, just a death, one more death, just one more.

Just the way I'm telling it, fertile little puppy dogs of my old age, that's the way I drove it home to Skinny the same afternoon I returned.

"Young man," said Skinny, after a pause that gave him a chance to lift a glass of water to that Strait of Magellan passageway that served as his mouth. "How many years did you say you had been away?"

Actually, just about all my life. I didn't add that extrauterine life, postpartum life was the least important part of our existence, an anticlimax pure and simple. It's a good thing, because that very night Pamela was going to alter my prejudices radically.

"And the business about the bicycle and the bread crumbs, how did you find that out?"

Stories, I told him. Stories that are going around about Manuel Sendero. When it comes to my sources of information, I'm like doctors and lawyers, my mouth is shut as tight as a clam.

"Stories you heard over there?"

Here, there, everywhere.

"Young man," Skinny repeated, "exile is like being in an insane asylum. Everybody believes he's been in the Battle of Waterloo. All that happened more than twenty years ago—what am I talking about?—thirty years ago. People make up a lot, especially about Manuel Sendero. Your version doesn't surprise me, although I've never heard it before. The last time I saw my buddy—although it wasn't the last time I heard him—he was on a bicycle like the one you say, and now, as if that wasn't enough, they've put one at the beginning of the story too. At this rate, everybody's going to be telling the tale soon. Then they won't be bread crumbs but bullets, and later instead of bullets they'll be messages or false IDs or something else. And a hundred years from now nobody will be able to tell for sure exactly what happened, they won't be able to distinguish truth from fiction. I don't think you've met Eduardo. Eduardo is one of my godchildren. He doesn't believe in the last song. He says the whole thing's an invention. That's what happens when you exaggerate and re-elaborate and generally stretch the truth. So, as for proof, young man, what kind of proof do you have? What witnesses do you have to corroborate that this is the way it happened?"

Then I decided to use my trump card, to really take the plunge. The time had come to reveal to Skinny my true identity. I took a deep breath.

"The fact is, I'm his son," Grandfather explained, trying hard to moderate his trumpeting alleluia tone. I'm Sendero's son, Skinny. How could I possibly not know?

And I held out my arms, ready to be embraced.

The hint of a smile of ridicule which he made no attempt to hide hardly fit on Skinny's toothpick face. He made no move to embrace me, he didn't relive one of their old adventures in my presence, he didn't rise off the floor like a helicopter at my news.

"Young man," he answered, as if I had not just revealed my origins, "there are three reasons which lead me to doubt your story. I'm going to give you all three.

"Three," repeated Skinny, raising at half-mast the corresponding number of fingers. "The first is that things didn't happen the way you said. From a distance you can weave a pretty tale, add a touch of color here and there, conjecture about motives. From a distance everything gets out of focus, and, as time passes, everything gets worse. But that's not the way it was. If you want to believe it, fine, that's your privilege. That's the way we build a democracy. But death was death, young man. It was cold-blooded and systematic and the only voices were the generals'. Afterward, yes, afterward, we've had our turn to speak, and, if you come to the demonstration, you'll see how far we've advanced. But don't come to me with mysterious choruses and magical bread. My second reason is more concrete. Manuel Sendero's mother had asked us to keep an eye on him when he got out. That's exactly what we did, because Manuel was like a brother, and, besides, we had a personal interest, you might even say an investment in his person. We had plenty of reasons. The last song proves that we were right. Someone you can't interview now, someone they killed many years ago, escorted him from afar, but discreetly, very discreetly, young man. That person didn't see any of these things you insist happened."

Kids, you little bundles of joy from my future, this grandfather who's speaking to you now started to tremble at that point. Why weren't you with me? Why hadn't you had the good sense to be born, to keep me company? How could I convince him? How could I march all my witnesses in front of his itchy eyes? How could I conjure up for him Papa, who had told me the whole thing with his hands resting on Doralisa's southern belly that same night? How could I fill his house with those voices that Manuel heard, our voices, mine and my friends', all the children's, all the ones who had refused to be born as an act of rebellion and who had participated in that first secret council? How could I resurrect the voices of some who had died and were floating around out there just waiting to take refuge in somebody's throat?

I, of course, had not been physically present, but we certainly weren't going to leave Papa all alone on that first day. We had an investment in his person too, and on this planet of ours there are plenty of children, standing in line, just waiting to be born. Were we going to just stand by and let Papa forget the mission he had been charged with? Hadn't that woman with the dancing-dog breasts dragged her enormous belly out onto the balcony? I was everywhere, in just as many places as the enemy sows his hidden cameras and electronic devices. And dear old Skinny, who had done so much to bring me into the world, almost as much as if he had planted the seed himself and, as an act of faith, dragged me out of the stellar darkness, yes, good old Skinny didn't believe a word his precious godchild had said, no, not a single word that your dear old grandfather was telling him. I hadn't expected that.

I felt like forgetting all my principles. I felt the fury settling into my fists and the overwhelming desire to pound him. I admit it, gentle children, I admit it, so don't look at me like that out of the darkness. I'm sorry. Your grandfather can make mistakes too, just ask Pamela when you have the chance.

I got up from the chair, a little out of control and trembling. Just a little while ago I had sought out this same man so that he could advise me on a strategy for making known the conditions under which the unborn children would agree to end their strike.

"And the third reason?" I asked, hoping it would be the weakest, trying to bring to my voice those gentle, purring, flutelike tones that I had used to communicate with this same adult, decades before, when he was seated beside Doralisa and on the right-hand side of my father, Manuel Sendero, yes, that same little kitten voice.

"The third is the most serious," Skinny replied, his face growing more and more ashen, uglier and uglier, and less and less an object of my devotion. He paused and then went on. "The fact is, young man, that Manuel Sendero never had a son. The only one he had, the one he and Doralisa were going to have, they killed . . . And don't ever call me Skinny again. That's a privilege reserved for my friends."

The child broke his silence for the first time the afternoon the Caballero came to see Manuel Sendero. *"Papa,"* and that word so typically childlike, the first word stammered out by so many little ones, that word would be the only one Manuel would remember, because what followed was a call to more serious business: *"Kill him, Papa."*

Of all the advice his son would offer Manuel Sendero, that was the toughest; it was clear to me from the beginning that there was no ground for accommodation with that devil. Bullets were the only possible solution, and the sooner the better.

But Manuel Sendero paid no attention. In prison they had taught him that they're the ones who generally provide the bullets and we tend to provide the bodies, so he prepared himself calmly for the imminent meeting. Nevertheless, many days went by, because the Caballero usually chose those few occasions when Manuel was out to come knocking at the door. The old woman informed him that her only living son had just gone out, sir, he went out to get a card; they say that's the necessary first step to getting a job.

"They're going to give him a yellow card, ma'am."

"A yellow card?"

A yellow one. That's what he deserves. He needn't think they're going to give him one to collect unemployment, ma'am, as if he couldn't get a job. No way. Sendero, like so many others, just didn't want to relocate productively. He was a good-for-nothing. A yellow card.

Manuel showed her the card in question that afternoon. They had allowed him to choose the reasons for his unemployment, because this was a free country: was he lazy, self-employed, or unsalvageable? He had felt like having them stamp *unsalvageable* on the card, he would even have had it stamped on his forehead and on his penis if he had had the chance, but he had realized that such small and sterile gestures of rebellion have to be paid for over many years and with many troubles, so he had decided to opt for *self-employed,* which, besides, was actually true, although neither the clerk nor the Caballero had guessed it yet: the family was feeding itself with the counterfeit bills that the old woman furiously produced every night.

"The business of the bills is the only thing this Caballero doesn't seem to know about," grumbled the old woman, glancing at the repulsive card that ratified the evil, almost omniscience of their enemy. "The familiar way he talks about you, as if he knew you. Are you sure you haven't run across him before?"

But nothing in the story his mother related to him offered Manuel Sendero the slightest clue, anything at all that would explain the crumbling mountain of a woman who had been his wife and who was sleeping in the next room, or the child that stubbornly refused to be born.

"It was a little after they carried off your brother's body," the old woman said. "He was a pleasant enough sort, yes indeed, the devil."

Night was falling and the streetlights cast their shadow on the wall like a sharp, white condolence.

"Is our Dora at home?" he asked, intimately, freshly.

It was a cold voice, the old woman would say. Like a big freezer that whines slowly and precisely.

Like a blank record, Papa. Just the barely perceptible noise of the needle in the grooves.

"Ma'am," said Doralisa, with extreme courtesy, "if you don't mind, I'd like to speak with this gentleman alone." It was as though she had recognized him, as though she was expecting him.

The old woman obeyed you, Mama. Why did she obey you? Why didn't she play the part of busybody mother-in-law to the hilt and refuse to leave? She must've thought the man was a policeman, that it had something to do with finding Manuel or with making burial arrangements for Uncle. But they never did bury Uncle, and he wasn't a policeman. When the Caballero wanted to go into the house, you stopped him, Mama; something like that old scream lit up your eyes and warmed my umbilical cord, and he knew beyond a shadow of a doubt that no, he should never go into the house, never.

So the old woman wasn't able to make out what they talked about. And I admit that I'm guilty of not paying attention. I must've been drowsy at that time. Later, when the twins confronted me, I pointed out, in my own defense, that Doralisa had already been pregnant nine or maybe ten months and I was just beginning to sharpen my wits for survival. So the old woman turns out to be our only source of information, and, given her tendency to exaggerate and to engage in flights of fantasy, and in view of the prejudice against the Caballero, which she shared with the son of Manuel Sendero, we really haven't been able to find out very much. She contented herself with spying on them through a window. They were speaking calmly enough, without raising their voices and without standing close to each other. The only noteworthy thing occurred at the end, when he extended his hand, long, like a sharp, icy stake, and in that hand were sparkling, multicolored pills, and he asked Doralisa: Yes? No? Yes? No? No? No? Yes? opening and closing his fingers like a neon sign flickering at night. She hadn't answered. She just received them, never once taking her eyes off him, holding her robe together across her enormous belly with her other hand, choosing each pill very carefully to keep from touching those arctic bones.

"OK," the Caballero said. "I'll come back another day." And then he turned to the old woman, whose eyes were pressed against the window, as if he had known all along that she was halfway present and that it was the most natural thing in the world to include her in the pact. "See you soon, Mrs. Sendero. See that Dori takes the pills every afternoon at six o'clock. Don't forget it. It's very risky, if she doesn't. Give my regards to Manuel when he returns. Tell him I can get him a job. Tell him to remember." He would repeat those same words, the ones referring to a job, on each subsequent visit, before saying good-bye, tipping his old-fashioned hat in an old-fashioned way.

Doralisa stayed outside awhile, watching his withdrawal, pensively rocking back and forth on her heels, and rubbing her pained waist with the hand that was free of pills. Then she went into the kitchen, filled the glass with the orange crocodiles on it with water, and swallowed the first dose right away.

The old woman questioned her with her gaze, but the answer she got apparently had nothing to do with the recent visitor. They were the last words she would hear her daughter-in-law speak.

"I'm tired," you said, Mama. "I'm really exhausted. I think I'll sleep for a while."

If Manuel, therefore, had prepared himself for his meeting with the Caballero, what he could not have anticipated was my voice, which pierced the atmosphere, climbing from Doralisa's womb, but really coming from an unconquered faraway place, from an island in time, where the verb *to fear* couldn't be conjugated. Manuel had verified that the child was alive just by his sense of touch a few moments after collapsing in his house the day he was released. Eleven months after he should have been born he still found himself in Doralisa's center of gravity, with signs of a life that echoed like a drumming double heart. Since the child didn't speak to him immediately, the ex-singer couldn't guess that his offspring—for lack of physical space—had had to start growing on the inside, developing his other faculties in abundance, as the afflicted often do, determined to exploit this unique opportunity to provide himself with the means and the talents he would need in his future life.

That was the way the relationship between Manuel and his son began, between my father and me, and, under the circumstances, it was going to be all the one was going to know about the other. Of course, we had started to establish what you might call privileged connections beginning that night more than a year and a half earlier while Manuel's body hummed and mounted and pushed and sucked, a microscopic fraction of me climbed up to meet my other round and juicy half that was descending from Doralisa. They say that Manuel's voice was so powerful that it held the sun below the horizon just so that dawn wouldn't break until his wife could rest assured that the child was on its way. Maybe. The fact is that darkness would always be between us like a curtain. I knew of him what I could make out through the misty keyhole of the umbilical cord, what I could piece together from the rumors that were endlessly whispered by the other little miracles from their posts of scanty observation in the world's womb: your papa is going down the street, your papa has just asked for work, your papa was throwing stones at a tin can. And of me he knew whatever he could imagine, searching out faces, exploring Doralisa's somnambulous skin, and, most important, what he heard on the least appropriate occasions: mindless advice, extremist suggestions, impudent insults, irresponsible remarks. What was to be expected from someone with so much passion, such excessive impatience, and such meager discernment of the boundaries between what is desirable and what is possible in this tricky world of ours? The only way to work this out is with bullets, insisted the child on that occasion—bringing down on himself the censure of all the other fetuses, who preferred nonviolence and who suspected, in addition, that we take upon ourselves the souls of the people we kill—and the only thing left to do, added the child, is to decide on the caliber. That's it. Where I come from—and to the Caballero's surprise, Manuel Sendero was smiling to himself like an idiot, because, really, where could this son of his be coming from?—there aren't rascals like this one. What is needed is for you guys to finish the cleanup. Do you want to use me as a broom?

So Manuel Sendero couldn't pay as close attention as he would have liked to the monologue with which the Caballero tore the singular terms of Doralisa's contract to shreds. He was too absorbed in the voice of his unpublished son, the joker who was commenting on every one of the adversary's propositions and demolishing his arguments, filling the air with statistics on infant malnutrition, levels of unemployment, housing shortages. Do you know that one out of ten children dies before the age of one? Did you know that, Papa?

The Caballero started by trying to calm Manuel down. These pills—and his tactic would always be to present himself as a Laboratory employee, just a functionary receiving orders, an everyday sort of fellow earning his living the best way he could—these pills wouldn't harm anyone. It was a matter of mutual convenience, a coming together of the individual and the collective interests. His company needed to measure the effects of a new drug, while she, Doralisa, and a few others, given her husband's absence, needed to make ends meet for herself and her unborn child during those long months, maybe even years or decades, that lay ahead. He was explaining the circumstances to him, not because he had to, but rather out of deference to Manuel, whom he had had the pleasure of hearing when he sang, and he did it very well too, if he wanted his opinion, though the themes led people astray, too popular and demagogic and even sectarian, a fact which had led the government to confiscate all the copies, but that should certainly not be interpreted as censorship of his songs. Far from it, he was sure that in high places, among the cultivated members of the regime, people who appreciated the difference between Telemann and Vivaldi, there were surely high hopes for the rehabilitation of Manuel Sendero and his re-entry into the social body from which he had isolated himself, and that the problem didn't lie in his vocal cords themselves, whose texture, richness, and vibratory capacity were applauded by everyone, but rather in the bad use to which they had been put by . . .

. . . when you sang, Papa, his son interrupted with a fervor of multitudes that reminded Manuel of that of his compañeros, *alive and dead, whenever they agreed instead of contradicting each other in endless meetings where they smoked until their own sophistries and harangues went up in a cloud. When Manuel Sendero sang, that was precisely when they were in agreement. There was a climactic moment when the chorus of those present would lose their sad oasis of solitude and would merge in a uniquely prophetic voice, and then Sendero, instead of going on drinking in the moisture of others, like a tree in sandy soil, quieted the animal that dwelled in his throat, forgot lyrics and tune, only moved his lips, so that it was the others who were singing through him. And what happened to them all, to him and to them, wasn't exactly a sound, but rather an exaltation of a different light, as if the touch of a blind man could make itself heard. It was as if all the ghosts of the world, Papa Ramón would explain to Pamela at night before she went to bed when she asked him for another story about Manuel Sendero, Pamela would tell it*

to her own grandchildren years later, all the hunger that had been piling up in living memory, would boil up all at once and start to become memory. Manuel felt complete, plural, used to the hilt, he and all the others, convinced that they'd been lied to all their lives. The newspapers had lied, the radio had lied, the textbooks, the statues of horses and heroes, the elementary-school teachers, the newscasters, everybody had lied every time they told them that no one is in control of his own destiny. Because those bridges in his voice pointed the way toward another future, another crossroads: history could be, would be, made by our very selves. And since that sense of power went far beyond any one person, no one, said Papa Ramón, can determine where the voice is coming from, if it's here or in the mountains or on the next corner. Around your uncle Manuel there arose a bell tower, a tidal wave, a fog of clouds. That was lucky, because the momentary effect on the enemy was tremendous. They were defenseless and for an instant they lost their morning makeup and the snake pits they were became evident for all to see. And their tongues got all tied in knots like cockroaches and they couldn't cover their nakedness with the traditional speeches and the usual corny poems dedicated to the fatherland and to the roses. They didn't understand what was the source of their fleeting misfortune. We could have explained it to them, dear grandchildren, my little eyeteeth. Adults stumble over words like magic *and* miracle *and* wonder, *but those of us who are close to the sources of life know that that's the way song has always been, ever since one cell fell in love with another and courted her with a serenade and the two of them together decided to grow. Good use, said the son of Manuel Sendero; the voice had been put to excellent use, said the little boy who was to be our grandfather . . .*

. . . the bad use that had been made of them, insisted the Caballero, and Manuel became alarmed—God forbid that this talking icebox should also pick up, as he could, the provocative voice of the child—bad use by the politicians of the past who had twisted the normal direction of his life and of those of so many others, leading them all toward disaster, creating slogans out of even the letters in their alphabet soup. And now the country was sick and had to be watched over while it recovered. Doralisa's contract stipulated the same thing. Here there were no time limits, just goals. His wife was going to wake up when, in the judgment of the company, a satisfactory result had been achieved. Meanwhile the future mother and present fetus, which, although it is not explicitly mentioned in the proposal from the Ministry of Health, is also covered under the contract by the phrase *and other residents of the mother's body*, enjoy the benefits of a Statute of Guarantees. It was good for Manuel to be aware of current legislation, so he wouldn't try to block Doralisa's access to her source of employment, in this case her pills. I'm going to tell you a story; we might as well be friends, since, after all, we're both involved with the same woman—forgive my frankness, and with all due respect, of course. Because there was a husband who didn't respect the terms of the contract, who brought some legalism or other to bear. I'm sure it was just a case of jealousy, jealousy of the pill, which, I'm sure, achieves levels of intimacy that we can't even predict. He flushed the pills down the toilet. His wife died two days later. She was awake during that period, actually a little less than forty-eight hours, but the only thing she asked for was to be returned to the world of dreams. He lost his wife, we lost our employee, as well as a good quantity of pills, and I received a verbal reprimand, despite the fact that the code didn't stipulate, at that time, the obligation of the contractor to notify the spouse about the agreement. Of course, that's just one case. Who is telling you, Manuel, that the pills are the real cause of her sleep, eh? It's possible she came to us because she had already decided to take to her bed and she knew that only our company . . .

Company? the child burst out. Company? Emporium, you mean. Emporium. Empire. Child abuser. Laboratory. Rat hole. Give me back my mama, you artery-suckers, you brainwashers, child-polluters, you heard what my immortal uncle said, supermarketeers, hearth-wreckers, profit-vampires, drug-fuckers, my papa's going to leave you without a leg to stand on, did you hear that, underagent, palmbroker, number juggler, did you hear that? you multirat in your multilaboratory?

. . . only our company, the imperturbable Caballero went on, could sustain her in such circumstances. It's possible she might not even wake up if you do take away the pills. Which came first, the sleep or the pill? Waking up or the antidote? The only moral is that you shouldn't interfere in the sovereign decisions of others. You, Manuel Sendero, were always too fond of sticking your nose in other people's business. It's a neat game, right? Advising others, inspiring them, holding their hands, playing your guitar, lifting your hands up to the mountains like a preacher. But afterward, Manuel Sendero, who pays? Here's your wife, look at her, listen to her sleeping. You planted the seed, Manuel, you convinced her you had to have a child, you bewitched her with pretty words. But when the hard times came, what could you guarantee her, not a secure job, not a country to your liking, certainly not the kind of future you had painted in your rosy-colored verses. You weren't even around to comfort her. And what about her pain? Could that be postponed? Now you come back and discover to your surprise that she decided to do something for herself, without consulting you. How was she going to consult you? Were you there beside her, perchance?

Manuel Sendero waited for the child to answer with his usual insolence, he waited for that rich and loving flood of invective. All lies, Papa, that business about the fellow who flushed the pills, just an invention to keep you from breaking the bottle over his head, for pity's sake. They talk about laws, these murderers who absolve themselves by decree when they're caught, sickos, who had to come out of their own mothers' asses, torturers, pushers.

Manuel waited for words like these to draw him out of his sadness, but he waited in vain.

I had to remain silent.

The Caballero's last recriminations happened to coincide with my own doubts, which had been gnawing at my placenta ever since a nearby explosion—it was the bullet that struck down Papa's immortal brother, just as my fertile nine months were drawing to an end—forced me to wake up and take stock of the damages and the perspectives. How could I attempt some counterattack of ridicule, if in a very disturbing way that dark drum was beating out the tune of my own criticisms? Wasn't that precisely the reason I hadn't been born yet, that the child couldn't be, didn't want to be, born? Didn't I wonder too what fool would keep on having children in times like these, oblivious to our lack of a future, hurling us out into the world like worms, just like that, to be beggars, illiterates, plotters, nuclear children, to stare into bakery windows or to stare at the closed curtains of the rest of the people, so we can watch our wives die outside hospitals where they won't admit them and then we're left to choke on our own fury, a fury that can only be released by killing a prostitute or by kicking a dog? And then, all of a sudden, things change. You take charge of the government, the poor take over, and one of those unique and miraculous periods opens up for the first time ever, and there's a real possibility of putting an end to the misery of all those kids whose brain mass and neura are shrinking from malnutrition, and for once the statistics predict happiness, they tell us that pregnant women have more milk and workers have more factories, and the most important statistics, those of the heart, indicate that more people are dancing, more fingers are playing instruments, and just at that moment, when the world is beckoning to us like summer welcoming the swallows, you all blow it, shit, you don't know how to manage the situation, fuck you, and they throw you out. And these sons of bitches take your place. Who's going to assure me, us, including all the ones who haven't even been conceived and whose interests we can legitimately represent in their absence, that they won't be in control for a millennium? And who's going to guarantee us that when they finally depart, you'll be able to get your act together so they'll never come back?

So these aren't times to just let the semen flow and the ova blossom and the universe recreate itself in every bed and then I appear in some two hundred-odd days like snatching a rabbit from a hat, like you had put me on a train that only goes one way; it's not enough to drop your pants, stick in your thing, and move your ass up and down, whispering sweet nothings in her ear and then let nature take its course, man. That's been going on now ever since Great-grandfather Adam, and we think it's time to put an end to the carnival. Gray Power, Teen Power, Poor Power, Indian Power,

Feminist Power, Gay Power, Proletarian Power. Well, now we're calling for Fetus Power, the democracy of the unborn, the true majority. *Power to the future,* that's our slogan.

That's what I should have told Papa. That they hadn't consulted me. It was the first of many antidemocratic acts they were going to impose on me, but in some way it sums up and contains all the rest. I would get up at night crying in, screaming in, chewing my fists in, terrorized in, dying a thousand deaths in the night of all nights without any day, and no one had asked me if I wanted to exist. Two beings who undoubtedly will come to resemble you more and more as each passing year allows them to mold us, they decide—and as often as not, not even they decide, it just happens in an adolescent fever, a pointless in and out, a rape behind the schoolhouse, a blind force like a river disappearing into a swamp—that someone will wake up years later dying that death of darkest night. From that moment on they've screwed you, all participation is illusory. When you come to power, forty years later, you'll be covered with scales (fear, resentment, rancor). They corrupted you, they already got you in line, the jig's already up. Unless. Unless somebody could be born already grown up—why not? Unless our generation, instead of laying a guilt trip on our parents after we're born, demand responsibility from them before the fact, impose conditions while we're still in the trenches, where it's easier to negotiate.

Do you understand, man?

But I kept quiet. I didn't add my voice to that of the Caballero.

It would take more than two decades to cleanse his organism of those bitter words. The words with which he refused to crush his father that day were whispered incoherently like a torrent into Pamela's little kitten ear, a way of keeping from hurling a more pleasant and less desperate torrent between her thighs, the same night he returned to the land of his roots. He dropped his irresponsible pants as if he were reincarnating the spirit of his own irresponsible sire, and he prepared enthusiastically to fulfill each step in the process, all except the last step of that ritual invented by man and woman, the ritual which, had it been allowed to culminate in its usual joyous and seminal climax, would have guaranteed right then and there that Manuel Sendero's grandchildren would have populated and inherited the earth.

But Grandfather diverted the flow, flooding a valley in the sheets and not a valley of children clamoring for cradles and beds in Pamela's warm corolla. She thought it was an act of consideration and respect, a sign of strength of character and of supernatural self-control, since she had discreetly mentioned in passing that she wasn't using contraceptives. But the reason was something else entirely, though he didn't tell her so that night. How could I bring a descendant into the world when I wasn't even sure of my own status, when my revolutionary friends withheld their own cells on the threshold of the air in order to negotiate the improvements that it was beginning to look like we'd never get? I would have been a traitor, a false inseminator, and would therefore have been disqualified from serving as the spokesman for our rebellion, and, what is even worse, I would have become my own father, repeating unreasonable and uncommitted acts, like the ones he had sweetened and performed inside my mama's eloquence. I had to bring my offspring into the light of day when our streets and our checking accounts were as clean as our hearts. Could I possibly admonish my own son now, like an adult, showing him the tricks of the trade and the traps and so forth, offering up punishments and compensations, me, could I do that? When we were, would be, twins, identical, almost Siamese; I had nothing to teach him and he had nothing to learn, he would hardly appear on the scene and he would have to join the babies' general strike. Outside of being able to tell stories, I wasn't ready for the role of father. No one ever is, of course, but you must agree that there wasn't room in this world for two like me, for three. Not yet. So at the first temptation the one who had sworn that we shouldn't be born until things changed couldn't feed a uterus with little white creatures and phenotypes and chromosomes and mirages and other such replicas of my cells.

I admit I had second thoughts. When I came into Pamela's galaxy the first time, I wanted, no, I needed, her to be the mother and the cry of my children, my sweet mama, my grandmother, I wanted her to cradle me, to uncover her left breast and, holding it imposingly against the horizon, to nurse us, me, it turned out to be harder to stand the solitude than the frustration, harder to stand the solitude than the sexual shells bombarding my insides, harder to stand your absence, my dear little fawns, the joys of my old age, as if you were already inside me, inside Pamela, calling for holy reincarnation and maculate conception, entirely in her, entirely in me, waiting to be joined, to breathe and to serve and to communicate inside me, keeping me company as you always have.

He had felt close enough to her to have given vent to all his helplessness. Before mounting that moon colt which Pamela, without prior conditions, offered him, he decided for the second time that day to tell the true story. Not all of it. He wouldn't be explicit with her nor with anyone about why he had come to that country. But he would tell her enough to test her, to force her to choose sides. Because if, as some sort of strange consolation for having lost Skinny, Grandfather met his dream girl, or rather met her again, he was not about to penetrate that miracle of nature unless first she knew with whom she was entering into a relationship, or rather, who it was that was entering her. He didn't want to hide any aspect of his true identity.

"Come," was Pamela's only response to the one who was still not our grandfather, but who, we wagered, would very probably be so before morning.

"Tell me first if you believe me," he asked, much too seriously for a fellow who was so devoutly naked.

She looked him over, taking in as much as she could in the semidarkness. According to the story she had just heard, this body, so complete and well put together, had been conceived by Manuel Sendero and Doralisa in a bed not far from this very garret where the two young people were getting ready for some sweet imitation. His parents had always put off procreation, because they insisted—they were both such mad fools, Mama and Papa were—that first it was necessary to be absolutely sure that the future bit of humanity would not have to endure the same penniless state. But the decision to summon him out of nothingness, like a match struck in the wind, had turned out to be a kind of challenge, to knowingly play a losing card. The world, far from moving toward renewal or ushering in the Judgment Day, was going from bad to worse; it was on the brink of catastrophe. Under such deplorable conditions the very planning for and carrying out the birth of a child was an unparalleled act of faith that he would come into the world with a miraculous multiplying loaf under his arm. They had conceived him as a final, irrefutable argument that things were going well. Someone would scarcely indicate some doubt as to the smiling of Lady Fortune or predict some massacre in the short term or count up the number of nuclear missiles in the world, when, like St. Anselm pointing with his finger toward the existence of God, Manuel would point to the expanding quadrature of the circle of Doralisa, to that portentous belly. Who says the people will lose? Who dares say that? As the world crumbled around them, they simply closed their eyes, muttered a prayerful *perhaps,* and put their best foot forward. Of course they put their best foot forward. But I was the best foot they put forward, plucked out of nothingness, with a one-way ticket and no place to buy a return passage.

"Do you believe me?" he repeated.

"They say that Manuel Sendero never had a son. I've heard the story that way I don't know how many times. Don't interrupt me. But if you say so, yes, I believe you. Why shouldn't I believe you? Yes, there is something else, something that's even more important: if he had had a son, he would be as cute and crazy as you are. Come in. Come in. Wherever you are. Come on in."

He came in.

He had recognized her at once. He had never seen her before, at least not with his eyes, and in the middle of the noisy demonstrators her voice sounded different, but he picked her out, sitting on the curb under a banner, her shapely legs hidden under a skirt which was barely stirred by a light breeze; and it must have been her aura or animal magnetism or astral movements or some such nonsense, anyhow he saw himself—just like that, with absolute certainty, step by step, as if someone had filmed the scene—undressing her that same night, his eyes melting with excitement, giving crazy, irreverent names to every delightful piece of unveiled flesh, just the way I had always dreamed you, and he foresaw that at just that moment she would shake out her hair, and, when she did, he moved, moved toward her. Attracted by everything that has been called mystery, enigma, vibrations, drawn onward by something that philosophers and lovers have been trying to explain for millions of years, by hidden currents, which the ancients had described as the well-known arrows shot from Cupid's bow, and which in medieval times they called dynamic and atomized, eye-to-eye rays, and which the Kamasutra more or less measured in dimensions, and which today we call electricity, vibes, sex appeal, butterflies in the stomach, whatever, all of it really useless interpretation, since he knew very well what was carrying him toward that woman like an oarless canoe tossed by the rapids, jostled by the angry shouts of the crowd that tomorrow would march to the cemetery in their protest against death; he held the key, why two beings who have never met recognize each other, and how they have completely unaffectedly accepted the fact that the clothes they are wearing must be shed like dead cells in a few hours, each totally surrendered to the other before the formal introductions have been made, that all that remains for them is to clarify the strategies for their coming together, the feints, the refusals, and the feelers, when after all it was so easy to do what Grandfather had done a few minutes later, that is, to elbow his way through the crowd like a barroom rowdy, crossing the limitless expanse of the demonstration, feeling the pavement intensely beneath his feet, and stepping directly in front of her, oblivious to the men who surrounded her, employing a tactic which—he would later discover to his own amusement—was far from in keeping with all her feminist notions and with her contempt for all seducers and macho men, and which in his case worked only because what Grandfather was was perfectly apparent, since his shining eyes, nervous hands, shaky knees (which caused him to knock over a banner on his way to that reunion), and stammering tongue all gave the lie to the image of Don Juan or supermacho that one would have expected from the classic line he pronounced:

"We've met before, but you don't remember."

Because she didn't remember, of course; there was no reason she should have been expected to remember; the son of Manuel Sendero had discovered to his own astonishment that birth is like death and that those who crossed over lost the rare privilege or perhaps the curse of retaining their prenatal experiences. She, on the other hand, immediately grasped two things: the first was that, despite her total amnesia, something told her that this young man was telling the truth, that in fact they did know each other; she had never seen him, smelled him, touched him, or caressed him with her tongue—all of which would take place to excess in just a matter of hours, as if to make up for lost time—but there was some essence in him that was familiar. And the second thing was that of all the lines that macho pirates had used to board her, this one was by far the most original; so, her habitually strong defenses were let down, especially since her usual male companions—remember, kids, Eduardo was not there—were all dedicated to the burning issue of coming up with a theory to explain why the government was responsible for the fact that no babies had been born in six weeks.

"I don't remember," Pamela agreed. "When was it?"

It was too soon to tell her since forever, although in their case that was literally true, so, in order not to lie, he answered:

"When we were smaller," without stipulating—he wasn't under oath, after all—just how small they had been, how ridiculously tiny and defenseless. He tried to maintain a neutral, dispassionate tone, but a movement of his brow and a kind of gentleness, like that of a newborn baby, of a real greenhorn, a novice, convinced her that he was accusing her of something, something that was painful. "We were smaller," he repeated, and he relived the absolute desolation, like being trapped on an elevator between floors, in which he had floated in the weeks following her disappearance, her voice growing fainter and more distant as a midwife's hands had torn her from her mother's womb, and the instant the transmission had ceased, when they cut the invisible lines of communication, when she departed the company of her own kind, my company in particular. It wasn't a question of condemning her; it wasn't her fault; it comes to all of us once in our lives, sooner to some, later to others, but she was the one who had departed, going away, going away, I can't help it, it's like an earthquake here inside me, everything is trembling, if I don't turn around, if I don't turn my head, if I don't start my descent, I'm going to die, help me, and he, they, we, all helpless, unable to prevent the inevitable, thus the first rebellion had already failed, afterward all the others would run off, she who had sworn to be the strongest, immovable, no conciliation possible with adults, we'll stay here till they change the world, she had not waited, she had shouted for him to come to her, not to forget her, don't delay, come, come soon, and he had whistled back that I'm going to follow you, I'll find you, I'll go back to my country for the second rebellion even if I have to camp for six weeks staring at the sky they promised us, and all of a sudden, total silence, as if someone with an ax had severed an arm from its body, you can't trust women, the twins had told him, that's not true, replied a girl who would be born blind, but who was one hell of a female when it came down to it, how much longer are we women going to have to put up with this discrimination? but he paid no attention to such childish prattle, he was trying to reach her and there was a void in his life, an emptiness where before her voice had whispered to him, that sister voice, his favorite among all others, and she had forgotten, you could swear to a lot of things, in the end all the promises in the world can fit into words, but neither she nor anyone else among them remembered anything, just look at her.

"When we were smaller? So you've been waiting for me a very long time, eh?"

She was joking to quiet the undeniable pounding of her ex-virgin's old *cuore*, but she felt a peculiar guilt weighing upon her, as if this man whom she had never seen before had some foundation for the silent accusation that was shining in his eyes, as if she had been unfaithful after fifty years of marriage, while he answered, with a passion that couldn't be a rhetorical game:

"A long time ago, love, long before we were born," the kind of announcement either you responded to with a slap in the face or you went along with the whole thing, ready for him to search out all the sources of those vibes that very biting night. Because now, instead of asking her "What's your name?" which would have corroborated the falseness of their having known each other years before, he asks her, "And your mother, what name did she finally give you?" and since she was staring at him in disbelief, he continued with his usual candor: "I mean, so I can call you by that name, right? Before it didn't matter but now, well, I've got to call you something." And the men all around her, who had besieged her for years with the hope of stealing her special fruit, of bleeding into her for a night, of savoring something more than a feel of breasts behind the bushes, all realized that they had lost, such is life, this fellow had bowled her over, building castles in the air, and that Pamela—they named me Pamela, what name were you given? and he, Me? oh, nothing, maybe Manuel, Mama wanted to name me Victor—that Pamela had rocketed into the stratosphere, nobody could bring her down, because now she was beginning to read his thoughts, a talent that, according to him, was a mere recovery of what they had shared, one more proof that what he said was true—my God, now he's thinking about the way I take off my panties, the way they cling to my hips, my God, now he's going to reach out to see if it's true that the warmth of my hand could hatch an egg—and if she didn't go with him now, who knows what would happen, and she got up from the curb, and, without saying goodbye to the others, they left.

Only later, when they finally sat down on a dilapidated bench, flanking the dirty, almost empty river, did she face him, feeling that the time had come to inject a touch of good sense into a relationship that would never possess such a quality:

"OK. In a word, what is it you want from me?"

And he: "If you let me touch your hand that'll do for now. Because it would be the first time I touched you. I'd like to know the temperature of your skin, just to see if it's as I had imagined. And if you like that, great, maybe we could go further. Reality must be infinitely better."

And she, instead of clearing her throat angrily, while he began to describe minutely the imagined sweetness of her ankles, the salty dampness of her pubis, the soft cry of her neck where the swan of her spinal column arched gracefully, instead of telling him to go jump in the lake, I'm no object, I'm no continent, I'm no field, said yes, that being, in fact, a very prudent and practical woman, as she was, she found reality definitely, undeniably, and infinitely better. And for that reason, since he seemed to have had so much experience, so many women captured and satisfied, she couldn't possibly believe that he was a virgin, just as she couldn't have believed his reasons for not seeding her, because at that point, she was already so turned on, as if she were a planet and he her first explorer, that she told him it wasn't true, that she could tolerate any lie except that one, who, what female vampire, had taught him to make love like that, but she wasn't surprised either when he answered that she was the one, didn't she remember, she, she had been the first one to talk to him about the birds and about the trees, which is, after all, an early way to make love, and she had pronounced the word *green*, a really cool word, and they had learned that all of it is in the very blood of that vastest of all lands, the one they had shared before this one, and that even this meeting was her responsibility, because she had told him they would meet for the second rebellion if this one failed, she had said it in jest because she swore that he would go out first, and then she asked him to shut up, that she believed him, she believed the whole thing, and all she wanted was to thank old Mother Earth for sending such an extraordinary and delirious example of manhood to mount her and penetrate her and nibble on her tongue and suck the spaces between her teeth, loosening what was left of the sandwich she had eaten for lunch, late in the day, precisely when Skinny was rejecting him three times over; that they had killed the child, and the lunch had descended to her ruminating stomach so its energy could course through her blood and she would defecate flowers and he could run his fingers through her hair and, with a penultimate thrust of his triumphant and totally concentrated body, he took her last breath and managed to ask her if she believed him while he was whispering sweetly into her glands, and she assured him that yes, she did, yes, a thousand times yes, that first night and all the nights to come Pamela believed the pilgrim, she was convinced that he was the son of Manuel Sendero, while, joined a thousand times, they conquered the serene world of inner doves which, if luck would have it, but still not that night, would be populated by children, by us, that's the way it was, my little heartthrobs, that's the way it was, don't be sad, Papa.

But Manuel Sendero would never know about Pamela. The abrupt silence of his baby forced him, now without any counterbalance, to immerse himself in the rambling discourse of the Caballero twenty years ago, still in front of the house, as if Pamela and I were not erasing him from memory, like a bad dream, as if the fetuses were not at that very minute resisting the pressures of nature and of adult blackmail to make them come out, as if at that moment men and women of all ages were not forming couples to try to warm up the climate with their love and with their choices to chase the echoes and traces of that shadow that still entangled the country's destiny, as if Pamela and I didn't exist.

Manuel Sendero had to swallow each and every word.

Besides, the Caballero said, becoming more deferential, Doralisa got the best possible terms from us. We're guaranteeing that she won't age, that is, the years won't be wasted, they'll be saved up in something like an age bank. If, at the end of the year, the balance is favorable, we've even discussed returning a few months as a bonus, something like interest. But that only goes for the ones whose relatives cooperate. We won't even speak of your mother. Don't be offended, but you know she's a stubborn old bird, though really the only effect that had was to reduce Doralisa's contract by two small points. We'll see, Manuel, old man, if you're any different. Because if you create problems for us, there's a clause that exempts us from all medical expenses. I'll let you know though: there never are expenses. Do you know why? Because our sleeping beauties never get sick. Aha. Maybe now you're beginning to realize how important your wife's work is. The only thing we can't provide is housing. We had considered another plan to provide a series of dormitories where the women could be more comfortable, less subject to petty annoyances, but the press here in the capital made us realize that to do that would undermine one of our most sacred principles, family unity, so we threw that idea out. At the same time, the men asked us to organize a section for them; there's already a long waiting list. Of course, it's impossible. This work requires a certain feminine quality. I'm telling you all this, not because I think you want to sign up. You couldn't anyhow. No, no, yes, don't say a word, you have other talents. If you need a job, I can help you. I'll recommend you to my friends. No, don't thank me. I feel almost as if this child were my own, like a godson, you know, you might almost say that you and I are buddies, right? Because if it wasn't for my pills, the kid could have been undernourished, maybe even have died, so I'm the one most interested in seeing you placed. Your wife's not going to sleep forever, and when she wakes up she's going to ask you for a close accounting. You'll pardon my frankness, Manuel, but we've come across people who get angry afterward when the woman opens her eyes. What? they say, so soon? they say. At first they complain, but then they get used to it, and then they beg us to continue it. The guy doesn't pound the table and threaten and shout anymore. He turns as gentle as a lamb. What am I going to do with this family, sir, and two, three months later, they show us a wife who's become a real fright, a kid who's been born, but without protein. Take us back, sir, put her to sleep again, that's what they all say. And I'll confess, that's what we do in the majority of cases. After all, we have our Christian values too, you know. We don't just think about profits. Of course, we check the client's file first. That's why I tell you it's so important to start off on a sound footing. We take family harmony into account. How do the others behave? Are they hostile or do they understand the problems of a working woman? That's what the pollsters ask us. Is the husband doing anything? Then I can recommend some temporary job to you, so you can take the best advantage of the situation and save a little on the side. The day she wakes up you have a little birthday cake all ready and waiting to celebrate all the lost years. And you come and get all the accumulated salary as well. Great deal, right? I'll tell you the truth, there are lots of people who would give their eyeteeth to have their wives accepted in our program. That's right, their eyeteeth.

"Kill him, Pamela."

But Pamela had fallen asleep when the sun was barely up and Papa was dead and, in my dreams, the Caballero kept on talking all night as if somebody had left a television on in the next room and couldn't find the button to turn it off. It went on all night and I couldn't get myself to wake up, I was back, cradled in the depths of Doralisa and she didn't wake up either and Pamela hugged me but she didn't listen, and if she didn't kill him, I'd have to do it, I would have to be the one.

Which was a way of conceding to myself the truth that I hadn't told Skinny and that I was even afraid to reveal to Pamela. If I hadn't dared tell him that I was coming, in the name of the unborn, to negotiate the unconditional surrender of the adults and the establishment of a supreme, if temporary, fetal government, how was I going to explain what I didn't want to know myself about my own designs and what I had never confessed to the other members of the Directorate: he had come back to this country, Grandfather had returned, with the express and unconfessable purpose of killing the Caballero. There, it was said.

Not even that day on the way to the cemetery did Grandfather want to admit that he didn't know why Manuel Sendero had lost his voice.

When the guards took off his wedding band, kids, then and there.

They undressed him without realizing that it was still on his ring finger, that useless scrap of metal that he and Doralisa had gone out to buy as a joke. Each prisoner grabbed some object that would remind him of, that would prove, his own previous existence; a little box of matches between the fingers, a button his mother had sewn, knickknacks that could not buy favors from the gods who ruled this subterranean world. But in those objects the prisoners held their boundary and their beginning, the only piece of unoccupied space in the world that they could dominate. On that boundary, that frontier, Manuel remained for hours turning the ring round and round before they came looking for him.

But what did they do to him, Grandfather? Tell us exactly what happened.

Oh, you curious, impertinent kids, don't ask me that, you really don't want to know. Don't even ask me what eight hands coming out of nowhere had to do to Manuel there in the dark when they finally discovered the ring and tried to take it from him. A donation to the cause of national reconstruction. A wedding gift to the fatherland. We'll show this ring on television. So they'll know you've had a change of heart, that you've decided to cooperate. Soon we'll have you singing "a chick-chick here, a chick-chick there" and "Little Miss Muffet eating her curds and whey." That was when his voice disappeared.

So they couldn't make a public exhibit of him, Grandfather. That's why.

Maybe. The trouble is, as always, Papa went too far. Not so much as a whistle came out of him, not an owl-hoot of a sound, not even the time of day. His enemies were determined from then on to make him say something, anything, my little chanting children. But his voice was going, trickling away in his urine, in the drop by drop of the screams he couldn't scream, spattering against the fifth wall of the room, the fifth corner, looking for an escape hatch, a place without the glaring lights and the questions, a voice so hidden that even Manuel couldn't coax it out later on.

So it was courage, Grandfather. He was a hero.

Do you know who you sound like with your soap opera words? Do you have any idea? Just like those *compañeros* of his that wanted Papa to sing again. They never understood either. They congratulated him on how he had tricked the enemy; they thought it was a question of courage, just like you, kids. He had saved his trophy in the midst of all the ruins. So now, it's back to work, they say. Because, according to what Papa Ramón told Pamela, the plan was to use that voice like an umbrella to cover all the rumors and the people's broadcasts, the jokes, and the gospel truth, the gossip and the instructions and the denunciations. Skinny figured that the whole problem could be solved in a jiffy. Just bring in Manuel's old friend Luis on his next visit, even though Don Ramón, an expert on rhythms, traumas, and sins, despite having abandoned the priesthood, suggested that they wait. Nothing that springs from shame or guilt can serve any useful purpose, he said.

Skinny paid no attention to Don Ramón. According to him, Manuel would change as soon as he penetrated Luis's gaze; those eyes of Luis would be as transparent as ever, clear and serene, sunset on a cloudless day, at peace. They had done something to Luis too, and yet the day after his release he was back in the struggle, in fact, quite the opposite of Manuel, his energy seemed to have redoubled. It didn't seem important to Skinny that farther back and deeper in, behind the eyes, there were dark glasses, the sort that protect you from the sun. Not out front, but way back. That was the price Luis had to pay, those dark glasses which, more than hiding what had happened from the others, seemed to serve Luis himself, like black mirrors against which his own questions, his own stare, bounced. According to Skinny, Manuel Sendero, upon seeing Luis, would touch the shame frozen in his own throat in a kind of reflex action and then they'll see how the springtime sounds flow out; that voice would cast out all the terror, little Pamela, just like overturning a glass of milk.

And how did Papa react? I asked Pamela, even though I already knew the answer, having witnessed the event.

He didn't say anything, Skinny informed Don Ramón and the others that night, while Luis half-closed those efficient, cloudy eyes in a sign of agreement. It was clear. He didn't even have the voice to say no.

Because, little lights of mine, the throat is not something you can call back, like a kite or a political exile. His *compañeros* couldn't accept the fact that, far from having been temporarily snuffed out, his voice could be dead, the voice dying instead of Manuel Sendero himself. How could they accept that possibility? You don't know where it is either, Papa? I asked hopefully, and he didn't answer. It was like throwing hook and line into a sea of pure salt. A total waste.

That morning, on the way to the cemetery, Pamela noted with relief that the account of Manuel Sendero's son was more or less the same one she had heard from her own people, similar to the accounts and rumors that were circulating among friends and relatives. Everybody agreed except Eduardo. Best not to ask Eduardo for his opinion.

Eduardo?

Yes. Now he would have the chance to make contact with him. They'd agreed to meet at the main entrance. And he shouldn't look so jealous. There hadn't been anything between her and Eduardo in a long time. And, of course, he shouldn't even hint at his true identity, Eduardo wouldn't believe him anyhow. He only believed what he could touch and measure and practice and read.

"I'm not going to tell the truth," he said. "Not to Eduardo and not to anyone else. Let him think I'm Doralisa's nephew. Just a spectator."

That so-called Eduardo could think whatever he wanted.

Grandfather would admit no rivals, not in his story and certainly not in his bed. What happened to his father wasn't going to happen to him, his voice was wise enough to protect him from all the perpetual Eduardos from here to eternity. Manuel Sendero had been ineffective. He hadn't prepared himself for the situation where it's not what you have that matters, but rather what's left when they've taken everything away, where all the innocence and sweetness and gentleness with which you've won over half the world and which have allowed you to survive without having had to pay off your debts are now nothing more than a spur to their insults, almost an offense to those anonymous men who, let's not forget it, dragged him through basements he had never anticipated in any of his songs. Oh, if only Mama had been there, if only Doralisa could have whispered advice into his ear, if only my own childish grandfather's hum, if only his voice, had been trained to analyze, to plan. But his music was nothing but gibberish all of a sudden, a mere decoration that could not protect him. Papa had squandered the years of his life prophesying victories that never came and doing dances for the people whose bones were now being broken one by one. There can be no doubt that, as he saw the horizon die within him, he wished for some other fate: to have spent those decades storing up wisdom, refining courage, learning to distinguish the real from the imaginary and good from evil, to have prepared not for Heaven but for Hell instead. But that wasn't the way it was, the way it turned out. And now Manuel Sendero was going to have to face life without that particular wonder of nature that had been his talent, that had camouflaged his vices and excused his mistakes. It was as simple as that.

"As simple as that," said Pamela, signaling to him that they should get off the bus, they'd have to go the rest of the way on foot, families and flowers filled the market street. "But the truth is that not even Manuel Sendero knew why he'd lost his voice, right? If he'd known that, he could've gotten it back again."

That was the moment for Grandfather to accept the fact that she was right. But he foresaw the figure of Eduardo, who would be waiting for them on the other side of the crowd, at its peak, and he realized, like a bolt from the blue, before he even saw Eduardo, who he was, this famous ex-lover of Pamela's, and Grandfather chose to remain wrapped up in his false cloak of infallibility. He was afraid. It wasn't so much the fear that a half-century or a century later we fucking supersleuths would make him see that he didn't have even the slightest confession or evidence from his father himself, that his story was inevitably a partial reconstruction, depending on the accounts of the other fetuses, who wanted Manuel Sendero to locate his fountain, to kill the dragon and to rescue them, no, not so much the fear of that accusation. No, it was the fear that someone, someone close, soon, right then perhaps, would say: it wasn't his voice that Manuel Sendero lost, it was his hope; that they would say that, and he would have no answer for them.

To banish the thought and its consequences farther away than those unmapped lands he had crossed during the last twenty or thirty or more years of his life, he said to Pamela:

"So we're going to visit your family?"

He asked her, even though Pamela had told him that morning in the shower—when, his eyes closed against the stinging water, he blessed the parents of that great big bubble of passion and of that inviting mouth, all the ancestors of that insatiable, sudsy sexiness, of each and every blessing his miraculous hand was caressing, searching out every opening, tunnel, turtledove, and grotto, front and back—and she put an end to his chatter by turning the water off and opening his eyes so he could observe something in her that didn't want to be uneasiness, but was unavoidably a source of pain she could never overcome: she had no family, no relatives, cousins, not one brother or sister, no one. And Papa Ramón, the one she talked about so much? Papa Ramón had brought her out of captivity when her real mother and father had, well, they'd died. Died in a manner of speaking, she turned the water on again, so they could rinse off, actually there weren't even any graves, she suddenly turned the water off again, feeling around for a flowered towel, all they knew was that both of them had been picked up together, secretly, in the middle of the night, five men in an unmarked car, she started to dry his hair, they just disappeared. Papa Ramón couldn't find out anything. The only sure thing was that she hadn't been born in jail. And, more important, she hadn't been conceived in jail either. Only after receiving these assurances had Papa Ramón handed over a large sum of money into a not very saintly hand. He collected and raised the eleven other children under identical circumstances, faithful to his vocation of ex-priest, except in his not-so-Christian insistence that his providers assure him that not a drop of the violators' blood was flowing through those young veins.

"You can rest easy," the son of Manuel Sendero told her. "We would have known if your mama's portentous belly had passed through the jail. She preferred balconies."

He wrapped her in the enormous flowered towel and took her in his arms, tickling her until she protested: she was all tied up and he had the advantage of two free hands. Poor thing, he consoled her, how could anyone dream that she might have anything to do with those bastards?

Nevertheless, Pamela thought the way Mama Teresa did. Ramón was wrong. Everything that's born, said Mama Teresa, has a right to life. You don't choose your parents. Any more than you choose poverty or IQ. They ought to help all the children who clearly had no family to care for them. Papa Ramón recognized the validity of those arguments on a theoretical level, Pamela heard the endless discussion that went on for years after they had adopted the last child, just because it was unresolved, and no doubt both of them would go right on with the pros and cons and this and that up there in Heaven, but it's quite another thing when you're cooking for them, added Ramón, in his house he wasn't going to have any offspring of those faithless, heathen angels of the Devil nor anyone who carried, transmitted, or was contaminated by their genes. His wife replied calmly: when they had set up this house there had been no mention of discrimination. Since some unscrupulous rascals had created this not-so-underground baby black market, they had to save the babies, to use her poor father's money, God rest his soul, to keep them from being shipped out of the country. Now if he wanted to revoke the unwritten contract between them, that was his business, but she wanted no part of it. And Papa Ramón: woman, let the military take care of their own bastards, we have enough to do to help raise the fruit that almost didn't make it because of them. Look at these children, these little miracles, we've saved. Mama Teresa looked at us, still unrelenting. Either there was a motherland for all, she said, or for no one. But finally Papa Ramón imposed his point of view with a trick. He said that, whatever Mama Teresa might say, he really could tell everybody's genealogy by means of inner vibrations; just by listening to their voices, touching their eyelids, he could sense where they came from, who their parents were. Pamela and each of the other children had passed the trial by fire, that is to say, the trial by voice and eyes, and the door of the house had been opened wide to them.

So when Grandfather asked Pamela about her family it wasn't out of ignorance and certainly not out of cruelty. As he watched her glide through the crowd, he thought she showed no signs of orphanhood, of solitude and isolation, that she had made the whole world her family, that the old fossil who was walking nearby with a bunch of wilted daisies in his hand and a not-so-wilted gleam in his eye was her father, that her mother was all the mothers there, whatever their ages, all dressed to kill, as if they were going to a picnic or to a fair instead of to a memorial service, in commemoration of all those funerals that had been prohibited. Pamela might not know the names and biographies of the man and woman who had cast her adrift in this world, but, on the other hand, she had a country where she was nourished and grew strong. If she didn't know where she came from, at least she was very clear as to where she was going, and that in itself was a miracle in times like these. Her reply confirmed Grandfather's intuition.

Visit my family? Today everybody was visiting, today there was only one family. That had been the idea of the opposition. Exactly one year after the last song of Manuel Sendero, they had called the march. The dead, at least, shouldn't be anybody's private property. Just as Manuel made us share our dreams for a little while, now we would share our ancestors and all those nights of love shared by those who in centuries past had conceived us even though now we don't even know where they're buried. Year after year on this date all the people carry flowers to the families which they forget are not their own, as a thousand years from now the unknown descendants of our brothers and lovers will come to visit our common ground. That's why Pamela was so calm. For better or for worse, she was sure that her parents, the rest of the family that I don't know, were receiving some offering. Out there somewhere, purely by chance, I may be putting flowers on the grave of one of them myself. Maybe not Papa or Mama. Ramón says they wouldn't have buried them around here; that's what the ocean is for, he says, or the countryside, the mines and the gullies. But maybe my grandparents or a brother or sister, there's got to be someone close to me right here in this place. Everyone cares for everyone else's dead, no one is alone today. Of course, if you have some specific interest . . .

Grandfather did have. Precisely. She had lived every inch of her life right there, in this land, and didn't have a single relative's bones to draw her like a magnet. While he. Yes, while he.

One day, Grandfather didn't know exactly when, they surrounded the house. Before dawn. You could make out the shadows of the policemen or maybe a cigarette flickering as it passed from mouth to mouth.

"OK," said one of them, when the last cigarette had gone out and the sun was just appearing. "Let's go."

"Sendero," shouted the other one.

Manuel walked out without putting his hands in the air, perhaps hoping they'd gun him down then and there and put an end to it; his head was downcast, as if he were one more suspect in a police lineup, instead of being alone there in the house with the old woman and the peaceful breathing of Doralisa and the kid who was stretching then, all ready to give advice: "Beat 'em up, Papa, show 'em what a real man can do."

"You're not the one," said the first policeman, looking at the picture he had in his hand. "This one is older. What's your name?"

"His name is Manuel Sendero," the old woman was going to say, but Papa had already handed him the yellow card.

"Oh, Manuel, the mute, the one who used to sing," said the

policeman. The one they were looking for was a Sendero too, but his name was Juan, they were looking for his brother.

"He's dead," the old woman managed to say this time. Not adding, they had done it themselves, right there at the door in spite of his immortal knees.

"We have an order for his arrest," they said. "That means we have to have him. Dead or alive, that's not our problem. Because it's certain or at least presumed that he's the ringleader of the gang that's going around defacing all the posters."

Mama Teresa had explained to Pamela that before she was born the authorities had decided to put up a lot of posters along their tidy streets. It was part of a campaign to encourage popular participation, the authentic democratization of the country. The posters included explicit instructions concerning the most definitive details of civic life. From then on, all citizens were informed they should not walk on the grass, they should add a new stanza to the national anthem, office hours would be from two o'clock until four o'clock, on a particular corner they should remember the soldiers who had laid down their lives for their flag, the unemployment rolls were permanently closed, they could get bank loans only with prior deposit, there would be no left turns, the only direction traffic could and should move in was the patriotic one, they should respect their elders, any letter mailed without a return address would be opened, and a thousand other regulations to aid the citizen in fulfilling his civic duty. The law was omnipresent, not hidden the way it is in other countries, all elaborately bound and stuck high on the shelves of Congress or floundering around in some fictitious freedom of the press, no indeed, here the laws were published and in full view of the common man, who could therefore feel secure in the protection of that eternal text as he went about his daily routine. The law tables and guides for conduct were hanging from every lamppost and anyone could consult them with no difficulty, the old woman said to Doralisa's womb, besides which you could call the Lawyers' Guild absolutely free twenty-four hours a day from any public phone and hear a recording of the latest legislation. Through this legal aid they hoped to lower the crime rate and to eliminate all subversive activity, which they claimed was due to the ignorance in which the left-wing terrorists kept the people.

That was the effort that Juan Sendero and his gang were sabotaging, the policeman growled, they had dedicated themselves to the antipatriotic act of turning posters upside down, or removing the ones showing preliminary drafts of the articles of the new constitution, or erasing the word *no* and the word *prohibited,* so that, as a result, people were pissing on loudspeakers, thinking that was what they should do to avoid judicial prosecution, and the spit was accumulating prodigiously on certain corners, because long lines of patriots were stopping to fulfill their civic duty, following the altered instructions to the letter, and office hours had become totally confused, because no one knew if the pertinent poster was authentic or not, and the phone number of the Lawyers' Guild was always busy and the consultant there was on the verge of a nervous breakdown because of the questions with which he was being inundated, and the pages of the Manual of Good Conduct had been mislaid and the provisions of the articles of the constitution were mixed up with daily menus. It was clear that someone was responsible, had to be responsible, for such a catastrophe. Within forty-eight (48) hours all the dangerous delinquents with similar acts in their dossiers must be arrested and duly executed, among them being the said Sendero, Juan, notorious for his excessive rebelliousness, accused and convicted of training schoolchildren to draw mustaches and crossed eyes and vampire teeth on the pictures of the President of the Republic wherever they appeared, and as a result not only in official portraits but even on television programs and in the movies those distortions were beginning to appear on his face, imitating whatever characteristics the children happened to be painting on him at the time, to the point that in the middle of a reception in honor of the Chinese ambassador his hair changed color three or four times and his eyes crossed in the middle of a speech and His Excellency began visibly to limp on one leg at the exact moment when some young subversive or other applied a charcoal pencil tourniquet as black as the Devil's heart to the thigh of his official photograph. The last time this nonsense had ended with the immediate execution of the traitor Juan Sendero, so now they thought that by carrying out that exemplary action for a second time they would stamp out all hostilities against official posters once and for all.

"Like I told you," said the old woman, "they already killed him."

But since she had no death certificate to prove her point, they proceeded to search the house.

Half an hour later they left without the immortal uncle, that's true, but with a very mortal flowerpot in hand.

"Lady," inquired the policeman who was carrying the trophy, "who are these flowers for?"

The old woman realized that the man considered himself a true rival of Sherlock Holmes, and she decided to play along with him:

"Every Sunday I take flowers to the cemetery, where I give them to the caretaker, who then places them on the grave where my son is supposed to be buried. They won't tell me which one it is."

The policeman took that detail in, without blinking or showing any sign of appreciation. Any help whatsoever, including odors, colors, and flower petals, anything that would brighten the death of that poster saboteur Sendero automatically made her an accomplice, and why hadn't she informed them earlier of her firstborn son's change of residence? Now they would divide forces. One would stay there in front of the house waiting for the criminal to come out of hiding, and the other would guard the cemetery entrance or exit, and other reinforcements would cover intermediate points, but this time he wouldn't get away, especially because now they were accompanied by an eminent surgeon who had sworn that this time his knees would bend, and that must have been why he hadn't died completely the first time but instead had gone on undermining public enlightenment and tranquillity, pretending he was in the great hereafter, when, in fact, he was hiding away in the great here and now, hoping to vote twice in the plebiscite against the Supreme Government, like the negativist that he was.

And I couldn't be quiet for another minute. Just let 'em wait till I was born, I'd show 'em a thing or two, his uncle was living over here with him, hidden here as comfortably as could be in Doralisa's cradle, you multi-idiots, and my papa might be mute for now, he choked on something, nobody knows what, but just you wait till he gets started, he'll sing things loud and clear and he'll put the frosting on the cake, yes, sir, rich and thick the way I'm going to like it when I get out of here, as soon as you all do us the favor of getting lost, not only out of this house but out of this world, out of the universe for that matter, and there's no way in hell you're going to get my immortal uncle on his knees, let that surgeon stick his knife up his own asshole, shit, and if they think the posters have been messed up so far, just you wait till I get there and some others like me too, 'cause we've had it up to here with this stifling atmosphere in here, we can't wait to see you disappear, instead of our parents, just you wait till yours truly gets a hand on those posters and constitutional pretexts and the whole batch of shameful and shameless decrees, 'cause you'll never catch us, we've had years of training and of working underground and we're immune to curfews and to propaganda and we blend right into the sunlight when it's bright and we're as persistent as the rain, we're a generation like you can't even imagine, sons of yourselves, get lost, beat it.

That wasn't the only time Manuel Sendero suspected that Uncle Juan had taken refuge inside Doralisa in order to escape definitive death. Because the kid had had to grow up so fast he hadn't even had time to acquire a personal coloration in his voice. The tonality varied, sometimes trying out registers and adopting inflections on loan from the living and from the dead and, according to what the fetus swore, even from those who were still waiting their turn to be conceived. Sometimes the slight bell, which Manuel Sendero scarcely recognized as his own, tinkled; at other times it occurred to him that it was his own father speaking, with an imperceptible lisp and a foreign accent that tortured the irrecoverable and wandering words, confusing the end of one with the beginning of another, wanting to converse rapidly in a language that wasn't his own; and most of the time it was the barking tone of his brother, especially when he argued the most controversial and aggressive points. It got to the point where Papa felt like he was being challenged by his older brother instead of by his son. He wondered again if Doralisa hadn't fallen asleep in order to gather in all the fugitives and the murdered, if perhaps she wasn't really involved in a secret mission, commissioned by the resisters and kept secret even from him, since if the authorities suspected her they would have stepped in and cleared out his wife's golden, smooth, and manuelous womb. It was certainly a more plausible and comforting explanation of her conduct, and one more in line with her previous devotion to the cause. Because in that case, we're the ones who are putting one over on the Caballero, and, with all his pills, contracts, and test-tube fingers, he is the real cuckold, feeding not only Doralisa and the child, but also Uncle Juan and others besides, tomorrow maybe even Skinny. It wasn't surprising that they were finding it so hard to catch the revolutionaries. Doralisa's vast domain had hidden them. The tigers of insurrection were floating like primitive cells in a plankton sea, within the nocturnal splendor of Doralisa and of other magnificent women. She had been, and in her somnolent state undoubtedly still was, a cosmically generous woman. My little Knights of the Round Table, there always had been an extra plate at our table and the pot was always boiling in case somebody came along: he could always stay and eat with us without giving it a second thought. It was good that that infinite cathedral of Doralisa was continuing the family tradition. It was a joyous vision, imagining her smiling at the crucified who had nowhere else to spend the night, knowing that somewhere in the city a little bit of the past had been preserved unchanged, and that Mama's warm hearth was inviting them to hibernate in her Big Bear Cave, and they could keep her son company, since he had refused to be born and was already learning naughty words, inexcusable in one so young, which meant that it would be necessary to advise Doralisa not to let those wanderers abuse our hospitality.

You're crazy, Papa, there's nobody in here but me.

Nuts. Loony. Off your rocker. My father and master, Manuel Sendero, was not at all pleased with the idea that a bunch of relatives and even unknown expatriates were wandering around his wife's prehistoric interior. The future army that would liberate his country might be quartered there, but he couldn't help but experience a very human wave of jealousy . . . Of course it wasn't Doralisa's fault. She had jumped at the opportunity the Caballero offered her a few hours after injustice had been visited upon my uncle, the opportunity to help him, and he, in his turn, had invited who knows how many others who were fluttering about like birds in a thicket, searching for some nest in which to enjoy themselves for a while. Pregnant women, being sensitive, now felt themselves driven, from within and from without, to open their uterine channels to the dead. At this point in the account, Papa no longer knew if that was good or bad, if it was harmful to me or useful for my education. He didn't know if it was Uncle Juan who was complaining in there or if it was his own favorite ventriloquist of a son. He didn't know if he preferred a heroic Doralisa full of ghosts or a cowardly Doralisa sleeping in solitude and sealed tight. He didn't know whether to call me brother or son or father. Or maybe it was he himself, his own incredible voice, that had taken refuge in that beloved grotto, and from there, from that vision, there was only one step to an even greater absurdity: who could swear that the kid existed at all? Someone else had taken advantage of the sleeping beauty to climb into her hotel, and from there he was mocking Manuel Sendero, it was some grotesque dwarf. Or maybe there was just a recording inside, a tape, and it was all just part of the Laboratory experiment, because how could he, in fact, prove that the one who was talking to him was really his son?

I'm going to come out now, old man, I lied to him, and relieve you of your doubts. Of course that was false, and you could hear the other fetuses protesting, led by Croupy and the twins, accusing me of having fallen into the trap of sentimental blackmail. But the one who was going to be born blind, and that vision of loveliness that would be Pamela, supported me. Little white lies, my two girls told me, are indispensable sometimes, and if the man was upset, who better than us to console him; we who have nothing but comfort to give. So I figured better safe than sorry and I didn't use immortal Uncle Juan's voice anymore, or, to put it more correctly, I asked him not to speak, as long as he was living in here. That's the price of asylum. Look, Papa is getting a little hysterical. And Uncle Juan, an honorary fetus, complied.

He had to comply. Several times during the next year men came looking for Uncle Juan, but now they were dressed in civilian clothes. They were furious. From the information they got from the grave-diggers, they had disinterred the body; they had repeatedly made him an example right there in the cemetery, so that the other dead and even the living onlookers would realize there was nowhere to escape the long arm of the law; they went on trying to bend my uncle's bony knees—not a shit of a chance, shouted the chorus of children from the bellies of Doralisa and of the other matriarchs of the future—but they were as stiff as ever. And as if that were not enough, furious, too, because the authorities had decided to withdraw the Manuals of Good Conduct from circulation and to receive no more suggestions for the preliminary draft of the constitution, blaming the subversives, as usual, for having undermined one more initiative of the new authoritarian democracy. More than furious, because someone had placed a bunch of insistent and stirring flowers on the grave of the said Juan, and they were sure it wasn't he, Manuel, or the old woman, because at that point she had already disappeared, or Doralisa, who was in an experimental state, and the idiots didn't even consider me; they had no idea of the nighttime adventures, and, decades later, the daytime adventures of which I and my lieutenants were capable. They supposed it must be Juan Sendero himself who came out to put a bunch of hyacinths there, since, according to the police reports, he had always been very fond of them, and therefore they would proceed to behead the flowers at dawn if the perpetrator didn't turn himself in. At which point, the kid exploded, threatening punishments from beyond the umbilical cord on anyone who dared touch the wreaths on his immortal uncle's grave; in the other world they'd spend eternity reading their own decrees, over and over again, endlessly, that was the punishment he condemned them to, and once we're born, flowers will no longer have any scent for you, you'll go around in the middle of the springtime as if you were stumbling through a desert or were stuck in a coffin, and when you look at a flower, not a single petal will wink back at you, imbeciles, you'll see reality in black and white, the way you've lived it. And I didn't burst out crying because those of us who have a double heart aren't capable of that, but my fine Manuel Sendero realized that I needed someone to comfort me. He went up to Doralisa's bed, undressed, got in beside her, and, caressing her skin, he was able to explain to his offspring with his hands that all that passion was fine, but that it was better not to react with such immediacy, that patience is a part of change, that of course those men weren't going to behead Uncle Juan's hyacinths, they were just saying that to frighten us, and that I should save my energy for the day that was going to come, yes, it would come, the day when I would be able to visit the four or five or six graves of Uncle Juan, all the different places they buried him each time they shot him; I had to survive until then and then I would see all the gardens that completely anonymous people would plant in his honor, and it didn't matter to me, little flowers from my garden, that I was the one who was lulled to sleep by Papa's hands, that Manuel Sendero went on as silent as ever, because Papa had curled up like a crustacean between Mama's legs, and, I thought, is he going to enter her, is he going to make love to her for the first time since they took him prisoner, is he going to send me some little stars, incipient brothers and grandchildren, because that's the way to wake her up. He started to caress her with his fingertips, lower and lower, his lips touched her nipples, promising a soft stampede of antelopes in her underbelly. And I waited without daring to move, with nothing Oedipal, no complexes, hoping that the two of them would come together the way Pamela and I would as soon as we could get rid of Eduardo and his people, that way Papa would wake her up with a good humping, pure macho tactics.

But nothing happened. That's as far as it went; the two of them embracing and sucking, father and son, both nursing, ancient, infantile, almost brothers, sucking milk from a woman who had none to give.

Perhaps Papa was afraid that such a ceremony and such a consecration would bring no change; she would go on sleeping afterward as she had before and during. It would have been a violation, like raping a doll, and that would be to accept from then on the fact that we had no salvation.

One time Papa opened an eye at a party. He was resting in another woman's skirts, when right before his astonished eyes Doralisa's magnificent ass appeared. Appeared? Let's just say its magnificence was confirmed for him, because his unhealthy curiosity had been stirred by rumors of it for months: in effect, the slacks that Doralisa wore hid nothing. To the contrary. She filled that second skin the way the wind fills two splendid, fleshy, and unfurling sails. Because Doralisa fitted so perfectly into her clothes, it was almost as if she were always naked, always ready for action, Captain: she was molded to her clothing or it to the folds of her flesh, and the only way to know for sure that she wasn't as naked as the day she was born was by touch. So she regaled any men who happened to be there with an entire banquet of Doralisas, of multiple tones and shades, all of them naked, all of them ready, Captain. Ready for what? Why, to embark, of course, to sail, child. But don't you believe it was just a question of shouting all aboard and that was it. She was very selective, really cautious, Mama was. Because the only problem Doralisa had never been able to solve was how to make love without undressing. She was sure that clothing hadn't been invented to hide anything at all, but rather that the divine mission which had been commended to it shortly after the Garden of Eden—besides protection from the elements, of course—was to reveal and to accentuate the natural curves and folds of that breathless and fragile exuberance that some fool had enclosed in the word *body*. To embark, so there was nothing between her and the air, between her and others. To sail, for, after all, that's why all those complementary organs of voluptuousness and pleasure had been invented. Dressing and undressing always put her in a bad mood. It was at such times that she was always reminded of her cloistered and decorative condition, and then with a crash, as though a dam had fallen on her, she was struck by all those unholy occasions beginning with her childhood when she had to submit to the humiliation of knowing she was distinct from her clothes and harassed by the elements, the camouflage that men and women put around themselves in order not to see each other. And Doralisa insisted that so many walls between human beings just wouldn't do: she wanted to romp around the way she had when she was four years old at the seashore.

This unswerving commitment to transparency, against hypocrisy, explains why Doralisa would search for a man who could love her whether she was dressed or not. She wanted someone who would understand her so well that he would melt into the depths and into the philosophy of her eyes, who would never commit the insult of assuming an alien perspective in her presence, who would not, at the climactic moment, fumble to undo some annoying and mischievous snap, shun her skirt while caressing her thigh, or catch his fingers in the stitching of her panties. She needed a flesh-and-blood man who, like ghosts, would go right through her clothes, who would pay no attention to the fact that her magnificent ass and even more wonderful front were veiled by some offensive fabric or other, but rather would go directly to the heart of the matter.

That man was Manuel Sendero.

"And you intend to abolish the death penalty," Grandfather said, suddenly, to Eduardo, surprising even himself at the bloodthirst in his voice, watching the flowers as they fell from his hand onto grave number three, the immortal Uncle Juan's, but even more alarmed at his own lack of control. He had managed to hide from the fetuses involved in the second rebellion his absolute conviction that the Caballero had to be finished off like a wild animal. They, on the other hand, unanimous and fervent in their support of nonviolent methods, and unaware, because of their late arrival, of what had been Grandfather's first and not so innocent words to his father, would have censured him categorically and might even have gone to the extent of withdrawing their authorization for him to act as a spokesman for the insurrection. And now, after the passing of so many years of discretion, all of a sudden he put it all on the line and opened himself up to the criticism of a much more ferocious adversary and one who on top of it all was alive.

"Exactly," said Eduardo. "That's one point of our program that we no longer discuss. It's what this march today is all about. To underscore that point."

"I thought it was to celebrate Manuel Sendero," Grandfather said. "Or to protest on behalf of the children who refuse to be born."

"What children?" asked Eduardo. "Bullshit. Just one more government maneuver to distract the attention of the people, to unify the nation in the face of a supposed catastrophe. We've been holding this march against death for years and years."

At that moment Pamela returned. She had been a block away talking to Papa Ramón and Mama Teresa. For a while she had considered introductions. What was more natural than that Doralisa's apocryphal nephew should interview for his book the friend that Manuel Sendero had visited on the night of his last song? But Pamela realized that her lover was evading the meeting, he feared it. Because if Don Ramón followed the same line of refutation that Skinny had followed, it wasn't just the apostle and last witness of Manuel Sendero's feat who went down the drain, it was the adoptive father of his betrothed too. It was better to avoid conflicts for now.

She saw that relations between Eduardo and Manuel Sendero's son were not exactly the best.

"You could also say," she ventured, in a conciliatory tone, in the middle as she would always be, "that we're marching so the children can be born, so that in the future they can come here and put flowers on the graves."

Unable to stop himself, Grandfather kept right on talking directly to Pamela and as though Eduardo were not there. "Everybody, you mean you're really going to pardon everybody?"

Eduardo knelt, arranging the scattered flowers with one hand.

"We're not pardoning anybody. But we're not going to kill. We're different from them."

"I could forgive them for what they did to me," said Manuel Sendero's son, as if he were speaking not to Eduardo or Pamela or to the others who were witnessing the scene, but to that same cold earth that sheltered the remains of his father's brother, "but I'll never be able to forgive them for what they did to the rest."

"And this one?" asked Eduardo, shaking his head. "What did they do to him?"

Grandfather looked at Pamela. "Someday my kids will be able to tell him," he promised.

"While we're waiting for that far-off day," said Eduardo, standing up, "it might be good for your friend to know that we don't want to end up being confused with the ones who govern us."

"So that the day after tomorrow those guys can do the same thing all over again, thinking we're weak. Is that what you want?"

"So that tomorrow and even today, I hope, we'll be joined by the ones who are undecided, uncommitted, and the ones who are afraid and by everyone who's ready to jump on the bandwagon when they realize they have nothing to lose," said Eduardo.

"Those kids who don't want to be born are right," said Grandfather. "This is no way to win."

Pamela intervened to keep the double monologue from prolonging itself. She took Grandfather's hand, and he had the satisfaction of seeing Eduardo grow pale. "You have to clean out all the hate," she said, but her smile and the unweeping willows and the chaotic and glorious clamor of the people who were starting to put down cloths for picnic lunches in the middle of the cemetery—as if it were the day of the final banquet and they were all inhabitants of the future and a troop of kids playing hide-and-seek among the tombstones and the sun warming even the bones of memory and the celebration, Papa, what a celebration—not all of that could convince him that the march had any meaning, that the dead hadn't died in vain, that the cement under our feet wasn't much more powerful and enduring than the bodies that would dance and feel each other that night. Cement as hard as the fist with which Eduardo spoke.

"Just get used to our way of winning," Eduardo spat out at him. "I wouldn't put my hopes on some kids who supposedly don't want to be born."

Because Papa didn't make love with Doralisa that night. The one who had covered her like soft, warm snow and had wrung sweet animal sounds from her until I began to take shape could no longer cross her inner world like a comet and reach me where I was. He refused to, he didn't dare to humiliate her, to humiliate himself, to treat her like an object. He must have known that was not the way to awaken her. That he had to kill the Caballero. But I was not the one to tell him that. He would fall asleep so near Doralisa's nourishing fountain, I wasn't going to ruin that rest, I didn't call to him from the future to inform him that we had placed a whole forest of flowers on all the graves of immortal Uncle Juan, or that I was so in love with Pamela that I had forgotten my original mission, or that Skinny was challenging my right to exist, I let Papa rest there between Mama's legs, as if I were protecting myself from the cemetery where someday my grandchildren would have to come in their turn to visit me or my reflection, I let Papa dream that he was in here with me, the three of us, like three flowers on a grave, like seven peaches still unrotting in a grave, the three of them slept together that night.

As for Eduardo's version, Grandfather already knew it. For how long? Eduardo said thirty years earlier, straining to leave his mother's womb, for how long? Eduardo said thirty years later, with his friends that same night, speaking as if the son of Manuel Sendero were not present, as if he were a bothersome headache that would go away with an aspirin, for how long? Eduardo would say in forty, fifty, one hundred years, Eduardo's children would repeat it when they were exasperated, his great-grandchildren, without even knowing the origin of the phrase, would repeat it, for how long?

Grandfather had noted that expression, that automatic phrase, for the first time when the fetuses who were meeting in the General Council had proposed sticking it out, not being born, opening negotiations for a better world. For how long? said that voice that they had never heard at any previous meeting, for how long this childishness, these silly conspiracies, this lack of realism? They didn't know his name, of course, but Grandfather guessed that it was Eduardo as soon as Pamela described him that day in the cemetery. He was the only one who declined the adventure of not being born from the very beginning. They could do whatever their consciences dictated. As for him, he had to hurry along. He'd been informed that his father was in a difficult situation and that his mother needed help, he might never be born if he didn't make the move right now. Besides, the struggle was out there, in the real world, not with infrared placentas and clandestine games, but rather growing and maturing and learning to change things where they counted, where the power was: out there, on the other side of the warmth of the amniotic and hypnotic sac. Even then, the baby who would be called Eduardo had distinguished himself by his irredeemable sense of what was and was not possible, his ability to sniff out the famous correlation of power, his devotion to the organizational, the measurable, the concrete, his scorn for anything you couldn't touch, his adherence to history as the exclusive territory where the truth or the weakness of a thesis could be proven.

For how long? Eduardo would say eighty years later, still angry. For how long are we going to keep on listening to the same old story of Manuel Sendero? This style, this vocabulary, this vision of things, none of it is worth a holy shit. I'm the majority, said Eduardo, I'm the reader of this story, I'll be the reader, I would be the reader, if you'd only let me. And I have an opinion, I always did have, I won't keep quiet and passive while this fraud, this fool that nobody knows, and who comes from God knows where, shows up with his dreams and all that charm of his and takes my Pamela away. We've got a right to speak up too, the everyday people who just want to be left alone to multiply in peace. I know we're not in style, that our lives are not exaggerated or fantastic, all of which is good for the literature business, I know I can't win over audiences or women with my life story. But Skinny was right, Eduardo told his history students twenty years later, that wasn't the way it was at all. Not so extreme, not so fantastic, not so confused, not so Manichaean, not so extraordinary. I know the country you're talking about; I was born there. Do any of you recognize the country? Other than a mountain range that's more like an anatomy lesson, is there any distinctive feature, any particular street you walk, some real name? At the risk of not surviving to talk about it, I participated in the social and political movement that ended the dictatorship. I don't feel represented in this version. The tyrant. The tyrant who ruled us. There is nothing in this story about the way he talked, his mediocrity, nothing. It's all veiled, foggy, allegorical, remote. Item: where are the political parties, the divisions, the rebellions, the dissensions, the purges, the screwups, the documents, the strength? Without all that, you'll never understand anything. Item: the unions. Or is somebody going to deny the role of the workers in the creation of the front that broke the back of the dictatorship, that brought about so many strikes and finally a general strike that was a lot more victorious and a lot more impressive than that intangible strike of the unborn? Item: violence. What about the problem of armed violence? Item: where's the new language—how we had to struggle just to keep the words from being poisoned, so the children wouldn't repeat the official lies, how to peel off the skin of the old words and not kill the old convictions, how to find a common vocabulary with slippery and precarious allies? Where are all those problems? What is happening is very simple, said Eduardo that night, talking about Grandfather as if he were a specter and not a spectator of his attack, this character can't talk about those things, because he only knows about them by hearsay. Metaphors, Eduardo complained decades later when he was revising the existing bibliography about that period: instead of narrating concrete, testimonial history, they dedicated themselves to swelling us up with fictions and vague symbols. Manuel doesn't sing, she doesn't wake up, the other one gets the idea not to be born, all pure negativism. Was that the real day-to-day of life in our country? Was the defeat really so savage, so tough, and so mysterious that someone lost his voice forever? And years later, equally as sudden, equally as magical and unheard of, they tell us that the same person sang a last song. Why the last? When somebody confronts the bits and pieces of his country's dreams, when he looks each and every mistake squarely in the eye, as we did, when he tames the wild beasts of his own mistakes, then, one must suppose that he keeps on singing, he doesn't stop. And what about the song? What was the rhythm? If it was so popular, how come nobody can tell me whether it was was a mambo, a cha-cha, or a folk song? No, no, and no again, ladies and gentlemen. Changing the subject: you write for a few, but in the name of the many. But I'm one of the many, and I don't accept it. I won't buy the book, I won't swallow the lies, I abstain from any favorable comment. That attitude of letting things pass, of not calling a spade a spade, of criticizing behind someone's back, of separating what we say privately and what we say publicly, that's what we had to overcome to get to where we are, because it's when people have the courage to look at themselves directly, to stop lying to themselves, that you get a nation of heroes. No, ladies and gentlemen, for how long do we put up with these parasites who make their living by stirring up other people's pain, decorating it with myths and fables to make it more marketable? I dare them to name dates and places, I dare them to put in the book all the circumstances out of which the story was produced, with all the causes and the attenuating circumstances, so then we can judge what they're trying to hide. But they'll never do it, they're afraid to. And it ends up being postcard literature, pure narrative tourism, Eduardo told his grandchildren, so they wouldn't be taken in by such fairy tales. The fellow was immature, like so many others, but, instead of admitting it as he should have, he invented that nonsense about not wanting to be born. Who doesn't have trouble being born? The fellow was a coward—and they were a dime a dozen—who would fall apart if someone didn't show up for a meeting with the resistance, and to disguise his own fear and make it more acceptable, he attributed it to this so-called organization of fetuses. The fellow was an exile, and there's no shortage of them either, and so we wouldn't shame him by pointing out that he was just coming back now, drawn by strange and sensational news, he came up with this even more distant exile, this rubbish of a faraway womb. And what about us? Eduardo asked his *compañeros* forty years later, when he was proposing to name streets for workers and squares for peasants and factories for schoolteachers, and what about us? Where were we in all those words? The ones who constructed the reality, shitting and sweating and molding the reality with our own hands and our guts and, please excuse me all you young ladies present here, Eduardo said to a group of splendid teenagers who had come to ask the venerable old man to speak at their graduation, and with shit up to our necks, Eduardo said, where are we, the ones who strained like women in labor, suffering to have their children, to keep the country from falling apart, to make sure there'd be a country and not just a big empty hole in the middle of nothing? What about us?

I know, said Eduardo that night at the party after the march against death—shortly after Pamela informed him why I had come, mentioning my supposed book about Papa—I know, said Eduardo, calmly sipping his beer and passing the bottle back and forth in front of me, as if I were a minor and therefore had no right to indulge in such vices in his presence, as if to say he wouldn't even share a drink with me—I believe I know, said Eduardo, in such a tone of voice that Pamela had to squeeze Grandfather's hand, because the fight was about to begin and she couldn't see any way to change the subject—I know the singer they call Sendero in this story of yours. Eduardo spoke as if it were already the next century and he were writing an article for a magazine, reviewing a recently published book from a position of arrogant neutrality. It's a good idea, before we go any further, to examine the real evidence, putting rumor on one side and facts on the other. We can't go on treating somebody's voice like an object with a will of its own. It's a function of the body and its paralysis is due to clear physical obstructions or to brain impulses. Manuel Sendero must be situated plainly and simply in a particular latitude and longitude, with a climate and in a chain of historic events.

They told him about his best friend's death, that's what happened to Manuel Sendero. It might have been before they arrested him or he might have been in jail already when he found out about his friend Gringo. They had given him that nickname because of those inexplicable blue eyes in the middle of a half-breed's face with a shock of black, Indian, or Arab hair on top of his head. Except it wasn't just any death. He had committed suicide. I know, I know. The government did a lot of that back in those days, killing prisoners and then announcing they'd killed themselves. We knew of proven cases, lots of them. But some of them really did commit suicide. It's true, Eduardo wrote in a heretical article in an underground paper, that to a great extent it can be argued that they were systematically driven to that extreme by their captors. But that means blaming the enemy for everything that happens, in that way confusing denunciation with analysis. If we don't stop exaggerating, if we don't substantiate our sources, they'll never believe us, that vast majority out there will never trust us. Credibility, that's the name of the game. For Eduardo it was absolutely indispensable to bell every cat that crossed his path. Some people commit suicide, he said, and others, in identical circumstances, control themselves. Far be it from me, said Eduardo, with a sign of bitterness in his voice that almost made Grandfather get up to comfort him as though they were still hidden away and swinging in their mothers' inner hammocks, far be it from me to attack those people. It's true they chose an easy, almost a conservative, way out. No doubt of that. It's always easier to die for a cause than it is to live for it. Easier to do away with your own conscience and your own body than to force yourself to painfully adapt them to a world that's unworthy of them. It doesn't matter to them that the ones they leave behind—family, children, friends, distant descendants—have to take charge of those leftover lives they didn't finish. So the survivors slowly destroy themselves too, in some other way.

That's what happened to Manuel Sendero, said Eduardo. And worse. Because he felt responsible for his friend's death. He was the one who put him in what was for the moment called prison and later would be called death and what had been called revolution earlier. He involved him knowingly, with all the enthusiasm of a friendly octopus, for which he was well known, exhibiting an example, a theory, or an argument in each arm. With so much smooth talking, so much pretty singing, so many walks at dawn, so much caressing their wives' empty bellies and then feeling those same bellies where something was imperceptibly moving, so much planning for the children who would perceptibly fill those bellies, so much dreaming a world where the occupants of those bellies could grow up happily, with so much this, that, and the other thing, Manuel had convinced him. Gringo started showing up at demonstrations; one day he announced he would vote for the candidate Manuel suggested, he even went so far as to paint slogans on walls with them one night and to ask for reading material. To use the language in vogue, Manuel raised his consciousness. He helped give birth to another Gringo, who existed just beneath the surface of the customs and the prejudices of the first, one who had been about to emerge anyway. Therefore, according to the wife and future widow of Gringo, Manuel Sendero was only the co-responsible party, a mere catalyst or interpreter for the forces that were floating in the atmosphere back then. Sooner or later Gringo was going to be radicalized anyway, so better to have speeded up the process, but if it had happened later, well, Gringo wouldn't have compromised himself so much, the coup would have caught him in his preliminary phase. In a word, if it had not been for Manuel Sendero's siege, he wouldn't have committed suicide some months later. Because when the bug bites, it bites hard. Once he had decided, Gringo went to the mark as straight as an arrow. It was all just too fast. Like all sudden converts, he chose to renounce his previous life completely, he shouted to the four winds that he wouldn't rest until poverty was prohibited by law on this planet. Gringo was a veterinarian. No more bureaucratic work for him. It was out to the countryside to join the oppressed who were taking the land from the rich. He asked to be transferred to the country, and his request was immediately granted. The personnel office of the ministry was full of requests from sensible people who wanted to move to the capital, and here was some fool who wanted to go in the opposite direction. Manuel Sendero suspected that his friend was being too hasty. Gringo refused to listen to his fatherly advice, how to avoid traps, deviations, easy and extreme solutions. That wasn't the way he'd planned the phenomenon, Manuel explained to Gringo's wife the night before Gringo's departure. Gringo is not a phenomenon, she replied, according to Eduardo, that night, what a shame he's escaping that course in political education you had programmed for him. Manuel insisted he hadn't brought Gringo into the revolution so that now he could go off half-cocked, crazy, and hotheaded. Gringo replied: Manuel might be his teacher, but he was lukewarm, reformist, conciliatory. Capitalism had to be squashed like a bug. Take it easy, Manuel Sendero told him. With what? he asked him. Not so fast, he said. But Gringo had already gone. The train was pulling away and the slow strides of Manuel and Doralisa and Gringo's wife had to speed up so that Gringo would catch their last words: be careful, be careful, he told him, they told him, but Manuel never knew, I don't know myself, said Eduardo, if Gringo got the message. That was the last time Manuel saw him alive.

That's how Manuel Sendero lost his voice. Because he wasn't prepared to continue the struggle, at least not with the politicians who had guided so many innocents—if one can use the word *guide* with no irony intended, meaning "to lead, to bring by the correct passage or path, to orient"—to the slaughterhouse.

If it had just been a matter of his songs, which were heard facelessly and anonymously on the radio and on the lips of the shouting crowds, if it had just been a matter of that, then maybe his voice could have been saved. But he had not taken responsibility for his voice. Gringo wasn't the only one he had involved in this mess. Manuel couldn't forget the others, all the others, who, one by one, through his personal intervention in every social circle to which his fame gave him access, he had harangued. His well-known energy knew no limits, oh what a splendid machine Manuel Sendero was. Let the unbelievers, the skeptics, the supremely cautious, come to him, send them on. Don't ask yourselves whether you know how to swim, Manuel would say, the only way to learn to swim is by swimming: one, two, three, take the plunge into reality. Manuel Sendero accumulated followers, friends, and militants the way some people collected photos, stamps, or bottle caps. Hunting trophies for the public to admire. Manuel was really a seducer, a political Don Juan: the mere sight of an independent made his mouth water; he couldn't tolerate anybody who was dubious, vacillating, or critical. At the present juncture, my friends, we can change the course of world history, the future of humanity. This is no time to stand around like cattle. Let's get moving. Get moving. Into the corral, come on, it's time for action. How could he help but inspire people if he himself was so possessed by the vision of dawn after dawn, coming over the horizon as if it were a brother, one sun after another, like a harvest that we eat before we've sown? Come on over here, little sun, the women called out to him without Doralisa interfering, go on keeping us warm. And he, sure, with pleasure. We can't lose, he said, weaving a tapestry of unity from person to person, we're too beautiful, we're too real. Real? questioned Eduardo, without getting an answer. How long did this last? asked Eduardo. Manuel was real as long as the dispossessed marched beside him, as long as they held him up like a banner. It was necessary to convert the unwary, so there wouldn't be even one dissenter near him. Often, during this crusade, Manuel didn't even argue: he distributed kisses, shook hands, painted rosy pictures, and the people believed in him, more than in his ideas. He was like a fetus too, said Eduardo, when he himself was one and wanted to stop being one and the sooner the better, said Eduardo, when he recognized the danger that his companions might stay in the uterus forever, yes, like a fetus that wants everything around him to be walls of milk and of love. Manuel believed in paradise, in the Promised Land, in the Golden Age. With no modesty whatsoever he presented himself as an outrageous example of the existence of such utopias, where there were no conflicts, where nothing could be criticized, where failures are only symptoms of an illness that's rapidly being cured. Manuel Sendero cast his hook into the depths of himself, and there always emerged a loudspeaker, a record, a birthday cake that was big enough for everybody. He was invincible, Manuel was. I'm invincible. We are. The people are invincible. Who could stop him? Who could stop us? Who?

Manuel Sendero was wrong, said Eduardo, before the Central Committee of fetuses, and now his son wants us to make the same mistake again. But his punishment, said Eduardo to Pamela and to the other *compañeros*, years later, speaking to another empty beer bottle, his punishment was infinitely greater than his offense. Everybody said so in those days, what have we done to deserve this? Doralisa said so, Don Ramón said so, Gringo's wife said so. In their mind's eye they examined minutely every act from their past and they found nothing there to justify or to explain all that suffering. The answer was so simple: they had lost. If their prophecies had been fulfilled . . . But instead of devouring showers of peaches under an open sky and of making love, and at that point Eduardo stared at Pamela's thighs, which he dreamed of exploring and sprinkling some dreamy and sultry summer afternoon, they found themselves, well, you know where they found themselves and how. There's a minimum requirement for so much enthusiasm: you have to win. To win, brothers and little sisters, Eduardo exhorted the fetuses as they met to discuss their strategy for the first rebellion. And Manuel Sendero, as if Eduardo's attack on the father of the one who was pushing for the strike was a way of disqualifying the son himself, made all those relatives who are nervously awaiting us in hospitals bet everything they had on a losing horse. He was like the Pied Piper of Hamelin, Eduardo told the fetuses, who liked such children's stories, except it wasn't the rats that got drowned, it was his own friends. He carried them off with his magical guitar, with the power of his voice, with the promise that he represented the future. At least, Eduardo said, years later at the party, staring at Pamela's hand as it caressed the newcomer's foreign hand, at least, Eduardo said, thinking that it was time for a small gesture of nobility to make Pamela notice him, at least Manuel Sendero didn't pretend everything was the same when that future didn't materialize. He had the guts not to turn his back on it. His *compañeros* came visiting to see if he would sing; Skinny and the others tried to make him feel guilty or to move him in some other way, but he just shook his head. That's why the legend is a lie. It wasn't something involuntary, a reflex action. It was a decision, just like his friend's decision to hang himself from the bars of his cell, just like someone cutting out his testicles after fathering the third defective child. Manuel Sendero would be the first, Eduardo told his grandchildren, as if he, Eduardo, had known him personally, the first to be shocked at all these foolish stories. What's the point of all the metaphysics, for example, to explain the matter of Doralisa? The woman is the one, Eduardo told his literature students, you really have to look at closely in this popular story, this piece of folklore. A sociological analysis of the woman, that's what we can get out of the whole thing. The tide had been general. But when history moves backward at full speed, the first one to get screwed is the female, said Eduardo, hoping to win Pamela back at the same time, sure that someone who spoke like he did would be considered an ideal father. Because if somebody had to be sacrificed, said Eduardo, looking at Pamela, lusting to get between her sheets, wishing he could jump over the beer and the empty wine bottles and the records and the cigarette butts, over the legs of the son of Manuel Sendero, who was presenting himself as only a nephew but who was holding the hand of . . . if somebody had to get screwed, there was no doubt it would be the same old second-class citizen, the same old doormat and maid it had always been. She was going to be filled, swollen, inflated with kids, filled up with the projects of men, not her own, said Eduardo, glancing at that smooth belly, where once upon a time he had deposited his useless and contraceptive seed, watching Pamela, who was so close to his thoughts and yet so far from his touch, that's what awaited Manuel Sendero's wife or any other woman in those days. Mistress of hearth and home, mistress of canned goods and frying pans, mistress of everything except of herself and of her own destiny, in that way Eduardo was really proposing an alternative to Pamela, saying that if she married him, she wouldn't end up like Doralisa, that if she married him, she'd never have to have anything to do with the Sendero family. Because this Manuel will never get us out of here, the future Eduardo told those fetuses of the past, we're going to have to find our own way, we have to help Mama get out from behind that apron. We could be different, said Eduardo the fetus and also Eduardo the man thirty years later, men could be more like mothers and women more like fathers, anything's possible. That's why Doralisa went to sleep in the legend, Eduardo added, trying to drain the last drops of beer from the last remaining bottle. Because they canceled her dream of ever liberating herself. Because one way or another, it was her fate to be immobile. It's a macho story, Pamela: it focuses on the woman only as backward, passive, and manipulated. But it does reveal a truth. Doralisa went to sleep to protest the treatment of women, her own subordination. She knew she was alone, sucked backward in time, and that her son wouldn't come to her rescue, that her husband wouldn't either.

"But you're forgetting the last song," Pamela said, suddenly fervent, clutching more tightly than ever the hand of that living song that was her own Sendero. "You always forget the last song."

Eduardo chose not to provoke her. He didn't tell her that when Manuel disappeared the alleged song was an excellent stratagem to make the singer a hero, a fine pretext for calling for the first march against death as a kind of repudiation. He didn't even tell her, in order to flatter her feminism and to confirm his strategy for regaining her bed, that if anybody had sung, it was Doralisa and certainly not the mute Manuel Sendero. He didn't say anything like that. He simply said:

"OK. The last song. But what a price to pay!"

A price to pay? A price to pay?

Eduardo had not expected the flash of panic in his rival's eyes. For the first time that night, the fraudulent nephew of Doralisa and the authentic son of Manuel Sendero released the hand of the only Pamela at the party, shook his head, and raised it from her skirt with a slowness bordering on terror.

A price to pay? those eyes were saying. What price?

"I wouldn't let them do that to my son," insisted Eduardo, failing to understand what nerve he had struck, but prepared to push his advantage. "Would you allow it, Pamela? Do you think a song is worth that?"

Pamela's response was to stand up.

"This conversation is boring me," she said. "You've been talking all night nonstop. We're leaving."

With that she hoped to put an end to Eduardo's provocation of the son of Manuel Sendero once and for all.

Not knowing that thirty years earlier Eduardo had already said it all. We're not going to go to sleep, said the baby that would be Eduardo, that would be Papa Eduardo and Grandfather Eduardo, as soon as he could get out, and assuming that Pamela would cooperate, we're not going to go to sleep and we're not going to commit suicide, said the baby that would father thousands of imperfect Eduardos and, it is hoped, millions of absolutely perfect Pamelas, we, the numberless individuals who want to be born because life is too short to waste it in here in the dark, and the darkness that awaits us down the line is too long to postpone this adventure, which promises very little light and a lot of struggle just to make sure there'll be more and more light. I choose to be born, said Eduardo, bidding them farewell, and without placing any preconditions or exacting any secret guarantees, like the father of somebody I know, I'll be born at my own risk and on my own, without asking anybody's permission, I'll be born because I don't want a bad end, like somebody I know, who's leading us all down to destruction just like his father did his friends, I'm not going to commit suicide, said Eduardo, kicking toward the light, not in here and not out there, and he started to be born, as his voice grew more distant, and when everybody follows me, then we'll have, and his voice faded away and they were left to their own breathing and to their own solitary conspiracies, then we'll have a country where we can finally look each other in the eye without fear.

Grandfather heard him go with pity, with relief, with the hope that someday they could be allies.

"I would've liked to have been his friend," he told Pamela as soon as they'd gone down the steps and were on their way to the garret to continue another kind of banquet, another kind of mouth-to-mouth from which the monothematic mouthings of Eduardo would be excluded.

"Difficult," said Pamela.

"True," said Grandfather, "but all that rage against my father just doesn't make sense," not daring to ask her what she and the other fetuses had been unable to answer when they were small, why all that urgency in Eduardo's voice, why such a hurry to get into the world, why?

"You'll never be friends," Pamela said, and it was an answer to that recent question of his, but also to that other more remote question that again he hadn't posed. "Didn't you know that Gringo was Eduardo's father? You really didn't know?"

OUTSIDE

"Eight years," Felipe says. "It just can't happen."

"It sure can," David answers. "Anything can happen."[1]

"I'll stick the suitcases in here," says Felipe. "Why bother to open the trunk?"

"Your house far from here?"

"Well, actually, nothing's really close here. We're in Polanco. On the other side of the city. With luck we can make it in an hour. I don't know how the traffic'll be on a day like today."

"How's the family?"

"Great. You'll see the two little devils. You won't recognize them. Simón is almost a man."

"What about Juanita?"

"Juana's changed. Naturally. Who doesn't? And your Gringa?"

"Gringa's fine, thanks. Or do you want me to tell you the truth?"

[1] Commenting on a text which is more than thirty thousand years old, of uncertain authorship and obscure national origin, requires a great deal of patience, a quality which we hope will be demonstrated by the archaeology students who were chosen by lot to take the course in Prehistoric Amerspanish III. But there is no alternative. From that remote period of infrahuman history, the manuscript known as the *Dialogue of David and Felipe* is the only relatively extensive literary text (one long initial chapter and seven shorter fragments) which has survived intact. Whether it was transcribed from an actual conversation or whether it is merely the result of a flight of fantasy we cannot tell. Generations of scholars have dedicated their lives to studying the points of controversy. To have to reconstruct an entire epoch of human effort by means of these fragments can be compared to the task which would face an extraterrestrial visitor from a superior civilization attempting to recreate our entire present culture by examining a kitchen recipe. The only matter upon which there is virtual unanimity among the critics is that the most obsessive, recurrent, and, one might say, annoying theme is the quest for permits to leave and to enter countries, among which the most important seems to be the magical country of Tsil, in ancient America, indistinctly referred to as Chile or as Chilex in the text.

The two of them laugh.

"That's a joke," David goes on. "A Paraguayan friend told it to me in Holland. Every time I see him I ask him how things are going. Fine, he says, or do you want me to tell you the truth?"

"Tell me the truth."

"Damn traffic," says David.

"You'll get used to it."

"I'll never get used to it."

"Never say never. If there's one thing I've learned out here—"

"—it's that anything can happen. And never say you'll never do something. And if you don't keep your eye on the ball. And out of the mouths of babes. They had to kick the shit out of us before we finally started to believe what we'd known all along."

"Well, old man, tell me about your Gringa. What's it like living with a foreigner?"

"Know what else I've learned? It's impossible to catch up. We could talk for four hundred days nonstop and we wouldn't even begin to scratch the surface of everything that's happened."

"I see you didn't sleep much on the plane. But what am I complaining about? You're the same as ever."

"Something that hasn't changed."

"What a mess I got myself into, inviting you."

"So who else could you celebrate the new year with, huh? And besides, I've got a little something for you in this valise."[2]

"You brought something? I guess you liked my suggestions."

[2] The first problem which we confront is temporal in nature. To what eight years does the beginning of the text refer? Archaeologists generally place the text in the last century of the second millennium (ancient Christian calendar), since there is irrefutable proof that the legend of David and the Dragon Pinchot, that marvelous story that we're sure everyone heard at some point as a child, dates from that period. Since the *Legend* is aesthetically superior and has the additional advantage of being complete, many critics have used it, overused it in our judgment, to cast some light on the *Dialogue*. But the similarity between the two continues to be minimal, however such interrelationships are stretched and twisted. We recognize, nevertheless, that in order to date the manuscript, it is necessary to ask, as in the classic example of the chicken and the egg, which came first, the *Dialogue* or the *Legend?*

"Instructions, man. What do you mean 'suggestions'? They were instructions you sent: 'Paula will do the drawings, think of something she can show off with. The point of the matter: satire. Country: preferably the southern cone. For sophisticated readers who have some political savvy. Style? Well, Paula prefers it to be really off the wall. She's been involved in advertising for years and she wants to go all out. Let your imagination go.' OK. I really let it go, man, not just run. I mean this is the real marathon, really far out."

"God, this guy thinks the world of himself! And to think, I've been nearly sick these last few weeks thinking you might not be able to come."

"I wasn't going to make it. I swear it. Damn visa. And we still have to go back out to the airport Monday to get my passport back."

"Take it easy. It happens all the time."

"I just don't like to be a bother."

"So what's the bother? Besides, I have to go pick up Paula. I told you she was getting here Monday, didn't I?"

"She postponed her trip? I thought she'd already be here."

"They were going to present a petition to the Ministry of the Interior. For Gonzalo, you know. She couldn't leave the country last week."

"She hasn't lost hope for Gonzalo, huh?"

"She says you never lose hope. It's been a long time."[3]

For a while neither of the two adds anything. They watch the

[3] There are, therefore, two different versions which may be used to determine what the eight years are to which the *Dialogue* refers. The first is the Historical School, which maintains that the manuscript is a realistic testimony of something which truly happened. This school suggests, although with little external evidence (see the later reference to Ronald Reagan), that the action would have taken place on the night of December 31, which the premoderns celebrated as the end of the old cycle, during some year of the decade from 1980 to 1990. The other school rejects this realistic thesis: these beings and events are totally imaginary and absurd, with no historical basis. The *Dialogue* would be a mere derivative of the *Legend*, an attempt by some unscrupulous Grade B writer to take advantage of its success using the same well-known characters, David and Felipe and the dragon. This has been called the Abolitionist School, because it demands that this dialogue cease being studied in the universities and academies.

traffic, which is gradually slowing down. Felipe asks: "So you liked the suggestions?"

"Later, Felipillo, later. Let's not talk business so soon. There are so many other things to talk about. When Paula gets here I'll tell you both about it. We'll be talking about Carl Barks for the next two weeks. So let's talk about other things now. Family, asparagus, pornography, the crisis of the political parties, whatever."

"So that's what's eating you . . . What have you got against political parties?"

"What about asparagus? Ask me the price of asparagus. The ones they grow in Holland are great. Or if you want to, what about the magazine? What do you say?"[4]

Felipe brakes the car.

"One question. Did you just say 'Barks'? Or did I hear you wrong? Marx, you meant Karl Marx."

"First tell me about the magazine, Felipe."

"There's really not much to tell. In my last letter—you got it, I suppose?"

"I got that one. It was the one before that got lost."

"I tremble every time I drop a letter in the mailbox. I'm sure it'll disappear forever. I swear I'm getting paranoid."

"It's the exile. It happens to all of us."

"It's not the exile. It started before."

"You mean you were always apprehensive about your letters?"

"Not always," Felipe says, braking and then coming to a complete stop. "It started when I had to hand over my letters to Juana and the kids to the commandant of the camp." He blows the horn once, twice. "You asked me about the magazine. There's really not much to add. You'll meet Ceballos the day after tomorrow. He can tell you

[4] An extremely obscure allusion. Dubrovsky-Pérez believes, sardonically, that it may refer to David's secret profession (a dealer in asparagus). Whittaker-Alonso cites the importance of the ecology movement in the so-called Netherlands at the end of that millennium. Jarkins's and Gorostia's interpretation, that we are dealing with a means of avoiding discussion of the political parties, is enjoying some scientific and literary support. (See notes 8 and 12.)

more. But things are moving along. Distribution is OK. The work teams are organized and performing well. The first contributions are coming in. And with no official subsidies. That's really difficult in this country."

"So how did you go about convincing them about the comic strip?"[5]

"It wasn't me, believe me. It's just in the air right now. It seemed right that we give it a try."

"A try?"

"Yeah, a try. I wrote you about that; it must've been the letter that got lost. People at the magazine couldn't agree on the comic strip. Some of the editorial board thought that our readers—the Latin American exiled community, progressive Mexican intellectuals, you know—wouldn't be interested. I thought they were wrong—and I told them all about the Chilean experience, when we were able, during the Allende years, to bring out some comic strips which were really interesting, combining art and politics. If we were going to start another experiment we had to bring in the best."

"I'm glad you think I'm the best at something."

"The best? I meant Paula, not you . . . Joke, joke. No, seriously, brother, that's why we're so screwed up in Latin America. We're always starting from point zero, as if we hadn't done things before. In Chile you and Paula had done some work in real mass popular culture. So we should bring you both here. And I get to see you—how's that for maneuvering?"

"I hope you told them that our experiment failed."

"Failed? I wouldn't say that. You learned a lot, people were educated."

"Failed, Felipe. Not one of the strips we did with Paula has any permanent value. I wouldn't publish one today. Not valid. And I don't see where we did much consciousness raising, do you? The

[5] Only a specialist in the mass media of said period would understand this allusion to a comic strip. It seems to have been a primitive form of combining images and words in order to narrate a sequence with comical characters or adventures, which was then printed in newspapers and magazines. The discussion here of the artistic as opposed to the political is incomprehensible.

people who kicked us out sure weren't convinced. So don't expect a miracle now. After all, I only have two weeks to work on this strip—and, as you said, it's got to be artistic and political and—two weeks. Listen, how come these cars don't move?"

"Two weeks is all we could get," said Felipe, stretching his neck to see over the line of cars.

"No extensions. They made me sign a paper swearing I wasn't going to stay even one day more than that. No possibility of changing to a resident visa either. They had me bring along five photos, special size, my residency papers from the Netherlands, fifty florins, and my round-trip ticket. I felt like a criminal. Fifty florins. Look, lady, I said to the clerk. Pinochet's the criminal, not me."

"And how did she answer that one?"

"Regulations, sir. She was just obeying orders. I felt like taking out a snapshot of Dad and telling her what some other people had done to him, just obeying orders, in Germany. Poor woman. She showed me the government telex. Two pages' worth. I had to go to The Hague three times by train. Three times."

"Is it far?"

"Not very. Now that I see this traffic jam. Sixty kilometers. It's just the fucking bother, that's all. All of a sudden you just want to give it all up."[6]

"Give what up?"

"Everything. Just take off."

[6] Traveling—or living for that matter—must not have been a very pleasant experience in that epoch. Today, it is hard to believe that someone who departed from his country could not be sure that he would be allowed to return. Distressing indeed. Perhaps it is for that reason that so much of the text shows the protagonists discussing and looking for visas, which were permits to enter a country for a determined period of time (two weeks, for example). To return to his own country, on the other hand, a visa seems not to have been necessary, but rather some other mysterious permit, which is apparently granted after a "bullshit paper" has been signed (see later). Nevertheless, even with such a permit, there were no guarantees that one would be allowed to return. It is understandable why David, later on, says that when he takes out a passport, he starts to sweat.

"Take off for where?"

"Just take off. Anywhere."

"It's the same everywhere. You always think it's better somewhere else, but by now we know it's the same everywhere."

"We're pariahs, man. Nothing but pariahs. You take out your passport and you start to sweat, you feel like hiding it. You're ashamed."

"It's not such a big deal."

"Every once in a while they make examples of us. The generals in such and such a country carried out a Pinochet-style coup. Or they say that this solution seems like a Chilean solution, that is, the worst one possible. You end up feeling contaminated. That's what we've come to."

"Don't exaggerate, David."

"Come on, Felipe. In a museum you bump into a fellow countryman, and you keep quiet, because you don't want them to recognize your accent. Gringa gets mad at me. Speak to them, she says, tell them they won't let you go back. Make them feel uncomfortable."

"Here, at least, that won't happen to you. There's no way a tourist from Chile is going to get in. You should've seen us getting a visa for Paula. Since she was coming from Santiago."

"Europe's full of Chileans. Half the country is traveling. Where do they get the money? All of a sudden, we'll get calls from the most unexpected people. Last month it was an old couple, grandparents of a friend of Victoria. Some miniature boxes that my daughter was sending me for Christmas. She made them herself. That kid has real talent, Felipe. And if you could see Nicola's drawings . . ."

"What about Lolo? How's he doing? He was the only one I never got to see."

"Hey, isn't this traffic ever going to move? We won't get there till next year at this rate."

"There must've been an accident. Just be patient. A couple of hours' delay."

"A couple of hours? This would never happen in Holland. Those sons of bitches really do respect traffic signals. You wouldn't believe how careful they are."

"You miss it already?"

"Sure. As if it wasn't enough to miss your homeland, after a while you start to feel homesick for other places. Except for Paris. Homesick for Paris, never."

Felipe avoids looking at David's eyes, at his hands.[7]

"That's because you're such a gypsy. You ought to settle down in one place."

"We've been thinking about it, believe me. My contract and residency in Holland are coming to an end anyhow . . ."

"It's a shame about Mexico. Two years ago we had everything worked out, then you changed your mind. Now the situation is stickier."

"It's the same everywhere. The doors are closing."

"You ought to look for a country where they speak Spanish."

"Gringa keeps harping on Austria. She's from there, so we could stay there forever. But I just don't want to."

"What would your mom say?"

"She never went back, you know. Not even for a visit. She wants me to go back to Chile. Says I have to go back before she dies. You know how old people are."

"It's really a shame the Mexico deal got screwed. If only you'd decided two years ago. Now, without the backing of a Chilean party . . ."[8]

"Yeah, yeah, I know. I'm irresponsible. But I was so sure I'd be

[7] What happened to David in Paris? Why does Felipe avoid looking at his eyes and hands? If we could turn to the *Legend,* we would venture an opinion, because one of its versions maintains that it was in Paris that David lost—but we prefer not to use this method, but rather to attempt to understand the text based upon its own fragments alone.

[8] This reference has astonished commentators. As if the whole matter of visas and returns and permits were not enough, now it is being suggested that the residency of an inhabitant of Tsil in a foreign country (Mexico) would depend on . . . Chilean political parties. Even Jarkins, who is always looking for hidden motives for disagreement between David and Felipe, thinks that such an affirmation (David has lost the backing of a party in the last two years and therefore can't reside in Mexico) cannot be true.

going back to Chile with Gringa and everything. Everybody thought they were going to let us in. Hey, doesn't this piece of crap move?"

"Not everybody."

"OK. So not you. Congratulations."

"I didn't sign any bullshit paper."

"I did, and so did a lot of other people. I promised to respect the established institutions and not to participate in politics. Look at me. Was there a thunderbolt from Heaven? Did I get my face dirty? See any harm done?"

"You knuckled under, David. That's the harm. They made you sign that piece of shit, and then they backed out; they told you to stuff it, that you weren't going to get in anyhow."

"So you'd rather rot out here."

"I'd rather rot anywhere than to sign something for those shitheads."

"And that's why you were stuck for an extra year and a half in a concentration camp."

"I didn't sign anything for them. I won't. Not a damn thing. Not even a check."

"And what about Juanita? What did she think of that extra year and a half?"

"She didn't say anything. What could she say? When she married me, I told her what she was getting into. I laid all the cards on the table. She has no reason to complain."

"Is that what she says now?"

"She's changed. I told you that."

The driver of the car behind them blows his horn furiously for several seconds. When the noise dies out, David goes on:

"I don't feel humiliated. And I'm not giving up. They never gave me a formal, written denial of entry. The consul advised me by phone that permission had not been granted. For the present, he said. For the present."

"For the present? David, you can't live like that. You just can't, brother."

"What alternative would you suggest? Stay here forever? Make

believe they'll fall tomorrow? They're the ones, man, they've got us by the balls. They're the masters of Chilex."[9]

"*You know how I live? Huh? As if I were never going back. And as if I were going back tomorrow.*"

"*Pretty words. I wish they were true. But you can't live like that, Felipe. There are two choices. Either you concentrate on what's happening there, or you adapt and put down roots here. Like the planets, man. They end up in one orbit. You can't serve two masters.*"

"*Now you're geting biblical on me.*"

"*Yeah. I read Exodus every night . . . It's not easy to go back to the Promised Land, you know? Lots of people stay outside. Forever. Some people never go back.*"[10]

"*If Pinochet falls tomorrow, I'll be on the first plane back.*"[11]

[9] The Historical School, which maintains the textual truth of everything, or almost everything, that is stated here, affirms that this strange deformation of the name Tsil, one which does not appear in the few other Amerspanish texts of the period, results from David's expectation that the allusion to the country will not be recognized, and that this will allow him to sign the story (see later, this obsession with signing papers) and at least return anonymously. Dubrovsky-Pérez, on the other hand, the leader of the Abolitionist School and an enthusiastic supporter of the thesis that the region of Tsil is a legendary and symbolic place, argues, basing himself on fragment 1A, that Chilex is an invention and the dialogue itself, false; they could not be selling Chil-children, Chil-dolescents, and Chil-women in that period, since it is well documented that slavery had been abolished there several centuries before. Fortuin-Hanna's suggestion attempts to overcome the limitations of both these positions by proposing a metaphoric place. This position is beginning to gain support.

[10] This allusion to Exodus is significant. The possibility of their being able to understand that biblical passage is equivalent to the possibility of our entering into their life experience.

[11] This obsession with Pinchot (written here in its less gallicized form) seems amply justified. (See also fragment 6A.) Besides the *Legend*, there are secondary references which have established beyond a shadow of a doubt that there was a dictator with a similar name who lived more or less in that time period. But, in addition, Middle-New-Amerspanish has preserved the term *pinsetear* (archaic spelling, of course), which means, as you well know, "to carry out extremely cruel, albeit astute, acts." There are even those who maintain that it is from this word that the verb *to pinch* (Primitive Amerenglish) derives. To this day, in the street jargon of the region which was once Tsil,

"What about Juanita?"

"Forget Juanita. I'll go tomorrow. With or without a job. I'd go back in a flash. Family or no family. She can decide for herself."

"There's one thing I don't understand."

"Just one thing? That's lucky."

"How can you be so sure of everything you say, Felipe? With all the mistakes that've been made, I'd be a little more careful about what I said. The one that ends up getting screwed is always somebody else."

"Great tactic, David. Since you really blew it with your strategy for going back, you want to cover up past mistakes by going on the offensive. Great tactic."

"My only mistake was leaving Chile, Felipe. And now the reasons why I had to leave are no longer valid. Would that be your opinion? I'd really like to know your opinion."

"My opinion is that they're not going to let you back in."

"And what if I told you that pretty soon there may be a good chance?"

"Are you making another petition, David?"

"Let's just say another avenue is being explored. Yeah. That's it."

Felipe is silent for a good while, as if listening to something, a radio blaring in a nearby car.

"Aren't you going to tell me what it is you're talking about?"

"Screwdicial power."

"Screwdicial power?"

"Yeah. You screw and screw and screw some more until the government finally lets you in, because your friends are kicking up such

---

when a child is given a position of leadership in a game by his playmates, he must promise that he will not be a "pinchot," that is, that he will not betray the confidence which has been placed in him by the others. A study by the Division of Anthropological Analysis has concluded that such a practice is not due to the influence of the *Legend,* since in it the Dragon Pinchot is portrayed as bloodthirsty and greedy, but not as a traitor. Therefore, the collective, childhood memory has preserved an oral testimony of the perversity of the dictator for more than thirty thousand years, paralleling the *Legend* itself and perhaps reinforced by it.

a stink inside the country, they would rather not have you outside anymore."

"Who's going to screw around for you inside?"

"Just people."

"Who exactly?"

"I'll tell you later, Felipe. Later."[12]

"Later. Always later. Ask you about Gringa, and it's later. Ask you about the comic strip, and it's later again. Ask you about the steps you're taking to go back, it's still later. I ask you about Lolo and you tell me nothing. You'd think we were enemies or something."

David opens the car door and steps out, walking up a little farther among the other cars. He comes back and sticks his head in through the window.

"OK. To answer your unfounded accusations, let's take a look at the comic strip. The traffic hasn't moved for almost an hour."

Felipe looks at his watch.

"Nine minutes. Only nine minutes. You exaggerate as much as ever, I see. But I accept the proposition. It beats sitting here blowing the horn."

"Or listening to the radio."

[12] Jarkins has stated that this whole long passage, the largest segment of the *Dialogue* that we have, is organized around two themes: David's obsession with returning and Felipe's obsession with discovering David's intentions. This interpretation assumes that the friendship between them is not as strong as they themselves would have us believe, and that, in reality, they are joined more by tension than by affection. Something, says Jarkins, happened in Paris, something which made David sign the document to gain entry, something which now means that he has lost the backing of a political party in Chile. Therefore, David does not respond to Felipe's questions and Felipe does not trust David. The important point in this analysis is that it therefore concludes that we are not face-to-face with a development from the *Legend*. The characters are not preparing an expedition to Tsil to liquidate the Dragon Pinchot and to rescue Alejandro, David's son, from grave danger. Far from it. But Dubrovsky-Pérez, based on his firm belief that they are identical to the characters in the *Legend*, argues in favor of an intimate friendship between the two men. The tactical differences between them, this investigator reminds us, occur in the *Legend* after it is known what has happened to Alejandro, not before.

"Right. So let's open up your Pandora's box and take a look at what my crafty David has brought his faithful Felipe."

"Fine," says David. "We'll open the briefcase of lies. Voilà, la comic stripette."

"La comic stripette," Felipe repeats, staring at the thick bundle of papers, notes, and outlines David has in his hand. "And what about the conditions, David? What conditions do you have to accept before they'll sort of let you back in?"

"Conditions? What kind of question is that?"

"I mean the comic strip. Are you going to sign your own name?"

"What's that got to do with anything?"

"Everything has to do with everyone. You're trying to get back in. So are you going to put your name on the comic strip?"[13]

"You were in such an all-fired hurry to hear about the comic strip, so do you want me to tell you about it or not? It's not finished, but . . ."

"OK. Lay it on me. If you don't want to talk about that little matter, I won't force it. So tell me about the comic strip."

"The first frame," David says, "fills half a page. The series title will be above it. Don't ask me what it is. I still haven't decided. I hope that among all of us we can come up with something good.

[13] The first fragment of the *Dialogue of David and Felipe*, the only extensive fragment that we have, goes up to this point. As can be seen, it ends with another question which has no answer. The drastically different results produced by the practice of signing one's name are astounding. David tends to sign, Felipe to refuse. The same occurs in the matter of the re-entry certificate, the permit to stay two weeks (visa), and for the departure from the camp (what camp?). But in the case of the comic strip the roles seem to be reversed: Felipe would sign, David has reservations. Such disagreements could be considered as supplementary proofs that we are dealing with two men who are unable to communicate, in accordance with Jarkins's thesis. Nevertheless, Kalki Gregor and Ferrowell believe that, on the contrary, in such times of insecurity, this preoccupation with one's signature was a means of compromising another person before the battle, based upon the primitive superstition that one's signature is identified with his spirit. We are dealing with brief skirmishes before a major expedition. Handing over one's signature is equivalent to surrendering his soul, a ritual of purification and brotherhood. (See fragments 2A and 5A.)

Maybe *Super-Agency* or *Supremagency*, something like that. In the upper-right-hand corner it says: 'In a hotel in Chilex somebody is dying.' "

"Chilex?"

"And underneath, in Paula's inimitable style, an enormous hotel room, converted into a hospital operating room. In the bed, a barely breathing figure, plugged into whatever machinery a sick imagination can come up with, as if the man were an appendage of the machines around him. The next five frames that make up the first page focus on each one of the patient's sensory organs, each of them barely working, connected to an electrical apparatus; for example, the eyes are hooked up to a TV set, the ears are attached to stereo speakers, and the mouth, down in the fifth frame, is like a tape recorder, and you can hear what are the first and perhaps the last words of Carl Barks, our hero: 'Bring Sarah. Hurry.' We turn the page: 'A few months earlier.' And we see an airplane landing in the Chilex International Airport."

"Hold on, wait just a minute, man. What's this Chilex business? Have a little patience with this poor, tired brain of mine."

"Chilex is something like a country. Any resemblance between that country and any other with a similar name or even a different name is purely accidental. If the reader insists on indulging in completely unjustified comparisons, the authors, not to mention the authorities, assume no responsibility for such distortion and indeed are prepared to prosecute the instigators judicially and in other ways. Don't say I didn't warn you."

"I'm used to being warned."

"Anything goes in this country. Ex-Chile: it was, but is no more. A trademark, a copyright, a department store more than a country. Like a supermarket of underdevelopment. Anything goes. Any experiment. Everything is ex-ported. A big *X* down on the ass of the world. A real Frankenstein's monster of a country. Anything you see, ladies and gentlemen, friends of both sexes, is within the reach of your pocketbook. Everything's on sale every day, twenty-four hours a day. Third World Shopping Center, continuous show, approved for viewing by old and young alike. Step right up. Step right up. A real closeout sale. We won't close the doors until the distinguished public has walked out with every last item of merchandise. Who'll buy the first Chil-child? Do I hear an offer? Look it over, try it out, and take it with you. And if things keep on going at the present rate, friend, I assure you, I swear, there'll be nothing left in no time at all. Nothing left to sell, nothing."

"The people in the car beside us are looking at us like we're crazy."

"We'll sell them some Chil-children too. Or maybe they'd prefer some Chil-dolescents or some Chil-women. Everything goes. All reduced."[14]

"Stop fucking around. Those guys can't take a joke. Especially in this traffic jam. Look, David, frankly I don't think Chilex will work. I suggested the southern cone, meaning you shouldn't limit yourself to our territory. Since it's two Chileans doing the comic strip, we have to be more careful. Our public is mostly Mexican, with some other Latin Americans."

"But it's a country like any other in the Third World, just a little exaggerated. It's a composite, a laboratory. But if you don't like the name, we'll change it. How about X-Land, South Hongo-Kongo, Fartantica, whatever you want? What matters is to keep it the same kind of country, the craziness of the place is what counts."

"So what about Barks? Who's he?"

"They invite him to Chilex. That's why, after showing him on his deathbed, we flash back to the press conference some months earlier. He participates in it when he gets there."

"Why do they invite him?"

"Ah, that's the problem. You find that out later. We'll show a different reason, another step, another job they give him, in each episode. They'll take him in little by little, without his even realizing it."

"But who is he?"

"He's a real-life fellow. A guy that's still alive. In California. An

[14] Fragment 1A. These four sentences (we do not know if they are spoken by David or by Felipe) are the ones which Dubrovsky-Pérez uses to prove that Chilex never existed, as mentioned in note 9.

old guy. He was born in 1901 in Oregon, the south of Oregon. He's done virtually everything to earn a living: cowboy, lumberman, printer, metalsmith, carpenter, barkeeper. But I can't use all that; I want somebody timid, no experience in life. What interested me is that he finally started to work as a cartoonist, so I stuck with that. He ended up being Disney's number one cartoonist. He's not so well known, though, just by a few fans, because he's not allowed to sign his work. He's the one that invented Scrooge McDuck and Gus Goose, lots of others too."

"Chilex. Carl Barks. You're crazy, David."

"Wouldn't you say I've got my reasons, Felipe? But I forgot—you're not crazy at all, are you?"

"Is this your first trip to Chilex?"

Carl Barks could only blink. He felt his head turning, first to the right, then to the left, then back to the right, slowly, looking for the person who undoubtedly would answer the question. Fortunately, the other members of the delegation could do that. Sarah would have known what to do, what to say, as she always did, but it would be two weeks before she would arrive. In the meantime, he'd be like the snails, who, after all, had survived lots of storms: he'd withdraw into his own shell, close his eyes, shrink and smile, just like right now, smiling like an idiot into the lens of the TV camera that had rolled up near him. Outside, the second plane had just landed and, according to the interpreter, world-famous personalities were about to enter, led by the one and only, the inimitable, Foilback, in the flesh, all of them people who had cut their eyeteeth on press conferences. So until those vedettes burst in, the wisest course of action was to smile like an ostrich that can't find any sand in which to bury its brains.

The interpreter hurriedly whispered a few words in his ear. "You, Mr. Barks, they're asking you. Is this your first trip to Chilex?"

"They can't be," said Carl Barks in surprise. "They're asking me?"

The interpreter, in a loud and imperious voice, asked them to repeat the question.

Now there was no way out. He must unavoidably put on an adult face and be polite to the female reporter who had formulated that first question and who was now repeating it. Who did the owner of that honey-toned voice remind him of? The way she lazily touched her hair? Those deep, lagoonlike, coffee-colored eyes? Like a flash of light in a fog, a woman's name appeared and disappeared, appeared and disappeared, a line from the Bible in flashing neon, and Carl Barks had no time to follow up the doubt, the loss, the resemblance. "Is this your first trip to Chilex?"

They hadn't warned Carl Barks that he would have to answer questions. No one had mentioned a press conference. Actually, they had explained absolutely nothing to him about what they expected him to do. Come as a special guest to our country, the letter from Chilex's ambassador in Washington had said, where you can take a well-deserved rest in our marvelously hospitable land. You can draw, if you like, the cultural attaché had added on the phone. Just have a good time, the honorary consul of Chilex in Los Angeles had whispered two days later, handing him an envelope with two tickets inside. Just be a tourist, added the interpreter who was waiting at the entrance to the airplane and who would accompany him throughout the trip, and observe whatever you would like. Then, said the stewardess who helped him fasten his seat belt, freely present your impressions. In comic strips, if you like. That would be fine, suggested the interpreter, who visited all the members of the delegation but who gave special attention to him, or perhaps in an article, an excellent idea, or if you'd like, by giving a press conference once you return to the United States. That's your business. Ours is a free country, just like the one where you were born, stated the Chief of Protocol, as he directed them to the hall where the reporters awaited them. Just let yourself be carried along, said the interpreter, who had re-emerged and had taken him by the arm, carried along by your own fresh, spontaneous, and faithful impressions.

Fine. He would draw, he would write, he would observe, he would let himself be carried along. Since, by some quirk of fate, someone had actually remembered him, drawing his name from who knows what old file or from some footnote in a book on the history of animation, he would take the trip. But this? This reception with thousands of handkerchiefs waving greetings, with giant letters spelling out BIENVENIDOX and WELCOMEX on the mountains, the flower for his lapel and the whispered promise that the keys to the city were on the way, while school kids and aldermen sang American folk songs in English. Perhaps it was a heartfelt homage to the other members of the delegation, important people, after all, to Foilback, who would now be getting off the plane with his arms upraised making the sign of the *V* for victory. But there could be no doubt now, as he confronted fifty reporters—see, there is freedom of the press, the interpreter drove the message home from behind him—he would have to answer questions, oh no, he surely hadn't expected that.

Carl Barks felt like running away. He should never have accepted the invitation. Sarah had convinced him. If someone has finally remembered you, you certainly aren't going to be so rude as to refuse the invitation. Of course, but Sarah wasn't with him, because she had considered the annual bazaar to benefit orphans on he didn't know what faraway continent more important. Sarah had stayed behind, promising to follow him, and so she had sent him off on this stupid venture. He was too old for this kind of jaunt. He was better off never leaving his little bungalow in California, cutting his lawn, pruning his favorite roses in his little Japanese garden, scraping together a few extra dollars by painting portraits in oils, better if he had never received that damned letter from the ambassador, and if he didn't have to answer that question right now. Of course this was his first trip. His first and last.

Carl Barks turned around. The interpreter's eyes were deep gray, friendly no doubt, but inscrutable, and there wasn't a drop of pity in them. "The consul didn't tell me I would have to do this," he said.

And then, right away, looking directly at the reporter, managing to wonder where, how, what that face reminded him of, he said:

"Yes, it's my first trip."

The smoke was becoming thicker. He saw the newshounds bent

over their notebooks. That's enough, that's enough, there's no reason to add anything else, he had done his duty now, but he felt that from the moment he had gotten on the plane, even before, since before he'd received the letter, everything had been leading him toward the need for just one more sentence, because his first answer had been brief, too much so for a man who had brought so much joy to the children of those same reporters, even though they might never have spoken his name. They were waiting expectantly, waiting like children, little ones, like tiny mice, baby pigs, bear cubs, on the edge of drowsiness, and he couldn't let them down.

"I'm going to let you in on a secret."

He enjoyed the almost subterranean whispers that spread over the group. It wasn't so hard after all. The tense muscles at the back of his neck relaxed. The public must be talked to the way one would talk to children, and Carl Barks was good at that, even though he and Sarah had no children of their own. Holding a press conference was a question of rhythm: once the script was ready, the characters sketched in, he was in charge, the only thing left to do was to deftly supply the appropriate suspense and write words clearly and in capital letters in the little bubbles over their heads.

"In fact, this is my first trip outside the USA," said Carl Barks, basking in the astonishment his revelation produced. He was sure they would fall all over themselves asking more questions, and that he had asked for it, for daring to focus attention on himself, stepping onto center stage for the first and only time since the day he was born, when he had also been center stage—he supposed—the day's star attraction. "My longest trip was to New York, when I was twenty. I've never even been to Canada, which really isn't that far from my native Oregon."

The murmuring faded away, and several reporters asked questions at the same time.

"One at a time," Carl Barks said, smiling.

"Mr. Barks will answer all your questions," the interpreter intervened in Spanish, "but please ask them one at a time."

"What do you think of your patron and teacher, Walt Disney?"

"Mr. Barks," said the interpreter, "thinks that he was a great man, a great American. He was like a favorite uncle to everybody who had the good fortune to work for him."

Carl Barks hesitated a moment. It was the answer they wanted to hear, like a happy ending, but it wasn't entirely true. You can never tell the whole truth, he had once told Sarah. But his intuition told him that she would have insisted on something more: just a hint of what really went on, so that those present would understand that life with the boss had not exactly been what you would call a honeymoon. Just an anecdote, the merest skeleton of a revelation, nothing to show, and he could hear the words slipping from Sarah's lips like needles, knitting a sweater for some nonexistent grandchild, nothing to show his egotism, his stinginess, nothing that would suggest—and Sarah did suggest it—the Great Magician's tyranny, nothing, in effect, that might detract from his brilliant legacy and his indisputable title as King of Happiness. Forty years of slavery, Sarah's voice sounded inside Carl Barks's head. He sighed. The only way to quiet that voice was by admitting that naturally he wasn't always, of course, like any genius, you understand, a man easy to get along with for the most part; then he realized that his slight hesitation, the silence he had invited, had allowed an indiscernible but decisive shift in his audience's attention. Those present were beginning to move uncomfortably in their seats, their eyes were blinking nervously, on the sly, they were tapping their feet impatiently, and there was widespread clearing of throats. That change in climate was only the first announcement of a veritable storm that was on its way. Even though one of the cameras was still focusing on him, Carl Barks understood that it was only a goodwill gesture: from now on his words lay on the periphery of the news. There could be no doubt. Beyond those closed doors, still invisible, but even in its absence exercising an overwhelming attraction upon all of them, the interviewees and the interviewers, the interpreters and the interpreted, the tourists and the guides, a powerful magnet was drawing nearer, extending its vast, trembling waters. A tugging, magnetic perfume began to flutter about all those present; it grew heavier and more biting, it made the air vibrate, an undertow of fingers that pulled at them. Magnet, perfume, undertow. Something even more powerful; a giant vacuum cleaner that sucked away at their will. People started standing up, as if all of them simultaneously had an urge to scratch but had no hands. From the corridor that led to the waiting room, a confusing quagmire of sounds reached them. There was a motor, voices, footsteps. Something unstoppable was coming down the hall, and that something was T. H. Foilback.

"Death, Mr. Barks. What do you think about death?"

The same reporter as before. She was taking advantage of this pause to return to the attack. Carl Barks pulled his attention away from the waiting room doors and that stereophony that continued its victorious march toward them, and contemplated her, more surprised than moved that someone still remembered his presence in the middle of all that hubbub. Imperturbable, she gave no indication she was aware that something in the atmosphere had changed. Her large eyes, the color of clear, perfect chocolate, drew him to her like a peaceful haven. Carl Barks didn't even make a stab at an answer. As if someone had phoned him in the middle of one of his favorite TV shows, not even he himself could muster any curiosity as to what his answer would be. Death? What death? Whose? Before he could flash a smile of recognition and of complicity, he realized that his head was turning, a pair of gentle forceps were slipping relentlessly into his muscles, turning his head until he was facing the waiting room door, as were all the others present there, something like a military band, ready to play, prepared for whatever was to come.

Suddenly the doors swung open.

T. H. Foilback roared in like an avalanche, seated on an immense motorized platform that seemed to be floating half a meter above the floor, surrounded by a trotting beehive of cheering personalities and a veritable flotilla of secretaries, led by the Chief of Protocol. A few members of the delegation had had the good fortune to hitch a ride on the triumphal carriage, where three glass plates, a long steel wall, and six guards assured the security as well as the peace of mind of T. H. Foilback. Behind that phalanx of men and women a mass of red hair could be seen, darting here and there, moving incessantly, obsessively, and hysterically, the up-and-down movement of a red, horizontal sun in a country where night never falls and where no one sleeps. Supported on a cushion of air that showed no signs of requiring wheels, surrounded by ubiquitous though hidden sources of multiphonic sound, covered with mysterious lights of unclassifiable colors that flashed on and off, all along its only wall there was a veritable tapestry of thousands of buttons, levers, nooks, wires, and contraptions whose use and description were difficult to imagine, and which T. H. Foilback pressed and filled, touched and pushed, twisted and turned, opened and closed, manipulated, pedipulated, and elbowipulated as though he were a light bulb that someone, he himself, was testing in every socket along the endless wall of a factory. Spinning like a radar antenna, softly humming with the centipede sound typical of a washing machine, centripetaling a telephone in each hand, speaking first into one then into the other, centrifuging a whirlwind of orders and recommendations to his secretaries, screwing and unscrewing himself as he moved, helicoptering correspondence with a remote-control pencil, T. H. Foilback nevertheless found time to thank the reporters, who stood applauding him and who didn't stop cheering him until he raised both hands over his head like a Roman emperor or a champion boxer, greeting them with a telephone receiver at the end of each fleshy and epic arm.

Everyone waited for some reporter to open fire or for the Chief of Protocol to make the totally unnecessary introductions. The energy emanating from the platform was almost visible. Carl Barks saw a fly, trapped in one of the air currents, swimming helplessly, trying to change its course. All for nothing. It ended up plastered against one of the impeccably clean windows of T. H. Foilback's vehicle.

"Foilback?" Felipe asks.

"Another real-life person," answers David. "You'll love him. He's the chief of the Latin American section of Exxon. I got the idea of using him because, besides what those assholes did to us, that fellow

visited Chile a few years ago when they opened a center for electronic and nutritional research. That center is going to be an essential element in the strip. Arnold AID and Milton FMI are along with him. Milton has come to see how everything is working. They always speak in rhymes and in double-talk, like a couple of chorus girls. Then I added the ex–Minister of Tourism from South Vietnam, and the Nobel Prize winner and father of the green revolution, Norman Borlaug, a French fashion-queen, a Christian Democratic member of the Bundestag, Vondertod's his name, from the Federal Republic of Germany. Originally Ronald Reagan was going to come too. He wanted to make a film with millions of extras; after all, in Chilex human beings are cheap: you can really kill them too, just imagine what a spectacular film that would be. But now it's more problematic to include him, don't you think?"

"I do think."

"And Major General Soro from the Pentagon."[15]

"Where'd you get that one? I never heard of anybody like that."

"Special Operations Research Organization: SORO. No 'Zorros' down here. Just Soro. Chief of the Division of Energy Studies of the Pentagon.'

"You're nuts. We can't put all these guys in a comic strip."

[15] Fragment 1B. This exchange between David and Felipe has been used tentatively to date the manuscript. Among all these names, the only one which appears in *The Encyclopedia of Illustrious Men of the Twentieth through the Thirtieth Centuries* is that of Ronald Reagan, President of what was then the United States. But the Abolitionist School counterattacks, observing that the same source mentions, en passant, an obscure actor with a similar name who probably lived twenty or thirty years earlier. They observe that David is referring to that individual, with all his cinematographic allusions. These arguments are reinforced by the fact that the other names mentioned, Foilback, Soro, Vondertod, Arnold AID, and Milton FMI (these last names are strange for that period) appear never to have existed, and they would prove that the author or the editor of the manuscript had no historic data upon which to base his work. They further add that the confusion between Karl Marx and Carl Barks (see the earlier reaction of Felipe himself) would lead one to doubt even the century in which it was written. In the face of this torrent of proofs, the Historical School can offer no more than the eventual existence of Borlaug.

"Why not? They can come to our country and praise the freedom of research, the free market, the freedom to sell; they can announce that human rights are being respected; they can say we have the cleanest air in the world, that they never saw so much peace and order, that a decisive leap is being taken toward superdevelopment; they can pollute our compatriots' ears with all that elephant shit, and we can't put them in a comic strip? Talk abut unequal flow of information!"

"They'll take us to court. For defamation of character."

"What they're doing is defamatory."

"Infamous, not defamatory. I don't think the readers will go for this, David."

"OK. Don't get all wrought up! If Ceballos insists, we'll change the names. But first you could give me a chance to show you what I want to do; then we can argue."

"OK. Fine. So what happens at the famous press conference?"

"Each one of them answers questions, explaining why he's come to Chilex. It really gives Paula a lot to play around with. Every one of them with his naive words of praise, what he hopes to take back with him, or what he hopes to buy or sell or to experiment with. Never before had a country placed its entire productive energy at the disposal of Western science. That kind of thing. And in the end, the element of mystery. A reporter who had already attracted Carl Barks's attention—she reminds him of a woman he knew and loved decades before—says that the country is buzzing with rumors, what can they say about a so-called X-Factor? A guilty silence. Pale faces. Foilback himself, who had previously answered through his subordinates, denies it absolutely and in person. There's no such thing as the X-Factor. Repeat: No such thing. The press conference is ended. But the last two frames leave the reader with the suspicion that something, some secret, is being covered up."

"I like that. We finally get to some action."

"For the first time we focus on T. H. Foilback's face, completely impassive and covered with makeup, except for one almost translucent drop of sweat on one side of his forehead. And when Carl Barks walks away and turns to look back, through a half-opened door he sees two men approach the female reporter as if to take her away."

"OK. And what the hell is the X-Factor?" Paula will say, or would say, if she managed to get here, Paula would have said if she were there in the car with them.

"To be continued," says David.

"Perhaps you're curious to know exactly why you were invited to Chilex, Mr. Barks."

"I am, as a matter of fact."

The Colonel sat back in his chair and pressed his hands together. "Tell me frankly," he asked, "what do you think of our country so far? The truth."

Carl Barks chose his words carefully. The man was sensitive on this point. "I haven't been able to take it all in . . . but what I've seen, I like."

"So you like it? And what about the climate?" the Colonel said expectantly. "What do you have to say about that?"

"Magnificent."

"Did you ever see such a blue sky?"

"Never."

"And what about our women? What do you think of the women?"

A veritable whirlwind of hair, skin, and eyes drifted through Carl Barks's memory. But all he said was: "Gorgeous."

"They're famous the world over. And what about the national anthem? Have you heard it?"

"I think so," said Carl Barks.

"It won first prize along with the 'Marseillaise' in an international competition," stated the Colonel. "And our wine? How do you like our wine?"

"I no longer drink at my age, Colonel. I was never particularly fond of liquor."

The Colonel stood up with determination. "You simply can't leave without having tasted a selection of our wines." He walked over to a cabinet, opened it, took out several bottles. "You can't refuse. Impossible."

Carl Barks found himself holding a glass containing red wine. He lifted it discreetly to his lips.

"How is it? What do you think?"

"I repeat, I'm not accustomed to drinking, but this seems excellent to me. For whatever my opinion is worth."

He set the glass down on the desk.

"Cheers," said the Colonel. "A toast to the year 2000. To Chilex in the year 2000. Did you know that by then every inhabitant of our country will have a car, several credit cards, and a television set? Every adult. A toast to our success." Carl Barks had to pick up his glass. This time he took a bit more into his mouth, it slammed into his palate, and descended his throat leaving a bitter wake. A warm sensation surprised his body. "But you're not drinking any," the Colonel protested. "Drink it down. That's the way we do it here in Chilex. A toast to you, Mr. Barks, and to all true friends of our nation, to all those who do not believe the lies of the international conspiracy. No, no, not like that. Throw your head back and don't put that glass down until it's empty. Not till you can see yourself reflected in the bottom, by Christ. That's the way. Yes, sir. No, don't put it down. There, now you've got it. That's the way we do it."

Carl Barks realized that gulping it down like that, so expeditiously, he could hardly taste it. It was in his throat and even farther down that a fresh, sweet taste was accumulating. Before he knew it, he saw the bottom of the glass, barely colored by what was left of the wine.

"That's enough," says Felipe. "I need a drink right now."

"Sounds like a good idea to me," says David. "A great idea. Do they have Chilean wine here?"

"We don't drink that wine."

"You mean the boycott?"

"Of course I mean the boycott," says Felipe. "We don't buy any products from Chile."

For a long time David doesn't say anything.

"Right now," Felipe announces all of a sudden, "somewhere in the world someone is refusing to buy. Out of love, David. Love."

David still says nothing.[16]

"You were explaining why I was invited," said Carl Barks.

"Slander," said the Colonel, "nothing but slander to rob us of our clean-cut image." He stood up again and returned the empty bottle to the cabinet. He took out two more bottles and four glasses. He set his booty on the desk and pushed an empty glass toward Carl Barks. "That's why we've invited you." He waited a moment, pouring the white wine. His voice acquired a sonorous solemnity. "We need your help, Mr. Barks. This country needs you."

Barks stared at the filled glasses with apprehension, but the Colonel made no move to touch them.

"Why me?" he asked. "I can understand how the others . . ."

"Correct. The others. This country . . . ," and a vague gesture toward the window indicated the waiting geography, "needs them too. We need all the understanding we can get, because we've been misunderstood. We need a virile friendship, like a father's; and we need a forgiving love, like a mother's. There's only one country in the world that can be a father and a mother at the same time. That country is yours, Mr. Barks."

"Thank you," Carl Barks murmured, but he was thinking about those words, *father, mother,* and he wondered what Sarah would be doing now; if, during the preparations for the benefit, she would be looking at her trim figure in a mirror, in a hall where portraits of

[16] This is fragment 2A. The boycott is truly an enigmatic custom. At this distance it is difficult for us to understand why Felipe places so much importance on the matter. Appel-Muus, in his now classic study, asserts, "We are dealing with a kind of reverse visa. The people who cannot enter a country respond with a kind of reprisal: they in their turn do not allow the products of that country to come into their homes or into their mouths." Ferrowell, in his commentary, dissents, pointing out that such a practice could be neither popular nor massive, and, therefore, that it was impossible for it to have had any real effect. He sees the boycott rather as a semisecret rite of a clandestine brotherhood, an act of continence, a form of self-punishment by means of which the warrior refuses contamination before battle. Nevertheless, these exegeses do not explain David's obstinate silence, his apparent neutrality. See our brief article entitled "David's Silence: Implications for the Interpretation of the Word *Boycott*."

children from several continents were decorating the walls, and realizing once again that the body had never felt the flutter of a new life inside it, a new life that . . .

"To the United States," said the Colonel, "where we're not always understood, but where the bulwark and the beacon of the West still stands firm."

Carl Barks had decided not to drink one drop more. He had studied the customs of the natives and knew it was a gross insult to refuse their typical food or drink. One of his characters would never break that rule, for fear of arousing the ire of the savages. But he was feeling the weight of the years, and Sarah had warned him above all to take care of his health. He sipped the wine timidly, brushing the edge of the glass with his lips.

"Shall we sit down?" the Colonel said, even though he was the only one standing up. "You, Mr. Barks, are a modest man. So you have no idea how much you can help us."

"I wouldn't like to get involved in politics," said Carl Barks. "My characters have always transcended such matters."

"We agree completely then. Completely. We know nothing about politics either. We've dispensed with it. There's no longer any right or left in this country. Just peace-loving and hardworking citizens. And the flag waving to inspire and unite all wellborn hearts. That's why they've attacked us so, because this is a model country. No rancor. No terrorism. No special interests. This is the sort of country you've always dreamed of."

"That's true," said Carl Barks. "That's true. I have always dreamed of a country like this one."

"Well, here it is. At your service."

"Thank you," said Carl Barks.

"No," the Colonel insisted. "I'm not just being polite. I mean it . . . We know everything about you, Mr. Barks; we even know that your most secret wish was to create new characters after you retired, but you couldn't do it because of your contract."

"How did you find that out? Why, the only person in the world . . ."

"We have our methods, let me tell you, Mr. Barks. We're very efficient." The Colonel nodded toward the cartoonist. "That is your wish, Mr. Barks. Well, we're going to fulfill it. We want you to take our country, to use it for your own pleasure, within the limits of our legislation, of course—we're very jealous of our sovereignty—and we want you to come up with a series of typically Chilenox characters, draw them in their natural habitat, and we'll publish millions of magazines featuring them in forty languages."

Carl Barks formed his words slowly. "You want to export a children's magazine?"

"For children, for adults, for old people. The only age that matters is the eternal age of the heart. We want you to do for Chilex what you did for Disney, Mr. Barks. That's what this native land that's never bowed before a foreign yoke asks of you. Look for those national qualities that are the best, the most timeless, in order to project a true image of what we are."

"And what about the Chilenox artists? Why don't you entrust this project to them?"

The Colonel laughed. "Mr. Barks, our artists have been contaminated for years by a gray and opaque realism or by incomprehensible experimentation. It will be at least a generation or two before anyone appears on the scene who would be capable of creating something like you could do. And you're more than Chilenox enough for us."

"He's right about that," Felipe suddenly interposes. "The Colonel, I mean."

"You don't mean the business about the gray and opaque realism, do you?" says David.

"I was trying to put myself in the place of the public the Colonel was referring to. It's your public, right, David? The one you hope to reach. If they had to choose between Barks and you, who do you think they'd choose?"

"The Colonel already said it. Barks is more Chilenox than we are. He's more popular, more capable of communicating with the masses than I am. And now even more than ever, what with the depoliticization, I mean. They wouldn't understand this comic strip."

"So they'd rather read Barks?"

"Why're you asking me these questions, Felipe? Is this your way of saying you don't like the strip? You can tell it to me straight."

"I'm interested in something else, David. All of a sudden I wondered who in the devil are you writing that for, David?"

"Who for?" says David. "I wish I knew. Who for? I don't have the slightest fucking idea."

"And if I don't accept, Colonel," said Carl Barks. "After all, I'm an old man now. I don't have much time left."

The Colonel seemed immense, casting a shadow more gigantic than his own body on the wall. "If you don't accept, you'll lose the place you deserve in the movement of contemporary history. I'm telling you, I mean it, the Communists have a hero from the nineteenth century, and they're always showing him off. His ideas stir up crises, his prophecies go unfulfilled, and his disciples fight among themselves. But we haven't succeeded in banishing his confused rhetoric from our world. Confronting that man whose name was Karl Marx, we celebrate you, a man of the twentieth century, the twenty-first century, a man of the future, Carl Barks. We're determined that history will preserve your name and not your adversary's. He had his model for society: totalitarian, obscure, oppressive, and impoverished. In the face of that model, we, you and all of us, seek a world full of joy, order, healthy leisure and ennobling labor, satisfied faces and sunlight. Which is going to be mankind's future, Mr. Barks? That's what I'm asking you. Which future will you choose?"

"The son of a bitch will choose to stay," says David, "not knowing what the hell he's getting himself into."

"You really do hate this poor guy," Paula would say. "This never happened to you? You never decided on something important without realizing what you were doing?"

"When I left Chile, Paula," David says, "you'd think I'd given that decision a lot of thought; you'd think I knew exactly what I was doing."

"That's not the way it was?" Paula would ask.

"Felipe can tell you," says David, "how it was and why."

"I'd rather you told me," Paula would say.

"Ask Felipe," says David. "Felipe can tell you."

"So you left without knowing what you were doing," Paula would say, "and Barks stayed without knowing what he was doing, but in him you insist on complete awareness."

"Please don't compare me with that guy," says David. "I'm not one of those people who wouldn't hurt a fly, like him. They're more dangerous than I am."

"But love can save anybody," Paula would say. "Don't you think so? I hope Sarah Barks can rescue him."

"Passion, I mean what you'd call real passion, was something Carl Barks felt for another woman, years ago. Of course. It was an affair. He didn't dare throw it all away and live without Sarah. So he bid her good-bye, along with a son or a daughter. She left for the Southern Hemisphere. But I'm getting ahead of myself. Barks is like so many others out there, proud of his small contribution, unsure of his own talent, suspecting he deserves more, maybe resentful that he isn't in *Who Was Who in the Twentieth Century*. They've exploited him all his life, and he doesn't seem to care. He doesn't even have any ambition."

"Oh, David, David! I wouldn't draw a character for the life of me, unless I really liked him. No use working with an unreal, empty caricature."

"And what if someone is essentially unreal and empty? A chameleon? What if, when we open him up, we find a shapeless mass, a lump of clay that'll take the most convenient shape, just one of God's little turds?"

"Who're you talking about?" asks Felipe. "Just any old opportunist? Or a Christian Democrat?"

"You guys haven't learned a thing," says David. "When the left won the elections in 1973, we should have reached an agreement with the Christian Democrats, that's what we should have done—allied ourselves to the political center. Instead you guys abused them during those three years . . . And I can see that now you're still repeating the same mistake."

"Abused them? You guys? So where were you all that time? As I recall you were the one that attacked them the most. And you were right not to trust them."

"When one of the characters I'm drawing does or says something

I don't approve of," Paula would say, "I . . . I feel ashamed. Like my favorite child was a criminal or something"

"Paula's a woman," says Felipe. "And since, on top of that, she can't have children of her own, she treats her characters like children . . ."

"That's right, Pedro's adopted," says David. "I'd forgotten. Listen, you don't think she'll believe Sarah Barks is based on her, do you? I thought of the character before I even knew Paula would be the artist."

"What do you mean 'based on her'?" asks Felipe. "On Paula?"

"Well, Sarah's sterile, like Paula. Of course Sarah is eighty years old and never adopted a child, because she keeps on dreaming of having her own."

"I hope you're not going to tell Paula she looks like she's eighty. She'll kill you."

"Come here, sweetheart," says David. "Come on over here, my sexy little old sweet-whore who looks like she's eighty years old, that's what I'll say."

"At least Sarah Barks seems to be a character with moral dilemmas," says Felipe. "The man in the strip should have been like that too. Why not create a Chilean cartoonist for your strip, one who comes back from abroad and they ask him to create a typical character, a fellow who betrays his cause out of fear or convenience or blackmail—how the hell should I know? Somebody like that. Sick at heart at what he has to do. That way we'd have an interesting character facing real moral decisions. Not this scarecrow . . . Listen, why the hell don't we call him Starks or Parks and avoid a lawsuit? . . . not this scarecrow that you've already condemned to death in the first scene."

"We've all gotta go sometime," says David.

"I propose a toast," said Carl Barks, suddenly moved. "This will be the last drink I take here, but I want it to be with you, Colonel."

The officer stopped.

"You have the floor, Mr. Barks. We're all listening."

"I toast my wife," said Carl Barks. "To Sarah."

"And the last frame shows the Colonel alone," says David. "He's talking on the phone, his back to the reader. 'Hello. Foilback? Yes, Barks has agreed to the first part of the plan.' At his feet there's a spilled bottle of red wine that no one has bothered to clean up."

"That's enough," says Felipe. "I need a drink now."

"Good idea," I say. And jokingly I add that we could leave the car in the middle of that endless traffic jam and look for a bar. The idea isn't really so off the wall. Felipe's broken-down Volkswagen is beginning to get on my nerves. At a table, sharing a bottle, maybe we would find a more amiable atmosphere for talking, Felipe and I, would be able to pick up the threads of a friendship that once joined us, the affection we still had for each other, that our last meeting in a bar eight years ago hadn't been able to sever forever. A good idea. No doubt we'd come back in an hour and the cars still wouldn't have moved. "Good idea," I repeat, and I ask, "Do they still have wine from Chile around here?"

A fatal mistake. Felipe's smile fades. It's an almost physical action from left to right, like numbers being erased from a blackboard.

"We don't drink that wine." It's a voice from the past, a familiar tone.

"The boycott?"

"Of course the boycott," says Felipe. "We don't buy anything from Chile."

He sits there, tense, his rigid hands punishing the steering wheel, waiting for me to answer, with a gentle murmur of dissent, to open the curtain on one more match in an endless series, Felipe versus the mistaken, Felipe versus the disloyal, Felipe getting ready to pounce on the revisionists with all the weight of his principles, while he stares fixedly at the rear bumper of a Buick as if it were the enemy, while he waits for me to avoid or to postpone the debate, as was my custom in the past, waiting for me to weaken, to fall silent, to give in.

During all those years, Felipe, we wouldn't have had occasion to argue. I went along with the boycott, my God, did I ever! I could see no good it did, but the leaders screamed up and down about international economic isolation and since you don't have the slightest idea what to do to stop all the killing and the torture and the arrests in Chile and it's not the time to question orders and we have the impression that someone up there, higher up, where? just higher up, knows more and has a clearer view, and since I'd gotten used to other people making up my mind, I, the then militant David, knuckled under. Not one red cent for the Junta. Chile, Chile, Chile, solidarity. No, no, we shall not be moved. I've repeated the slogans with great fervor all these years, buoyed by the chorus I needed, hoping those sounds would reach the walls of Jericho and Pinochet's drums would come tumbling down. At every meeting and on every street I shouted those formulae of faith with which Felipe will overwhelm me if I dare confirm that yes, I, I buy, apples, wine, even seafood when I can afford it. My taste buds wander through the fruit section as if they were in a forbidden garden, scrutinizing the place of origin of all the wines out of the corner of my eye, dying to exchange all the "Midis du France" for one little "Centre du Chili," or all those dusty Greek grapes for that burst of light that means a delirious bunch of our own. As if the only, and secret, passage that would take me across the mountains and deposit me near my children and my mother, without need of passport, were hidden on the other side of the green glass of that bottle of Undurraga or of that can decorated with a Robinson Crusoe crab. Not to buy them was like burning a round-trip ticket home. But I didn't buy.

Until one day I found myself face-to-face with the next to the last tasty, shining apple and I was Adam and Eve wrapped up in one, Cain without Abel, I sold my soul for thirty nibbles, I took it in both hands as if it were a woman's head and I felt its gravitational weight. I nibbled, I swallowed, I paid. It's like when you're going over the speed limit and you hear the siren and the fine is inevitable anyhow; I accelerated, I accelerated, my good hand raked native products from the shelves and my bad hand pushed the cart up to the cashier in the supermarket. Back in my apartment I spread out the spoils of war. Only then, with my table running over and my pockets empty, did I feel my body chilled by the cold sweat of guilt. A stench that permeated my underarms warned me that something grave had just happened. At that point most Chilean exiles were buying products from back home. They had started it slowly, secretly at first, then with less embarrassment, finally as a matter of course. They would simply say they couldn't stand it anymore.

Couldn't I repeat those same words?

I could not.

Because in stealing that apple in the supermarket of good and evil, I had crossed an invisible, symbolic line; I was, in fact, making a confession to myself.

We shall not be moved? They moved us, Felipe, Gringa. They moved us.

I had consoled myself in the face of defeat, embracing all the gestures and the rituals. And breaking with the boycott was finally accepting the fact that those gestures and those rituals could no longer protect me from skepticism. Breaking with the boycott was reducing myself to my body that digests and defecates. Breaking with the boycott, in a word, was admitting that I had lost faith.

Without realizing it, I allowed twilight to fall with that gradualness with which it happens abroad when you can't muffle the shouts of children in an unknown language. Maybe I imagined that, with the absence of light, all the rest would disappear: shouts, children, aromas from the neighboring apartment; I would even have liked the unfamiliar chirping of the birds in that zone to have faded away. And I would be there alone with my pirate's hands, thrust headfirst into reality, caressing the skin and the flesh of a peach like a blind man who eats by means of his fingers, hoping that that unique certainty in my gut would deceive me with the wisdom that dark, inner things possess, whispering to me that it wasn't true, that neither the fruit nor the wine nor my poor body had traveled thousands of absurd kilometers in order to meet and come together, that when I opened my eyes I would be over there again, back there where those plants had grown and where those bottles had been filled, back there, on the other side of the world, in that place which now no longer had any prominence in the newspapers but where the same sun still kept coming up every morning even though I was not there to see it.

Suddenly a scream of artificial light flooded me, my memories, and my friendly foods. It was Gringa. She blinked. She didn't understand anything, a fact which in our case was not in itself strange, but then she gradually came closer to the table where my treasures were spread out and she eyed every label and every piece of fruit with a look which, like Felipe's now, was trying to hide her reproach.

For an instant it occurred to me to begin a political argument with her. Tell her that the majority of the people back in Chile didn't understand the boycott, as far as they were concerned we were all antipatriotic. To add that a boycott can only work for a short time, when an active struggle or a massacre has galvanized public opinion. After ten or twenty years of dictatorship no one will even remember where that country is that once was so much in the news. To tell her that, on the other hand, an economic boycott or an arms embargo could work, if . . .

I turned my thoughts off. I wasn't going to say a word.

What possible good could it do to try to justify myself, to argue, to debate, when the problem was me, the problem was that they had defeated us and I had lost my faith that we were going to win?

"I suppose," said Gringa, examining each piece of evidence of the crime with her fingers extended to avoid contamination, "that you won't even consider the possibility of returning all this."

I shook my head. I would eat, drink, suck, swallow, sweat, piss, and shit every last drop of alcoholic liquid, every gram of sugar, every drop from that sea, and every fruit of that land.

She turned around and I realized with relief that our ideological exchange would go no further than that. For once she wasn't going to try to convert me to her cause.

But I didn't get off so easy. Gringa gave me her real answer a few hours later in the form of a poster she had spent all night making along with her friend Hans and old Helene, benefactress of Surinamese, Moroccans, Uruguayans, and Indonesians, prepared to take any action for the liberation of the people. I listened to them in the next room, chattering away and tracing letters. They excluded me from their cabal. Gringa must've told them I was sick or involved in some task of supreme political importance. You mustn't tell Hans about it, she whispered to me, as soon as she heard the doorbell, the first words she had uttered to me since the rupture of diplomatic relations between our two countries, whispering as if Hans were already present and not down below, blowing his hands in the cold. Not to Hans and not to any other eternal buyer of *empanadas* in our solidarity meetings. It was Gringa, then, who led me along the path of hiding my decisions. She thought, with her implacable logic, that it was preferable to lie to our friends, rather than disillusion them. Anyhow, her choice in the matter coincided with my own dislike for altercations and for seeing pain written all over the faces of the people I admired.

A poster. I brought along a dazzling copy in my suitcase. "To my comrades, Felipe and Juana, who stand as tall and firm as oak trees," read Gringa's dedication. And then in blood-red silk-screened letters: EAT CHILEAN APPLES. THEY ARE AUTHENTICALLY FASCIST. And there was a sinister swastika in the heart of a piece of fruit that looked something like an apple, but not one of those glorious and now traumatic apples that grow in our orchards.

So at three in the morning, Gringa's sleepy movements awakened me, as she took down my favorite Klee and prepared the tacks for an assault on the wall. Shit, right over the bed, that damned fascist apple would be right over the bed. All I had to do was open my eyes at daybreak, when your body wakes up and doesn't know what in the hell country it's in, open my eyes and there they would be, sparkling in the miserable light of a pestilential sun, there would be the teeth of Hitler, my teeth, my very own incisors, biting into a fruit "made in Nazi Chile." Making love beneath Marianne's versatile though compact weight, and glancing out from behind that flowing hair of a tender young Valkyrie on the point of erupting, soon I hoped, beyond the crazy, dark ardor of her tush, above and beyond and behind, there would be Mr. Poster, winking at me, Comrade Poster, the Categorical Imperative, the Ought-to-Be, the face of my father who art under the earth and sacrificed yourself for others and for humanity and who never made a mistake, the prosecuting attorney, future judges, the political vanguard that would never leave me alone until I turned my back on that accursed fruit and returned to the fold. Felipe was the one up there on the wall, joined in that magnificent fraternity of the true, the blue, the pure in heart. The inflexible in heart.

From the time of my adolescence, I had accepted their company as part of my solitary destiny; I had surrounded myself with the simple and the downtrodden who believe in a dawning in spite of the fact that everything confirms the contrary, who can say with unfashionable passion, today we must plant the seeds so that tomorrow there will be trees. From the time of my adolescence, I felt at home with them, they provided a frame of reference, a window from which to observe and to understand the universe. Now with even greater reason, as my country grew more distant, as its borders and its memories faded, they constituted my last contact with myself, with the person I had dreamed of being, they were a second and a third and perhaps even an infinite land, like that Promised plot of Earth I carried within myself.

I had been inaugurated into that vast sect of believers years earlier, when I most needed it. It was during the 1958 election campaign when Allende almost won the presidency the first time.

In those years I was a plague on my teachers. This crackpot didn't do so bad on written tests, but when the tests were oral, I always got tangled up in the subject like a person chewing gum with false teeth. I could never finish a sentence. I didn't exactly stutter, every word came out as clear as a bell. It was more the whole conceptual structure that seemed to flounder. I mislaid my verbs, one idea seemed to lead to its metaphor, and at the end of that many-tailed kite there were veritable labyrinths of commentaries upon commentaries, culminating in a flood of scattered vowels, of OKs and you knows and let me put it this ways and I guess what I mean ises, until that blender in my brain even forgot the subject we were dealing with, and I sat staring at my inquisitor as if he, or I, were a statue, unpardonably silent. I was what my mother called a cute little fool, what my enemies called an idiot, what the guidance counselor at my high school referred to as a pathological case, and what my few friends called an eternal romantic. Not one of these diagnoses, however, penetrated my sense of being a stranger in the world, my need for a group to which I could belong, with words that I could make mine, make familiar. Nor did the teachers make any effort to rescue me from my solitude. Under the leadership of Old Cookie, the tough old geezer who taught history, they were more interested in proving that my halfway decent written efforts had to be the result of unbelievable cheating, since I had never been able to repeat out loud what I managed to write down on the sheet of paper. You're playing tricks, Wiseman, Cookie would swear, you're playing tricks, and one of these days, I'm going to catch you.

He never caught me. But the garlic smell of his breath on my neck made me nervous, while the rest of the class traded answers right and left, without his even noticing. And my meager knowledge shriveled even more under his scrutiny. "Now that I'm keeping an eye on you, Wiseman," said my persecutor, "your written tests aren't so hot. I wonder why that is."

What could I say? That I couldn't possibly remember the consequences of the Treaty of Versailles, because the gentle falling of my teacher's dandruff on my totally blank page kept me from concentrating?

Like all this world's weaklings, I took refuge in my dreams of a meticulously plotted revenge, a revenge that would reach out even to my tormentor's grandchildren, until one day Cookie himself handed me a not-so-distant occasion to humiliate him publicly.

Our smart-ass history teacher had decided that the only way for us to really learn about the elections that were taking place that year was for each one of the candidates to be represented by a student, who would expound upon his virtues and his program in front of the class. Afterward the students would vote.

"Alessandri," said Cookie, and fifteen hands shot up. Everybody wanted to recite the wonders of the right wing's flag bearer, the one who promised the people austerity and promised the powerful even greater earnings. "Céspedes," Cookie decided dryly. The class bully, the only intelligent part of him being his fists, accepted the applause of the rest of the class as if he had just knocked out Lenin himself in the first round. "Frei," Cookie went on in his monotonous voice, as if he were intimating that, if worse came to worse, at least the Christian Democrats could stop Allende. That goody-goody Jérez indicated his interest and was promptly chosen. Nor was it difficult to find someone to speak for the other two minor candidates. And what about Allende? Naturally. Cookie had left the infernal Salvador Allende for last.

"All right. Allende?" he asked coldly, indifferently looking at each and every mophead.

I waited for someone else to volunteer. Don't misunderstand me. At that time it was no longer a crime to be a left-winger. For all legal purposes, the year before Congress had publicly repealed that damned law with which the former President, González Videla, had sent thousands of Communists packing to concentration camps up north. But it's one thing to be legal and quite another to be socially acceptable and respected. To support Allende, especially in places like my high school, was . . . how can I put it? . . . in bad taste, low class, they said. It was like being part of the underworld, with a license to steal, to loot, and to freely violate every law on the books. For example, nobody would have wanted his sister to dance with an Allende supporter.

But even though I couldn't easily admit it to the girls whose not-so-docile breasts I tried to brush against in the confusion of the "cheek-to-cheek," that's what I was: a dangerous Allende supporter. Without intending to, those five- or six-year-old kids who sing on the bus for a few coins had brought about my conversion. I remember, one of them sang out of tune. He was trying to stir hearts and purses with his rendition of "Smoke Gets In Your Eyes," and, instead of giving him a coin I took him home with me. Mama gave him something to eat. The next day he came back, he and a few others. Affection is contagious. They were fed. Two days later things got worse: my protégé's mother showed up along with a baby only a few months old, then there were some other little singers, and stories of tragedies, migrations, abandonments, leaky roofs. There was a real beggars' convention just outside our door. "This just can't go on, David," my mama said, referring to my works of charity; there were just too many poor for us to take the whole matter in tow. For once I agreed. This "matter"—this society, this humanity, this situation—couldn't go on. Drastic solutions were required to do away with poverty and to change the whole country into a home for its citizens, and a garden and a kitchen as well.

"Allende?" the teacher repeated.

No one.

"The fact is," whispered Céspedes hoarsely, in that voice of his that had never had to sing on a bus to buy milk for his little brother, "that fag's not going to get a single vote."

In the middle of the stubborn silence that followed his words, I noticed with remote astonishment that the insolent hand that shot up was my own. Cookie yawned, as if I didn't exist.

"Nobody wants to represent Allende, then?" he asked, yawning again. Somebody had found out that Cookie was teaching night school in order to earn a few extra bucks.

That thief Wiseman, Wiseman the thief. Thief because the Socialist Allende was going to abolish private property. Wiseman the thief. That chorus of voices, jeering, contagious, howling, forced him to take my candidacy seriously. Cookie couldn't mask a frown, more of displeasure than of surprise.

"You, Wiseman?" he asked, contemplating the orphaned lines of desks to see if he couldn't induce someone else to make the sacrifice.

"Yes, sir."

It would be great to be able to claim—and sometimes I tell the others that that's the way it was—that this, my first political act of alliance, my ideological baptism, was rooted in superior principles, in the defense of those hungry children I was still giving pieces of bread and other leftovers on the sly, passing them through the grillwork in the fence of our house, to proclaim that my raised hand hid a fist, prophetic of future acts of courage. I would be lying. A vague, almost mischievous sympathy for rebellious and utopian causes was directing my path toward revolutionary positions. Later, study, practice, the patient presence of my *compañeros* would deepen my commitment. But at that time, I had not advanced enough to raise my irreverent and cowardly arm. My motivation was more personal. Rumor had it that Cookie was an enthusiastic supporter of Alessandri. Why shouldn't Allende have a defender? Was my voice all that bad? Was I all that illiterate and scatterbrained? So nobody was going to vote for that fag Allende? Here was David. By means of some miracle, I would mesmerize them with my brilliant delivery, worthy of a tribune. As you can see, the old saw about "Know Thyself" has never been my forte. With no foundation whatsoever, with nothing to bring to bear on the task at hand, not even the words of my mouth, I envisioned myself carried on the shoulders of an enthusiastic multitude of converted students, all shouting "Allende, Allende, the people will defend you." Screw yourself, you old shit-ass. After that performance he wouldn't be able to accuse me of anything, because then it would seem like political persecution. He'd make a fool of himself.

"Wiseman," said Cookie, with a stoop of infinite fatigue in his shoulders. "Are you sure?"

"Positive," was the reply of this rascal, happy at last to see him so uncomfortable.

"That's OK, sir." Céspedes interjected his big mouth. "Just like his candidate, nobody can make sense of what he's saying."

I watched Cookie write my name with that parsimonious, slow, threatening hen-scratch of his that always seemed to bode ill. You could see that something inside him, way down deep, wanted to explode, right then and there, a sleepless teakettle, desperate to drop off, was about to boil over.

"Wiseman," he said, as soon as he'd finished inflicting my name like a scar in his class book, perhaps in anticipation of future bad grades, "I want to see you after class."

"You really blew it, you dope," cackled old Nosey, Céspedes's right-hand man, who it was my misfortune to have as a benchmate. "You really blew it this time. Bye-bye love, bye-bye happiness."

Nosey, enlisting the Everly Brothers in a bad cause, was right for once. I lost my breath. In an instant, all my dreams of Robespierre and of Robin Hood came crashing down and I wrapped myself in the rags of the eternal victim, poor little me. Cookie's speedy, almost violent reaction, his direct uppercut to the chin, indicated that, in effect, in just a few minutes I was going to get it. His summons had been issued in the full and ever patient view of the other students, without the usual hypocrisy with which pedagogues take their actions, leaving a prudent interval between the transgression and its punishment. No objectivity here, no high principles. Cookie was going to grind me up and spit me out like a spoonful of instant coffee. Right then and there. How was he going to do it? With that bag of a thousand tricks and those two thousand sadistic eyes of the omnipotent teacher in the jungle called an educational establishment, where there's no such thing as habeas corpus, freedom of speech, or release on your own recognizance. Who could defend himself against that garlic breath and those eagle eyes that would harass me in the hallways, make me flunk this year and the next, set up ambushes at faculty meetings, in accusatory letters written to my mother, in the vice-principal's office, in the principal's office, or on my report card? Who could save me? Who would defend me when the dandruff of his foul vocabulary poisoned the minds of the other teachers, who certainly hadn't formed a fan club for me up to that point?

"Because you're an imbecile," added Nosey, while Cookie started to declaim, for our civic education, on the constitutional guarantees that would never be applied in my case.

Because I was an imbecile. Exactly. This was happening to me because I was an imbecile, not because I was an Allende supporter. I was slowly learning the famous Law of the Most Powerful. I learned it so slowly that, twelve years later, when Allende finally did win the elections, when it would've come in handy for me, for all of us, to have known that law backward and forward, to have framed it and bowed before it; years later I still hadn't succeeded in fully coming to grips with it. To screw the owner of the cage, says the provable hypothesis of that merciless law, to screw the owner of the cage or of the stick, or of the revolver, or of the key, you have to have power at least equal to, and, it is hoped, superior to, his own. I looked at my hands. Except for a Bic pen, broken at that, they were empty. Fifteen years later, when the coup against Allende came, they would be no less empty.

According to the second axiom of that famous law, precisely the one we would ignore years later, when your hands are empty and the enemy is on the point of declaring total war and of annihilating you, the only option is to withdraw from the field of battle.

Maybe that's why Cookie had kept me after class. To offer me an honorable escape. After all, he would say, you already have enough problems, look at your grades, and then there's discipline. Why take on even greater responsibilities and thankless tasks? Don't you agree? To my surprise today, to the joy of the children and grandchildren of my son, Alejandro, tomorrow, in a universe that offers a very small quota of heroes, the answer was no. I didn't agree. I wasn't prepared to compromise with the enemy. Again, you'd be wrong to congratulate me on the strength of my convictions, at that time rather meager really. I'd call it simply decency of youth. That's a nice word. Decency.

Because there is a secret clause, an additional one, to that Law of the Most Powerful. When defeat is imminent, says this law, which could be called the Law of the Weakest, and which only the weak happen to know, after defeat, the only thing left to feed on and to leave as a legacy to those who come after us is our dignity. Otherwise, you really screw yourself. If you lose that, I thought, swore, supposed, in those days there was so much that I thought, swore, and supposed, then you really have screwed yourself. I could not know that fifteen years later, in 1973, when the coup came, when everything was lost, we would invoke that same law, just as so many defeated revolutionaries in history, from Spartacus on. Go down standing up, at least. Don't let them humiliate you.

The bell rang and the rest of the class fell over themselves rushing out for recess, leaving me to my Waterloo. The last lucky back disappeared through the door. I squared my shoulders, as if someone were going to take my picture for a future biography, ready to savor my epic misfortune with blind enthusiasm.

Cookie didn't give me the chance.

"So you like Allende," he said, before I could move from my place. "Is that why you volunteered?"

"Yes, sir," I told him, because it was true. But I didn't add: and also to make your life miserable, Cookie, that's why I volunteered.

He walked over to the window. Then he spoke without looking at me.

"You like Allende," said Cookie's melancholy voice. "Well, you know something? So do I."

He did too? Cookie?

Why did I feel so stunned?

Didn't I know about Pisagua? Hadn't my mama condemned Pisagua in her loud Germanic voice? That disgrace, Mama had said, leading me by the hand down the street. Concentration camps in this country. Who would believe it? After all we've seen in Europe, now the concentration camps again? Hadn't I hidden my preferences so as to avoid the jokes and so they would keep on inviting me to their dances? The old fox had much more substantial reasons than I did for keeping his affiliation secret. Mine could be interpreted as just more silliness from one more black sheep. It would go away. While in his case, what would go away was his own family's welfare, especially if the principal of the school got wind of his ideas. After all, you don't send your kids to a private school so they'll be indoctrinated with subversive theories. Who better than I to understand the reasons that had moved Cookie to take a cautious course, I who, a few moments ago, had been assimilating the bitter law of who is most powerful, the law which had probably governed his own disguised and dissident life for who knows how many years.

"We have a little problem, young man. Just a little bit of a problem."

"I don't see any problems," I told him, barely disguising my hostility, still smelling his garlic breath on my skin.

And he, calling me David and not Wiseman, speaking gently, as I would never have imagined he could, putting a hairy hand—the same hand that stuffed itself on my mistakes—on my shoulder, he told me that unfortunately for us—for us, no less!—Céspedes was right, at least in what he had said about me. Because Allende could be understood, only too well, but as for me, not a word, and that was the truth. "You're going to have to do a lot of improving if we're going to carry it off, but we're going to carry it off. The two of us. The two of us together." I felt like pinching myself to see if I was awake. Five minutes ago the world had been so simple and so neat. My enemies were the ones I was rebelling against. And now that old bastard was including me in a brotherhood that I had no desire to share with him, both of us members of the same seditious and recalcitrant band, both of us victims of persecution. "You're going to have to work hard, very hard, David."

"I don't need to work at all," I told him. "I can make myself understood perfectly."

"Do you believe in God?" he demanded suddenly, out of nowhere, changing the subject dramatically.

Since I'd already admitted to supporting Allende, I figured I could confide the totality of my perversion. Maybe in this camp, in the theological one, I could recover my pugnacity, my insolence, could separate myself from him, and confront him.

"Absolutely not," I told him.

"Neither do I."

As you can see, it was a day for confessions.

"You don't believe in God," said Cookie. "OK. Then we'll use the Martian approach." In spite of my anger at Cookie, which was stil gnawing away at my gut, I started to feel the first nibble of curiosity. "Since you can't imagine a Supreme Being, you have to suppose the existence of another being, we'll call him a Martian, up there in the sky or just over your shoulder. He's recording everything you think, say and do. He examines each word of yours and tries to understand it. What do you think about that Martian?"

"He must be going bananas," was my peevish reply.

"No doubt," Cookie agreed. "With all your vagueness, your incoherent and unfinished sentences, your pointless arguments, your slips of the tongue and your long silences, your nonsensical references. Why wouldn't he be bananas?"

The raking over the coals made me blush. But it also relieved me. Even though we were both rowing in the same boat, my oratorical skills still didn't impress him. And then for an instant a peculiar truce reigned between us. As if his attack had given me back my identity, my desire to fight with him again. And paradoxically, that allowed me to see things from his point of view. To him, a convinced, unshakable supporter of Allende from way back, my raised hand must have seemed like an affront. The most tongue-tied student in the history of the high school was volunteering to praise, but really to braise, his candidate.

"I understand myself," I said. "That's the important thing. I like myself just the way I am."

"The world is made up of other people," he answered. "To find a way for those other people to understand us is important. Especially if you're a supporter of Don Salvador Allende. If you want to change history, if you want to row against the current, you have to speak clearly; every idea has to be in its proper place."

I just couldn't believe that Cookie could be talking to me like that, so calmly, so paternally. For just a second, I really wished for a return to the conflict that had characterized our previous relationship. But there was no going back. No chance at all. Deep down in my own personal chaos someone had listened to him, someone was still listening to him.

"So what about the Martians?" I realized that it was my own voice formulating the question.

"Oh, the Martians," said Cookie. "That's just a device that usually works. It really helped one of my daughters who was a real disaster . . . Just a method, David. A way to get yourself organized. That's all. What you have to do, David, what we're going to do, is train you."

"Here at school?"

"No, boy, at my house. Nobody must know. It's fairly easy. Every time you speak in public you have to imagine that the one listening to you is that Martian. Someone who knows nothing about you, who sees you as some kind of curious object, almost a bit of folklore. To convince a Martian, you have to start out with really elementary things, teaching him his ABCs. And prepare well. Classifying everything in your head beforehand. That way even an extraterrestrial can understand you, and above all, be on your toes; because in this world of ours, being an Allende supporter is like being surrounded by Martians, son."

Could I pull it off?

I did it. I didn't want to accept his advice. I didn't want to owe him anything, to cross his threshold, to smile at his daughters or to accept their tea and biscuits. But I'd spent my adolescence in front of a mirror, one of those carnival mirrors that distorts everything, thinking I was my own best friend, that if I understood myself, that was enough. As hateful as he was to me, Cookie had, nevertheless, penetrated the secret of my inner chaos, that solitude of an alien that corroded and clouded my words. I could reject his offer and lock myself up in my dream world. But something told me that Cookie's mental Martian, whom he had conjured up and substituted for the God that neither he nor I believed in, would be capable of disciplining my tongue, and even more important, would prove to me that I had a place here on earth. Because I really did need help.

But why did Cookie have to wait for me to declare myself an Allende supporter before he had come to my rescue? If I had been an Alessandri supporter or a Christian Democrat, didn't I still have the same deplorably urgent need for someone to guide me? Or does charity always begin at home? Is there no other way to get ahead in these times of repression and catacombs? Is it necessary to worry about our own first, to organize our own first, to take care of our own first, always our own first?

I don't think I asked myself even one of those questions. I took advantage of the opportunity that presented itself, with anger, with distrust, with embarrassment, not knowing that years later, both of us, Cookie and me, along with millions of others, would each suffer the Law of the Most Powerful that Cookie had applied to me before I learned to share with him the pernicious, lovely, necessary, effective, idiotic, biased, abusive, inevitable, living reality of the sect, before we started to belong to the same brotherhood.

I had no idea my inauguration into that collectivity of which Felipe and Paula were at the time already a part, along with the Law of the Most Powerful (back to that again!), would lead me someday to this bed which, in fact, could have been on the planet Mars, that I would find myself turned into some kind of walking dictionary, having to clarify with utter explicitness the etymology and origins of my conduct to people who acted, as far as I was concerned, as if they were real extraterrestrials. Or, worse still, maybe I was the Martian now, fearful of being absorbed by these benevolent and helpful foreigners, longing for the sect to which Cookie had welcomed me, as it grew more distant, more remotely irrecognizable.

"Don't tell Hans," Gringa had asked me, looking after her own, and now, suspending her interior decorating, no longer hammering a tack with my own contaminated shoe, my Martian, my Marianne, repeated it: "Please don't tell Hans you're going to eat those apples. Listen, it'll really break his heart."

I won't tell him. Hans had closed his checking account in protest, because his bank gave some kind of loan to Chile. He wrote a long letter in Dutch, an indecipherable copy of which is lost somewhere in one of my cardboard boxes. For the Solidarity Museum, Gringa says, so they'll name a children's playground somewhere in Chile for Hans someday.

She shouldn't worry. What can I say to Hans? That he should cease and desist? That one drop of fresh water won't transform a latrine? What can I say to him to keep from breaking his spirit? To him, who at midnight sits translating lists of the disappeared or human rights petitions, for María and Sepúlveda and some Gonzalo or other, letters which nobody answers, to him who sat with his legs crossed in front of the embassy and unfurled a Chilean flag with the star in the wrong place and who was on a hunger strike for ten days, all for our cause? What do I say to those little people who don't ask for grand results, but instead concentrate on their daily, monotonous, anonymous tasks, all those everyday people in solidarity with us? What do I say to that taxi driver in Tunisia, to that peasant in Perugia, to that butcher in Krakow, to those simple people whose eyes light up when they find out we're from Chile, and Jara, Jara, they say gutturally and almost incomprehensibly, Stadium, Stadium, years after the coup, millions of unknown people, repeating in chorus in forty different languages, Allende, Neruda, Allende, Allende? What do I say to them?

Dead heroes, I mutter to myself in that Amsterdam apartment. Wishing I could just disappear from the face of the earth, thus ending the discussion. Wishing I could break that bottle of Chilean wine on the table and then drink what's left, broken glass and all.

"We don't deserve people like Hans," I say.

"You may not deserve him"—Gringa spat at me sweetly—"but your people do."

She's a tricky devil, because she knows that by invoking the name of the people, the "We Shall Overcome" people, my old friend the people, always there, those "We Are Not Afraid" people, she knows that by doing that, she's already won the argument. I can eat the forbidden fruit, but I can't indulge in the luxury of living without that paradise of hands that harvested it and put it in boxes, I can't live without the consolation of invoking the name of the people. I don't dare run that risk. Even if I have to hold on to my belief like a drunk who's lost everything in the rain except the name of his dead mother. Deep down inside me, buried under frozen layers of skepticism, that David who raised his hand in old Cookie's class must still exist, the David who hoped for a freer world for the great-grandchildren he would never know and for the children of those street beggars, the David who refused to leave Chile when they were killing them in the streets, the David who made the rounds of all the newspapers in Europe to push for the release of prisoners. I'm afraid that David might die on me, might die and leave me without a country to go back to.

I'm afraid, Gringa. Please. Let's not talk anymore.

As if she'd heard my secret prayer, as if the people really were defending me, were defending me and were with me, she didn't say another word. Her warm and soft bladder, the one that didn't have a drop of that damned Chilean wine in it, needed to relieve itself, and off she went, strutting like a stork, leaving me there, leaving me here months later facing Felipe, with the same questions and without the same answers.

"At this very moment," says Felipe suddenly, "somewhere in the world someone is refusing to buy. Out of love, David, out of love."

I say nothing.

"As for me," Felipe goes on, "I'm with them. I won't drink a drop of Chilean wine until we go back. And then I can celebrate with a clear conscience."

I tell him: "It may be you'll never drink any, Felipe."

"I'll be in good company."

For a moment we contemplate each other. Suddenly I realize that he doesn't have any real desire to go on with this debate which each one of us has settled in his own mind, like two recordings that are played every night in the same room with the volume turned down so no one can hear. There are things he would rather not tell me, he'd prefer not to remember.

"Cheers," I say, as if I were saying I'm not going to get involved, I'm not going to commit myself on this one, with something bitter on the sad tip of my sad tongue, toasting with an imaginary glass in the middle of the blaring horns of thousands of stopped cars.

"Foreign readers won't understand what you're talking about," says Felipe. "Get rid of all this obsessive shit."

"If you insist," says David. "I have one whole espisode where our Carl is looking for his character. He asks them to tell him about the legends and the customs of Chilex, local flora and fauna, that sort of thing. You can imagine the fun Paula'll have with that. A parade of condors, sea urchins, Chilean abalone, locally known as crazies, *kids with faces like copihue flowers and hands like lucuma fruit. An avalanche of dignitaries volunteer, as in the days when warriors would offer themselves to impregnate women for the future strength of the race, only now they offer themselves as models of what's typical, of the essence of our people. After that, child-zombies from Valparaiso, Chiloé dwarfs, mysterious Easter Island idols, one long-buried Indian who comes out and wanders at night . . ."*

"It's always a good idea to have an Indian in a comic strip," said Carl Barks.[17]

"You know, David," says Felipe, "you've been away from the country for a long time."

[17] Fragment 3A, the most indecipherable passage of all. As if the obscurity of the references were not enough, an additional participant in the dialogue, Carl Barks (?) makes a unique and surprising appearance. The Abolitionist School has suggested, with irony intended, that of all the allusions, the key is the word *crazies*. "In effect," affirms Dubrovsky-Pérez in a powerful invective against the *Dialogue*, "let us imagine that from an epoch we have inherited only the hieroglyphics scribbled by a madman in an asylum; only the fragments of a speech made at the tomb of an unknown bureaucrat; only the mutterings of a savage who knows nothing of our civilized system. Can we really justify the study and the reading of such a spurious product? Aren't we then the crazy ones?" Whittaker-Alonso's reply is eloquent: "Humanity has learned not to be intolerant of races, minorities, sexes, foreigners, animals, trees, old people, children. Let us then not be intolerant of the supposedly dead past. Who knows what will survive of our own labors thirty thousand years from now?"

"You don't say. If anybody knows I'm out here, it's you. Thanks for reminding me."

"I'm serious. Why force everything that makes you homesick down our readers' throats?"

"Your poor readers should realize, while there's still time, that what happened to us can happen to them too. They can lose their country, not know how to get it back, search for it forever. One's country can be stolen in the blink of an eye."

"Oh, it can't be stolen that easily," says Felipe.

"Oh no? Are you going to tell me you still know what Chile is?"

"Chile's something permanent," says Felipe. "It's not just mountains and grapes and folk dances. It's people."

"Sure, sure. Chile's the people, and their struggle," says David. "Like what we used to say when we were asked to define ourselves, the Englishmen of South America. We were, man, Chileans were the Englishmen of South America. Except the kind of Englishmen we were had nothing to do with the ones who smoke aristocratic pipes and wipe their lips with the corners of their handkerchiefs. The English in India, man, the English beating the shit out of their own workers in Manchester, the English looting Ireland, that's the kind of Englishmen we are."

"Keep on making fun of me," says Felipe. "What I'm saying may not be fashionable right now, but it's no less true for all that. Chile is the sum total of all our people who have hope for the future. That's what we are. We may be a long way from the goal, but we'll get there. Ask Paula. Her answer will do you good."

"So what about Pinochet?" asks David. "Is he part of Chile?"

"Yeah," Paula would answer, hesitating. "I think so. Lamentably, yes, I think he is."

"Absolutely not," says Felipe. "Pinochet's an aberration, just a parenthesis."

"A parenthesis," says David. "Well, that's a piece of good news. It's nice to know our armed forces are really constitutionalists, everyday people, only in uniform. It's nice to know nothing's changed, nobody's crying in Chile, as the old song says."

"If you'd been a prisoner, David," says Felipe, "you'd understand about the real country, the real power that's still there."

"Chilex, Felipe, Chilex is the real country. Everything is exportable, everything's for sale, even the people. One more province in the great empire. A thousand years from now nobody'll even remember where it was . . ."

"What do I care what some idiots think in a thousand years or in two thousand for that matter? I'm alive now. You want to know what Chile is, David? You'd know it by instinct if you didn't feel so alien, so . . . foreign. It's like recognizing a smell or the sound of rain falling or a kindergarten song."

"Foreign?" Paula would say. "You shouldn't have accused him of that, Felipe."

"Why not?"

"Because David wasn't born in Chile," Paula would say.

"He wasn't born in Chile? That wasn't what I meant. How could you think that, Paula? I had even forgotten about it. I was just referring to the intellectuals, the pompous creators of theories and that kind of shit, who get further and further from the people. They're foreigners, cold, skeptical observers; it doesn't really matter where they were born."

"Who's more of a Chilean, Felipe?" asks David, suddenly looking out the window at the car beside them. "Me or Pinocchio and his Chicago boys?"

"Sensitive son of a bitch," says Felipe.

"He was right," Paula would say. "They always made him feel like a foreigner. In a thousand different ways. In high school, at his job, on the streets, in the Party, everywhere. Then later, there was Cecilia. Saying, don't try to hide it, anyone can tell you weren't born over here. Every time they quarreled, she threw it at him. And the sad part was that there was a grain of truth in it: there were subtle little experiences he lacked. Things that are passed from generation to generation, that only David's grandchildren could possibly understand . . ."

"If I have any grandchildren," says David. "And not even then.

How many centuries was my family in Germany? And then one fine day, bye-bye, out you go, this isn't your country . . ."

"And when he got involved with Gringa," Paula would have said, "Cecilia, who always finds everything out, said: OK. He went back to Europe. He'll never come back here again. Good riddance. It was a historical accident that his mom turned up in Chile. Now he's correcting the mistake."

"How old was he when he got here?" asks Felipe.

"Two."

Felipe laughs. "Two years old, eh? Freudian thesis—nursed on Austrian milk and all that."

"Don't make fun of David," Paula would say. "We take our country for granted. But he needs a refuge, a place to stop wandering. Even if he has to invent such a place. And one fine day his convictions begin to crumble, and he doesn't even know what he's going back to. Do you ever ask yourself that kind of question, Felipe?"

"Never," Felipe says.

"What is this country, Paula?" asks David. "What are we, anyway?"

"A Jewish immigrant who came over when he was two, running from the Nazis, with no father and with an inconsolable mother who couldn't speak a word of Spanish," Paula would say. "How did you answer him?"

"Don't you know what Chile is, David?" says Felipe. "It's the country you want to go back to. It's as simple as that. It's a place in history."

"And what if it's not there when I get back?" asks David.

"We'll build it all over again," says Felipe.

"And what if they destroyed everything, wiped it out forever?"

"Then we'll start from scratch," Paula would say.

"Chilex," says David. "I hope you realize that of all the countries in the world, the one I'll have to go back to is Chilex."

"Enough arguing," Paula will say. "We simply can't call the country Chilex."

"Why not?" asks David.

"The owners of the agency have put up with everything up to now," Paula will say. "My hunger strike when Gonzalo disappeared, the business with the Committee of Relatives of Missing Persons, everything. But if I do a comic strip that's this obvious, they'll fire me for sure. And the authorities won't let me back in. Is that a good enough reason?"

"So don't sign it, that's all," says David. "Nobody has to know."

"Decided," says Felipe. "Unanimously. We'll call your infernal laboratory 'Swastika Land' or 'Fifth Reich' or 'Third Asshole,' whatever you want. As for the search for the typical character, you do it, David, if you have time, when you go back, if you do manage to get back soon. Meanwhile, we'll give the readers action and suspense. How did the third episode begin?"

"During the next week," David reads, "Carl Barks is . . .

DURING THE NEXT WEEK. CARL STARKS IS BUSY TRYING TO GET TO KNOW THE COUNTRY. NEVERTHELESS, ONE MORNING . . .

FIRST FRAME: The telephone rings: RING-RING, RING-RING.

SECOND FRAME: Starks's arm and hand reach for the receiver, as the phone continues ringing. Water is dripping, indicating that Starks has just rushed from the shower.

THIRD FRAME: The receiver is next to Starks's dripping ear.
Voice: "Mr. Starks? You don't know me, but I need to talk to you."

FOURTH FRAME: Starks, completely naked.

"Front view," says David. "It's important to see his genitals, worn out, drooping, ancient."

With the receiver in his hand, a puddle at his feet, thinking.
Overhead: But Carl Starks recognizes the reporter's voice. The voice that reminded him of another voice he would like to forget.

FIFTH FRAME: The reporter's face and bust, calling from a phone booth. "You must come, Mr. Starks. It's urgent."

SIXTH FRAME: Half an hour later. IN A DOWNTOWN CAFÉ. Carl Starks and the reporter, seated, facing each other.

The reporter: "Did anybody follow you here? Are you sure?"
Carl Starks: (His hand near hers.) "Why all these precautions? I really don't understand."

SEVENTH FRAME: Some fear shows in the reporter's eyes.
The reporter: "I feel like I'm being watched."

EIGHTH FRAME: Starks and the reporter seen from a distance, as if someone were observing them on a television screen.
Carl Starks: "I think it's time for some explanations, Miss."
The reporter: "Call me Becky, if you like. That's what my friends call me."
Carl Starks: "Explanations, Becky. Explanations."
The reporter: "Mr. Starks, I wanted to speak with your wife. But it seems she still hasn't arrived. So I'm coming to you."

"But who is this chick, anyhow?" asks Felipe.
"Buy the magazine," says David. "And you'll find out."

NINTH FRAME: And then Carl Starks heard the first of many strange stories that he would hear in that country.

"A couple of months ago, Mr. Starks," said Becky, "a friend of mine who works in the Customs Office called me. Suárez is his name. He told me he had information for a story. There are people coming into the country from the USA, he said, without going through normal channels. They get off the plane by the front door and are rushed into special cars. Even at a distance you can see they're really worn-out types, in wheelchairs or walking with canes. Their faces are worn. He took some pictures from a distance, without being seen. They weren't all old people, but all of them showed signs of wear and tear, they were horrible looking, really unpleasant. Like mummies or something, my friend said. So what? I asked him. I don't see anything of interest so far."

"I don't either," said Carl Starks; he had barely heard her words, he was so taken by the high, hoarse quality of the voice itself, at once wanting and not wanting to remember the last time he had heard it.

"Three weeks later, Suárez photographed the same people as they left the country. The same people, Mr. Starks. Except that now they were different."

"Different how?"

"It was as if they were a hundred years younger," said the reporter.

"And she . . .?" asks Felipe.

"She's collected evidence that it's true," says David. "Groups of tourists are coming into the country in rotten psychological and physical shape, and a few weeks later they leave completely rejuvenated, and as happy as larks. Nevertheless, she needs help to continue her investigation now. She doesn't know where they take them, what they do to them, what the treatment is that they receive. She asks Carl to try to find something out, to ask his wife to speak with her too when she gets there."

"What about Carl?"

"He doesn't commit himself one way or the other. He's a guest of honor, after all, so he feels he should stay out of that kind of thing. But the girl fascinates him."

"Why?"

Carl Starks waited until she was out of sight; he sat playing with the crumbs on the table and stirring the coffee dregs in his cup. Until several minutes had gone by and he was sure she wasn't coming back. Then, with all the deliberateness of a paralytic, he took a wallet out of his pocket and opened up the photo section. Sarah and him. Sarah's father, his own father, so yellowed they hardly seemed to have existed. Carl at that indefinite age when he had tried to enlist in the army. Sarah, fifty years ago, forty years ago, thirty years ago, Sarah today. He felt behind the wallet's cover; between the gold, silklike folds of its lining, there was another picture. He hadn't taken it out in sixty years. Now he took it out, using a fork to break some threads sewn a half-century ago. Before he looked at the picture that his fingers guessed at in its hideaway, his memory was already flooded with fragrance; he closed his eyes and recalled, like an avalanche of blossoms, Agueda's tanned face; he closed his eyes, not knowing if, when he opened them, he would find Agueda's features in the photo or Becky's, out of his immediate memory, the same face that had just disappeared, after asking for his help, something wounded and fearful in her calandria eyes, just as there used to be in Agueda's.

It would have been so easy to burn that picture or to tear it up or throw it into the sea. But Carl Starks had feared that, at the very instant of its physical destruction, instead of erasing the proof of his memory of that woman, he would end up giving it form and admitting it into his imagination forever, and from there it would be even more difficult to banish it, so, like the prudent man that he was, he had preferred not to run the risk. That tactic had worked. Until now.

FINAL FRAME: Behind Carl Starks, the shadow of the interpreter, in the café.

"Beautiful," says the voice. "Who is she?"

"My mother," lied Carl Starks.

"So do you want the picture and the reporter to be identical?" Paula will ask.

"Not exactly," says David. "The resemblance should be striking, but you can change the hairdo, the expression. The reader has no way of knowing whether the relationship is real. Whether it's the same woman, for example, sixty years later. Or her granddaughter. Or whether Carl Starks is projecting his own guilty obsessions onto her, dreaming of the woman he betrayed and abandoned with a child."

"Or if she's a government agent," says Felipe. "To convince him that the Fountain of Youth really exists. Or part of an act of revenge by women against men."

"Paranoid," Paula would say.

"When somebody paranoid is really being persecuted," says Felipe, "what then?"

"Starks really doesn't know what to think," says David. "Because, when he gets back to the hotel, he begins to have some pains that prevent him from drawing."

"Pains?" asks Felipe. "What kind of pains?"

"In his hand," says David, without looking at Felipe. "The right hand. The one he uses to draw . . . So they call Dr. Garay, who says it's nothing, that it'll pass. Starks wants to go back home on the next available flight. Patricio Marras intervenes, you know, the Managing Director of the Research Center, that laboratory we talked about before. He raises a gloved hand. He always wears gloves, that's important. He says not to worry. While he's recuperating, Marras has a plan whereby Starks can collaborate without having to draw."

"Another plan?" asks Felipe.

"Marras asks Starks to imagine a newborn baby. No features. Nothing predetermined. And instead of just the Three Kings, every inhabitant of the country would grant that child all his most outstanding virtues. As he grew up, says Marras, he'd be a prototype of the best that we have. Let's imagine, just suppose, says Marras, that that supremely typical man we are looking for doesn't have to be a mere cartoon character. That the characteristics that are discovered, the chosen features, can be directly injected into a human being. What would you say if I told you that the research being done in our center indicates that such a possibility isn't so far-fetched? A superior man, synthesizing the best qualities and merits, representing the highest possibilities this country has to offer. An all-star team, not only of soccer players, no, one that would compete in the most transcendental of contests, in life itself."

"Some language, for a comic strip," says Felipe.

"Concentrate on one person," said Marras. "On one family, one champion: the best voice, the most perfect skin, the most handsome features. The son we've all dreamed of. The best horseback rider, the strongest fighter, the biggest he-man of all. But why limit all this to a drawing, only an artistic reproduction? We use reality to create the character, and he'll be someone the international community will immediately identify with this country. A human being far more recognizable than a flag or an anthem. Something like Chiquita Banana."

"But of what use can this be?" asked Carl Starks, and Felipe, as if in echo, asks the same question.

"Of what use?" responded Marras. "Tell me, what's going to happen when machines have done away with all our problems? What are we going to do with the leisure time? Shall I tell you? That's when the poor countries will really come into their glory, that is . . . if they've prepared. None of the usual stupid tourism, you know, natural wonders or useless historic dates. Psychological tourism, Mr. Starks. Here, every foreign family will have the chance to come and relax with a native family, to really get to know them. They'll adopt children and grandparents, they'll get interested in local problems, they'll contribute to cultural exchange among nations. We already have sister cities; now we want to pair off families."

"And what do I have to do with all this?"

"We have to attract tourists, just like in an amusement park. We have to experiment, build models, look for entertaining and emotion-packed situations, drama, comedy. Like taking part in a soap opera, Mr. Starks, except that it's real."

"My hand is aching," said Carl Starks.

"Then don't draw right now. This temporary setback is really a blessing in disguise. You can dedicate yourself to more important projects."

"I don't understand," said Carl Starks.

"Someone like you," Marras continued, "can define the characters, the situations, the story lines, that later we'll translate into reality. An assembly line."

"I still don't understand," said Carl Barks. "Please forgive me."

"Starks," says Felipe. "Get used to it, David."

"Please forgive me," said Carl Starks. "But I assume this program won't interfere with anyone's freedom. I wouldn't like to . . ."

"Mr. Starks," said Marras, "exactly what are you accusing us of?"

"Nothing at all," said Carl Starks. "I just wanted a clarification. That's all."

"A group of volunteers. Patriotic men and women who are going to study a role. Like in a play, Mr. Starks. Is there anything wrong with theater?"

"No, no, absolutely not," said Carl Starks.

"I insist. You should ask your own countrymen for their opinion. From the private sector, from government. You can talk with Major General Soro or with Mr. Foilback."

"But that's entirely unnecessary," said Carl Starks. "The thing is I don't want to stay here if I can't be useful. At any rate, I wouldn't make such a decision without first talking it over with my wife. With your permission, I'd like to call her, collect, of course, to . . ."

"That won't be necessary, Mr. Starks."

"I can pay for the call, Mr. Marras."

"I wasn't referring to that. The thing is that at this very moment your wife is on a plane en route to our country. We took the liberty of calling her as soon as we learned of your slight indisposition."

Carl Starks felt that the courteous response required by such an act of thoughtfulness stuck in his throat. They were being too kind. It was beginning to bother him that they anticipated his every wish even before he had time to express it.

"That was very kind," said Carl Starks. Although he also added: "But I'm afraid Sarah will be very worried. She'll take me back on the first flight."

"Do you really think so?" Marras's gloved hand touched his shoulder.

"Yes, Mr. Marras, that is my opinion."

"You know your wife better than we," said Marras, "but I think she's going to want to stay here. Perhaps we have some little thing that will interest her, some surprise."

TO BE CONTINUED

"So you really don't know what Chile is?" asks Felipe.

"Really."

"And you've never known?" asks Felipe. "Because, my friend, countries are a lot like women. If you really want to get to know a country, the only way to do it is when she's at her best and when she's at her worst."

"I know. I know. In sunshine and in showers. Thanks for the consolation."

I say it indifferently, as if telling him that I know the showers all too well, now when do we get the sunshine? But we already had the sunshine, and now I get his drift, I understand what he's talking about. Because there was a moment when I did know, when I found out. Not really a long time, just a period of maybe a few months, or weeks, one night in particular. Yeah, if I have to choose, it's that night. And Felipe is going to back me into the corner of that night; he's going to draw it out of his hat like a bankrupt magician who after many years only has one trick left to make people applaud.

"Do you remember that night?" asks Felipe, as if he has read my mind. "The night Allende won, the night we won the elections?"

There are certain memories that with the passing of the years become more real than the people who lived them. They're rare memories, different from the common, everyday variety, because you don't wear them out with use. That's the way it was with the night of September 4, 1970. All of a sudden it seems to make no difference whether it's Felipe or myself or some other lost and forgotten person who's remembering those brief hours. They end up having their own separate existence, as if it were the dead who have, once and for all time, frozen what happened and no one and nothing can change it.

I know that if I were dead, that is the one night I would want to remember. Too many of those who overflowed the streets in a mad, dazed dance are no longer with us, murdered in the coup and the years that followed. Maybe our dead do remember it: how we roamed downtown Santiago like wild horses in a meadow.

I was strolling through the center of the city with my friends, with my eternal Cecilia by my side like a trophy, as if we had won the marathon and still could walk some more, scornful of sidewalks, thoughtless of how we would multiply the loaves tomorrow, because right now we were multiplying our vocal cords, Gonzalo and Felipe stopping perfectly anonymous marchers to force them to join in their song, hugging and congratulating the most absolute strangers. Not one person refused to sing along with them, when asked. Boys and girls who had worked in the campaign until they were ready to fall from exhaustion and had somewhere found the strength to form a dancing chain, boys and girls who, hours later, one hoped, would find themselves tangled up in each other's private arms, bringing the night to an end in the usual not so godly way. Old women, fat from so many beans and so much washing of other people's laundry, holding the hands of their flocks of bewildered, whooping kids. Young workers from the factories sporting little paper hats and plastic horns, as if this were everybody's birthday. We were like medieval troubadours, I felt, troubadours who might be slightly out of tune and off key, but, nevertheless, troubadours, getting the city ready for a rich and fertile night of love, celebrating the end of a plague which was as old as any of us.

By three, it may have been four, in the morning, we had come to rest our sleepless legs on the high solemn steps of the most powerful bank in Chile, the Banco de Chile. Other couples and even whole families with Great-grandfather and their stray dog were already camping out there. Nobody had ever had a picnic on these steps. And nobody knew what Santiago looked like from up here—partly because Santiago had never looked like this before. It was the first time in the history of mankind that any of us—and especially the poor—had been able to explore our own city in this way. I had often noticed how poor people would take long detours not to pass through the center of Santiago, as if they sensed that it was somehow an alien space. But tonight they belonged. I can remember a textile worker sitting on a bench in the Plaza de Armas with his hands behind his neck and his lungs taking in the clean, clear air up there: he felt absolutely at home. I'm not going to move from here, he told us, when we sat down next to him for a minute. I'm going to wait for dawn.

"We're not going to sleep tonight either," Gonzalo told him. "And I know who else isn't going to sleep."

The enemy, of course. To ensure that Gonzalo's as yet unformulated prediction would be fulfilled, a few hours earlier we had driven through the rich neighborhoods of the *barrio alto,* blowing insolent car horns so loudly they would have awakened the dead and certainly those scared-to-death people who had been the lords of Chile's wealth and power and who now mourned Allende's victory behind stony windows.

Before heading back downtown, we passed by Jerónimo's house, which, like so many of our own homes, was smack in the middle of right-wing territory. Our hearts might be on the left, but that's where we lived . . .

Jerónimo received us with the news that Santiago seemed to be calm: no troop movements, no worrisome signs of trouble. He had volunteered to man the telephone. So many people, like Jerónimo, who watched over us while we celebrated, so many people ready to get going in case of an emergency. Now Felipe wanted to relieve him. But Jerónimo, who was single at the time, insisted on staying home. "You guys haven't seen your wives in days," he told us. "You go on back and have a good time. I'll take care of any soldier-boys trying a takeover. You can count on me."

Felipe didn't give in easily, so while they traded theories and vaticinations, we kidnapped a little coffee and some cookies from the kitchen and when those were spent we managed to drag a fatigued Felipe off, shouting to the owner of the house that we would be back by dawn.

"You'll never make it here before the sun rises," Jerónimo called out to us.

I went back to where he was—standing there in the doorway. "Tonight," I said—and how I loved to fill the air with prophecies in those times—"the sun will come up for everybody or it won't come up at all." And I pointed like a preacher in the direction of the mountains where, between yawns, we would make the sun come from the usual horizon, calling it comrade, calling it a member of the tribe.

"The sun comes up whether we're there or not," Jerónimo answered.

I was surprised to hear a touch of melancholy in his voice, an anticipated weariness, which abruptly contrasted with my own joking solemnity. I didn't realize then that Jerónimo's tired smile was inviting me to many similar nights, in which instead of celebrating something we would be trying to hold on for dear life to that swinging trapeze that the country had become, nights when we waited without sleeping for the inevitable phone call, like the one Jerónimo was waiting for that night, like the one that didn't come that night because the telephone took three years and a week to ring with news of the coup. Before it came, there would be long hours standing guard in different party locales or going out to paint our slogans on vast factory walls. There would be polemics and documents and plenary sessions and emergency meetings and discussions about how to stop the right-wing offensive and plans for voluntary work in the slums, until daybreak cried out for mercy and the day asked for a couple of extra hours and wives and children begged for just a little attention and we begged our wives for some as well because they were off doing their own political work and the only answer was to speed up the process, to speed up in order not to lose the clearness of mind and the energy that come from traveling on a train that has lost its brakes but not yet its sense of direction, to speed up without mercy in order not to feel the temptation of getting off at the next station and the next station is just another moving train and the peasants will take over the land and there'll be no way to stop them and everything is in motion and the business community is getting frightened and will sabotage everything and there'll be no way to stop them either, and the only way that lies open is always forward, as if we all couldn't wait to find out how this thing is going to end. Until the train would jump the tracks. That telephone call that Jerónimo answered three years later, that I answered, that somebody and everybody answered: it seems the coup has started, it seems the army has rebelled, the Armada has just disembarked in Valparaiso.

The enemy must have started to make plans that very night. When we passed by their mansions in Las Condes and Providencia, the latest model cars piled up in front indicated they were having their meetings too. "Look," I said, still obsessed with the idea of dawns and auroras and mornings, "look, they're conspiring to steal the rays of the sun."

Felipe, whose knowledge was of a more specific, economic nature, suspected less metaphoric intentions. "They'll make a run on the banks," he predicted. "A financial panic, that's what they'll try to create."

But we were oblivious to those dangers. Back in the center, we let our pirate eyes stroll over each bank, really touring Chile itself, each bank bearing the name of a province or of a city, Osorno and La Unión, Valdivia, Banco de Concepción, Llanquihue, as if in there, now Talca, Banco de Curicó, was enclosed, in those giant strongboxes in false Doric style, poor imitations of Paris or New York or Chicago, the country that had been stolen from us for centuries.

They're going to try to screw us, Gonzalo warned, glaring at the bars of the Banco de Chile with Bonnie-and-Clyde eyes, they'll try to screw us with every means at their disposal—and they've got lots of them. He was saying this to a Christian Democrat friend of his who had climbed the steps of the Banco de Chile and who really didn't know whether to sit down with us and join the orgy or just shake our hands urbanely and offer his congratulations. Without you people, Gonzalo told him, we may lose. Gonzalo was making him an invitation—let's work together. But nobody else invited the fellow to sit down, no pretty girl offered him a skirt to rest his head on, so he went his solitary way. Gonzalo watched him make his way down the steps and into the throng of frenzied marchers still milling around. We should've invited him to share the night with us, Gonzalo said reflexively. A guy like that who came all the way down here to congratulate us, we've really got to work with him. Even if we don't agree on everything. If they join us, we're sure to win. And Felipe: We're going to win anyhow. With them or without them. They join us, or they'll find themselves with no votes. And I added—I can still hear the arrogance in my voice: That sort of guy really bores me. Too damned tight in the ass. And Juana: They're going to betray us. I feel it in my bones. The first real reform, the first growl from the United States, and they're going to run off with their tails between their legs. And Gonzalo: Then we'll have to make our reforms with their participation. And Felipe: As long as they don't throw a monkey wrench into the works. But I wouldn't just lie back with my legs spread out for them and tell them to have a good fuck. And Cecilia, I felt her thighs stiffen under my neck: What a vulgar image!

The same people kept passing the Banco de Chile again and again, as though they were riders on a merry-go-round or a worn phonograph record. It seemed that, as we could not immediately expropriate the banks, we were going to expropriate each other, and perfect strangers now found themselves dancing the *cueca* together, oh, my Lord, as if they were trying to pound dust out of the marble. If one of the owners of the bank had shown up there by some chance—instead of cowering and conspiring in his *barrio alto* residence—I think we would have stared at him the way you would stare at some leftover, extinct species. To us, they were already relics: bones in a museum, amnesiacs, invisibilities. That's the way Santiago will be, Paula whispered softly, in ten or twenty years. Every person who lives by exploiting others will have gone.

For that to happen, for us to take over those banks and that country in reality, and not merely with our eyes and our imagination, hard work would be needed. I might have been saying hello to the new country that night, but I was also saying good-bye to my old carefree life. I already knew that, in the weeks to come, I would join a party. Felipe and Jerónimo had extended an invitation, and it was time that I took the plunge. You could only defend Allende's victory if you became a militant, if you became part of an organization larger than yourself, if you accepted discipline and obedience. If you really wanted to expropriate the banks, there was no other road. But that meant that there might never again, for years, be moments like these, this shared innocence of irresponsibility, exploring a city like children or—better still—like a father who picks up his newborn son and snuggles nose and mustache and tongue and begins to describe each object, even though the little one has nothing even resembling a vocabulary yet. I didn't want to worry about tomorrow. I wanted to record the deed of ownership of this city before it evaporated, explore it along with the extravagant, gentle, greedy cartographers who were wandering through the streets.

From one end to the other, from north to south, from east to west, we were taking possession of this land of Santiago del Nuevo Extremo, in the name of her majesty, the People. School textbooks proclaimed that Diego de Almagro discovered this land, that Pedro de Valdivia founded the country, and that innumerable other leaders built it. That's what the old historians reported. OK. So what about us? The new, the recent historians, the ones who weren't going to read history, but make it?

Yes. Us. I said *us*.

I who had arrived at the age of two, who was conceived in an Austrian bed by a father who was only a pale figure in a photograph on my nightstand and a mother who still stumbled through Spanish with a Central European accent, I said *us* again and again that night. I felt possessed by the silent voices of men and women who had breathed in that land for hundreds of years and who were as excluded as I was, even though some of their ancestors had lived on the banks of the Mapocho before the arrival of the Spaniards, even though they'd built every building, built and razed every building in styles hawked thousands of kilometers away, and monuments as well, and keys and locks and mausoleums and barns for wheat and rails to move nitrate and copper and iron and coal and also the names in capital letters and looms and cement and fruit.

Us, I had spoken of us, placing myself in opposition to the continent where by chance my body and those of my parents had been born. Us. Sometimes in life, not often, but sometimes, one belongs where he decides to belong: to have his children, to tremble with love, to take to the streets for a cause, maybe to die.

At last I was in my own home.

This city had always been ours, it was just that others had held the title and residency permit, others separated it from us, they held it over us as a forbidden and hostile wasteland. Now was the hour for new conquerors, other Pedros and different Diegos and—why not?—a delirious David, to put their dirty, sweat-soaked feet on the threshold, time for us to tear down the DO NOT ENTER signs. Build the city here inside yourselves, *compañeros*, if I can do it, you can do it, since you've had more practice and more patience, always remember it like it was tonight, tell it freely, syllable by syllable, along the *senderos*, the pathways; explain it right away and in a voice that will travel as far as your great-grandchildren, because tomorrow we are going to have to pay dearly for standing upright and for this walk we are taking.

To pay dearly. I never imagined the price. I now rested between the legs of the one who had borne my two children, as if the generosity of that night could rescue my broken relationship with Cecilia, as if we could stay in love like that forever, like in fairy tales, as if we were on a picnic at five o'clock in the morning, looking over, along with Gonzalo and Felipe and all those other messengers from the future, all of our eyes with insatiable irreverence roaming over the colonnades, the iron gratings, the pigeon shit drying whitely everywhere, lingering here and there; let me tell you, you don't found a new city just like that on the ruins of the one that's still standing, on the solid ruins of the old city, still standing there. You pay.

Could it be that we were intoxicated with our own power that night? Could it be that we believed everything would be like this eternal Sunday afternoon stroll, going down the hill to drink water from a nearby lagoon with our beloved? That we could not possibly lose? That we could eternally be like a bridegroom watching his future wife sleep the night before the wedding, but not making love, not even awakening her, just contemplating her as she sleeps, surrendering to the gentle breathing of her body and exploring it from afar, lighting a cigarette with anticipation and certainty. Did we believe that moment could last forever?

In any case, the illusion was short-lived.

Three years later, the whole city would be invaded anew. This time it was no voyage of discovery. It was a voyage of extermination. At this very moment, though we had not the slightest suspicions, someone was taking our itinerary down, marking the very reflection we were leaving in store windows. Someone was taking down names methodically, and among them, heading the list, Gonzalo and Jerónimo. So that nothing would remain of them, of any of us.

It was getting cool, and Cecilia shook with a sudden chill. After all, winter was still not over. It was time to go. Felipe was getting impatient: there was a promise to keep, Jerónimo waiting next to that phone.

A light fog rolled in as it always did at that hour in Santiago, just before dawn. But for one final, infinite moment, we kept on seeing things as if this fog didn't exist, and the capital lay transformed and clean at our feet.

Gonzalo stood there, on the steps of the Banco de Chile and, extending his arms like some god, he cast one last, towering glance at this building—the building we would have to inherit. The affection, the dynasty of love in his gaze, surprised me. I saw how he took Paula's hand and squeezed it firmly, as if she were an anchor and he a sailing vessel. Damn it. The city might be ugly, but we were beautiful. The beautiful lovers of this flushed, feverish city that would wake up tomorrow like a disfigured woman who knows she's going to be a mother. Knows it more deeply than the nine months in her womb. Knows it's going to happen even if she has to wait ninety years. We inhabited that niche in time and space as if it would never repeat itself, so that the city would know, like a cathedral knows, the secret of who was who and who among us would share the insomnia of future births.

Because the city was also pleased that we had finally come. After so many centuries, at last her favorite children, her true native sons, her heirs, among whom I included myself, had reached her borders.

We will return, we told the stones. Gonzalo and Felipe and I, as we went down the steps, Paula and Cecilia and Juana, as we withdrew from the center of town, we will return. Someday this march would begin again, but in the meantime we will have earned every stone and every grandchild, we will have taken something more than a weekend excursion, something more than this playfulness, we'll be adults when we come back, the feet of Gonzalo and Paula, Juana and Felipe, Cecilia and David, walking down the steps, we're going to have to do a lot of living, to mature until we're bruised and battered, to grow until we're young, to learn to hate cleanly and without rancor, before we can put up our tents and establish our descendants forever on the banks of this river; it was a promise we had made to each other, we would return.

The first street sweepers were already beginning to sweep up the debris of the celebration; when somebody would pass here tomorrow or the next day there wouldn't be even an orphaned scrap of confetti to prove that this parade had taken place, not even an echo of these songs to bear witness, tomorrow, that there had been more than an orange peel or drunken embers, there had been a victory. Tomorrow, the day after, in four years, or in ten? Some serenity, some radiance, some memory? Would anything remain?

The violence of my own anticipated nostalgia surprised me, the sudden, sad, dirty rain that was soaking me from the future as if the sweepers were piling up my own ashes along with the cigarette butts at the door of a bar, waiting for that noise of the approaching garbage truck, that we all recognize, that sudden incineration. I could have no idea where I would be in ten years, no one could have anticipated this infernal marmalade of cars in a city on the other side of the world, but such a question smelled of defeat to me, it confused me like a slap in the face. I succeeded in shaking it off, as with everything else in all those new dawns, with a smile on my lips and my hand in another hand to give me strength against the ebbing tide, and with the undeniable evidence that if the sun just couldn't wait to appear and the mountains were beginning to move away and men were beginning to turn into the mothers of all things, who was I to contradict them?

I refused to confide that doubt to anyone.

What their response would have been was clear. Gonzalo and Felipe and Jerónimo and Elías and Paula. To throw my doubts away like pieces of stained cotton. To have faith in the people.

Everything was so clear, so clear back then. What difference did it make that the sea had erased the footprints our feet had left on the beach? The sand knew we had walked there, it knew it on its cold, damp, smooth surface and it knew it farther down in its warm, dark heart. The sand knew, the city knew, Gonzalo knew before they killed him, Jerónimo knew when they came for him, even the bastard brooms the street sweepers were using knew, that we would keep our promise. Felipe and Paula could have repeated it word for word with their eyes closed, that promise that Jerónimo made before he died, Gonzalo before they finished him off, that miraculous, whispered promise that we would return.

And what about me?

"That night," Felipe insists. "Do you remember?"

I raise my eyes to the parked cars, thousands of them paralyzed in that intoxicated Mexican sunset, but I don't look at Felipe's face.

"There are experiences that won't be repeated," I tell him. "It's easy to be a prisoner of the past and then everything ends up tasting like nothing, just rancid, tired."

"So you do remember," says Felipe.

"Do you want to go on like that? Spend your life being loyal to something that only exists up here in your head?"

"In more than one head," says Felipe. "But you still haven't answered me. Do you remember? Yes or no?"

"I remember," says David. "Unfortunately, I still remember."

PART II

Maturings

INSIDE

But the event that finally placed Manuel Sendero at the mercy of the Caballero was the disappearance of his mother. The child predicted what was going to happen and informed his father of it the day they stole all the clocks in the house. He further added the evident fact that at that very moment a group of men was going out the back door with Doralisa's sewing machine, three of his immortal Uncle Juan's shirts, and the cradle his parents, defying all superstition, had acquired prior to his birth.

The evidence, then, was undeniable. They could come for the old woman at any time.

At first, it's true, the soldiers sacked the houses of their victims after the arrests, with the usual conqueror's logic, but now that the arrests were being made far from the victims' houses, in order to avoid witnesses, the agents had decided they were being deprived of their rightful booty. So, provided with a looting order from the Court of Appeals, from then on they exercised their right to invade the domicile prior to the arrest. A few weeks before, for example, Dr. Arismendi had reluctantly come to visit Doralisa. His diagnosis wasn't going to change, he said, fatigue showing in his voice. Even if there were something to be done, he had no instruments, as they could see. Four men had taken his stethoscope and several syringes. They would come for him and his valise and cough medicine soon; then they would take him, the only instrument that was left. "Why don't you ask for asylum, hide somewhere?" the old woman asked him that day, advice she herself wouldn't follow weeks later. The doctor thought the authorities wouldn't be stupid enough to offer someone such an unmistakable forewarning of his own arrest. Exactly. So the population couldn't read its own future just by an inventory of diminishing possessions, so they wouldn't start to construct a secret language of equivalences and predictions in which two stolen chairs today implied the arrest of a brother tomorrow, the government, after consulting with the Supreme Court, had wisely chosen to issue more search warrants than the number of people who were being threatened with arrest. The disappearance of a television set today didn't necessarily mean that Great-uncle would be carted off tomorrow, nor was the stealing of a heater yesterday an indication that shortly its owner would be approached in the street by a gang of thugs who would ask him to come along with them. On the contrary, it was almost a favorable sign, a good omen. It was whispered about that these agents, to give the lie to the dectective novels, never went back to the scenes of their crimes. It was almost desirable for them to plunder us.

"I hope to God you're right, my boy," the old woman told the doctor, and she repeated it to herself when the clocks disappeared, in that way trying to convince herself that she couldn't be the victim of such bad luck, especially now, when her family needed her the most.

So she went out to look for bread that afternoon without saying good-bye to her son, without a tear in her eyes, not wanting to admit they would never see each other again. For his part there really wasn't anything Manuel Sendero could do, in spite of his son's protests to the contrary, and he decided to go out to look for work, perhaps without realizing that now he really would have to find some way to earn a living. He waited in line for hours to see if they would pay him for pushing a float in the Summer Festival Parade, but the organizers finally announced that they had decided to mechanize the floats this year, because two of the employees who had pushed the float representing "The Passing Spring" the previous year had eaten all the fruit, piece by piece, before they'd even left the garage and, when the signal to start the parade had finally come, the float theme had become a living, or, to be more correct, a dying exhibition of "Winter Reigning in Our Stomachs." It looked like the chimpanzee cage at the zoo, peelings and seeds and empty branches everywhere. So there would be no work; the 3554 applicants could come back next fall.

The child didn't have to tell him that the old woman hadn't come back. Two blocks from home he already knew it. There was only the gentle butterfly of Doralisa'a breathing and the invisible little voice of the future Sendero, who with no need for the stolen clocks was counting the seconds he had remained in his unjust confinement, and if they wanted him to come out, they should destroy all the nuclear bombs, did they hear that? There was only the child and Doralisa, but of his mother's rustling skirts and of her inexorable will to print counterfeit money, there wasn't a trace.

That's why they'd taken her away, however much the kid might accuse the Caballero. It was the counterfeit money that had done it.

That night the Caballero had scarcely gone, Doralisa had scarcely fallen asleep, the old woman had scarcely realized that the immortal Uncle Juan would return only in memory, when she locked herself in her room to write letters on the peso bills, protests, insults, threats and challenges, harangues and demands for habeas corpus, slander and just plain nonsense. She recounted what the wife of General So-and-So was doing with Air Corps Second Lieutenant Such-and-Such; she repeated what everyone knew about the stealing of drinking water to fill the swimming pools of the wealthy; she insinuated rivalries between the intelligence services. With abundant detail she related the defections among industrialists and also what was being published outside the country concerning cellars, false closets, and secret houses that in better times had housed libraries. And oh, the insults! There were no dictionaries of obscenities that even approached her inventory. In her sophisticated and untraceable handwriting, her curses reached out to their ancestors and their buffoons and parasites, leaving little room for doubt as to where her still unborn grandson had gotten his impudence. She promised financial losses, predicted the general strike which years later would bring down the dictatorship, and presented counterarguments to the affirmations of peace and order from the Interior Ministry. Because if the old woman hadn't gotten all of that out of her system, she would've exploded. One day, according to what she told Manuel, she got tired of being shut in until dawn with the light turned on under an enormous sheet made of four of her widest skirts, and she didn't write, and at three in the morning she awoke swollen up like a toad and on the point of exploding, so, as quick as a flash, before the cataclysm occurred, she ducked under the sheet, one trembling hand managed to turn on the lamp while the other grabbed her indelible ink pencil, and, when the first word slipped out, she felt that internal pressure between her ribs relieved, she felt her own hatred diminishing, and she discovered that she would have to exercise her handwriting and her rancor every day if she didn't want to go the decisive but for now impracticable route of dynamite.

Therefore she wasn't discouraged, kids, dear unpublished editions of mine, when one day, simultaneously, or one after the other, two events occurred that would have blocked the effectiveness of any normal person. The first: the authorities prohibited the circulation of paper money with anything written on its back. And the second event, more drastic in nature, was that she had run out of money. But, far from being frightened, she told the breathing corpse of Doralisa and this very much alive Grandfather who is here speaking to you in person, that she had seen a providential premonition in such an astrological conjunction of events, the prohibition of public money and her own rather private dearth of funds. So they wouldn't be getting any more letters from her, OK, so what? So she couldn't get into the most secret places and into the most isolated districts, fine, she wouldn't do it, but if they really thought they had neutralized her, oh, no, they had another thought coming. And that very night, said Grandfather clapping his hands in glee, as if he were in the theater and the actress they had just killed in the previous act had stepped out to receive the applause of the public, she set herself to counterfeiting bills. Since she knew nothing about electronic techniques and had no idea how to use a printing press, it occurred to her that the only solution was to patiently copy by hand all the lines and curls and signs and marks and she decided to use a kind of trash paper that no one would ever have thought could have been used for that kind of nonsense. She had asked to borrow a bill, one of the big ones, from a close friend of hers, Don Ramón—and at this point Grandfather fervently suspended his narrative in homage to the adoptive father of his Pamela, but we made him see that we weren't interested in romantic melodramas and told him to speak of his and our Pamela later, and what had happened to the old woman? And Grandfather said: the old woman had promised him she would return it to him in a week or so, and seven days later she kept her promise, with a shiny bill, neglecting to tell her friend that this was the counterfeit one and that she was holding on to the real one in order to continue her illicit operation. That wouldn't put Don Ramón or Teresa in danger, because the bills would never have been detected, such was the old woman's skill, if she hadn't persisted more or less in the period when Manuel returned from jail, and, after having lived almost a year with those well-gotten gains, if she hadn't persisted in spelling out under the words SUPREME GOVERNMENT, the words OF SHIT in invisible letters that blossomed in four or five days, when no one could trace their origin. For once, accommodating and pragmatic, I was of the opinion that it was insanity, kids, for once, I was being prudent. The other fetuses, idem. The most basic thing in that period was to have an oasis against the Caballero, for Manuel not to fall into his trap because of the search for a job, as happened, in effect, when the old woman was carried off. But the financial fraud wasn't enough for her. She had to continue her information campaign. Silence is collaboration, she said, watching her son out of the corner of her eye.

Therefore, her disappearance didn't really surprise Manuel. He had been expecting that disaster for so long that, shortly after it happened, it was as if it had occurred a thousand years ago. It was doubtful that the old woman would survive. She had never been able to hold back the truth, which always tickled the top of her tongue, and there was no reason to expect jail to alter her habits. She might be able to tolerate a discreet silence for two or at the most three days, but by the fourth day she would confront her captors with all the contempt that had been piling up between her gums, and then, while she spat out the best-kept secrets of the security services and the most creative abuse, erupting in a veritable flood of insults and demands, they would realize that only she could have been responsible for the torrent of rage that had invaded so many bills; it would be like having the voice itself there in front of them, reading those letters that had needed no stamps, no envelopes, and no mailboxes to reach their addresses. So Manuel went through all the required motions, without any real hope that they would be successful. He presented habeas corpus petitions, which the courts rejected or passed along to the authorities requesting an investigation that would never be carried out; he visited hospitals and the morgue; he hung around the police barracks. In fact, it was the same routine that first Doralisa and then the old woman herself had gone through shortly before, when they were trying to find out about him, the same streets that twenty, thirty years later his son would haunt in search of some sign of his father, the same temples and barracks and offices. Manuel supposed his mother was as dead as his own voice.

But she was alive, children of my own impenitence and grandchildren of my curiosity, she was very much alive. Even Manuel had to recognize it, even Eduardo would've recognized it. One day a veritable pollen of shredded paper began to fall at the feet of the people and on each tiny piece was written GOVERNMENT OF SUPREME SHIT, supremest shit, and on the other side another insult, another rumor, and they were so small they clogged your nostrils or got in your eyes and stuck to your fingers like taffy and they demanded to be read, and that meant that his mother was still at work in some secret corner of the city, that somehow she had managed to evade her captors' most severe measures and that every evening and even until midnight, with superhuman strength and with the fan of her own ill will, she was blowing out by the hundreds those tiny messenger bees that were raining upon the streets like biblical quotations. That's where the old woman was: she would arrive, on board tiny airplanes made from last year's newspapers; she was infiltrating schoolchildren's notebooks and bus tickets and the classifieds, telling the captain's wife about the goings and comings of her faithful and epic spouse between the legs of bound female prisoners, turning the high command against the upper echelon and the lower echelon against the officers and everybody against everybody else, making denunciations in front of churches, repeating critical testimonies, showing such a vast and scientific and tenacious discord that it engendered automatic replies and excuses and disclaimers on the part of the persons alluded to, which, of course, no one believed. Manuel Sendero could imagine his mother's skin emanating plots while she sat, in front of an open window, sweating her letters like insects, with nothing more than her own body, wearing herself out in a fury that knew no bounds. Until one day the flood dried up.

"Grandmother?" asked the son of Manuel Sendero in a whisper. As though he were hoping that one of those tiny pamphlets would fall into his hands, even though not one of them had ever contained a single word of encouragement or of stimulus, even though she wrote only with invective and never with love, against those people who had counterfeited not money but an entire country. Still waiting twenty or thirty years later to hear those messages that no museum, not even a living memory, had preserved. The son of Manuel Sendero, searching the streets like his father before him, looking for some sign that the old woman was carrying on her activity, answering from the very gates of the cemetery, from her remains floating down a dirty, whispering river, from way down in the gully where they had dumped her along with fifteen others.

"Pamela?" asked Grandfather.

She had protected him against his own doubts. During all his half-life in the saddle, an immobile emigrant, like a child born on a ship that will never reach land, Grandfather had appeased his sense of foreignness by the certainty that in some hemisphere, maybe on the other side of the world or on the other side of Doralisa'a wondrous foliage, awaiting him were familiar avenues, intonations of a language that was a remembrance, a way of smelling the sun and of inheriting grapes and other foods that were, would be, completely his own. He tried not to remember that the only experience he had of that promised banquet was borrowed, just hearsay, second-hand. Even though Eduardo had excluded him, not only in the present, but also in advance, from the future, denying him the right to return, making everything ominous and threatening, even in those moments when everything was alien and lacked a name, it was enough to close his eyes in that open darkness inside Pamela, next to Pamela, and to let her lead him by the hand like a little child being taught to walk; Pamela was enough to make everything familiar again, to make everything family. But she scarcely had left him for a few hours:

"Don't go."

"It's just that I have a meeting I can't . . ."

"Don't go, Pamela."

"You're like a little boy. I'm coming back, silly."

"Pamela."

"I'll bring you a surprise, you'll see. Don't worry. Nothing's going to happen to me."

Not to her, of course. It was to him, me, that something might happen.

As soon as she had rounded the corner, her figure swallowed by a bus that roared from among the cars, as soon as the horizon had kidnapped her, when the son of Manuel Sendero felt the silence growing around him, and, in the center of that silence, the same silence that had surrounded his father and that he began to understand for the first time, he felt something like panic, the dizziness of solitude. He had a sudden urge to run back to that sweet caravel that was Doralisa, to fall asleep secure there inside, to peek out timidly from that fortress in the desert in order to remap the streets, from there to photograph those faces that told him nothing. He wished to be born with a clean slate, with no prior memories, without the weight of the dead, with no mission in the world, to be able to skip aboard Doralisa and to be able to dwell with Papa in Grandmother's womb, to live side by side with his immortal uncle for the prescribed nine months, just as he had offered a refuge to his uncle when they were looking for him to bring him to injustice for the second time, to exchange one belly for another, to enter the world as a normal, everyday Eduardo. But for what purpose? To find himself, like my father, Manuel Sendero, wandering the streets twenty years, or a thousand years, before, on another planet, through another wasteland of the planet, searching for some sign that his mother was still alive, still sending the butterfly messages even though there was no longer any hope.

Through these streets, looking for work. In these offices, along these galleries, through these markets. Here on this corner.

Pin a little sign on himself, laryngeal cancer, and a stringless guitar at his feet. Papa stretched out his hand with difficulty; Papa stretched out his hand, hoping for a coin.

The shadow appeared, cold, definitive, that shadow.

"A trick, just a trick, Manuel old buddy," said the Caballero.

You had to have a medical certificate, and it was perfectly clear to any hospital that Manuel Sendero was physiologically sound. If he had decided to make no use of the nightingale the good Lord had blessed him with and he didn't want to earn his daily bread by the sweat of his voice, that didn't authorize him to beg in the streets. Such activity fell under the Antimonopoly Law, because so many hypochondriacs, so many disguised agitators, so much spoiled humanity, left no room for the working out of free enterprise among the legitimate beggars, the real professionals of charity, and only served to sully the image of the country abroad. Just any old lazybones who wanted to take advantage of the situation, all these anybodies with their other talents, even if they were hidden or passed over, were excluded from the guild and enterprise of the mendicants. "So you're trying to put one over on us, Manuel old boy," said the Caballero, his voice dark and cold like black snow. "Go on, get moving, you could earn millions with your voice."

Papa drew his hand back, kids, he drew his hand back from the public thoroughfare.

I looked at him from the future; I saw him from the train station that was Doralisa, where we all were: I stopped on the same corner and all I see is his empty hand and nothing else.

And the father felt, the son felt, they both felt the accumulation of sadness rising without appeal and on the point of devouring itself and of rotting the world, and Manuel Sendero wasn't able, didn't know how to, say anything, not one single word of rebellion or of rage, as if the old woman had expropriated them for herself without even leaving him a beachhead from which to roar, simply withdrawing his hand there along the public thoroughfare under the antarctic hum of the pill salesman, and then Grandfather sent his first confidential report. We'd told him to send it if necessary, if the going got rough out there, the mere fact of sending something, even though we couldn't answer him, would be a help in the face of adversity, but he, so sure of himself, thought it wouldn't be necessary: I'll tell you about it when I get back, or I'll tell you when you come to see me, fully born and whole, when I hand you the keys to power. Grandfather was insolent, all right, wasn't he? But here he is, downcast. First confidential report, and underneath that: to my other *compañeros* who decided not to be born, to the grandchildren who are awaiting my words, to be read by the illustrious dead as well as by the anonymous dead. Before anything else, he thanked all those mentioned for the confidence they had placed in him, offering him this exploratory mission. He doubted, at least right now as he silently composed the report, watching the passing traffic, he doubted he could carry it out. He had originally sworn he would never go into the land of his forefathers without first having gotten guarantees and assurances that things had changed and that the inhabitants of the world of the living were well on their way to wiping out poverty, ignorance, racial as well as sexual discrimination, and other evils that Grandfather would enumerate in greater detail in an appendix, so the readers of his report wouldn't get bored and also wouldn't accuse him of demagoguery. A profound modification, recalled Grandfather, careful to avoid the word *structural*, which was so much in vogue in those times. Changes that wouldn't just touch the surface but that would signify the automatic inability of people to lie to themselves: that would be a real revolution, by golly. That had been his pledge. But they, that is, we, the alliance of fetuses, grandchildren, the dead, and others, had convinced him that the time had come to put aside rigid positions of principle and to show more flexibility.

What was happening was that the fetuses had finally agreed on a course of action, a second rebellion.

The first one had failed, that we knew. Just as Eduardo had predicted.

Grandfather indignantly rejected the version that said that the first rebellion, rather than a failure, had in fact been nonexistent, no more than a fabrication of the unborn babies. According to these rumors, each supposedly rebellious fetus was in reality controlled by one of the Caballero's frosty fingers on a button and would begin to take its place in the gynecological line of existence when the Company decreed that the experiment had reached its antinatural end.

A pair of bored twins and a little girl who was going to be born blind anyway and therefore had nothing to lose had invented the first rebellion as a way of relieving the prolonged confinement and soothing their wounded pride, the way the insane make believe they are in charge of the asylum. No wonder nobody ever paid attention to it.

I am not and never was a test tube, said Grandfather as his only commentary on these versions. He was certain, and we tried to sympathize with his positions from a distance, that the primary and most evident reason for the failure of that initial baby strike was lack of unity. Since inside there was neither day nor night, just twenty-four hours of being cloistered and of continuously spinning tales, we whiled away the hours in meetings and in nonstop jam sessions. The babies were divided into two main bands. One of them, which called themselves Realists, felt that the only stumbling block, the determinant of all other ills and subsequent sins, was the strength of the rich and powerful. According to them, it was merely a matter of replacing the ruling class with the poor and the disinherited, and then everything would shift one hundred eighty degrees. The others, who considered themselves Radicals, had fewer illusions as to the perfectibility of the human species. Although they didn't deny that society's oppressed could, given the opportunity, be our natural allies, since they were being treated like children by the lords of the earth, the solution was not to put the victims in the place of the executioners, since the new masters would end up resembling their recently ousted rivals. A more categorical, not to say a more apocalyptic, solution was called for: adults in general should abdicate.

This strategic division—not so different from that which existed in the already-born of the human species—obstructed all unified action. Until the Realists, unwilling to heed the warnings of their rivals that future generations should not align themselves with any living group, no matter how underprivileged, launched the first rebellion. We can't wait for Judgment Day to see justice. Now, let's act now, they told the pessimistic Radicals, who were holding back from that struggle, now before they differentiate us, before they say: you, over there with your skin, you, over there to stammer and stutter alone; you, poor little thing, ten sailors are going to rape you; you, Croupy, your parents won't have money for medicine and that cold is going to turn into pneumonia; to the corner, you, and you, you'll get a pony first and then someday you'll get a Cadillac. Shut down everything now! All power to the Poor, Orphans of the Earth! Right now. Before they paralyzed us. Before we started repeating like parrots whatever they forced us to say just to get food and love. Drink that juice. Drink your milk. Drink that stagnant water. Don't shit on the floor. Kiss your auntie. Don't look at your father that way. Don't get so close to the fire. The things they would force us to do for our own good but that would end up making us just like them. The well-known consummated acts. Don't put your hands in your pockets . . . So now, let them watch out. If they didn't pay attention to us, the future would simply come to a grinding halt, there just wouldn't be any more babies, not even a tadpole, in the world.

That fetal insurrection failed miserably.

Because the Radicals were in possession of an irrefutable argument with which to answer those who had launched the strike without consulting them: all the Radicals had to do was to set about being born to destroy it, vitiating any possibility that the demands of the remaining babies would be seriously attended to. Scabs, yellow-bellies, Milquetoasts, crybabies, what didn't we call them when they were getting ready to leave? The accused answered from the great beyond of life, rudely sticking out their radically real tongues. In a little while, they were going to be able to do more than that: they could beat the laggard-babies up, rip them to pieces when they finally and reluctantly arrived, because their most stubborn adversaries had no other choice but to follow them into the damned light of the sanatoriums and, still later, onto the hard playgrounds of schools where their rivalry would express itself in terms both less peaceful and more forceful, and where the advantage of a few months or years of life counted a great deal. Of course, before being pushed toward the waiting hands that would give them a painful welcome on their rear ends, each one of the bands indoctrinated the youngest, those from four months upward, so they would carry on the debate in their stead. But the youngest disciples soon tired of this debate: it took them months to really understand what was being argued, and when they somewhat apprehensively joined in the deliberations and felt in a position to have an opinion or to act, lickety-split, it was time to say bye-bye, to be born, and so long, it's been good to know you . . . , and so several years went down the drain futilely without their being able to reach a consensus. And what was worse, now they were divided not only by their vision of the future, but also by accusations and recriminations about the past, weighed down by different interpretations of history—not remembering exactly who of the first insurrection had done the betraying.

This could have gone on for thousands of years—and some say that's precisely what had been happening ever since man and woman first distinguished themselves from the Neanderthal and invented inequality—if the remote heirs of the first rebellion, anxious to repeat it with some chance of success, had not chosen, having brought together their rather depleted ranks in a meeting, to do honor to their self-styled realism and accept their rivals' strategy. If the abdication of adult power was the only way to get all the fetuses to unite around a single banner, if that broad front was what would guarantee a triumph, then, forward, march, get on the ball, babies all. The remnants of the first rebellion told themselves that their first effect of a victorious insurrection would be to bring down the dictatorship, which is what the original Realists had always sought, and since a transfer of government, first that of the republic and later that of the planet, to the innocent could not be accomplished in the wink of an eye, as the unborn would need administrators and representatives, it was probable that the living adults elected to those posts would be the poorest and most excluded sectors of society. With shouts of unity, unity, the banner of the second and, one hoped, the last rebellion of the unborn was unfurled.

Grandfather had kept himself at a prudent distance from all these controversies. Having been the fetus who in all the history of the universe had held out the longest, he was and still is the favorite child of all those citizens who spend months floating in a state of weightlessness, and he refused to place the weight of his considerable popularity behind one or the other position. No one remembered that, along with the twins and the blind girl, he had led the first rebellion, because he was the only survivor. Besides, he had slowly become convinced that those who accused the movement of being overpoliticized and too one-sided were right. In some way, Grandfather implied, this passive conception of our role, that we were a support force for the living and those already suffering in the world, weakened us. It wasn't just a matter of turning the tables on the powerful. It was a question of abolishing the tables themselves. He not only liked the idea that the second rebellion proposed a more ambitious goal for itself, all power to the unborn, but also that it had a fixed time to be carried out. To test the good faith of the adults, the rebels demanded the immediate fulfillment of three drastic measures. Correction: they were three very extremely drastic measures. Once they were convinced that the effects of those measures had become irreversible, they were prepared to begin to undergo birth. But these kids were really suspicious. To ensure that the recent arrivals wouldn't be bribed or taken hostage, an efficient and continuous rotation of power was instituted. Those who were born handed over the reins of authority to those whose turn still had not come, who would then remain vigilant from their mothers' wombs, watching for any sign of deviation or of treachery, certain they couldn't be tempted by the latest-model cars because they still had not developed habits of consumption and are home-loving and immobile by definition; certain that they couldn't be bought with offers of fame because they haven't forgotten that the only opinion that counts is the one had by someone who loves us; certain that privileges would be no temptation for those who had already rejected the first and principal privilege, birth. As the new contingents, with practice in collegiate government, went out into the world and grew, the unborn would have living and uncorrupted allies, more and more of them, until the last of the old adults had died and there would only be adult infants left. In the span of a human life, a few generations, the world would be clean. Without firing a shot, without shedding a tear.

Nevertheless, before this could happen, it was necessary to overcome another weakness of the first rebellion: if no one had ever responded to the demands of the children, it was because no one had ever met them. The little ones had remained silent inside themselves and had never known how to obligate anyone—with the exception of Manuel Sendero—to listen to them, much less to represent them. The second rebellion attempted to get around the problem by designating Grandfather as the negotiating expert who would present their points of view to the respective authorities.

Don't think for a moment, though, that, when he advanced his candidacy and moved to a neighboring border, don't think that approval was automatic. They still delayed six weeks mulling the matter over, and would have delayed six centuries, if we hadn't gotten an ultimatum from inside that country: decide once and for all to send someone to voice the purposes of our rebellion, because both the government and the opposition were beginning to show signs of using the scandal for their own ends and, if the matter were delayed any longer, several of the children-to-be had announced they couldn't stand it any longer and would cross to the other side at any minute. In the face of that alternative, all doubts were silenced, and the son of Manuel Sendero, our grandfather who art in the cellular memory of each one of us, came, saw, and, so they say, conquered. But those six weeks were endless.

Although it may seems strange, the doubts had nothing to do with Grandfather's ability. They still didn't know something that Pamela would learn during those few days, with more tenderness than irritation, something they wouldn't have considered important anyway: Grandfather, like anyone who has lived reclusively and inconclusively for a long time, was clumsy by vocation. He inevitably got lost, broke any object that fell into his hands, burned his fingers with matches, left the change with the cashier one day when he went to buy bread. One shouldn't be surprised, then, by his slowness in discovering the whereabouts of the Caballero, nor by his inability to talk to him when he finally found him. If they had known it, the members of the Directive probably would not have condemned him: after all, they were equally inept, and for the same reasons. And, on the other hand, Grandfather possessed one faculty which they lacked: the freedom to move around in the world without impediments. He was the only unborn person in history to have mastered the mysterious art of external space. OK. We can already hear your objections, my dear rational little grandchildren with your tiny Euclidean triangle faces. If this version seems too far out for you, let's put it another way: he was the only born person in the universe who still remembered and lived looking backward to the womb; I had remained psychologically trapped in that intrauterine reality.

If you'd rather we tell the story in this less fantastic way, that's all right. Who cares? The end result is the same. Being born ancient, very grandfatherly, was like not being born at all, and reality slid off him like water off a duck's back. So adults would leave him alone, and, in order to protect the intense aquatic world that was swimming just beneath the customs that everyone wanted him to adopt, he learned to repeat those minimal gestures that would permit him to pass unnoticed. He learned to vocalize the alphabet, not to mess his pants, to greet people politely, to ask for more cookies, to distinguish colors. When we ourselves tried to corner Grandfather about these experiences, he scoffed: always classifying, he said, always sticking Latin names on new species. What do you want? Do you want me to show you Pamela's well-bitten breasts or your own undeniable existence just to prove mine? All human beings are like me, except that in me that inherent tendency was exaggerated. They lived like that for nine months; I stayed that way all my life. There's not a single creature of our lineage who hasn't suddenly felt that influence in dreams, in hallucinations, in coincidences, in music, in the peace that comes with some insuperable ethical moment, and they forgot that for me, for some of us, for those unborn children that everybody has in his future and who were in the loves of his past, that was the habitual way we stumbled around the planet. So, very simply put, Grandfather was made differently from the majority of his fellow citizens: he was a misfit. Because if they remembered little of the world prior to their births, for him, on the contrary, what was hard to remember was the present; he was an amnesiac of his present circumstances.

Absentminded, foolish, a dreamer, a poet, what didn't they call him, notes on a medicine bottle that explain symptoms, but not causes. In love, clumsy, crazy, egotistical, everything but a prophet, they never called him that. Why not a prophet? asked Grandfather, angry, in one of his lucid moments, he asked the other fetuses and marginal beings on the shore of his conscience. Because prophets, we, his grandchildren, explained patiently, fulfilling the duties of an encyclopedia of history three centuries later, act in the world; they're men—and women, added an indignant Cassandra out there somewhere—men and women, the chorus quickly corrected, men and women whose words, we continued, are tied to the very essence of an enterprise; they radically modify the conscience of their epoch, whether by threats or by promises, pointing out with the simplest of all fingers what's desirable and possible and even unavoidable but what the majority doesn't dare suggest even in a whisper, perhaps out of fear or perhaps as a matter of convenience. And if he didn't hurry, we weren't going to be able to wait for him; we'd have to look for another grandfather to inseminate our mothers' fountains. If he wanted us to remember him as a prophet, and not as a weaver of fairy tales, he was going to have to live for the future, and, unfortunately, the only way to do that was to get through this miserable present, crossing the female divide and testing his mettle in the land of his roots. Our advice didn't fall on infertile ground. He himself was already tired of his own intransigence. Slowly, without wishing to admit the withering of his hope, he had accepted the possibility that the same thing might apply to his country that applied to his father; that he would never know it, that when he finally decided on the visit, the landscape would be so unfocused and discordant that it would take the rest of his life to adjust to it. He had spent years pushing that fear aside, telling himself that his friends had gotten lost like rotting fruit in a forbidden orchard, that there was no point in asking himself where or even if the twins, the blind girl, or the little woman that Papa Ramón and Mama Teresa would baptize Pamela were waiting for him, fooling himself like an exile who has spent so many years without tasting his mother's cooking that he begins to believe that the local fare is just as good, consoling himself with junk mail when the mailman no longer brings him letters from home, munching flavorless food and leafing through inadequate catalogs, as if that were life and he had a thousand meals and catalogs and lives to squander. Years of not giving in to his emotions, years of making believe he was as firm as a dam, pretending the cracks and the impatience were not there. Making believe he was tough? Grandfather had become tough in reality, and where other people had tear ducts, he was afraid there was nothing left but empty shells. He had told himself that, perhaps, if he didn't look at the map of his country, it would stop hurting him. And this pain, this burning to go back, he emphasized to the Council the day they started to discuss his candidacy as spokesman for the second rebellion, what is it? Explain it to me.

This eloquence earned him the admiration of the other fetuses, but it also reinforced the faction that suggested, and rather wisely so, that the son of Manuel Sendero was the least likely candidate for the mission, because he would be tempted by his native soil, would entangle himself in the search for his own genealogy, in spite of his own desires. Although he was the only viable candidate, the doubters had to be convinced one by one. Since it was impractical to exert physical pressure on the critics, and since they emphasized achieving unanimity whenever possible, so the adults would appreciate how easy it is to respect the rights of the minority, and since the fetuses were, after all, on the way to being human, they jumped at the opportunity to distract themselves from their idleness with an in-depth debate. And, let's remember that they didn't even know, since at that point Grandfather probably didn't know it himself, that he would follow the shadow of the Caballero in order to erase him from the memory of all time.

But Grandfather was advised that the experience could be a stormy one. The message was, we hope that what happened to the others who took the immortal leap won't happen to you. You remember. They ended up being more faithful to their own pleasure than to the pain of others, dazzled as they were by the light and by the taste of ice cream.

It won't happen to me, don't worry; I'm as tough as pig iron.

If he wanted to, we told him, he could send back reports so he wouldn't lose touch, but security regulations made it impossible for us to answer; after all, the government or the Caballero might trace them and discover the Directive's hideaway. He was going to have to fend for himself.

For myself. No. Never. I'll be able to lean on my father's friends, who, as you know, kids, were the best and the least wolflike men alive.

How could I have guessed that it wasn't going to be like that?

And Skinny's triple denial had thrown me into Pamela's arms, as if I were looking for a mother's comforting. Nothing's going to happen to me, but what had happened to me was Pamela. I'm incorruptible, I told them. But love, if they had only whispered that love is the final, irrefutable corrupter. I was risking staying here forever, in love with everything that Pamela touched, fascinated by the secret density of the real, as if Pamela were a synonym of pampering, of slippers, of a woman's precious form. It was possible that I would stay there, that I would settle down under the palm trees and the pines, calling to my children and my vision to meet me beneath the starlight of nights, drinking a mug of beer with Eduardo as old age approached, never again being the protagonist of anything, a prophet in my own little corner, savoring the sweet anonymity of one who has placed all hope and all waiting in the hands of others. Contamination, contagion, the amorous cancer of living life, I foresaw happiness in being out to pasture, in the quiet of the afternoons coming home from work; I discovered that I'd be ready to forget all my promises, all for the dawning of Pamela's two feverish lips.

But perhaps those lips didn't tell me that booty that isn't used ends up rusting at the bottom of the sea. And I found you again in Pamela's soft and electrifying depths, little fish of my future, my Sargasso Sea grandchildren, little treasures of this buccaneer who would have to go out to rescue you; luckily you needed to be born; you needed a world and some sort of victory.

Be careful, we had told him. And his first report confirmed to us that his difficulties were greater than we had ever imagined.

He felt like a wild animal that's been taken from its cage and dazzled by the vision of a gentle herd and of sunshine and freedom, and the passageway leads to another cage where everything's the same, except more solitary and more bereft of illusions; that's the way he felt when he reached the land of his seeding and no one recognized him; the mother that is in other people's eyes refused to welcome him; no one celebrated his coming and they couldn't corroborate even one of his stories. If that happens in a strange land, fine, that's natural. But in his own home? With the people who had listened to the last song of Manuel Sendero?

You want to know how it is, said Grandfather, using the terminology that obsessed both him and his public. It's like babies feel when they're born. The jungle. It's the jungle. We're cornered and gasping; there's hunger, but it's not just in the pit of the stomach; it's in the whole infinite machine; it's cold, but the cold's not in your lungs; it's in the lungs of others who are taking away your oxygen. Understand: the others are starting to be your enemies. And you have to go back to the shelter; but there's no place to go and no way, and you still haven't found out with whom; the only direction is toward and upward and downward and a knife and never getting there. Can that be the moment when babies commit suicide? Grandfather meant something that Eduardo couldn't even guess when he said good-bye, so sure of his will to live, something that medical science with all its paraphernalia certainly doesn't even suspect, and that is that every newborn kills himself, destroys the bonds that link him to himself, to the months of pregnancy, to the dead who kept him company and warmed the darkness there, to the future brothers and sisters who will occupy that space, to the parents who before them were identical and mirror images and tiny in Grandmother's concavity, and to Grandmother, who also once filled a dark, warm hole that wasn't in a cemetery and so on, back through time, the lie that there is a particular uterus not a constellation of uteruses where all meet and succeed each other and change places. To break the fingers of the hand that links us to that place through which all living men and women have passed, where your father met your mother, through which will pass again for one instant in the abyss on the roadway to death, brothers, nephews, relatives, and everybody else.

But not me, said Grandfather in his confidential report; I'm not going to kill my memory just to make room for life.

Not him. Not his memory. He wasn't going to kill himself, but he was in Eduardo's country, and in that country nobody says what he thinks; the inhabitants put more effort into suppressing thoughts than into expressing them, and you had to be like Eduardo to survive, you had to learn how to make calculations before you extended your hand in welcome to a stranger. You had to be like Eduardo in order not to be trampled underfoot, in order that the person you handed your soul to wouldn't become your master, a pimp in charge of your most intimate self. Therefore, Eduardo had to be strong; that's why he had been in a hurry, because he was going to need every year and every minute of his life to defend the baby inside him, his potential for being transparent.

Grandfather should have suspected it was going to be that way when the immigration officials, then the police, the customs officer, each and every one of them looked at the document, then looked up to compare the picture with the face, looking through the body in front of them, as if it were glass, as if Grandfather were not crossing the official boundary of a nation but rather the tenuous barrier of regulations that separates dream from reality, the living from the dead, the future from the past. In spite of the fact that they stamped his passport, lazily searched his suitcase, asking if he was bringing some terribly dangerous disease with him, he had the impression that they really were not seeing him, that he was somewhere else, still watching them from the narrow, glorious watchtower of Doralisa, as if he were still inside that gloom, unable to leave.

I thought, said Grandfather in that first confidential report, that it was a trick, that in some infamous way the Caballero had discovered my landing, and that just outside the airport or the bus station he would be waiting for me in that jeep that knocked over the kid on that bicycle that first day of spring. But nothing like that happened. The glassy stare, a television stare, a stare of celestial absence, was awaiting me in other corners of the city, including the hostility of Pamela's friends, some of whom should have recognized me because we had been together in endless sessions planning the first rebellion, discussing strategies. They pass by my side and I identify them as if their voices were recorded in my head; I want to embrace them, to sit down with them, to have a glass of juice and enlist them in my cause. They don't greet me. They're suspicious; they've learned to play the game of hiding your real intentions and dreams. The other person is there only to be used, to render service, to accumulate influence. Is that why they reject me? As if I were a threat, as if my presence reminded them, like a burning coal, that life isn't to be wasted like this. You won't survive, Pamela told me, brushing back my hair to measure the fullness of my forehead, as if she were doing a phrenological reading. This place wasn't made for us.

Not made for us! Who was it made for then?

I know how short life is. I know it better than any other amoeba who wants to endure; I know that death is an endless file filled with useless papers, where everything will end up in the garbage dump of words and actions that never took hold in another being, that it's a senseless storeroom, a library full of books in a forgotten language, nothing more than a catalog of rusting, useless objects. How could I not know that, being who I am, coming from where I come? But those few moments of light, what are we going to do with them? Are we just going to let them fade out? Is it possible time after time just to act as if we were already dead and defeated? Is is possible that the only way to survive is to duck your head when someone throws a punch, to be constantly measuring your adversary's strength, to learn to say thanks and to smile when they punish you until you're the one doing the punishing? And if that's what life is all about? If that's all there is to it?

And then the question he didn't want to ask, but asked anyhow: Can this be my country?

And the answer that Pamela would not have given him, but which her absence forced him to give to his own question, the answer in that period of time without Pamela inviting him to populate it with future: it was the country Eduardo had inherited and the one that would be his grandchildren's if we were lucky, and if things went badly, it would be the Caballero's grandchildren's, depending on who was stronger and more cunning, it would be the country of one or the other, but it would never be his country.

He tried to calm himself down, thinking that the same thing happens to every traveler who returns with anticipated nostalgia after years of distance and finds that someone has poisoned the wells in his holy places, that not even one site is intact. Somebody stole my world, friends, someone stole the autumn in which I should have been born, someone snatched the memories to which I have a right, someone kicked down the wall where Papa snuggled up with Mama's body to borrow a little of her warmth. Little brothers, the bread has no aroma in this square's orphaned light.

But it was too late to blame the distance now. It was as if he had been resurrected two thousand years later and couldn't find even one of the love notes that someone had carved for you to read on the tree trunks. Everything in that peaceful whirlwind seemed unreal and adrift to him. In Eduardo's country, grandmothers don't sweat peso bills, fathers don't lose their voices, mothers don't sleep perpetually, uncles don't come back from the dead.

And for the first time he asked himself without mercy if Skinny hadn't been right—it was impossible, the mere fact that I was thinking it, that my mind existed to ask the question, belied it—if Skinny hadn't been right when he had assured me that they had killed the son of Manuel Sendero.

But we couldn't answer his doubts or silence his darkness. Some of us, because we still hadn't been born; others, because we hadn't even been conceived; some, because we were locating in foreign countries with unpronounceable languages; the rest because the dead don't speak.

We didn't utter a single word.

He had invented a country for himself. Now let him learn to live in it.

This time he was going to have to solve his problems all by himself.

All by himself only up to a point.

The prophetic and impenitent grandchildren would have said the same thing about Manuel, that without his mother, with his wife in dreamland and his son in Eduardo's country thirty years later, beached on a corner, that Manuel too would have to work it out all by himself. They would have said so, they did say so, and they were wrong. Because then, always at that moment, Grandfather would tell them, would tell us, the story of Esmeralda.

Manuel didn't recognize her at first. She had been enormous the last time he had seen her, the afternoon he had come to offer his music in an electrical products plant which had recently been nationalized in favor of its workers. Esmeralda had been the cook. You give them something to listen to, she had explained to Manuel with such a full-moon face that there wasn't even the wrinkle of a smile. I'll give them something to eat. We're not very different. Open your mouth.

Now her body was still the same size, but her breasts had grown tremendously. Inside, in the great emptiness where children would never again float, the great kitchen still bubbled away. What she gives you isn't milk, they had confided to Manuel in one of those lines of the unemployed: it's baked chicken with bacon strips, complete with parsley, lemon, golden potatoes, or maybe beef stew or potpie. Only one course, the special of the day, that's for sure. Inside, Esmeralda was still cooking.

It didn't matter that the first thing the owner had done, newly reinstalled in his office after the military government had returned the company to him, was to accept her resignation. All he'd had to do was to announce that from now on the kitchen was closed, and Esmeralda had decided to leave. Once again the workers would bring their sandwiches, soup, whatever they wanted, but there was no reason for them to be eating free with money that was needed to expand the business. Kids, just imagine the humiliation, said Don Ramón. Imagine having to say, yes, boss, sure, boss, of course, boss, after they had been running their own company. But she told him no, that the kitchen was going with her, the wood, the pots, the utensils, since he wasn't going to be using them. That first act of rebellion was just a sample of what was to come.

You remember that little child, just a vegetable who couldn't say a word, a body that never answered a single one of our questions? Well, it was the death of that angel, it was his stillbirth between Esmeralda's legs that would demonstrate the true temper of his mother. She didn't understand a thing about politics. She announced to whoever would listen that it was a matter for men and that she just voted because the men she admired or with whom she had shared fleeting moments in bed believed it was her duty. No, that wasn't her duty. It was another, simpler one. It was to feed them, to spoon out the portions herself, so that everyone would get the same amount of gravy, to cook for the hungry as if they were all about to be shot, as if they were off on their honeymoon, like bidding farewell to a son who's going off to war or like a welcome home party for a son who's come back safe and sound.

She had discovered her vocation the afternoon that someone was passing through the lamps section looking for a volunteer to organize the meals schedule and to administer the meager budget available for the workers' nutrition, and she had reached into her eternal knowledge of everyday cooking and from that moment on she no longer tested the quality of light bulbs but went to tasting food instead.

Go ahead and fire me, boss, she had told the owner of the factory: I'll find a way to keep on doing my duty. And if you want me to stay, you have to keep the kitchen open. If you don't, I wouldn't stay even if you begged me.

The factory owner was in no mood to beg anybody to stay. He let her leave without accusing her of being insolent to the authorities. After all, she seemed to be just a harmless nut.

Not even one night had passed after the death of her little angel when she felt her breasts growing enormous again. It would be the last child she would try to bring into the world, the final failure of her fertility. She wouldn't try to have any more. But maybe for that reason, kids, my little mind readers, there was room in her heart for all candidates to limbo. She gathered in the depths of her great, bottomless kettle all the tenderness that might have been, all the fullness of life that had ever emerged and that, instead of evaporating, sought to move out toward other human beings. And it's true it wasn't milk that came out of her: every day she changed the menu outside the door of the shop where she had set up with the help of the Committee of the Unemployed. Come on, little Manuel, come on, son. I'll take care of you, you're not going to die. You're going on a trip, even though you don't know it. You're going to need the nourishment.

That's how she had come to this wasteland. From town to town, getting ready for the banquet of Judgment Day, a day when someone would have to cook the same meal for everybody, when finally there would be something to celebrate, disposed to reach out to the very last uninhabitant of the country there on the church steps, always ready to unfasten her bra, growing until she scarcely fitted in the cart drawn by two horses which she also fed, because she was always ready to serve any living thing, irrespective of race, age, or species, anything that was hungry and couldn't be fed by ordinary means. She knew. Her breasts knew. They knew by the way the lips were half opened, by the little child's yearning in his breathing. The false poor couldn't deceive that pair of colossal breasts. They closed at the first sign of fraud; they closed before the greed of anyone who went back for seconds too quickly, they closed for whoever wanted to take a sample for analysis in the Laboratory. Inside, the great kettle was working, seasoning, adding salt and saffron, cooking up a storm. Rising through her glands, inflating her breasts until they almost smothered the helpless, was milk in a thousand different flavors. Without giving in to the temptation to entertain more than one visitor at a time, even though she had so much food and so little time.

Manuel Sendero came in. He didn't recognize her at first, Grandfather repeated. That's how bad off he was.

"Oh, Manuel, it's you." She sure knew who he was. "Don't you remember? Don't you remember when you came to the factory to sing for us? I was making a stew; we were peeling some carrots as big as my arm."

When he left, for the first time, there was something like the tears of another person in his throat, something alive; it was the heart of a newly hatched bird that was beating in him. Don't think that was enough, kids; don't think that was enough to make our not-so-holy father sing. But Manuel Sendero humbly lay down beside the delicate earthquake that was her body.

She put out the lantern. For an instant he was dazzled by the darkness.

Then she started to hum to him, as if he were one of the dolls that were decorating the bed. Manuel closed his eyes, stretched out his arms, enveloping the breast that was as large as a smooth, warm melon; he listened to the voice that stopped humming in order to speak to the outside, to the people who were patiently waiting in line: you can go. Please leave. The two of them would be there all night. Come back tomorrow for breakfast. Be good. That's all for today.

You too, she told him. You can come back tomorrow, she told him. Come back every day until you're cured, Manuel.

But Grandfather says that Manuel knew she wouldn't be there the next day. Everything he touched became contaminated, forbidden, vulnerable. The same thing would happen to her that had happened to the old woman. At that very moment the Caballero or his Superior Caballero was writing the name of Esmeralda on a list, was giving a final order; the Laboratory agents were on their way. With luck, she would leave on her own, so that her food could go on being shared in more places, here one day, there another; she alone didn't have enough for all the needy, and after several days the lines in front of her tent became endless; people started to fight; there were uprisings; abusers appeared. It was better to move on like some small-time circus. She wouldn't advertise. She would just set up her tent, usually beside the parish church, with the serenity of one who knew that in a little while her guests would arrive, guests who would always be welcome.

So Manuel Sendero wasn't surprised when he came back the next day at twilight and the tent was no longer there. Just the little holes where the stakes had been. The faded grass that had missed the sun for a time, the smell of horses in the air.

Everyone was whispering, sniffing the ground to catch the trail and to follow her, to follow her until Judgment Day, until their mouths would chew on the promised banquet, with the streets full of tables and trays, people bringing their pots and chairs to the avenues, one cooking beside another, mixing recipes, tasting sauces, offering new concoctions, exchanging delicacies, yes, she would be there anyway; she was already preparing the feast.

"The police didn't cart her off," said someone. "They wouldn't dare."

"They've sent her north, to the desert," said someone else.

"Where to?" asked a third.

Manuel had nothing to say. He just rubbed his throat as if someone had cut it again, like cutting the throat of a corpse with a knife made of blood. The warmth, that's true, the warmth was still there.

We fetuses, I remember, were divided as far as that incident was concerned. Like so many other times. That was one of the last, if not the last, plenary discussions we would have before the movement fell apart, before we lost what we now suppose was a battle and not the war. Some predicted that the encounter with Esmeralda would save Papa. Besides receiving a shot of protein, which he really needed, he was suddenly alerted to the fact that everything had not been wiped out; he allowed himself to be surprised at the number of people around him who hadn't become disheartened, the struggles that he hadn't had the time, the perception, or the will to notice before getting lost, in spite of himself, in his own labyrinths. This, they insisted—and in that chorus the one who insisted most was the one who would be Pamela and would dampen and thereby adorn Mama Teresa's generous diapers, all of which led Grandfather to feel himself being strictly seduced by those positions in the debate—this was, said the chorus, so healthy it virtually guaranteed Manuel would recover his voice in no time at all. Which was of no small importance, since up to that moment no one had answered the unclassified ad they had sent out: "Wanted, a spokesman for MOFAR, Movement of Fetuses Against Repression," just their luck, the only adult who could hear the transmission of the job offer was the very same mute who officiated as our own father and unemployed person. If my father, said Grandfather in the first confidential report, had recovered his voice before the failure of the first rebellion, well, kids, I wouldn't be here surviving and going under on this corner where Pamela left me; I wouldn't have to be the frustrated intermediary of a second insurrection now. So it definitely seems that the others were right, the ones who thought, on the contrary, that the pain of Esmeralda's absence, even the sense of renewed guilt at being the probable cause thereof, ended up throwing him into the Caballero's arms even more than the disappearance of the old woman had done, convincing him that it was useless to go on turning down the solicitations of the Laboratory representative.

According to Eduardo—if he had been present to give his point of view, instead of running away to his about-to-be-widowed mother—according to Eduardo, years later when the story was going around, that story of Esmeralda was a beautiful way to express the female participation in the resistance, the immeasurable power of women, who were able to feed that inhumane country and to keep a home going in the middle of the worst of calamities. A shame that once again the storytellers had relegated to the woman the subsidiary, support role, as if motherhood were the only use for her body and cooking the only use for her hands. In that sense, said Eduardo, reviewing various anthropological texts, the figures of Doralisa and Esmeralda turned out to be strangely complementary. It was as if the legend could not conceive a whole female, both active and dedicated to motherhood: that immense fountain of a woman paid for the nourishment she gave to others and her participation in history by being sacrificed on the altars of sterility, and, in contrast, the only mother in the story had to go to sleep, an example of extreme apathy, in order to be sanctified as a nest of fertility.

Eduardo could analyze whatever he wanted. Grandfather, even after Pamela left the womb, went on believing that the children that Esmeralda couldn't give birth to spread their voices in her milk, and Manuel could thus begin to hear the stories being woven in the tunnels of the future or of death, which is the place, according to our legends, where music, and therefore his song, originates. Or maybe you prefer the less fantastic version—that, just as his son would do thirty or so years later, Manuel refused to go on compromising those who wanted to help him. But the important thing, emphasized Skinny, confronted with our urgings, is the result. And the result is that Manuel bumped into the cold, walking and talking figure of the Caballero, not waiting for him at the door of his house as on so many other occasions, but rather, as if to punctuate his newfound power, in the bedroom itself. Do you want to know the tangible result of his encounter with Esmeralda? Whether it was because he felt stronger or because he now saw himself as absolutely helpless, Manuel Sendero accepted the first job they offered him.

He was never a pollster, as is mistakenly stated. He was polled, which is quite a different matter. Anyhow, I seem to be picking up a slightly reproving tone out there. It's easy to hold him up to scorn now, dear grandchildren who will never lose your jobs, now when it's all over, when the dictatorship is just a memory, so don't talk to me about collaboration. Lots of *compañeros*, really good people, were pollsters. There were worse things. They set up businesses, sold stocks, imported foreign can openers, participated in the promotion and exportation of unusual and typical objects. They had no choice. Back then, if a job was offered you, you took it. At first, there were limits: within the bounds of decency, just up to a point. Did I say jobs were taken? I should say the offers were devoured. Pretty soon decency was forgotten along with all other limits. It hurts to say it, kids, with your full bellies and your pretty, bright pajamas, and all your latest records, it really does hurt. Because the first obligation was not to die. As simple as that. Every *compañero* had the basic obligation not to die. If you had to take polls to manage that, then on with it. If you had to answer questions, then answer questions.

And the Caballero's company had no lack of questions. And answers too. The frosty representative unfurled a sheet of paper from which tumbled a veritable waterfall of statistics. What did he tell him? Hadn't he told him? Eighty-nine percent of those interviewed said their home life was more pleasant since their wives were taking the pills. And that wasn't all. More than sixty percent of the parents whose children were not born on time concluded not only that the delay was not prejudicial to their health, but that in fact it turned out to be a pedagogical advantage.

He's alluding to me, said Grandfather. He's suggesting a sputtering strike, with no punch to it. It's true that up to now our movement couldn't count on the desired unanimity. But if everyone will join us just for a week they won't be able to cover the thing up with the fraudulent manipulation of birthrate statistics and visits by experts on demographic control. Then the Caballero will shiver in his shoes, and it won't be from the cold. On no. It won't be from the cold.

As for the unemployed, the white, untrembling shadow of the frozen Caballero went on undaunted, another category to which you belong, Manuel old lazybones, ninety percent of them are ready and willing to move into an elevator. And in the category of freed ex-delinquents, another one to which you belong, fifty-three percent, that is, an absolute majority, recognize that their period of confinement was beneficial for them and that they won't repeat the offense. Eighteen percent, which is still intolerably high, affirm that it was harmful both to them and to their families; twenty-nine percent didn't respond, because they were in jail again or it was impossible to question them, for which reasons they were put down as having no opinion. I must point out, of course, that of that eighteen percent two-thirds don't believe, or hope, that the same experiment will be repeated with them. That means that at least sixty-five percent (fifty-three percent plus twelve percent) look to the future with optimism. If we add to these figures the number of those who cooperated with the authorities during their term in prison, well, the result speaks for itself. I'm sure that you, Manuel old Nobody, will finally join the category of those who cooperate, and from there proceed to those who affirm that their period of punishment was beneficial, and from there to getting out of the category of ex-delinquents and to being able to aspire to something more than a yellow card is only a step, oh, yes, my little Manuel, we've considered your case, and we believe you're going to walk and sing your way along the straight and narrow, yes, sir.

Of course, Papa didn't look at him. That was the only way to keep from wringing his neck, I think. Papa was drawing concentric circles, each one the prisoner of another, on a piece of paper.

Just one week, I told Papa. Just one week of unity and we would all be on the other side. Who's not ready to give up seven tiny, insignificant days of his life to do away with that rascal? When it's a question of several years, I have to tell you, man, the spirit's weak, only the most determined . . . there's a little girl that if you saw her you'd go crazy and you'd fall in love with your own future daughter-in-law, she's the one who talked to you from that balcony and kept you company the day they released you; she's as tough as pig iron, right up there in the vanguard. But the majority are weak. They spend their time figuring out how long before they can get out, like the idiots who watch a film on television when they already know the ending. Or they compare which parents have made more purchases, already consumers at that age, would you believe it? Even the most advanced argue about whether their parents should or should not make love while we're watching. Don't blush. How could we possibly not know about these things, when we're so close to the source of life? But they go no further than that; everything revolves around their own umbilical cords. What's induced labor? What's a transfusion? What's a cesarean section? You try to explain something about the world to them, what's waiting for them on the other side of the incubator, and they refuse to listen; they accuse you of proselytizing, of ideological terrorism. They think the world is one big womb, and candy grows on trees, and little lambs dress us with their wool directly. With that level of consciousness, with this organization, the most we can aspire to is some moral support, if you get the picture, pretty speeches but not very much action. So when they're finally born, at the first slap, the first time a breast is withheld, they forget their rhetoric and they knuckle under. Whereas, while we're here on the inside, we're untouchable. Nobody can hurt us.

Without looking up, Manuel Sendero stopped drawing. The Caballero's voice went on monotonously, citing the importance of such and such statistics, maybe he would be interested in getting a temporary job, but one that pays well, of course, he could be included in the next sample, but it wouldn't be easy. That's the way officials were: their ears were always tuned into the people, the pulsations of the popular ear. Voting for a candidate every three or four years, just so he could do whatever he wanted irregardless of his promises, was demagoguery, pure and simple, nothing more than bribery with nonexistent, future influences of political schemers. In our country we vote by poll. It was a mandate for the authorities. That's why antidemocratic elements were sabotaging those consultations, which were truly plebiscites. They considered their own voices the voice of the people. Participating in the poll, as perhaps would be the case with Manuel Sendero tomorrow, if he accepted this job, was a serious responsibility. Along with ninety-nine other people who would respond to exhaustive questionnaires. The answers, duly tabulated, gloriously synthesized, would come to rest on the desk of the executive, legislative, judicial, fiscal, military, consultative, and constituent power, that is, the President of the Republic, at dawn the next day. It was he, good old Manuel Sendero, who would, along with ninety-nine of his contemporaries, direct the destinies of the nation during that period. He didn't even have to use his voice. One tap, yes, two taps, no. Three taps, no opinion.

Manuel pulled his chair closer to Doralisa's bed and arranged the blanket more comfortably, sticking the edge under her leg so that if she turned over she wouldn't be uncovered. He didn't want the kid to sense his fears, the five sick, dirty bulbs that had flashed like an omen when his son had announced that there inside they were untouchable. Curled up in the bed sheets, the child would end up giving in to the consolation offered by the darkness and would fall asleep, he wouldn't be able to watch his father's slaughterhouse sweating.

Every time he covered us that way, tighter and tighter, it was because he was trying to avoid my irrefutable arguments. But they don't buy me off with thirty-seven pieces of silver. And especially now when I was going to offer him a job too. Because my colleagues' problem isn't insurmountable, Papa. If you could describe the world for them the way it is, if you could describe it the way it could be, if they could understand, these dear grandchildren of Pamela's, then they would have no choice but to work together. Even the children of the rich. Since they're the best fed, they often take the lead. The twins, for example, if they were born they'd own half the country. But others vacillate, and when it comes time to act together, at exactly twelve o'clock all the babies are going to shift to the right, let's start practicing, well, they were lazy, let us sleep, that's the way they complained. I don't deny the logistical problems, the period of indoctrination being so unavoidably brief: to organize that floating mass, always on the move, always naked. But language, kids, there was the heart of the problem. The original nucleus of innocents grew up too fast, among ourselves we squandered a language that became more and more distant from the grunting and jabbering of the youngest. The same one always ended up being convinced and the rest only paid attention when the blind girl spun yarns and legends and flights of fantasy. We don't need to be so pessimistic, said the one who would be Pamela—even then she stood out for her hopeful nature—we're the newest and the youngest detachment of our people, and it's petit bourgeois, said the one who was very petite and not at all bourgeois, to forget how much we've advanced. Of course, we're right, answered one of the twins, but even if we are, when the time comes, the mothers give birth and the children all fall in line, jumping out head first. And the son of Manuel Sendero, humbly for once, asked his father if he couldn't teach them, or maybe Skinny or Luis of the dark glasses could, some organizational skills, working-class savvy in building alliances; I think what we're lacking is a representative structure; we need trained militants, man. You could help us. Couldn't you give us a couple of little lessons?

Papa didn't respond to that offer. But he did respond to the Caballero's, one affirmative tap accepted the job, because Esmeralda had given him the strength to enter into negotiations, intractable, rebellious, insubordinate, to be sure, but negotiations all the same. Was it possible that Manuel Sendero was harboring some plan? Was it then that he realized that the only way to get out of this situation was to get close to the Caballero, to steal his confidence, to get into the Laboratory, to search for the antidote to the pills? If that was the case, Papa had been seeing too many American films. Maybe his son's last statements had frightened him. He had to hurry to get the kid out of those meadows of the intellect, because he was getting too dry and erudite; he would end up being a brainy dwarf, which might be the Caballero's true mission, to underdevelop an entire generation, an entire continent, turning its most conscientious inhabitants into diagrammers and users of other people's formulas, before any life experience could make them think for themselves.

I'd rather suggest, nevertheless, that Manuel's decision was due more to heretical, orthodox, driving necessity. They turned off his lights, his gas, his water, all that was left was for them to come and take down his house board by board, carry it off in payment for some debt or other, an eviction carried out by stripping the place bare, leaving it the way it had been before he and the other *compañeros* had come as squatters, returning the land to weeds and wild brush, the roof open to the stars, and now it was being rumored that in a little while a bulldozer would be operating in the area. Did he see, or did he think he saw, the possibility of avoiding that? An affirmative tap, neither that fantasy nor that job would last very long, but meanwhile. Meanwhile he didn't answer us; we were going to have to build our organization from the ground up. The twins boasted they could find a volunteer within twenty-four hours, but the only one who could listen to us was that inhabitant of the grave, that silent Sendero, and in a few days the first rebellion was burning out, because one woman, twenty years later—or was it a century after a dismal time that can't be figured on a calender?—I would be waiting for her on an unknown corner in a city of sewers; it would take decades to find some stumbling answers for ourselves to the problems of communication and strategy that my father had not been able or had not wanted to transmit as a solution.

Sensing the nearness of Pamela, who was approaching, pale, tanned, and upset, I tried to give the first confidential report a less personal, less melancholy touch. I still haven't found the twins, or the blind girl, I told them. Maybe they're different. But I believed that the ones who left in the first wave would help us, that they would have managed to learn something during those years. If not, why had they left? But the truth was that they didn't seem any closer to running the world better than their parents had been. It was as though it were all the same whether they had been born or had decided to stay with us. Eduardo, she, all the others, had nothing to bequeath us, nothing to teach us, and at the very moment I sent that mental message, the figure of Pamela made me jump out of my skin; I just couldn't contain myself, such was my territorial expansion, belying with my body the cynical notes I had just sent, since Grandfather realized with relief that even if he recognized no one else on the face of the earth, it was enough to begin with her, eventually it would be possible and necessary to remake the world from top to bottom, that same world which during the afternoon had gotten away from him and had turned into an alien land, that world could flow once more around him, like mother's milk.

"How's it going?" I asked her, while I put a final optimistic note in the report, they shouldn't worry, I would observe all the terms of the mission, I would make our nonnegotiable conditions known at the very first opportunity, not knowing that Pamela herself would force me to fulfill my words to the letter in just a few minutes. "Did the meeting go well?"

She collapsed on the bench beside me.

"Badly," said Pamela. "Things couldn't have gone worse."

The baby strike was at the bottom of her mood. Complete censorship of the news had just been declared, and the city was rife with rumors. As always, some were saying that the government was on the point of resigning, but they had been announcing that tasty bit of news ever since the day the government had been established, so their predictions shouldn't be taken seriously. What did seem certain was that a foreign delegation would arrive at any moment, packed with specialists who were offering advice, mobile hospitals, and food to confront the catastrophe, apparently under the illusion that it was an earthquake that had laid waste the region. Eduardo had emphasized that the government's supporters seemed divided. One group in power, the hard-liners, said Eduardo, thought that the only solution was to crack down, declaring a state of emergency, accusing the opposition of attempting to discredit the nation's most sacred institution, marriage. The subversives, according to the hard-liners, unable to undermine conjugal love directly, had now enrolled the unborn children in the campaign in favor of contraception and free love. Like any other terrorism, it was necessary to attack fetal terrorism with all the force of the law and, of course, with all the force of some other little things as well. The other group, on the other hand, the soft-liners, again according to Eduardo's information, wanted to negotiate. As the catastrophe was demographic, affecting all citizens, rich and poor equally, this was the perfect moment to open a dialogue with the opposition, forcing them to recognize that only the government could confront the emergency.

"Fine," said Grandfather, though he was beginning to notice that it was not only the unborn who hashed and rehashed the discussion of tactics and counterstrategies; he preferred to focus on the way one of her nipples was pressing against a little flower in her blouse rather than on the intelligence of her arguments. "So the government is divided. Great."

More or less. Because if it was true that the government was divided, it was just as true that the opposition groups were even more divided.

"That's something I'm familiar with," said the son of Manuel Sendero enigmatically, as though that was the way it had been since the time of the pharaohs, but also as though he, and not just Eduardo, disposed of secret information that guaranteed—and he did have it, didn't he?—that in a little while such conflicts would seem anachronisms, that less conflictive times were coming.

Pamela, on the other hand, didn't have access to Grandfather's sources of information, and she felt desperate. The opposition couldn't even agree on the existence or nonexistence of the strike in question. There were some, led by Eduardo, who insisted that it was surely a government trick to justify the declaration of martial law, to stall the process, slow as it was, of what could be called a certain liberalization. We should denounce the hard-liners, he said, for wanting to unleash a new wave of repression, and we should refuse to negotiate with the soft-liners, and we should ridicule them both for suggesting that we are ingenuous enough to believe that there is such a baby strike in the first place.

But other opposition figures, among them Don Ramón, affirmed that it could not be denied that an appreciable number of women were entering the tenth and eleventh month of their pregnancies. The opposition should blame the government, capitalizing on the anger of the people. Eduardo counterattacked: whether it exists or not, they're going to blame us anyway, because we don't control television and television will offer the final version. Eduardo felt that the opposition could not trust their fate to the baby strike—and his intransigence redoubled later when he found out that the supposed spokesman for the rebellious infants was none other than the intruding lover with the absentminded gaze and the fast hands.

"They're not going to repeat what they did to the first rebellion, are they?" asked the son of Manuel Sendero, forgetting that it had passed by with no blood and lots of sweat and tears, that the only remaining trace was his own drifting conscience, and quickly, before Pamela could answer him with an unknowing, blank face which he could not have stood, he added: "And what's the enemy going to do, then?"

The hard-liners were preparing a policy of aggression which finally, according to Don Ramón, would drag the soft-liners along. The son of Manuel Sendero remembered how the Radicals had foiled the Realists in the womb and he wondered if all politics is not condemned to repeat the same infernal pattern. But then he realized that these politicians were more dangerous than the babies. Their decisions could end up hurting people. The hard-liners were contemplating, Don Ramón had told Pamela, nothing less than an intervention: against the opposition to begin with, naturally, but also an operation of a surgical nature against the refusenik infants. The only thing that held the hard-liners back was the Church: it had reminded the government that no assault on life was justifiable, that no intervention which might be construed as an abortion should be practiced upon the babies.

Grandfather had been following Pamela's confused story without really paying close attention, still half caught up in the daze of the afternoon, which had lost all semblance of reality, but the word *abortion* touched a raw nerve. He grasped that he had wasted his only days on personal problems, just as some of us had predicted, and now a sword that wasn't exactly of Damocles was hanging over the Council and all the participants in the second and final insurrection.

He hid his concern.

"So what do you think?" he asked Pamela.

"I don't know what to think. All the arguments end up seeming the same after a while, it's so confusing." She took a notebook, swollen with useless notes, out of her handbag. "But one thing I do know: the government is capable of doing anything in order to stay in power."

Grandfather resisted the temptation to reopen the first confidential report and to add an urgent postscript: Be careful; watch all isolated entrances; prepare for a commando attack. But he decided there was nothing his *compañeros* could do to protect themselves. They had no place to run except in the direction of a painful birth, so it was better not to frighten them. Instead, it was up to him, as the only one of them with any mobility, to come to their defense and to threaten the enemy—should they dare to open a womb or to prepare a nail to close a coffin—with inheriting a planet where a baby would never again be born.

"And what if neither of the two was right?"

That's what they say Grandfather asked in a loud voice.

"I wouldn't be surprised at all," said Pamela, fatigue showing in her voice. "When they're talking, you know, they never seem to be wrong. But as for whether things really work the way they suggest . . ."

Grandfather closed his eyes.

"I mean, if it really were true about the babies," he said. "If nobody was twisting the truth, neither the government nor the opposition. If they really had decided on their own to rebel."

Pamela laughed for the first time that afternoon, and he remembered when she used to laugh like that, from way down inside, especially when the blind girl would add a happy ending to one of her stories to liven up our waiting there in the dark.

"It's a pretty story," Pamela admitted. "What a shame we can't prove it."

The son of Manuel Sendero swallowed hard, almost choking on his own silence. The time had come. He was going to speak the words he should have left with Skinny; he was going to finish that conversation. Let's speed it up, kids, Grandfather murmured, as if that were the real postscript, a message to fill us with enthusiasm, and not with panic. But he still hesitated. By now he had learned that in this country everything favored distrust and cynicism. He was going to give himself to that woman the way someone burns a ship or erases a border, but he tried to be sure his confession wouldn't involve a break between them, that it wouldn't leave him standing out again on that same damn corner, this time without her protective, feminine company.

"It's possible you won't believe what I'm going to tell you now. If you do believe me, fine. But if you don't, I don't want you to argue or ask questions or anything like that. Just tell me, I don't believe you. That's all. And that'll be the end of it. We'll go on as if I hadn't mentioned it. Promise?" So said Grandfather, thus protecting his flank.

She measured his seriousness and confused it with the turmoil men go through just before proposing something wild like marriage or eternal love, so she promised, without realizing what she was getting into; she simply went ahead and promised.

"I," Grandfather told her, "am . . ."

And while he was inflicting the truth on her, Grandfather realized that if she didn't believe him, it wouldn't be possible to go on as if nothing had happened, that if she didn't believe everything, absolutely everything, he would have to get up and leave her; it would all be over.

He shouldn't have been so worried. Pamela was too involved to turn back now. After all, it was easier for her to believe what he was telling her than to choose the opposite course, at the end of which she would have had no alternative but to doubt everything else he had told her, and his love for her, and even his physical existence. And if she could accept the idea that he had loved her before they were born, what was the problem in accepting that he was still in touch with the . . . and here she didn't want to finish the sentence. In some part of her brain, or was it her past, a voice assured her that she shouldn't betray him a second time. A second time? Where did she get that idea, if she didn't remember the first time?

So at the end of the story, her automatic reaction was to open up all her instincts and her arms and to offer them to the son of Manuel Sendero like a blanket, a spring, and a roof; she covered him like a mother hen gathering in her chicks in the middle of a rain shower.

"My poor little Sendero," she said, half singing and half sheltering him, neither of which displeased the said Sendero, who was feeling terribly needy and deprived after the purgatory he had been through that afternoon. "What can we do, child? What are we going to do to save your *compañeros?*"

Thus, resting on her shoulder, the way Manuel had rested on the landscape of Esmeralda, taking advantage of the panic to let his frolicsome head and hands slide downward, toward that fountain of futures, grateful that at last he was transformed into what he did best, a terminal of affections, Grandfather allowed her to propose the various alternatives for action that they could follow. Almost dozing, as if that way he could forget the urgency of coming up with a quick solution, as if we ourselves were not asking his own grandson: but didn't your grandfather realize that they were threatening nothing less than a surgical intervention? Why didn't he hurry? He savored a few moments more of happiness, as if bidding it farewell, because however much Pamela pondered the matter, in the end, he already had the answer; he had had it ever since he was conceived and awakened by a black, slaughterhouse smoke that cloaked the beating of Mama's warm and cozy heart, there inside; kill him. The

Caballero was waiting there at the end of Pamela's ramblings just as he had been waiting for him all his life.

Pamela first threw out the possibility of the press. Even under a different regime, news like this would be published only as a joke in the parapsychology section. She had a friend—and the image of the little girl they used to call the Gossip, years ago in the womb, flashed through Grandfather's mind; her tongue never stopped for a minute and for a while she had even vied for the position of head of the Information Section with the efficient twins—who was really daring; she practiced journalism to the limits of the tolerable, but only a centimeter from the limit, and if she . . . But there was the matter of censorship. No point in going that route.

Pamela raised her brow. "What about Skinny?" she asked out loud.

Grandfather's pressure on her thighs refuted that idea. The one who hadn't deigned to accept him as the illegitimate and illegal son of Manuel Sendero could hardly be expected now to sanction and to swallow this apparently even more absurd story. It was more likely that his instinct would cause him to see in this young man with his outlandish ideas not just a nut or an opportunist, but a government agent. He'd call Eduardo and say: You're right. It's conspiracy. There's the proof. They want to convince us to support a nonexistent insurrection, so they can decimate us afterward. They really must think we were born yesterday. And Grandfather, who was the newest of them all, who, for all practical purposes, had been born yesterday or at least the day before yesterday, wanted to keep the door open for future collaboration with Skinny and with all that incorruptible part of the country, the best part of the country, which would be necessary for tomorrow.

"When we're in power," said Grandfather, "then they'll believe me. And then we'll need them to help us establish order."

Pamela ignored the judgment and the arrogance it concealed. The last remaining actor was the Church. She had some doubts about the role the Church was playing now, but Don Ramón still maintained his contacts, which . . .

"Too dangerous," said the son of Manuel Sendero. He jumped

up, as if he had just been measuring all the consequences of implicating Pamela and her family in this matter. Dangerous for Don Ramón, and dangerous for her and for all her adoptive brothers and sisters. Contrary to what his father had done in the case of Esmeralda, it was up to him to keep Pamela at a distance from that kind of entanglement. If the enemy discovered that Pamela knew what was going on, if they found out, he saw a shadow approaching this woman's door, a hand with pink pills in its palm, a white presence climbing the steps one by one. If they were preparing a maneuver to get at the babies, if they were capable of that, what wouldn't they do to Pamela? And Grandfather swore—it was us, me, the one telling this story, kids, I was the one who swore—that the certainty and the sanctuary of Pamela's womb was something to be protected at all costs.

Dangerous? The word didn't seem appropriate to Pamela. The Church was ambivalent, confused, maybe. After having been in the vanguard, after having protected the raped and the violated and the fallen, the Church, thought a lot of women, was now revealing its sexist prejudices. If it was defending the unborn babies, it was doing so in order to attack contraception, abortion, and, at the bottom of it all, women's liberation. After all, it was the women who were going to give birth to those children and where did the ecclesiastical authorities come off, all of them men after all, deciding what women were going to do with their own bodies?

"Abortion?" asked Grandfather. "Who the hell can be in favor of abortion?"

"Me for one," said Pamela. "Who can be against it?"

"Every life is sacred," said Grandfather, and he didn't even mention his cousins the trees and his brothers the dolphins.

"My dear Senderito," said Pamela, surprised, drawing closer that little body of hers that she wanted to be as free as any man's, "you're a reactionary, a conservative, that's what you are! Of course life is sacred. But some life is more sacred than other life. I'm sick and tired of the people who are so concerned about the ones who haven't been born yet and who couldn't care less about the ones who are already here. I'm not accusing you of that. You don't know those people. Once the babies get here, those same defenders of life in the abstract leave the little ones to fend for themselves. They don't care if they're hungry or abused. Senderito, I'm more concerned about the living."

Kids, as torn as he was by that admission and facing the first and hopefully the last disagreement with his beloved, it was up to Grandfather to convince her of her error. But he realized that time was pressing. The one who had stated that opinion was one whom the fetuses would undoubtedly have considered an ally, and an enlightened one at that, and that kind of lapse from her tongue showed the degree to which the government's plans for a purifying operation against the innocents could meet with a disarmed public opinion, one which was perhaps indifferent and certainly divided. The whole strategy of the second and last insurrection depended on the military not daring to carry out a massacre of the innocent.

"Priorities, my dear Sendero," said Pamela, like an echo of what Grandfather was thinking. "We must never forget our priorities."

"One of my priorities," answered the son of Manuel Sendero—trying hard not to look at the roundness of her belly and praying that a knife would never tear at its borders, speaking slowly to his sisters and to their children so they would survive in that interior—"is for nothing to happen to you. I have other priorities, and maybe they're not yours. I'm going to ask you to do me a favor, to find somebody for me. After that, we'll separate and you'll be out of danger. There's one person, one who can—"

"Can help us?" Pamela interrupted, suggested, plunged in.

Far from it. Only one person to whom he could present their conditions, one who would take the rebellion of the fetuses seriously, who would at least accept it as a reality and not an invention. Not untouchable, much less invincible, those fetuses, but at least real, and that was a real step forward. He had to locate that someone.

"Someone?" He should describe him to her. She would be discreet . . .

That was precisely the problem. Describing him.

Don't you see, my little teddy bears? After all, you do open your eyes and you put all you have into your seeing, as if it were something natural and self-evident. Don't you realize that the son of Manuel Sendero had never seen the Caballero; he had what might be called a hearsay relationship with him. Only his voice.

He could only give Pamela a climate. No name. Just an atmosphere.

That man had taken such a definitive leap into evil, that when he opened his eyes he was an island in the middle of the sea, separated from the rest of humanity by too much water. For obvious reasons, Grandfather enjoyed aquatic metaphors. A mastless horizon, he said incoherently, while Pamela loyally took down his words in her notebook, and the Caballero, explained Grandfather, had had to search within himself for that shadow of ice that was his own shipwreck, in order not to sink; and he loved himself because there was nothing else to love.

Pamela cleared her throat.

"Of course. But did he do something? What did he do to end up like that?"

At some point he had made the decision, or the decision had taken control of him, to betray or turn in the person closest to him, and from that moment on, he wanted everybody to be just like him. Do you want to know what he was like?

Pamela wanted to know. She devoutly raised her pencil.

He was as far from a baby as you could ever imagine, that's for sure.

"So what were his weak points?" Pamela floundered. "He must have weak points."

She didn't know that in this way she was repeating a question she had enunciated so many years before, when the fetuses involved in the first rebellion were debating precisely that point. The son of Manuel Sendero had been urging all of them to concentrate their thoughts on the midday sun to see if that would melt away the glacial presence of the Caballero. That won't work, suggested the twins, whose intelligence service rarely failed: the guy has got an inner shield. He's untouchable, said the son of Manuel Sendero now, from Pamela's lap, patient with her and with her chromosomes of forgetfulness. No weak points, he said, because there was no remorse in the man. The slightest morsel of doubt would have acted inside him like a heat wave: he would have thawed out immediately, leaving nothing behind but a salacious puddle in the ground. But the man was now too far gone. There may have been a time when he lived among us and smiled while he gathered information about us. But in order to smile at the very moment when he was contemplating betrayal, he had to have built up a block of ice inside himself, and when he realized what he was doing, it was too late. He had awakened on an iceberg, floating in a frigid sea, and at this precious moment Pamela put her pen down, because she didn't want to go on taking down Grandfather's maritime obsessions.

She didn't want to wound his sensitivity, but the truth is that that kind of description was not enough.

"What?" asked the son of Manuel Sendero, trembling. "There are lots of people who fit that description?"

"Lots," came Pamela's affirmative. "Tell me more about what he did, what kind of work he was doing, what he's doing now."

He was a salesman, an accountant, in a laboratory. He collected people. Like insects, stuck on pins, like microbe slides, trophies. He wanted to find couples who would betray each other, that's how the Sendero dossier had fallen into his hands, all three of them, and he had planned, up on his mast, under his drum, floating on his morgue, in the last hole of his file, he had planned his strategy: She's so spirited, so passionate, it doesn't matter; I'll tame her fallopian tubes. And as for him, he's never uttered so much as an *Oh*. So what? We'll have him in an elevator and singing at the top of his lungs in no time at all. And as for the baby, I think the best thing to do . . .

And at this point Grandfather remained silent for a while. He was silent in the powerful, smooth mire of Doralisa; he remained silent in Pamela's lap; he was silent in the face of his favorite grandson, who right now is speaking to you, telling you everything, adding nothing of his own invention.

"What's the matter?" we, his grandchildren, the other babies, Pamela, asked him, even Doralisa gave a half-turn and sighed, as if to question him.

"What do they say about me?" he asked Pamela. "What stories are circulating about the son of Manuel Sendero?"

An airplane doing exercises zoomed overhead, leaving the air heavy and tough like the inside of a soccer ball.

He insisted.

"What do they say about my birth?"

Remember that she was incapable of hiding her thoughts from him, that he could delve into her confused brain the way he had plunged his triumphant tool into that kettle of maternity she carried between her legs. So she let the thought lose itself; she was still, quiet, until its last echo had disappeared.

"What do you care what they say? You tell me. Where were you born? What was it like?"

How could Grandfather answer her? How could he accommodate the whole truth and nothing but the truth? How much would this woman put up with? How many revelations can you allow a man on a fall afternoon?

"I'm looking for a place too," he told Pamela, as if that were an answer. "If you can't take me to the man, maybe you know the place."

When he started to describe it, Pamela noted with relief that it wasn't aquatic in nature, that, at least in this sense, he was changing his tactics. But he was no more exact in this case than he had been in elucidating the figure of the Caballero.

Hundreds of buildings, one after the other, and elevators, thousands of elevators. The important thing was the elevators. Did she know of a place like that?

"You could be describing any city, any neighborhood in any city."

"You don't remember, of course," he said. "Not even the last song, I guess. You don't remember that either."

"I was little," she said, "but I remember. We all remember"—she was about to go on and tell him everything, and then she felt a wave of fear sweep over her, fear that as she spoke, the story might disappear, if she didn't watch what she said. "We remember its effects," she said. "Everything else is speculation. Skinny and Papa Ramón saw him go up to . . ."

"She couldn't remember the elevator, could she?" said Grandfather, speaking of Pamela as if he were speaking of a third person, someone remote, as if he were now telling us his reaction, chatting with the twins when she left.

That procedure exasperated Pamela.

"For a person with so little experience"—she bore down on him, coming dangerously close to a conflict—"you should be more tolerant of others. If you could be more specific, maybe I could help you. This way, sweetheart, to be honest with you, I can't make heads or tails of anything you're saying."

She wanted me to be more specific, kids. Never be born, kids. Your eyes devour everything else; they make you blind. Look, I would've recognized her under ten thousand masks, worm-eaten, after a century underground, ripped apart by bullets; I would recognize you, Pamela. What's his name? That's always the question. As if knowing a name were really knowing someone. What's the Caballero's name? I'm describing him to you. I'm X-raying him for you. I'm handing him over to you, as if I were showing you his fingerprints, and you're telling me there are lots of men who fit that description, thousands, an infinite number.

"No, not an infinite number," said Pamela. "But a lot, yes."

Dear children of my own infinity, I told Pamela that more than one of that species is enough to immortalize it.

"Fine," said Pamela. "So you've given me a perfect description, to the letter."

We babies have scant capacity for irony, and at first Grandfather almost concluded that she was serious. Good. They would finally be able to locate the Caballero. But he had realized—maybe it was the days he had spent in that country, days filled with insinuations and double entendres; maybe it was that desolate afternoon that had taught him everything, even the painful realization that there are times when things aren't called by their names—at any rate, he had realized he could spin one story after another, without ever being any closer to imagining the Caballero or to finding him.

The twins had already warned him. That man was protected by

his own evil. So far removed from what is human that he defies description.

"The one who was far removed was the one who was looking for him," Eduardo preferred to explain many years later when speaking with Pamela. "Isolated by his own innocence, perhaps, but nonetheless isolated. He knew nothing about evil. Evil is the norm. It's doing the cruelest things just the way you'd give directions to a lost motorist. It's shining your shoes while someone else is vomiting in the next room. It's a mistake to think that our hair will stand on end whenever someone malignant walks into the room. Evil is precisely the fact that our hair doesn't stand on end, that we don't recognize it."

"He was afraid," said Pamela.

"We're all afraid," said Eduardo, "and everything has an explanation too." Eduardo was one of those people who believe that everything can be explained if the causes are investigated. "He didn't understand, and it is hard, after all, to understand that some people give orders and don't carry them out. They just walk off and smoke a cigarette or write a postcard to their little girl, while someone else methodically carries out the orders for which they don't feel responsible. He couldn't accept that schism between the head and the hand, that distance, and he joined both roles in a single figure. To top it all off, the legend he created was ineffective, because that kind of person doesn't consider himself evil. If you ask them, they have all kinds of justifications, and, besides, they love their families. Doubly ineffective, because he couldn't answer the only question that counts: Was that man part of our country? Was he born out of our history? To put it more urgently: Can he come back? Or was the famous Caballero just an accident? It should have been decided: Was he middle-class, technocrat, military officer, imperial adviser, or was he the empire itself? Or a demon, the wind of death, a soul-snatcher? Everything and nothing; that was the Caballero. On a masthead? A drum? Didn't he tell you he was on an unwashed baby's bottle? Wasn't that the way he described him?"

"There's only one thing in the world, my dear Eduardo," said Pamela, "that's worse than using irony with a little child who doesn't understand it. And that's using irony when he does understand it." And she turned, years earlier, and told our Grandfather, who was musing at her side: "We'll find him, love. We'll find him, Senderito."

"I'm not going to find him," said the son of Manuel Sendero. "He'll come looking for me, as soon as he knows I've come."

"Where?" she asked. "How will he know?"

"It's just a matter of his seeing me," Grandfather answered. "But first I have to show you the place where I want us to meet again. The elevators I talked to you about . . . They're special. Big. For passengers. But really big, like freight elevators. A whole family could live in one."

Pamela raised her arms and let them drop, in defeat. Why didn't he express some desire that she could satisfy?

"In front of the building I talked to you about," said the son of Manuel Sendero—as if he were describing to a sick woman a picture in an album that she had once taken—"there is a pair of statues. Not really in front, sort of diagonally opposite, on the other side of a square. A post office," he said—as if he were discovering or had recently realized the name of such places. "The main post office for the neighborhood or for the whole city or maybe even for the country. In the distance, diagonally, crossing a couple of streets and a square. That's where the statues are."

Our grandmother Pamela was going to say something, but she didn't. The son of Manuel Sendero had his eyes shut like a lizard and he was evoking the memory of the statues and the site as if they were not his own, but instead were hers, as if she were the one whose memory had gone astray and the one who was asking foolish questions.

"So the statues aren't there either?" he said, drinking in the negative in her feminine silence. "Not the building, not the statues, not anything . . . And isn't there a neighborhood called 'The Messengers'?"

"Yes," she said, happy though astonished to be able to answer him. "Of course there is. In the south of the city."

Take him there.

But what had happened there that was so important? Had he been born there? Had his father sung there? Had his mother awakened there?

"It's a place that belongs to me," Grandfather answered. "A place that apparently only I know about. If you really want to know, it's where the first rebellion failed."

"The first rebellion?" she asked, and then: "Why did it fail?"

And he didn't answer her the way he answered us a half-century, a century, a millennium, later, that it was the lack of unity, the need for a spokesman. He answered her, brutal in a way he had never been before, and as he never would be with her again, permitting himself the luxury of cruelty as the city and the infection of its life grew around them, having to tell her because he had kept that answer inside himself throughout his semiexistence, feeling himself adulterated, unexplained, vulnerable, as he said it:

"Because you decided to be born. That's why we lost. That's why."

OUTSIDE

The journey of Sarah Barks—let's call her that—was more troubled than her husband's had been the week before. To begin with, her mind insisted on keeping her body awake. Since she refused to attribute the ravages of insomnia to her age, which was advanced by the standards of anybody who was ruled by things like birth certificates, she had to come up with other causes. Above all, her concern for Carl's health. But Carl was indestructible; for all practical purposes, immortal. It was probably a minor indisposition that would disappear once she brought him back to Los Angeles.

It was also true that the nonsmoking section, up here in the front of the cabin, was full of matrons, all of them over sixty, who were chatting tirelessly, exchanging their most intimate secrets along with their lipsticks. Yes. That was bothersome, but pleasant too. It kept one from falling asleep.

But above all, it was impossible to doze off because a premonition had infiltrated that center of rectitude which was a kind of invisible spinal column for her conduct. Next month she would reach the magic number—eighty years of age—and this trip, so untimely in its coming, could only be a providential adventure. Something was about to happen that would solve the dilemmas, or rather the single dilemma, which had tormented her throughout her admittedly long existence.

She exhausted topics of gossip, commentary, and generally juicy tidbits with her two neighbors and then with other venerable travelers within a discreet range, until, to her great surprise, she found herself inquiring about their children, grandchildren, diapers, and school notebooks, begging for pictures, anecdotes, and memories of baby bottles. All the questions, that she herself could never tolerate, or that she had learned to evade so eloquently, but which now boiled and whistled in the tired teakettle of her own mouth. Not a single one of the women, who by sheer chance were traveling with her, had any progeny, and that was evident even before her questioning. It could be sensed in the tired dryness with which they withered in the face of certain themes. Oh, I do, Sarah lied, incapable of consenting to her inclusion in this group, to being one more dark mirror in that gallery of wasted bodies. I do, feeling mean, although she could comfort herself with the certainty that deep down something real remained in that fiction: someday, she prophesied, she had sworn it, she would have the child that doctors, hospitals, and men in general denied her. My mother didn't name me Sarah for nothing, she argued to Carl, the way you would teach a schoolchild to read. At the age of ninety that bibilical woman had a baby, and that's the way it happened sometimes to women named Sarah. She invoked articles from the *Reader's Digest*, quotations from the prophets, letters from the *Ladies' Home Journal*, homeopathic diets, and female legends of diverse origin, auguring a solution in the not-too-distant future. Barks never answered her. She read his doubt in his silence, but an innocent doubt, like all else in her husband, free of cruelty, filled with the hope that her wish would come true. If it had been physiologically improbable earlier, when she had joined him in the delicious flowering of youth, and then later in her sensual maturity, how could the miracle happen now, when her womb had withered and her breasts had traded in their splendor to become a couple of shriveled cherries, and when they no longer shared even a spasm in a corner of the marriage bed and had not done so for more than twenty years? She answered his invocation of the laws of cause and effect and of material wear and tear, praising her mother's wisdom in giving her that miraculous name, and rereading the pertinent verses from Genesis. "Yes," said Sarah, "he was a beautiful, chubby baby," not wanting to go on in order not to hurt her faded traveling companions, afraid of seeing the recurrent envy of other women, afraid of seeing in them her own expression, when, while she was crossing the street, she ran into mothers with their broods of little roughnecks in tow.

But none of the women reacted that way. It was as if for them, even at that age, there was still the certainty that in a little while they would conceive, or rather as if they had absorbed the stubborn madness that she, Sarah Barks, predestined to give birth at the age of eighty, according to her, or ninety, according to the Hebrew language, thought she had monopolized during these tedious years of her sterility. As though she were no longer facing those old women that she usually met, showing off smiles they really didn't feel, ready to nurse bitter doll babies in order to deceive the sadness of their own worn-out wombs, promising a last-minute salvation that would never happen, no, not the usual companions in misfortune, but rather she herself, multiplied, the true Sarah, authentically robust in the face of a misfortune that was, apparently, one more of the stratagems that the good Lord had concocted to test her faith.

"The episode opens with Sarah Barks in the airplane," says David. "Surrounded by childless old women who, like her, have not lost hope. She can't sleep."

So Sarah Barks had more than enough reasons not to close her eyes. She lost herself in her knitting with such vehemence in order to erase the sensation of irreality which had invaded her when she didn't know for sure whether she was the one traveling or whether her personality and aspirations had been expropriated by these ladies; she moved the needles with such fury, stitch after stitch, that it was almost inevitable that the ball of yarn would treacherously and playfully escape her grasp and roll under the curtain that separated her from the first-class compartment. Her pursuit of the fugitive brought her into the austere presence of four draconian passengers, two male and two female, who didn't seem to notice the intrusion. Sarah Barks asked them courteously, as was her custom, to forgive her usurpation of their private space, nodding agreeably toward the little ball which had occasioned her rudeness. Not one of them answered her. They looked at her in unison, as though someone had snatched them from a common nightmare. Sarah Barks felt like a cockroach in a spotless hospital. One of them stretched the angle of an insecticide finger to call the stewardess, when some turbulence rocked Carl's eternal wife and threw her on top of the other man.

"Oh, excuse me," Sarah repeated, dropping the guilty ball of yarn again, and about to add another string of apologies, when she noticed that those hands of ancient pigment, trembling like dry leaves in a storm . . .

"I want the hands to occupy almost an entire page," said David, "so they'll be completely recognizable later, when we meet them. The same thing I told you about the faces: paralyzed masks where, nonetheless, there would be some identifiable characteristic that time would not erase."

"Fine," Paula will say. "The hands. As if somebody had pulled out every hair, the pores covered over by an epidemic, an affliction, a wasteland. Hands emerging from a mist. A close-up. Agreed. The readers won't forget them."

"Don't scare them too much," says David.

"Whatever you say, boss," Paula will say.

The hands had left the refuge of blankets, not to catch her in her fall, but to crawl and jump like two snakes toward her neck, the site of her breathing and of her voice, with the voluntary and premeditated intention of strangling her, the thumbs already resting at the base of her throat, when the stewardess appeared and disentangled her from that mortal embrace, the hands disappeared again beneath the blankets, four pairs of eyes captured again in the straitjacket of a horizonless panorama, while the stewardess assaulted her with words that would have given the lie to the proverbial hospitality of the country to which she was going.

"This section is reserved exclusively for first class, miss," with emphasis on the last word, as if she were speaking to one of the old maids who were chattering a few meters away in their economy-class asylum. But the balsam of knowing she had been freed from those boa constrictor fingers led her not to respond to the insult.

Squeezing the ball of yarn as if she had to punish it, she directed her voice to the pale, drawn face of the owner of those murderous hands:

"We shall meet again," said Sarah Barks.

But her prophetic ability, in this, as in other details, was not to be fulfilled. At least during the next hours.

When the plane landed, she stood up before anyone else, ready to leave by the first-class exit and to bury those four passengers under an avalanche of caustic and biting words that she had been rehearsing, mulling over, during those last sleepless hours on the Boeing, but, to her chagrin, she ran into a wall formed by the backs of several airline employees, who, like a second curtain, kept her not only from descending upon her victims, but even from observing them. "We shall meet again," Sarah Barks reiterated, thinking that in immigration, in customs, in the health center, at the airport exit or the hotel entrance she would have the chance to condense her fury into two or three well-chosen sentences, much deserved by that caliber of barbarian. But that wasn't the case. Not a sign of them. As if they had someone to facilitate their entry into the country.

Not the warm reception, full of verbosity and of honors, offered by the interpreter, or the impression that Dr. Garay was sincere in assuring her that her husband's illness was perfectly under control and trivial, or the indispensable concentration on hanging up clothes, hers and Carl's, in the place provided, or even the moderate happiness of once more protecting her little man and of resuming the comforting habits of a lifetime, nothing allowed her to ignore the perfume, or was it a scented wave, of evil, that was still hanging around her. Until, a little before falling asleep that night, she realized that, due to the overexcitement, she had neglected to ask something that was of even greater urgency: What were all those barren women doing in that country and where had they been taken?

"What a strange old girl," says Felipe. "Where do you come up with these characters?"

"In here," says David, pointing at his head. And then lowering his hand toward the left side of his chest. "Sometimes here. And sometimes . . ."

Felipe contemplates the right hand that is still descending.

"The old woman wouldn't be one of your pickups, I suppose."

"Who do you think I am? Tomás?" says David.

"Tomás? Is he picking up old broads as well as men?"

"Ask him."

"I have no desire to ask him. It's enough to know what Enrique writes me . . . He says his brother's half-baked. What with Hindu

philosophy, happenings in Piccadilly, ecology, women's lib, he's even turned out to be a fag, it seems. I don't want anything to do with a bunch like that."[18]

"Then I guess you can't ask him," says David.

"So Mrs. Barks isn't one of your broads?"

"Pure imagination. Physically she resembles a nun I saw at a meeting for Uruguay once. They were all together, singing really nicely in the middle of a terrible cold snap. Open-air mass with wind accompaniment. I don't know why, but one of them stuck with me. She was singing so sweetly, her eyes closed. She was a Maryknoll. Later when I heard they'd murdered the two nuns in El Salavador, I always thought about Sarah Barks, you know. A woman who can't bear children, but who can bear other things. Who hasn't dried up."

"I'd never imagine her that way. I tend to identify characters with people you and I know."

"But you don't know the ones around me now. Not a one."

"True. In spite of the picture you sent us, I still can't picture your Gringa. The way I always picture you is with Cecilia beside you. The last time I called you, remember? To tell you your visa was ready?"

"It wasn't ready."

"OK. OK. To tell you they told me it was ready . . . She answered, with that heavy accent of hers, but without a single grammatical mistake. I almost hung up; I thought they'd given me the

[18] Fragment 4A. All of sudden, the past is like a foreign country. Of all the shocking characteristics of this *Dialogue*, the one that appears in this section is the most repugnant to readers. The Historical School has attempted a weak defense, stating that we are dealing with exotic and entirely transitory customs, typical of societies without the material means of overcoming prehuman prejudices. Such arguments do not seem seem valid. It is no mere folkloric manifestation that Felipe denies to his fellow human beings the right to use their own bodies as they see fit, just as we find it difficult to understand that in those barbarous times there were people who had too much to eat and others who had nothing. This contempt for women, homosexuals, ecologists, and Hindu philosophers strengthens the case of those who proclaim that these are not the same heroes who confronted the Dragon Pinchot in the *Legend*.

wrong number. The famous Gringa. But I was still thinking of you with Cecilia."

"Don't you think it's about time you stopped that?"

"How is she? Cecilia, I mean."

"You don't know?"

"How am I supposed to know?"

"Through Juana."

"Juanita doesn't tell me a damn thing. How's your cousin? I ask her whenever a letter comes. Fine. Fine, under the circumstances."

"Only fine? Doesn't she say, 'Everything's wonderful,' so you'll write me with the news? Now that Cecilia's finally rid of this beast . . ."

"She doesn't tell me anything."

"Just like a good journalist. She's an expert in communicating with the appropriate public: she arranges for me to hear the rumors, that she's become a real wonder woman, you know."

"Think that's true?"

"At first, the only thing she let me know was that she was in terrible shape. So I'd feel like a real bastard. So it must be true now. Why not? Since Lolo went back, she has everything she wants, right?"

"Yeah. That's what she complained about most. That man, that's what she called you, that man kept my son. Can you imagine what he's teaching him?"

"Lolo wanted to stay. I didn't influence his decision one way or the other. You believe me, don't you, Felipe?"

"We all know that, David. Nobody paid any attention to Cecilia. She was crazy. It's something that happens to women sometimes."

"Naturally," Juana would say. "Once in a while we just decide to go off our rockers."

"He wanted to stay," says David. "Later he decided to go back. I respected his decision."

"There was no way that could work," says Felipe. "That's what I told Juana. Of course she thought you'd manage. She was furious at you because of the business with Cecilia, but when it came to Lolo she really defended you. Why? she asked me. Why can't the man take care of the kids? And I said: Because we can't, that's all.

We aren't made for it. We don't have a womb. We weren't brought up for that. We carry them for nine months, she said. We give birth. We nurse them. It's about time you guys take charge."

"I was really glad to take charge," says David. "And if I'd stayed in Paris, Lolo wouldn't have gone back. But we couldn't live like that. The first two times I had assignments abroad I left him with Tomás in London. The offer from Edinburgh came up, then the producer in Holland turned up; I couldn't drag the kid all over Europe with me. He needs some stability. Right?"

"What David didn't tell you," Paula will say, "is that it just wasn't working anyway, Felipe. One day David would be a real authoritarian and the next day he would be a pushover. A really tense time was starting . . ."

"Are you sure Juana isn't telling you anything?" asks David. "I'd sure like to know how the kids are doing."

"All diplomatic relations have been cut," says Felipe. "Cecilia went back to Chile disposed to break with all your friends, David. All of them."

"Our friends, Felipe. They were ours. Friends we made together. They could've helped her. They could've, anything . . . Oh, you know . . ."

"I don't want to owe him anything; that's what she said. She said they were your friends. They would defend you. If they have to choose, they'll choose him. Since he's a man, they'll forgive him everything. And I don't want that man's representatives in my house. *Spies* was the word she used."

"Spies. Of course. I'd really love to have a couple of good spies now, to find out what the devil's going on in that house."

"But Lolo must've kept you informed."

"At first, yeah. We wrote each other pretty regularly. But lately, not a word. I haven't heard from Lolo in a month."

"That's the way kids are. They forget to write."

"No, Felipe. Something's going on. Ever since the medal business, ever since then, I haven't heard a word. Mom sent me the newspaper clippings about the award ceremony, and later Lolo's statement. Did you read that?"

"Cecilia sent it."

"Not one word about his dad. Didn't that seem odd to you? As if I didn't exist. Just his grandfather, the retired colonel, in a photo."

"Maybe they wouldn't let him say anything."

"Then he shouldn't have accepted the medal, Felipe. I wrote him. Refuse it, I said. He shouldn't have let himself be put on display like a circus animal. Because they end up believing in the circus, Felipe, kids without their fathers."

"And with that grandfather of his . . ."

"And with that grandfather; they're really impressionable, easily taken in. The fatherland, the little soldier, the military band, the Medal of Honor, the big he-man. He's old enough now to reject all the glitter."

"Don't get yourself all worked up. Look at it as recognition from the community. He deserved the damn medal. You should be proud, really."

"He could've made a statement. 'I saved those old people's lives and that's all the honor I want.' Nothing else. He shouldn't have let himself be put on display, an example of the good, clean-cut youth of the new fatherland. I wrote him what he should do."

"And he didn't pay any attention."

"Of course he paid no attention. He didn't even answer my letter. Finally I called him . . ."

"You could've done that sooner."

"I could have. Of course I could have. There are a thousand things I could've done. But I didn't. I just didn't, that's all. I waited till Christmas. I had to call for Christmas anyway, see. Person to person. In his name, to be sure I'd be able to talk to him. Cecilia answered, naturally. She insisted the kid wasn't home. I'm sure I could hear his voice in the background. Then she hung up. And when I asked the operator to connect me with Victoria or even with Nicola, she couldn't get through. They don't answer, sir. I was really desperate. I thought Cecilia was stealing my letters. She's capable of anything."

"Anything at all," Felipe agreed.

"But Gringa calmed me down, and we called Mom, since the person to person hadn't worked, and she tells me that the kid's fine, that he went camping, that I shouldn't worry."

"You see."

"I should be there, Felipe. I should be with him. Because Cecilia must be happy with all that hoopla. She'll help push the old man's idea of putting him in the Military Academy. And when I try to talk, she's there listening to what Lolo says. She interrupts so I can't influence him. She could think about the kids, about what's best for them. Don't you think?"

"That's what I told her."

"So what did she say?"

"What does that man care about the kids? she said. He always did sacrifice them for other things, more important things. No, she was heading straight for a break, at a hundred miles an hour. She carried the conversation in a direction where there was no common ground. Look, she got back two days after I left Tres Alamos. Remember?"

"I remember," says David.

"Imagine the state I was in. I'd better not say anything. Peace. All I wanted was to be with my people forty-eight hours a day. But when I found out Cecilia was coming, I told Juana we had to go meet her. That was the time when I was afraid for Juana to go out in the street, man; I didn't want her to leave my side; we were like a couple of old people, holding on to each other's hands. But I told Juana to go to the airport. She's going to need you, I told her; I remember it as if it was yesterday. But if she wants to come back here, she's got to come without the Colonel; I wouldn't stand for that. They arrived a few hours later. You can imagine how much Cecilia wanted to see me. She was almost hysterical, grabbed me and kissed and hugged me; I wasn't sure if she was congratulating me on getting out of the camp or for something else. She was really wound up. I felt really bad. She didn't tell me you were in the hospital. I don't know; we talked about trivial things, nothing to do with anything. Victoria remembered me, can you believe it? She climbed up in my lap. And Nicola called me Uncle right off the bat. Then Simón asked about Lolo. Just at that minute Juana had gone to the kitchen for coffee. Cecilia chooses that minute to open her briefcase and take out twenty handwritten pages."

"The letter," says David.

"She'd spent the hours between Paris and Santiago writing non-stop. Read this, she told me. I started to read."

"The whole thing?"

"It was hard, even though the writing was amazingly neat, you know, like her anger forced her to write well. At first I tried to read every word, looking up once in a while to measure Cecilia's reaction, as she watched me, completely motionless. So when I started to skip some sections, you know, reading faster, she interrupted me. Read the whole thing, she told me. Don't you like it? You're not finishing it. I'd spent nearly three years behind bars just waiting for the moment when I could be in my own home and say whatever I felt like saying. I was in no pitying mood and wasn't about to sugarcoat anything. No, I told her, frankly, Cecilia, I don't like it at all."

"Thanks," says David. "Thanks, brother."

"She held out her hand, without a word, and I gave it back to her. Men are all alike, she said. What do you intend to do with that? I asked her, as if I didn't know. I'm going to send it, she said. So the whole world will know. And I: David isn't the enemy, Cecilia. Why should you treat him as if he is? It's better to save your energy for the real enemy."

"It's good to know," says David, "that I'm not the real enemy."

"At that moment, Juana returns. Excuse me, Juana, she said, but it's time to go. The Colonel—that's what she called him, I swear it, her own father—the Colonel's waiting for me. See you tomorrow, she said to Juana. She said good-bye to me like I was a convict; kiss your uncle, she said to the girls, then she kissed our kids and left. I was really taken aback. All diplomatic relations with my territory were broken."

"But she kept on seeing Juana."

"She needed help, and Juana, Juana and some other women, gave it to her. But I don't get a drop of information. Gossiping is for women, according to you, Juana tells me. Don't be a busybody; hey, this is for women only."

"So did Juana receive the letter?"

"Everybody got it, brother."

"Everybody. Even people in Nairobi, the kind of people you meet at a cocktail party, you know, and write down the address on a napkin, just in case. Cecilia was meticulous. She carried around a regular catalog of addresses. She really called out the cavalry on me."

"She didn't influence anybody. I already told you that. Didn't I? I call you up and I still expect Cecilia to answer the phone. So you see."

"And Juana, did she believe the whole thing, when she read the letter?"

"Yeah. More or less."

"Everything?"

"Yeah."

"So what did she say?"

"That if somebody had to be born again and was going to be born a woman, it'd be better to die first."

"What about you, Felipe? Did you read it again?"

"Yeah."

"The whole thing?"

"Yeah."

"So what did you think?"

"I told Cecilia, David. These things are best not aired in public; they're private, personal, between you two."

"But you didn't tell David what you really felt," Paula would observe. "It's one thing to defend him and quite another to condone his actions. True, Felipe?"

"They were bad times, Paula," says Felipe.

"But you wouldn't have behaved that way, would you?" Paula would ask.

"I'm not David, Paula," says Felipe.

"David behaved badly, Felipe," Paula would say. "And he knows it. First that business with Patricia."

"But David sent her a message. He had to leave Chile abruptly. He told Cecilia not to come to Lima. She came anyway, with the two kids. And then she wanted to follow him to France, Paula."

"That's not the way she tells it in her letter, Felipe," Paula would say.

"I don't give the benefit of the doubt to any woman who leaves her husband under those circumstances, when David had that accident with his hand, or to any woman who forgets her political ideals because of love problems," says Felipe.

"And if they weren't going to stay together," Paula would say, "why did he father Nicola, poor little thing?"

"You should ask why she wanted to tie him down with another baby," says Felipe.

"You all think," Juanita had said, "that you can separate your public and your private lives, that you can be a hero or revolutionary in your public lives and a piece of shit with your families and that there's no contradiction. That's what you think."

"Me?" says Felipe. "That's what I think?"

"Your friend David," Juanita had said. "But you go along with it. You slap him on the back. You don't tell things the way they are. Go on then. Tell him he's a son of a bitch. Tell him."

"By mail?" asks Felipe. "Or by telegram?"

"When you see him," Juanita had said.

"And what if I don't agree with what he did, but I still don't think he's a son of a bitch?"

"What's his mother got to do with anything?" Paula would ask.

"Just one thing, Felipe," says David. "What's your opinion about what happened? I mean, objectively. All friendship aside."

"People lose their heads, David."

"The business with Patricia, that happened, Felipe. And the other women. But I did send her word. Not to come to Lima. Not yet. And she came on her own and then wanted to follow me to France, Felipe. I swear that's true."

"That's not the way she tells it in her letter, David," says Felipe.

"So who are you going to believe? Her? Or me?"

"I believe you, David. Always. But even if everything she says is true, what difference does it make? Are your friends going to love you any the less for it? We are the way we are, David. And you've got Gringa."

"There were problems with Gringa," Paula would say. "She wanted to have David's child. It was now or never. Her age, you know. But David would have none of it. He said that if she was such an ultrafeminist, so liberated, what did she need a kid for, it would just tie her down and fuck up their lives."

"For a foreigner to think like that is one thing, but for a Chilean woman like Juana, that's another matter . . ."

"But," Paula would say, "Gringa believed that David and she could share the care of the child, you know, according to the latest theories . . ."

"Like Tomás," says David.

". . . so it wouldn't be so hard for her and she could stay with the ballet," Paula would say. "But David said he wasn't going to go through that again, that he wasn't ready to bring any more babies into the world. One day Gringa told him she was pregnant, and David really blew his stack. He accused her of betraying him, said if she had the baby he was going to leave her. And he would've done it, you know David."

"She needs me," says David, "more than I need her."

"Arguments up one side and down the other," Paula would say. "It seems that broke a pact of honesty between them. David told her that if she was so modern, why didn't she join up with a man who wanted a kid, but that it was unfair, typical female blackmail, was the way he put it, and you can imagine her reaction. He used all the arguments on her that she had been preaching for years. I don't know if he convinced her, or if in the end David's love was more important to her."

"You can't imagine how that woman loves me," says David, "more than a mother loves a child."

"The fact is," Paula would say, "she had an abortion, and the next day David went to a clinic and asked to have a vasectomy, you know, an operation to be sterilized."

"Without a word to Gringa?" says Felipe.

"Exactly, while she was still recovering. And David, instead of comforting her, decided to put an end to temptation once and for all. Neither she nor anyone else would play any tricks like that on him again. Let her have somebody else's kids."

"That's what David said anyhow," says Felipe. "Whether or not he believed it himself is another matter. Nobody likes the idea of someone else sleeping with his woman."

"The things men say, my boy," Paula would add. "The fact is he went to the clinic and waited his turn. They told him to come back the next day, that it was painless and fast, and there would only be a small scar. Almost invisible, yeah, just about. David went home and didn't say a word about it to Gringa."

"He could've told her," says Felipe. "That was the least he could have done."

"The next day," Paula would say, "he went to the clinic again and everything went fine until a few minutes before the operation. They're all sitting there, getting ready, I don't know, it's hard for me to imagine something like that, and the doctor asks him: 'Don't you want us to keep some of your sperm?' You know they can keep it for years, even centuries, if he wanted."

"For thousands of years," says David.

"And David answered, without even thinking about it, absolutely not, that he wanted to be sure that no more of his children would be running around out there. Although who knows if he said it just like that, he knows so little Dutch. Then they were about to give him the anesthesia, things had gotten to that point, and all of a sudden he announced that he didn't want it done. He explains that it's because of Gringa, that it wasn't fair without telling her. I think it's more likely that he got to thinking about his three children, the three of them, and he felt sad, nostalgic, sentimental. He gets up as politely as you please, puts on his underpants and his pants, and explains to the doctor that for now he's changed his mind, to please excuse him. The doctor didn't get angry at all."

"He was probably used to that sort of thing."

"Of course," Paula would say. "Don't worry. He understood; these things are really delicate. What does he care as long as he gets paid?"

"It takes courage," says Felipe, "to cancel the operation right then and there, doesn't it?"

"Courage," Paula would say. "That's really important for you guys, right? So tell me. Exactly where is this courage of yours located?"

"So nothing happened," says Felipe. "Our David got away by the skin of his teeth."

"Wait a minute," Paula would say. "He told Gringa all about it that night. And know what she did? We're really dumb, you know, Felipe. We women are superdumb."

"Please," says Felipe, "tell Juana that."

"Gringa told him that if he was so all-fired eager to do it, well, to go on and have the operation, that he could cut it all off if he felt like it. She wasn't going to stop him. At that point, David was really scared. Can you believe it? And I think he really hoped Gringa would change his mind. He wanted to back out, and that idiot went and gave him unconditional freedom. So the next day he went back to the clinic and had the operation. What do you think of that?"

"He didn't breathe a word of it to me," says Felipe. "I wish I'd known."

"Mr. Foilback," said Carl Starks. "I need to consult you about something."

"New York," the secretary announced at that moment.

"Just a moment." Foilback winked at Carl Starks and at Marras, covering the receiver with his large, fleshy hand as if it were the mouth of a doll. "T. H. Foilback to the rescue, boys, as you can see. Please sit down."

And then in a computerized telephone operator's voice, uncovering the receiver: "Foilback here."

Pain crept along the other arm, the healthy one. For an instant Carl Starks thought he could massage himself, protect himself, inject a bit of warmth. But just the idea tired him more than the pain, and he collapsed into a chair.

"So long as I don't resemble Carl Starks," says David.

"OK," said Foilback. "What can I offer you?"

Carl Starks saw, with astonishment, that a bottle of Coca-Cola was chilling in the entrepreneur's hands.

"Mr. Foilback," Carl Starks said again. "I don't know if they've informed you that I'm somewhat ill. I need to talk to you."

"Ill?" said Foilback. "Illness is an illusion, Carl, just an illusion. Have you ever seen a machine that was ill? No. Of course not. Because machines were appendages; they were, well, you might say they extended and perfected functions of the human body. Now the moment has come to reverse the process. Let's start to imitate the machines. Look at Foilback. That's the only way to never feel tired. Don't fight it. Integrate yourself with the machines. Plugged into the electricity, à la Foilback. That's the secret of success. Who can stop Foilback? Who can keep him from producing? So look to the future with optimism, Carl. The optimism of someone who's in with machines."

"Men get tired, they wear out," said Carl Starks. "Machines do too."

"Sometimes I forget," said Foilback. "I forget that all men don't have a machine's miraculous rhythm. And even some machines lack the overcharge I was born with. If he doesn't move, if he doesn't act, Foilback simply explodes. That's no joke. The doctors have warned me. They want me to will them my body when I die. But screw them. Because Foilback has no intention of dying. Imitate machines, Carl. They need very little sleep. Just like Foilback. I explain to the doctors that they don't need my body. Don't be annoyed by machines. Be stimulated. If we could count on our own source of energy, and then give it, like Foilback's, to humanity, all these artificial problems would come to an end. One day soon, Carlie, we're going to find the solution. The solution to that dilemma." He brought his face close, a face that was burning like a shining toaster. "Much sooner than some people imagine."

"Mr. Foilback," said Carl Starks. "This aptitude of yours seems highly admirable to me. And your plans too. But I don't think your advice is valid in my case. I want to go back home to convalesce. They've suggested that you might give me reason not to do so. The doctor has told me . . ."

"Nothing to fear. Nothing. Nothing at all to fear. The doctor said so, and it's very well said. A good diagnosis. Foilback fully concurs. You should stay."

Where was Sarah? Why was she talking to the reporter instead of coming here with him, helping him solve these grave problems? What could that Becky be telling her? Why stay, Sarah?

"Why stay, Mr. Foilback?"

Foilback rotated like a radar antenna.

"What do you know, Carl, about the X-Factor?"

"Close-up," says David, "of Carl Starks's face. Astonishment. He doesn't say a word, but it's evident that he's remembering the conference, Foilback's denial, Becky's words."

"Promise me you'll never tell this to a soul. Not even to your wife."

"In our character's favor," says David, "the guy does hesitate. He doesn't like the idea of excluding Sarah. But Foilback convinces him. You know. Scout's honor. Pledges of allegiance to the flag. Secrets of State. The Confraternity of Good Old Boys. Leave the women out. You know. That sort of thing."

"I know," says Felipe.

"And poor Starks swears silence."

"The X-Factor," murmured Foilback's washing-machine voice. "If it's found, and if it's exportable, injectable, takable, pillable, then Chilex . . ."

"Hong Kong South," Felipe corrects him.

". . . this country," Foilback continued unperturbed, "will go down in history. The X-Factor is the ultimate, the definitive, the decisive factor that makes men no longer satisfied with their fortune in life. It's the motor of unhappiness. What keeps people from living at peace, loving one another. We, Carlie, think it's possible to isolate the X-Factor. Only a hospitable place like this, that doesn't stifle foreign investment, can advance toward the X-Factor. We can split the atom; we've reached the planets; we're on the point of freezing genes. But human society still can't control itself. Every time we try to put an end to misery and pain, alien, rebellious, impertinent factors intervene and sabotage our efforts. It's the X-Factor that interferes, that upsets people and makes them forget their true interests."

"But this X-Factor," says Felipe, "is like life itself."

"Earlier," Foilback answered, "the X-Factor was confused with life itself. It's true that it gives force and drive to things. But it's not the same. We don't know where it's found. In the head, the hands, the sex organs. You need an entire country to locate it. To extract it and to prescribe the necessary quantities to plan for universal welfare. You need a country and many years. This is the country and these are the years."

"But what's it for?" asked Carl Starks.

"In one part of the world there's too much X-Factor, and elsewhere there's not enough. If, Carl, we could take this serum to our tired, hopeless people. Like fertilizer for tired land. And take it out of a land flooded with excessive water. A two-pronged project. For our mutual convenience. For you and for Foilback, Carl. This country has agreed to contribute all its resources to reach these goals. Never before in the history of the world has there been a possibility like this, a government so willing to cooperate."

"And what about me?" asked Carl Starks. "What can I do in this attempt to save humanity?"

"When the X-Factor is found, Carl, my boy, when it's found . . ."

"Yes," said Carl Starks.

"We need a model for the man who lacks the factor. We need to orient him, mold him, give him direction, toward a happy life. Meaning, Carlie."

"And that man . . ."

"He's the one you're going to imagine, the one you're trying to draw."

"Then."

"Yes, that superman. That man will be re-educated to resemble your character. He'll be completely at your disposal, yes, at your disposal. The man you dreamed up."

"The man I dreamed up."

"Felipe," says David. "Look. This damned traffic jam is finally moving."

"So it seems," says Felipe, turning on the ignition. "Only an hour and a half. A real miracle."

"Blow the horn," says David, "like the others. And accelerate."

"So you see," says Felipe, "everything works out."

"What?" says David, trying to hear above the cacophony of horns and shouts.

"When your grandparents came to the United States from Germany," said Foilback, "wasn't that why they came, Mr. Starks? To dream of another kind of man? Wasn't that why my great-grandparents emigrated from Ireland? Am I right?"

For the first time that afternoon, Marras spoke.

"Our friend has reservations," he said, raising a gloved hand. "Would you allow me?"

"I'm tired," said Carl Starks. "Please forgive me. We would really love to stay, really, but I just don't have the strength. I'm sorry, gentlemen."

"Did you ever hear anyone speak of El Dorado?" asked Marras. "Before your grandparents or Mr. Foilback's came to America, other men came to these lands in the south. They were the ancestors of my grandparents, Mr. Starks. They came in search of a city of pure gold. The city of the Caesars. And also the Fountain of Youth. When you drank from that fountain, the years melted away, you became young again. They didn't find them, Mr. Starks. But they weren't wrong. That fountain exists. And the gold too. Right here in this country. Now we can find it. I'm not asking you to imagine the future of mankind. Imagine your own, your wife's. We've always been blocked from scientific advancement because of false humanitarian notions. But here, Mr. Starks, we're in a position to push the experiment to whatever limits are needed. Do you understand?"

"Everything's going to work out," says Felipe, raising his voice.

"What?" says David.

"Lolo," says Felipe, almost shouting. "Don't worry about Lolo."

"You're right," says David. "Hell. Fresh air at last. Speed up, man, the new year's coming and this year's going to be out of sight."

"That's my old David," says Felipe. "So now it's up to me to tell you to calm down, like before. We still have to cross the center of the city."

"The X-Factor," said Marras. "Like the Fountain of Youth."

"Fresh air," says David. "It's great."

"So?" asked Sarah. "Did they convince you?"

"I accepted," said Starks. "I said I'd stay."

"If I agreed, I assume."

"Yes."

"All right, if it can be done, I'd like to stay too. If your hand isn't bothering you too much."

"She convinced you," said Starks. "What did that journalist tell you, Sarah? What did she tell you?"

"Convince is a strong word. Let's just say I'm curious and disposed to help her. I met her daughter. She's a very pretty little girl. Did you meet her?"

"No," said Carl Starks.

"If your hand is better, I'd like to stay."

"My hand," said Starks, "is the same. And I think the other one's starting to hurt. But that doesn't matter. If you want to, we'll stay."

"We're staying then," said Sarah. "It's your decision."

"How much farther?" asks David.

"It depends on how it is downtown," says Felipe. "Let's take advantage of the time. What happens next in the comic strip?"

"Major General Soro," says David, solemnly, as if he were introducing a marquis at the Royal Court of France. "A military officer who's longing for peace."

"Peace, Mr. Parks," said Soro. "That's why we have to be strong; that's why we have to prepare for war. For our children's peace of mind."

"Because," says David, "far from the magnetic aura of Foilback, Parks has some doubts."

"And world peace, Mr. Parks," said Soro, "doesn't depend exclusively on our goodwill. The international panorama is volatile and there are vulnerable points, countries like this one. You touch a sensitive spot, a pointless rebellion starts up, the Ruskies stick their noses in and confront us, and *Boooom,* the whole world blows up. Fortunately, that can be avoided."

"Fortunately," said Carl Parks.

"So Parks is going to accept an invitation to dine with Soro," says David. "In a downtown restaurant."

"We have to eliminate the tendency of these countries to be irresponsible," said Soro. "To do that, economic development isn't enough. You need a rational population, disposed to accept a prolonged period of stability, so the effects of progress can be seen and will trickle down generously to the less fortunate inhabitants. There are notable exceptions—Mr. Marras, Dr. Garay, people like my colleague, the Colonel—but in general these people are pretty primitive. If they were innocent, that would be admirable . . ."

"Like little animals," said Carl Parks.

"Little animals, exactly, Mr. Parks. But these people aren't.

They're violent. They don't behave the way you would predict. They're fanatics."

"I don't like fanatics," said Carl Parks. "But we're not going to force them to do things against their wills, are we?"

"The American's need to feel he's innocent and good is really touching," says David. "Don't you think so?"

"We all need to feel that," Paula would say.

"Why, the very idea, Mr. Parks. The legitimate government has asked us to come and advise it. The thing is there are sectors, minorities of course, who don't participate in the electoral process, who just act like madmen, with no understanding of their own interests. So we have to find a way to make them like us, individualists, westerners, pragmatic, conscious of civilized norms of conduct. And do that without their losing their own idiosyncrasies. We mustn't repeat the Iranian disaster or what happened with those savages in Vietnam."

"And right there, hidden by a mountain of food, brought in by servants," says David, "the guy introduces the X-Factor. If you extracted a little bit of X-Factor from every aggressive native of the underdeveloped world, they'd have just what they need to be normal, reasonable, and industrious citizens. In a word, they'd be educated, turned into good adults. Thus avoiding war."

"Well, what do you know?" said Carl Parks. "I learn something new about all this every day."

"By controlling the X-Factor," Soro continued, "we could reach a strategic agreement with our enemies, and thereby persuade them to stop assuming such totalitarian and antihuman positions. They'd know it's useless to subvert the internal order. They could no longer count on having cannon fodder; they wouldn't have these barbarians with too much X-Factor. Without that factor of adventure, that factor of the unexpected, there would be no more wars."

"It's good to be a little rebellious," Carl Parks interrupted, closing his eyes.

"Right here," says David, "we see the face of Becky or Agueda. And in the next frame, Sarah Barks at the airport."

"Mr. Suárez?" inquired Sarah Barks.

The customs officer turned around.

"Mr. Suárez, could I ask you a few questions? About some photographs I believe you took."

"Photographs, ma'am? I don't know what you mean."

"A little bird told me that you do know what I'm talking about. And if you prefer to speak in the presence of your superior, that can be arranged."

The panic in the eyes of the customs officer would have occasioned a truce if his opponent had been Carl. But Sarah Barks's serene determination would admit to no such sentimental blackmail. Men, my dear, must be treated like small children, always on the point of sticking their fingers in the electrical socket or of pushing a button that will blow up half the world. Be firm with them; they don't know what they're doing. Those were her mother's very words, the words she intended to pass on to her own daughter-in-law in twenty years or so. Meanwhile, she was practicing what she preached. Suárez made one last attempt to save himself.

"This is dangerous," he said. "For you, ma'am, but especially for me."

"The photographs." Sarah Barks held out an expectant hand, palm up.

"What are you going to do with the pictures?" asked Suárez. "If I give them to you."

"You will give them to me, have no doubt of that," asserted Sarah Barks. "And I'm going to look at them and then return them to you. After you answer a couple of questions. Assuming you tell me the truth, of course."

She didn't say another word until her fingers had caressed the photographs twice.

"I don't know these people," she declared didactically. "But I think I've come in contact with similar people. And I don't hold them in very high regard. Did you see two couples, similar to these, get off the flight from Los Angeles the day before yesterday?"

"The day before yesterday?" Suárez mumbled. "No, I don't think so."

"You don't think so?"

"I'm sure I didn't. Maybe they arrived, but I didn't see them."

"To lie without getting caught," said Sarah Barks, "the rest of one's conscience has to be very clear, Mr. Suárez."

"But, ma'am, I swear, I . . ."

"Don't swear. Our Lord's name shouldn't be invoked in matters of scant importance. Because of your lies, I could keep your photographs. But I'm going to give you another chance. We'll see if you get your merchandise back."

The customs officer wet his lips like a high-school student about to do badly on an exam.

"Tell me the name, and, if that's not possible, give me a description of the driver, along with the model of his car, the one that took those couples from the airport."

Suárez gave her the description, the model, and the license number.

In exchange, Sarah Barks offered him some advice.

"If someone decides to be brave, young man, he has to go all the way. Today, tomorrow, and yesterday. It's the only way to win over the ladies. Whether they're single, widowed, or married."

Suárez accepted the pictures, but not the advice. Even before Sarah Barks left the area, she could already smell the smoldering matches in the air, and it made no difference to her that the proofs she had just examined were going to disappear from the face of the earth in just a few moments. Just then she recalled that once again she had forgotten to verify the whereabouts of those lively if sterile ladies who had accompanied her on the plane. And Suárez would give her no more information. In his life.

"It's good to be a bit rebellious," Carl Parks repeated, as if the Major General had not heard him.

"Yes, a little, but not uncontrollably. Because whoever possesses an extra quota of X-Factor will inevitably end up being antisocial."

"And what about nonviolent opposition?" asked Carl Parks.

"There is no opposition," said the other.

"You shouldn't put that," says Felipe. "It's too contemptuous."

"It's what they think," says David. "They think we're incapable, inefficient, divided, indecisive. As far as they're concerned, we don't live in the real world."

"And that's why they repress us so much," says Felipe, "because we don't represent a threat."

"They're afraid of us. I didn't say they're not. But as for respect, not a chance."

"Because we're not murderers like they are."

"Because we're full of theories and know very little about the way the world of business works, the world of factories, agriculture, banks. The world where you have to command. Even you, Felipe. Look, it's hard for you to realize how important this magazine is to me, the fact that they've given me the chance to write again, but I don't understand what you're doing mixed up with it. When I was leaving, a Dutch friend, an old fox with too much money and a left-leaning heart, asked me about the profession of this friend of mine, Felipe. I told him. And he told me: That guy, if he's an economist, why doesn't he take advantage of his stay over there to really get into the financial world, why didn't you become an entrepreneur, he wanted to know."

"Thanks a lot for the suggestion," says Felipe. "You've just hit upon a new route to Socialism. I'm going to propose that we take it up at the next cell meeting."

"I'd feel honored," says David.

"The opposition," Carl Parks repeated. "The people who are against the government."

"They're just mischief makers," said the Major General, "who've never done a good day's work in their lives. In countries like ours those people end up in mental asylums, in penitentiaries, or living on welfare. Down here, on the other hand, they organize. The Communists get them organized. They offer these good-for-nothings heaven, and, what's worse, earth. They turn a bunch of minors and women into terrorists."

"My God," said Carl Parks, looking around him.

"You could leave that comment out," says Felipe. "You're making Parks too much a coward, too stupid. I don't know if poking fun at the rulers in a comic strip isn't the ultimate confession of our own impotence. They shit on us in history. We shit on them in a comic strip."

"They shit on us in the comic strip too, man."

". . . and, what's worse, earth," said the Major General, and he added emphatically: "They turn a bunch of minors and women into terrorists," waiting for a reaction from Parks. But the old man didn't say a word, pressing his lips together as if some guard were forbidding him to comment on that eventuality or even to get alarmed about it. Soro even noted a strange, almost unaccustomed distrust in his face. "A terrorist, Mr. Parks. A man born with an overdose of X-Factor. Where's he going to channel his resentment if not into vandalism and destruction? Cutting down innocent human lives."

"What a caricature!" Paula would say. "Even with everything they've done to me, I can inform you that the military aren't like that . . . Tell me something. Have you ever known one of those fellows? Really?"

"Only my father-in-law," says David. "And he's retired."

"Cecilia's father isn't like that," Paula would say. "He's conservative and rigid, but not like that. I went to talk to him about Gonzalo. If he could find out if he was still alive. He was very polite."

"And who told you this guy has anything to do with Cecilia'a father?" says David.

"And if there aren't any more wars," Carl Parks said all at once, "what would you military people do? Is it in your interest to control the X-Factor?"

"I'm an expert on energy," Soro replied. "And I'm going to answer your question in that capacity. According to futurologists, our civilization could crumble if we don't soon find an element that will enable us to solve the energy crisis. They talk about the sun, the atom, other planets. We prefer to look for the solution within the resources that we have closest at hand: the human resource. The X-Factor, being a residue of condensed and chemically pure human energy, could be used as a fuel. Substituting for petroleum, liquidating international terrorism; those are the Pentagon's goals, after all. Just imagine achieving both at the same time. And there's still another advantage that's going to . . ."

"Precisely at that moment," says David, "three masked men armed with machine guns burst into the restaurant. 'Hands up, shitheads!' "

"That's it!" says Felipe, enthusiastically. "About time. The only way to get rid of these bastards is with bullets."[19]

"Bullets?" Paula would ask. "To do that you have to put your lives on the line. Your lives, my boys. Any volunteers?"

"None of that," says David. "Those fellows go right up to the table where Parks and Soro are sitting. Parks goes pale. He's the one, says one of them. He's the one we came for. But Soro goes into action like one of those karate champs you see in the movies, and, after a spectacular battle, disarms and captures them. Soro hurls the usual epithets at them: Take that, animal . . . This'll teach you to come uninvited into a respectable restaurant . . . Didn't you come for dinner? Well, eat my fist . . . And other pretty phrases from Soro's repertoire. Everything should be coarse, exaggeratedly so, so that the reader will begin to suspect that the 'terrorists' are really men on Soro's payroll. His purpose: to frighten Parks."

"As I was saying, Mr. Parks," said the Major General, taking his seat at the table again and picking up his napkin delicately,

[19] This fragment (5A), the next to the last of those which we have inherited, which consists of only these three short sentences by Felipe, has nonetheless been the one which has raised the most controversy, due to the fact that it is the only one that mentions violence, supposedly as a possible response to the Dragon Pinchot. Those who uphold the connection between the *Legend* and the *Dialogue* base their theory on this fragment: according to them, it proves that Felipe is preparing for total warfare against the enemy. Those who support the opposite thesis are more numerous, however: the *Dialogue* is a gray and mediocre exchange, with no perspective of heroic denouement. Although they do not go as far as Vescovar's rash affirmation to the effect that fragment 5A is apocryphal, added to the text many centuries later by a second and false scribe in order to strengthen the similarity with the *Legend*, they do tend to maintain that this fragment, flowing, disconnected, and hermetic as it is, cannot contradict the persistent multiplicity of other signs that the protagonists were not planning any kind of epic action.

"there's a further advantage. But let's go on with our meal, my dear friend . . ."

"I'm not hungry," said Carl Parks.

"Another advantage," Soro continued. "The X-Factor would solve the problem of atmospheric pollution as well. For people who love nature, as we do, a fuel that doesn't destroy parks and rivers would be a real blessing."

"My Lord!" says David. "We just picked the wrong world to live in! That's why everything is going so badly for us."

"Things aren't going very well," Felipe admits. "But we've got plenty of ammunition."

"Against the grain, man. We're going against the grain. We're on the wrong track."

"The people," Paula would say, "still haven't shown up in a single frame of this comic strip. Could that be because you're so tired, David?"

NEXT TO THE LAST FRAME OF THE EPISODE: Carl Parks, convinced that he should collaborate, returns to his hotel room.

Parks's hand can be seen on the doorknob, trying, without success, to open it.

LAST FRAME: Carl Parks's back; farther away, inside the room, Sarah is sitting, waiting for him, in an armchair.

Sarah: But Carl, what's the matter? You're so pale!

Carl: My hand, Sarah. My left hand. Now I can't move the other hand.

The other hand. The left hand.

Felipe doesn't look at me; he doesn't need to look at me for me to know what he's thinking, not just now, at this moment, but what he's been thinking all this time, ever since the moment we gave each other a bewildered embrace at the customs exit.

If only he'd asked me straight out. Does it hurt, David? How do you feel? Just like that. Matter-of-factly. Not making a big deal of it. Tell me, David, tell me how it was, why it was, David, your left hand? But I would have to ask you what you were doing, Felipe, on the day this happened to me, on the day I did this to myself, the day I made it happen, the day when your footsteps didn't climb that Paris staircase, when your presence at my side . . . But no, there were no footsteps; you weren't there when I needed you. I learned to live as if you never were going to be there. Deceiving oneself at first, wanting to believe that the new faces, faces of the recently shipwrecked and of kindhearted supporters, could compensate for the loss of past companions, losing the habit of real contact until there was nothing left but manipulation. Deciding first not to talk about what's happening to us and later the more dangerous maneuver of not feeling what we are talking about, and finally withdrawing from experience, so that what we ought to talk about or to feel won't happen to us. Everything would be different, we whisper to ourselves, in another place, with other people; in the past it was different. If Elías or Paula or Felipe . . . And we turn to nostalgia, the way the rich use their bank accounts; we use it to convince ourselves that distance is a matter of kilometers and not a question of spirit. But by the time we meet up with our friends, Felipe outside the airport, Paula at the beginning of a comic strip, face to face with the bodies in the photographs of your album, unable to write a letter in order to camouflage the differences, by the time they demand that we pick up the relationship as if it were a road left unfinished because of a budget deficit, by then you have realized that lying is pointless—it just doesn't work anymore.

It's difficult to fix when you understood that fact. There comes a moment, call it a point of no return—when, instead of blaming bad times or bad luck or bad history, you are forced to ask yourself whether it is not a question of bad life, mine, the one chosen by me entirely on my own. When was that point of no return? When did I look back and see no horizon—feel that I was absolutely on my own? I've often wondered if it was not at my birth, something that took place in that unique and irreversible moment I can't remember. Or maybe even earlier, further back. When my father made the mistake of betting against the undeniable beast of history and against his own death and took pity on his loneliness and made himself a home inside my mother, inside the momentary darkness. But why blame others? The point of no return is the moment when you no longer blame anyone else—the moment was that moment in Paris, Felipe.

The same day they freed you, were going to free you, Felipe, I was far away, watching a group of children leaving a school on a mediocre Paris afternoon; the French children were leaving the way kids leave schools all over the world.

The first one to appear, breathless, a few minutes before the others, the first to appear, as we had agreed the night before and confirmed that morning at breakfast, was Lolo. He was walking head down, sulky, maybe nervous or afraid, but our eyes had scarcely met when something inside him lit up, as if I had been James Bond to the rescue. We didn't say anything to each other. We crossed to the other side of the narrow street and stood facing the school, both of us with our hands in our pockets, leaning on a car like a pair of gangsters. From that point you could watch the French children, who in increasing numbers were beginning to fill the front door of the school, the advance guard of a vast and noisy contingent making its way, more and more of them, until they overflowed the space itself, as if they were the ones being freed from a prison and not you on the other side of the globe. Felipe, gesticulating, shouting obscenities, and making dates, greeting mothers and aunts who constituted a group neither dispersed nor compact, a group of which I had formed an anonymous and indistinguishable part only a few moments ago . . .

Lolo grew tense at my side.

"Which one is he?" I asked. "That one?"

He shook his head. "This is my class," he whispered as if it were a secret of state. "The older boys come out a little later than we do."

"Son of a bitch," I said. "Let me know. As soon as you see the son of a bitch, you let me know."

Contrary to what I had expected, I didn't recognize him. Lolo grabbed my arm and squeezed it.

"That's the one," he said.

"The one with the tan sweater?"

"The other one."

"Which one? The one with the blue tie? That one?"

"Yeah, Dad."

I didn't want to register my own suprise. He was heavier, more solid, than Lolo, two years older, and at that age the years count, but even so, he was much smaller than I had imagined, and an impartial observer would have found something pleasant, slightly sarcastic or rebellious, in his face. I could hardly believe that this same punk had waited for Lolo at the school entrance every morning for the last ten days and had tormented him mercilessly.

"Let's go," I said.

He was with a group of classmates, three or four of them, talking animatedly, not knowing that Lolo and his father had heroically crossed the street once again and were following them.

It was ridiculous to call to them, but that's precisely what I did.

"*Attendez,*" I managed to articulate. "*Attends*."

Not one of them turned his head. He was telling a joke, and they were dying laughing. They didn't even know I was calling them.

I stepped off the curb. I dodged out of the path of a car driven by a lady with her offspring, and, half running, half walking, I stood in their path.

When I tried to say something, I'd forgotten what I was going to say. I'd rehearsed two different speeches, depending on my mood at the time; I'd gone over them in French and Spanish or something in between for the last half hour, almost the whole ten days since Lolo had come home fighting back the tears and I had dragged the truth out of him. Two simultaneous speeches, more like a pair of contradictory prayers than a strategy for persuasion. In one, aggressiveness was the primary stance. Look, you little shit, if you're so brave, why don't you fight it out with me now? You like to fight so much? You want to take on a Chilean fag? Well, here I am. I'm a Chilean fag. But just a little bigger than this one. No? Well then, leave my kid alone. Do you understand? That was one. The other was an offer of peace. Look, boys. Why do you want to fight? What's the fun in beating up a kid smaller than you? Men don't do that. Shake hands and all's forgotten. What do you say?

Neither speech came out. I stammered a few impossible and surely unpronounceable words, completely blinded by a rage that was mounting in me from someplace in the galaxy that couldn't be the pit of my stomach, my heart, my guts. Just at that moment some devil had stolen my tongue, a dark hold installed itself in the unfathomable center of my brain, just behind my chin, leaving me with only this pair of mercenary hands.

"Son of a bitch," I said slowly in Spanish and I saw those two hands that had always been mine grab him by the lapels and push him against the school fence. He didn't weigh anything.

"I'm going to kill you, you son of a bitch."

If I'd let go, he would have splattered like an egg, coming apart like something fragile, dismembered and yellow between my fingers. How easy it is to break a bone that's been growing for eleven years and nine months. How easy it is to break the bone of someone else's hope, the backbone. So completely at my mercy, so absolutely in my power; I felt, I believed, I could have him, I did have him. Hanging from the ends of my arms, as if from a butcher's hook.

He could've tried to get away, twisting himself, moving his shoulders. He could've gotten desperate and called for help. Maybe inside he was sick with terror. But he didn't show it. He didn't seem to accept his own defenseless condition. He, at least, hadn't lost the notion of who he was, what country this was, what was the language that should be spoken here.

I guess it was the calmness of someone who is born and grows up, goes to school and plays soccer, eats ice cream and learns his colors in the same land that his parents did, in the same land that his own grandchildren will. Could that be the source of his calm? The calm of a child who doesn't have to leave his home and his friends at the age of eight for reasons he doesn't understand? The calm of a child who has older brothers and sisters, aunts and uncles, grandparents, friends of his father, friends of his mother, to protect him, to watch over his dreams at night? The right to dream at night and during the day? Could that have been the source of that calm that permitted him to look at me as if I were nothing more than a car, banged up in the street?

A final, animal undercurrent climbed up to my mouth.

"Son of a bitch," I repeated. "I'm going to kill you."

I would've done it.

I saw myself from a distance, the way a spectator or a mother would have seen us from a balcony: a grown man pushing a child against a school fence. I saw a woman go by, on the point of saying something, or stepping in, opening her mouth, then passing by and going on her way. I saw my own son, surprised, worried. I saw the other children, gathered around us, absorbed by what was happening. I also saw myself the way he was seeing me; from the surface of his eyes, in the pupils, in the calm whites of his eyes; I saw myself reflected, adult and enemy and epidemic in the round liquid corners of his eyes, a man that was me.

That man's teeth clenched to avoid a heart attack, his fingers twisted the lapels with enough electricity to torture an ox.

"*Monsieur, s'il vous plaît, vous me faites mal*."

The damned automatic translator started to work: "Sir, please, you're hurting me."

Sir, I'm French. Sir, you're not French. Sir, I'm a child. Sir, you were a child too. Sir, what did I do to you?

The hands that my mother bore released the child. Almost gently. The way you place a bride in the marriage bed.

Where were you, Felipe? What patriotic words was some captain proclaiming to you in farewell?

I was left empty, empty and trembling, barely surviving. My hands wouldn't fit in my feverish pockets, my hands wouldn't fit anywhere.

Without another word to him, I spun halfway around, and I left.

I must've walked ten blocks, fifteen, twenty beastly, feverish blocks with Lolo behind or beside me, half running, his book bag on his back, rising and falling with his trotting motion, trying to imitate my gait, simply near me. I don't know where we went, what corners we turned, what our route was. At some point I must've stopped to buy *Le Monde*, must've glanced at the "Amériques" section, taking note like an automaton that they hadn't published the news about the disappearance at the hands of the secret police of a labor union man in Chile, which two, maybe three days ago, we had asked them to print. It must've been so, because the newspaper was open and wrinkled in that section. I found myself with the newspaper in my hand when my feet finally decided to halt their movement. You always walk in circles. Once again I was a block from Lolo's school.

"Dad," said Lolo.

We were a block from his school, and, yes, along the same path, but some thirty or maybe twenty-five meters away, the children were coming, the kid and his friends were coming, talking, so intensely, so concentrated, that they didn't even see us right away. They were coming with a French policeman to whom they looked up with admiration and with almost familiar reverence, escorted by a tall, shining, and powerful policeman, a black policeman.

There was nothing else to do. Just wait for them like a couple of blossomless trees that don't know how to move. That's all.

At that moment, the kid saw me, touched the policeman's elbow or sleeve, whispered something, pointed in our direction. "That one?" the policeman asked, possibly asked, because the kid nodded his head, the others confirmed the identification with their fingers and with exclamations.

I don't know if I really don't remember what happened next or if I prefer not to; I don't know exactly what happened. What did I tell the policeman? What did I say to the kid?

He must've asked me where I lived; he asked me if I knew what I had done; he asked me if it was true; he asked me my status in this country. How did I answer? Could I have given him our address? Because we were in that district illegally. We had moved without advising the authorities in order to have a house in Paris from which to clandestinely receive and send off *compañeros* to and from Chile. Did I hand him my *carte de sējour*, the document for foreigners who are residing temporarily or permanently in France? Did I hand it to him? Why, then, didn't he ask me what we were doing here, when our official address was on the other side of the city? Or did he ask me for it and did I invent some story, turning aside his doubts?

I don't remember anything.

He was black. That I know. I told myself that fact the way someone invokes the peace of a cathedral. He's black; he's a brother; he's just as screwed as we are. He'll know what it's like to be persecuted, what it is to be choking with rage. How many times hadn't I seen people of his race harassed by the same police, in the metro, along the streets of Montparnasse while they were selling knickknacks supposedly from their tribes, collecting garbage at five in the morning, the Algerians and the Moroccans at their side, making merry music on a flute in some dead-end street of the Latin Quarter, while another one, thin and sad, played a tambourine? Blacks from La Martinique, from Haiti, from other islands of my America, from Senegal and farther south. Could I have tried to transmit something of this silently to him? Could I have thought about them in order to throw myself on his mercy that miserable afternoon in Paris? Can he have sucked in something in my eyes, something ancestral and beaten in my tortured eyes? Or was he a hard nut to crack, someone who had seen infinite offers of brotherhood without ever having been moved, so that now he no longer even recognized them?

Lolo, nearby. That I remember too. As near as if I were being born right then and had to be helped to draw my first breath. Lolo seeing his father apologize, stammer in his poor French that the whole thing was nonsense, just a childish prank; his father trying to gather resources so they wouldn't carry us off or accompany us home or ask us to follow them, send us back to Santiago on the next plane. Lolo witnessing his father, humiliated, wishing he were someplace else, lowering his head, slumping his shoulders.

The kid was looking at me without triumph, without vengeance in his glance, as calm as before, more curious, a bit self-satisfied to be sure, but not really gloating over his victory. Instead, looking at Lolo, all of them staring at Lolo behind me, all of them and Lolo listening to my tumultuous words, to the fear in my esophagus, the evidence that I had lost still another little battle in another war that we had lost long ago, Lolo who had gotten me into this mess just by being on the pavement under the feet of children older than himself, forcing him to spit out "I'm a Chilean fag," Lolo who'd gotten me into this mess just because he existed, Lolo entirely alone, unable to take my hand that afternoon, Lolo beneath the scrutiny of the others, Lolo thinking about school tomorrow, when they would watch him crossing the courtyard, when they would witness the patches on his clothes inherited from French supporters, notebooks mended with Scotch tape, rumors of the violent, irascible, crazy old man he had.

I didn't see an ounce of sentiment in the way the policeman treated me, the way he took down the information, the way he closed the notebook with decisive finality.

He should have answered my prayer.

Beyond us lay Paris. I didn't even know the city. I'd had no desire to visit a museum, a monument; I hadn't even entered Notre Dame. As far as I was concerned, I could have been in any other part of the world. The Eiffel Tower was cardboard; the Seine was a fictitious river. Cecilia and I had shut ourselves into our own world, alien to Paris, casually walking streets that appeared in Hemingway, on postcards, in Balzac, along which by some strange coincidence Gene Kelly had danced and Jean-Paul Belmondo had died, but which in the final analysis had nothing to do with our poor, exiled bodies that had to look for work, contribute to solidarity, send money back to Chile, discuss strategy, raise three kids. Paris wasn't this place where we had to buy meat. It was a Hollywood set, a place that went on existing, perhaps waiting for the day we might become tourists; it went on existing out there, in books, in films, in paintings. I was sure that behind the facades of buildings there were nothing but vacant lots, the facades were held up by scaffolding, like an abandoned town in the Wild West, a ghost town. Paris was someplace else, a place marked by Sartre and Matisse and Debussy and the Commune, not that kid, that policeman, me, Lolo, Cecilia, Nicola being born thanks to public charity. I had lived there for almost three years without the city affecting or even touching me. That policeman was as foreign there as I was. Neither he nor I nor his hand nor mine had built the city. We had come there from a world where Paris was cheap reproductions of Renoir on the walls, drawn there, he and I, for different reasons, driven by easily distinguishable historic winds but identically alien to that

French child, who was the only one with real roots and therefore with the valid right to accuse, judge, and someday to procreate in the shade of those blossomless avenues.

He was nobody. I was nobody.

But they'd put a uniform on him.

"Come with me," the policeman repeated. "Unless . . ." and he put his hand on the kid's shoulder.

The pity that the policeman didn't have was exercised by the victim. Incredibly, unbelievably, he intervened in my favor. Was it the natural generosity of youth? Was it one more gesture of august power, the taste of dispensing absolution or pain? The discomfort of seeing a grown man in such a denigrating situation? Or some note of panic that he read in the set of Lolo's jaw and that was unbearable for him?

He didn't want to press charges. That's what he said. He was happy everything could be settled amicably.

The outcome was so fast I didn't have time to get used to it.

We shook hands, the kid and I, the kid and Lolo, Lolo and the others, as though someome were filming us for "The Great Treaties" series. The policeman offered neither his hand nor his opinion. He stayed there a little while longer, beating that notebook full of my data against the palm of his hand, open and rosy colored, as if he couldn't decide whether to abandon the spot.

I walked slowly to the next block, conscious of his unyielding presence, and only after we had rounded the corner did I speak to Lolo.

"Not a word of this to your mother," I told him.

"No, Dad."

"Promise me. You're never, never to mention this to your mother. If she got wind of it . . ."

"No, Dad, I told you. I won't say a word."

"I mean it, nothing. She'd be really upset, understand? Do you understand?"

"Sure, Dad."

The elevator in our building in Paris was one of those ancient cages that goes up in plain and shameless view, through the somber and poorly lighted interior of a rococo stairwell that in its day pretended to be an imitation of something elegant and that never, even for the inaugural trip, succeeded. It was as decrepit and run down as everything else in our neighborhood, as was our apartment that cried out for repairs, a coat of paint to combat the smells of decades, that literally screamed for a little love. If it hadn't been for a French law that required that the elevator be maintained when there were six stories, the owners would've closed it down years ago or, at least, would've allowed it to fall into total and much deserved disuse.

I pressed the button that with a groan set the whole mechanism in motion, the pulleys, the hairy, black cables that could be seen dimly in the lazy darkness of the hall. From above you could hear the asthmatic, metallic protest that indicated the elevator was on its way.

"Bet I can get there first," Lolo sang out, bubbling over all of a sudden, as if nothing special had happened that afternoon.

It wasn't hard for him to win the bet against that prehistoric cage, but it was always fun to accept his challenge, a head-on race that gave the passenger in the elevator the chance to exercise his comedic talents, peppering the stair-climber with advice, jokes, clowning, shouts to make him lose his breath, and therefore the race.

"No," I told him that day. "Let's go up together."

"But, Dad . . ."

"No! Together!" I blocked any possible protest by raising my voice. "How many times do I have to tell you something?"

I pushed the iron grillwork doors with too much force and they bounced back. Lolo went in without saying a word.

I don't know how Cecilia realized the door of the apartment was opening, since the night before we had oiled those intolerable hinges, but she must have been listening for a long time, because we'd hardly entered soundlessly when we heard her voice from the living room where we slept with Nicola:

"Alejandro?"

"Yes, Mommy," said Lolo. "It's us."

I went to the telephone and picked up the receiver. In that apartment you could even hear the flies take a shit. Every movement by every member of the family, every sigh, was public property. I listened to Cecilia's footsteps behind my back—she was dragging her feet, as if she were in pain—and, along with hers, the lighter steps of the girls, Victoria and Nicola, coming to see their brother, their daddy. I started to dial the number. I didn't need to turn my head to know that Cecilia had stopped in the doorway to the other bedroom.

"David," she said from there. "I have to talk to you."

I didn't turn around.

"Wait until I . . ." At that moment I heard the operator at *Le Monde* answer. I gave her the number on the extension, covered the receiver, and looked at Cecilia. She was just as I had imagined, blocking the stingy light, leaning against the doorway, with Nicola snuggling against her skirt, her head just at the level of her mother's sex. "Wait till I finish this call, then we'll talk . . ."

"I'm leaving, David," said Cecilia. "This time I'm serious. This time it's no joke."

"That extension doesn't answer, sir," said the operator.

"Could he have gone home?"

"I don't know, sir. Would you like to leave a message?"

"I have the tickets, David," said Cecilia, pointing toward our room. "I picked them up this afternoon."

"Just a minute, miss." I covered the receiver again. "Please, Ceci, hold on just a second, would you? Everything will work out. Let me finish this call. OK?" And then into the telephone in French: "Yes, miss. Thank you. Tell him to call David Wiseman. Yes, that's right, with a *W*. About the . . . no, better not tell him anything. Just that I called, Mr. Wiseman called."

"We're leaving tomorrow, David. This time we're really going."

"Try again later, sir," said the operator. "He's usually here at this time."

"Thank you, miss, thanks a lot. You will give him the message?" I hung up.

"We can't go on like this, David. Alejandro!" Lolo had gone to the kitchen; we heard the refrigerator door close. "Alejandro, come in here. I want you to hear what I'm going to say."

I took a deep breath.

"Why do you want to mix the kid up in this, Cecilia? Let's talk things over calmly, like adults."

"You're not an adult and I don't want to talk anything over calmly." There was no aggressiveness in her voice, just fatigue, as though she were speaking to me from the top of a hill or from a tower. "Daddy sent me the tickets and I picked them up this afternoon and we're leaving tomorrow. That's all."

It wasn't true. We were going to have another free-for-all, with endless mutual recriminations, with the kids running around like animals in the zoo, until I would finally find out what the problem was this time, what sin I'd committed, and would promise her I'd never do it again, that everything would be all right, she would see. She would half believe me, there'd be a week of relative peace, and then once again the threats to leave. It wasn't true, but like an idiot this time I really wished it was, that this time she'd just leave, disappear from my existence, that every minute we'd spent together would be suddenly erased, that only I and the three kids would remain and she would be just a picture on the mantel. The last drop of affection had dried up years ago and we kept on pretending that by some miracle, by some higher intervention, by some lottery number, we would find the way, not to love, but to a certain tolerance that wouldn't make our home a battlefield. That's the way it had always been. For ten years, day after day, telling ourselves, as Cecilia had just said, that we couldn't go on that way, but observing it in passing, between spoonfuls of soup and dirty sheets, before buying medicines, or when the phone in another house was busy, threatening an imminent break as a way of getting the other person to leave us alone—she was leaving, I was leaving—playing at running against the stone wall of the other spouse, playing at reconciliation, and, when we were on the point of falling apart, something persistently returned our faith or distracted our attention, emergencies, big, small, and middle-sized, Lolo's birth, then Victoria's, until the sheer weight of the years and the kids was the best argument; it was too complicated to separate; there were more urgent things to do; the excitement of Allende's thousand days, Victoria's accident that we faced together, Cecilia's hepatitis, the sudden death of her mother, always tomorrow, the day after tomorrow, as though in one room of the house was all the goodwill, all the affection, all the pleasant company, and in the other room we were building up all our rage, and you could go in and out of each room with impunity as if the other one didn't exist, next week, next month, next year, like two armies that never show their nuclear arms and end up forgetting the probability of extinction. We were far from each other at the moment of the coup, but, paradoxically, the military's assault brought us together again. It was stupid, but we confused the pain we shared for our country as it was being destroyed with an act of love. The sense of danger, of death, of suffering, the sense that everything was irreconcilable, except for the two of us and our children, perhaps certain wisdom, anticipating that it was going to be impossible to get through the sterile years ahead without a stable companion, a small circle of peace in the middle of the collapse. We took refuge in each other, like an embassy, and Nicola was born.

"I'm not going, Mommy," said Lolo.

"Me neither," said Victoria.

Nicola, poor thing, didn't say anything. She didn't know what the hell was going on. She shook her head a little as though asking those voices not to shout so much.

"Children have no opinion in these matters," said Cecilia. "We're all leaving. Tomorrow. And if you want to know why, ask him."

Now we were going to argue about whether the kids would go or stay. Even though the trip, this time like all the other times, would never take place. Just for the hell of it. Like a soccer game that's never official, where all the plays are voided.

"Did anybody call?" I asked, to see if I could change the direction of things. I saw her hesitate.

"Natalia," she finally said.

That was all I needed. Natalia was the woman, the dotty old

maid, a friend of Tomás's, who was lending us the apartment. Every once in a while she descended on us, her adoptive family, the Chileans.

I waited.

"She wanted to come and see us tonight," Cecilia went on. "To see how we were. If we needed anything."

"What did you tell her?"

"Not today, that Nicola had diarrhea, that she could come tomorrow."

"Tomorrow? Why tomorrow? Didn't you tell her we couldn't?"

"You'll need the company, David. Natalia can keep you company. Or is she too old for you?"

My God, it was one of those days.

"Call her," I said. "Explain that we can't."

"You call her," she said. "It's your house. What do I have to do with it?"

I let my fingers tap the wall, calming down.

"OK. I'm going to call her," I said. "Anyone else?"

"What?"

"Anyone else? Did anyone else call?"

Again something like a doubt clouded her face before she answered.

"Did the television station call?" I asked her.

"Yes."

"What did they say?"

"I didn't really understand. I asked him to speak more slowly, but the fellow refused. It seems like they may need you this weekend. He's going to call back."

"You see. You see," I told her. "I'll get a permanent job. I told you they would call me. These guys really like the camera work we do."

"What they like," Cecilia declared, "is that you cost half what a Frenchman does."

"But once they give you a contract they raise your salary a little. What time did he say he'd call?"

"I don't know. Tonight, I think. I didn't understand him."

"How do you expect to understand if you never go out? How are you going to learn French that way?"

The children were paralyzed, quiet, not even a blink, as if they were attending a play which they had seen in rehearsal, and now this was the real performance, opening night.

"Never? I never go out? I go out to clean other people's toilets. That's what I go out for."

"Never is just a manner of speaking."

"Just look at my hands. Would you look at my hands? I never go out."

"I mean go out with me, with the kids."

"I don't need to learn French. I'm not a foreigner like you," said Cecilia. "I'm leaving tomorrow. I'm never going to speak another word in this damn language for the rest of my life."

Again.

"OK. Fine," I told her. "All I was trying to make you see is that if you stay closed up here, you're not going to learn the language. That's all. I just said it for your own good. Just some simple advice. In this house you can't even say something as innocent as that . . ."

She interrupted me brutally.

"Today I did go out, David. Today I went out and stopped by Air France and I have four tickets in my purse. And I spoke to the girl who waited on me in Spanish. And I confirmed my reservations and everything. And we're leaving, David. You won't believe me; you always refused to believe me. But we're going."

"I'm staying with Dad," said Lolo.

My mouth felt dry and bitter. Something undigestible lay heavy on my stomach. It was coming out my pores, my skin, my nails: the taste of cheap food, the kind served by fat, bored matrons in university restaurants in outlying neighborhoods of Paris, where anybody can have lunch, with his hunger and his buck and a half, where you don't need a student ID to go in.

The phone rang.

"Meanwhile," I told Cecilia, looking joyfully at the receiver, as if it were a fairy godmother who was going to suspend this imbecilic exchange, "you'd do well to learn the language. That's all. Since we're probably going to be staying here for a few more years, until your dad's colleagues gave the country back to us, maybe it would be worthwhile to make a little effort."

"Are you going to answer that phone?" asked Cecilia. "Or shall I?"

I reached for the receiver, but went on talking: "Because since you're always leaving, you forget to study French."

It was Charles, the reporter from *Le Monde*. We spoke Spanish. I explained that I was worried about the matter of the labor union leader who had disappeared, that if the news didn't get out, it would be hard to stir up a campaign.

"They cut the article," said Charles. "You know how these things are. They decide upstairs."

"So what do you think?"

"If it doesn't come out tomorrow, it won't come out," said Charles. "It'll be stale news . . . But that's not why I called you, David. I have something here that's going to interest you. It's a cable from Chile."

"Don't tell me Pinochet fell," I said with irony.

"It's your friend Felipe Cuadra. The one we ran the campaign for last month."

"What's happened to him?"

"Apparently they've released him. They released ten prisoners from the Tres Alamos Camp. That's what the cable calls it. His name is on the list."

When I hung up, there was no one in the hall. Cecilia and the two girls had returned to the other room, Lolo was looting the refrigerator again.

"Lolo!" I shouted. "Lolo! They released your Uncle Felipe. Lolo! Cecilia! They released Felipe!"

No one answered.

"Lolo!"

From the kitchen came Lolo's voice, disguising his enthusiasm and his interest: "Great, Dad!"

I dialed the number of Esteban, the friend who was in charge of the Party in Paris. Busy.

"Cecilia, didn't you hear me? They released . . ."

Our living room–bedroom was a disaster area.

Cecilia was on her knees, like a scrubwoman, bent over one of four or five suitcases scattered around the floor. Beside her, on the bed, she had piled all her clothes and the kids'. It looked like a burglar had ransacked the place. Also on the bed Hurricane Nicola was entertaining herself pushing socks, shirts, skirts, blouses, bras, while Victoria made vain attempts to return each piece to its place.

Cecilia was folding the clothes calmly, efficiently, and meticulously, paying no attention whatsoever to the war going on around her.

"Love," I said to her, kneeling and taking her by the arms, trying to coax her up, "they've released Felipe, love."

"How nice," she said, imperturbable. "Do you want me to take him a letter?"

I managed to get her to her feet; I took her in my arms like a new bride; I waltzed around the room kicking shoes, trampling slips, turning over a sewing basket.

"They released him," I told her. "They released him. He's free. They let him out. He's alive. Alive and free, darling. They freed him."

Her body remained stiff in my arms, her eyes fixed on Nicola.

"Nicola," she said. "Get down from there. Right now." Nicola threw a glove triumphantly. "Victoria, take your sister down from there. And see if she needs to be changed."

"I already changed her once today, Mommy."

"I can't do everything, sweetie. Somebody has to cooperate. David, put me down."

I tried to recapture my euphoria, like a drunk who thinks that one more drink will sober him up before they close the bar.

"To the park," I shouted. "Off to the park, kids. Lolo! Get the ball. We're going to the park to play. Let's go. Victoria, put Nicola's jacket on her. Come on, Ceci! Don't be mean!"

All I wanted to do was to celebrate the fresh air, the free air, my air and Felipe's and Lolo's, to make a party in homage to Felipe and all the others we had saved, to kick a ball among the leaves of that splendid autumn day in Paris, shouting in outrageous Spanish without caring about the peace of those Frenchmen who would be going out at that hour to walk their dogs. Shit! We were alive! To laugh our heads off at Lolo's clowning, to teach Nicola dirty words and then to try to get her to repeat them in front of Mommy, to run from her and then to let yourself be caught, to disguise Victoria as a monster, covering her with dry leaves so she could chase us, me jumping around like a sheep, and giving Tarzan yells when I was caught, and then back to the ball again, here comes the bogeyman, ready or not! I'm counting to ten, and then I go out, running after the three of them, off to the statues, visiting the ducks in their pond and explaining to Nicola why you don't throw stones or acorns at them, here comes the bogeyman, getting closer, ready or not, absorbing ice cream until you're ready to pop, in honor of Felipe, until the twilight drove us home, sweaty and exhausted, ready to devour the dinner Cecilia had been cooking.

That's how it should always be, that's how it would have been, perhaps, without the coup or without Allende, that's how we had planned it to be at some remote time in the past. We had dreamed about it when Cecilia was in my honeymoon arms the same as now. I was certain—and in the midst of the waves of that certainty I was swept by a flood of sexual desire toward that organism whose moist and mysterious inner membrane I wanted to explore once more, a desire similar to what I had felt that night in Lima when we conceived Nicola and she didn't return to Chile—the enlightened certainty that we could still rescue our marriage, that life had to be lived like an interlude in the forest, like the play of children, that the bogeyman would never get you, as long as you hid well enough, that anything was better than being alone, without her, without Lolo, without the girls. It was enough to get off the roller coaster on which no one knew how we had gotten, to take time to calm the beating of our hearts, to slow down a little, recognizing mistakes, and, with just a little dose of goodwill, to wake up the next morning without a headache.

"To the park," said Victoria.

"Pak, pak," said Nicola.

Cecilia made a convulsive movement.

"No one's going to the park," she said. "Although I'd appreciate it if you'd take Nicola . . . David, would you please put me down?"

The telephone rang.

We heard Lolo answer.

"It's for you, Mommy. Madame Wiseman. From Air France." He pronounced his *R*s like Racine.

"Would you let me go, David? You're hurting me."

For the second time that day someone was asking me that. For the second time, I did it.

Cecilia went to the phone. Sitting among the ruins and the clothing catastrophe, with Nicola trying to put one of her bonnets on me, I managed to hear the intermittent conversation. The man spoke Spanish. Very good. Yes, sir, one adult, myself, two children and a baby. Yes, the baby was still not two. She'd be two on October 15. Yes, it really was lucky, right? A few days' difference and a free trip . . . An hour before? Of course. Thank you very much, sir.

Why didn't I intervene? Why didn't I take the telephone in my two ogre's hands and tell that guy to stick those tickets up his ass, that my wife wasn't going anywhere, to cancel the reservations? Why didn't I take Cecilia in my arms again and carry her to the park, why didn't I take them all out of that place, stumbling down the stairs to avoid the elevator?

I don't like to think about that. But if that same afternoon I hadn't used up my entire capacity for violence, all my persuasive talents, all my energy for the next twenty years, all my hopes for the next century, maybe I would have found some way to explain to Cecilia, maybe I would've ripped out the telephone cord, who knows what I would've done? But the kid was there by the school fence, I was facing a uniformed man, Felipe was walking out into the polluted air to Santiago and not the false air of St. Germain de Près, Felipe was walking out into that vaster concentration camp, the whole country, where in a few more hours my children would disembark. For one day, for one afternoon, it was too much for me and I was silent.

"Where are you going?" asked Cecilia, with something resembling alarm. Was it a fleeting spark of disquiet or was I mistaken?

"Out," I told her.

"Go ahead," she said. "Go see Patricia."

"That'll be hard. She stayed in Lima, just in case you've forgotten."

"Go to the others then," said Cecilia. "Go and see the others. Let them wash your underpants."

"I'm going to the park. Does it matter so much to you if I go to the park?"

I opened the door and rang for the elevator. Absurdly I calculated that its arrival would be as slow as always, that something might change in those moments of waiting.

"I told you, David. This time it's true. I told you. You refused to believe me. But you can see, they called from Air France. You see it's true."

"Cecilia," I said to her.

She looked at me. Behind her skirts I could see the three children, like a band of angels. It was hard for me to believe that between the two of us we had produced them. It was as if nothing remained of the woman I'd married. Not even one night of that woman.

"Cecilia," I said to her. "Please."

"Please what? David," she said.

"Let's try," I said. "Cecilia, they released Felipe, Cecilia. You see. They freed him."

"I was taught," she said, "not to close the door in anybody's face. So will you please hurry up and get out of here once and for all?"

I stepped into the elevator like someone going into an oven. We stood like that for a good while, just observing each other, without saying good-bye, as though we were recording the scene for some album that we would burn, both of us somehow wanting to prolong the moment.

"If you want to go, go," I said to her. "But I'd like for you to stay."

She wet her lips and picked up Nicola, so I could see her well, as though that were the proof of something or of someone. She had one of Lolo's soccer shoes in her hand.

"There's nothing in the world you can do," she said, "that will change my mind."

I imagined her going down the plane ramp in Santiago, offering a look of gratitude to the soft ferocity of the mountains; I imagined her with the children by the hand, greeting her family and friends who had come to meet her, talking with Felipe, before I could do so, silently receiving my mother, weeping in the arms of her father, the Colonel. Every time I had thought of that sequence she was beside me, both of us were returning, not so much to that country, as to that other country, which is the past, which is the capacity to deceive yourself and to hope.

"Cecilia."

"My God, David, don't make all this any harder. Think of us, for once, will you?"

There wasn't a single tear left in my throat for myself, for her, for the children, for the whole damned universe. There was nothing in the world I could do to make her change her mind. I thought about the trip to the airport tomorrow, about her back as it left, about the kids turning around for the last time, going through immigration in Charles de Gaulle Airport, leaving France behind. I would stay there for hours, screwed into that place in front of that hallway that has only one direction, exit, and never entrance, waiting for a miracle, as always, a woman who would turn around and smile at me, some kids who would come running, to wake up one day and find that the country is my own, that I'm not myself but someone else, standing there for hours until hunger or fatigue or ridicule make me react, taking the reverse route to this apartment and its telephone and its Miss Natalia, returning along those fraudulent avenues, past those cardboard buildings and those museums I would never visit.

"My father," Cecilia said suddenly, as if to herself, and as if I were not present, "will make sure you never go back to Chile. Never."

I pressed the ground-floor button with the index finger of my right hand. The elevator went into motion with a sick shudder. And then, deliberately, fully conscious, in front of my wife and the three children I had had with her, as they disappeared from my view, I stuck the fingers of my hand, the left hand, deep into the metal grillwork door of that son-of-a-bitch elevator.

"You're so quiet," says Felipe. "Is anything wrong?"

"No. Nothing," says David. "Nothing's wrong."

"Don't worry so much," says Felipe. "I'm sure Paula is bringing you a letter."

For a while David watches the cars passing by and doesn't say anything. Then: "It's better that Lolo left," he says. "Before it was too late."

"Too late?"

"I lost Lolo, but at least he's in his own country. When I go back, we'll both live in the same city, we can see each other every day. When you're Simón's age, you never go back."

"Simón doesn't decide for himself. When we go back, he'll come along with us."

"Tell me that in another ten years, when he has children, when there are a wife and friends and a profession to deal with . . ."

"Ten years," says Felipe. "Damn but you're a pessimist. Listen, don't come over here and subvert my family. I've already got my hands full with Juana saying she wants to stay here, that she's gotten used to it. She's stubborn."

"She's gotten independent on you," says David. "Once a woman gets bitten by that bug . . ."

"Felipe was the one who refused to adapt," Paula will say.

"As if it were my fault," says Felipe, "for everything women have suffered for the last million years. As if I were responsible for the biological differences."

"So, whose fault is it?" Juana would ask. "If we don't start at home, where do we start?"

"But why be so aggressive?" says David. "Felipe was right. We've got our hands full just to survive, man, he told me. Stirring up this business of total liberation for women is playing into Pinochet's hands. Everybody lost something, he told me. The workers lose the unions, the people lose their democracy, the parties lose their legal status, the students lose their freedom of speech, we all lose something, and yet women want to have more than they started out with. It's impossible, he told me."

"Wild ideas," says Felipe, "foreign to us, imported from outside. Gringo ideas, ideas from industrialized countries. What do they have to do with the aspirations of the great mass of the people, with our country, with our particular idiosyncrasies? Or with the Mexicans for that matter? What would a working-class woman say, or a peasant or a laborer, when she doesn't even know if she'll have milk for her children tomorrow? Or a domestic worker? Or some *compañera* in El Salvador? She wouldn't understand any of this. All she'd want would be for her husband to be out of danger, for him to have a job, and for her children not to be carried off. Go on, ask Paula what she thinks."

"A woman who lost her husband?" Juana would say. "I'm certainly not going to add to her pain by asking stupid questions."

"If they had killed me," says Felipe, "Juana wouldn't have all these problems. That's what I say. Let her ask Paula what it's like to be without a man."

"But in the end," says David, "you have to adapt a little, Felipe. You have to give a little. If I didn't pay any attention to Gringa, my life would be like something out of Dante's *Inferno*."

"Who made you marry an Austrian, huh? But I didn't. I chose a Chilean woman. I didn't go off to Edinburgh to find her either. It's *gringas* like yours who put crazy ideas into the heads of women like my wife."

"Juana didn't learn those things abroad," Paula will say. "That's where you're dead wrong."

"Why all this urgency?" says Felipe. "What's the big hurry? Old habits aren't perfect, they may be useless. OK. But at least they keep us going along, they save energy."

"That's where you're wrong," Paula will repeat. "When Felipe got out of Tres Alamos, he didn't realize that Juana had changed. It had been a wrenching experience for her. But at the same time she'd discovered that she could be without him, that a woman can survive without a man, that she could do certain things well, things that he'd always done before. How long was it? Almost . . ."

"Almost three years," says David.

"Felipe, Felipe, all she thought about was her Felipe," Paula will say. "My man. She didn't leave a stone unturned to get him released. She spoke with generals, majors, bishops, captains, cabinet ministers. Her theory was that, in the end, they'd release him, even if it was just to get her off their backs. So, when he did get out, imagine how happy she was, so happy that, well, you could've predicted that it was going to be a honeymoon. At first," Paula will say, "maybe he didn't know how to read the signals. Or maybe back then she wasn't sending out any signals for him to read. She treated him in a special way. Those first weeks she left him alone. It might've happened the way it did with so many other wives who went back to subordinating themselves to their husbands' lives, their interests and their priorities, gradually, without even realizing it . . ."

"I wish you could've seen her, when I got out, David," says Felipe. "She was a jewel."

"All we want," Paula will say, "is for them to come back. It doesn't even occur to us that there could be a fight, a difference of opinion, that a husband could beat his wife or be unfaithful or go out drinking. In time, you forget the real human being and it's as if we were waiting for a saint and not for a flesh-and-blood man. So it's only natural for us to give in to his every whim. Then the wives wake up one fine day and realize they've lost that . . . what would you call it? that autonomy they had won during their husbands' absences."

"That must be tough," says David.

"It's the sort of anguish," Paula will say, "that they didn't give me the chance to go through."

"Later, things got really tense," says Felipe.

"From then on," Paula will say, "Juana refused to cut back her work schedule, and for Felipe that was almost an insult; he felt like he was superfluous in the house, that he was no longer the undisputed boss. Juana explained to him that it wasn't necessary to look for a job right away, that he should wait awhile. But he said he was the breadwinner in that family. The whole thing blew up when he managed to get work in that economic consulting firm. She asked him to accept just part-time, because somebody had to be at home. Said she'd been doing it for a dozen years, so now it was his turn. This isn't the time for a war between the sexes, Felipe said. We're involved in another kind of war."

"Yeah," said David. "That's what he told me. That Juanita didn't understand that in the struggle against the Junta, the kind of work he could do was more important, more significant, shall we say. I'm like a cannon, and you're a machine gun, he told Juanita. Let's establish our priorities. First we have to liquidate Fascism. When that victory's behind us, we'll take a look at this matter of male and female roles. And besides, they were paying him more than they were paying her . . ."

"In those days," Paula will say, "the DINA solved the whole thing by arresting Felipe again. This time they were going to expel him without any further proceedings. With or without a signature. Imagine his surprise, when she gets to the airport and tells him she doesn't want to leave. That she'd be screwed out there. I don't know what Felipe told her. Whatever it was, the fact is he convinced her. Within a week Juana and the kids followed him to Mexico."

"She was wise," says David.

"No doubt," Paula will say. "Women talk a lot about liberation, about living on their own. But in the final analysis nothing's more important than our man. When you have to choose, David, and there's almost always some moment when we have to choose, we choose to be loyal to our man."

"All of which doesn't mean," David observes, "that once they were in Mexico, Juana didn't make life impossible for Felipe."

"Impossible, man," says Felipe. "A fight to the finish, everything I say, do, or breathe. Over the kid's education, my work schedule, salaries, the chauvinistic, male-dominated structure of political parties, over who'll wash the dishes on the maid's day off."

"If we'd had a maid," says David, "Cecilia wouldn't have gone back to Chile."

"Impossible, man," Felipe repeats.

"I wouldn't say impossible," Paula will correct him. "Juana simply decided she'd given in on the most important matter and that from now on she wasn't going on that way. She announced that she had a new personality and that she wasn't afraid of separation. That's what she wrote me."

"And what do you think?" asks David.

"Men are real egotists," Paula will say, "but I don't think we're going to change them very much. Not in one generation anyway, not in my opinion. While everything else is falling apart, our hands are tied."

"She was in Chile," says Felipe, "and she didn't want to leave. Now she's happy in Mexico, studying the health of working-class women, planning, studying computing, so naturally she doesn't want to go back. But she'll go back."

"You think so, huh? You really think she'll go back?" asks David.

"What would you do?" Juana will ask.

"I would do anything, Juana, to keep from being alone," Paula will say.

"Like Tomás," says David. "You know who would get along well with Juana? Tomás."

"Please, David," says Felipe, "don't put Juana in the same category as Tomás."

"How can you say that? What do you know about Tomás? Did you know that after the coup he spent more than three years doing militant work? Did you know that?"

"So what happened to him then?"

"You wouldn't believe how efficient he was," says David. "He always said you had to move like clockwork. Results, he said. The only important thing is results. He got whatever they asked him for. Passports, money, housing, contacts, printing presses. Places for *compañeros* to live in Paris, for example."

"But Enrique wrote me that he was living in London."

"That was later. Back then he didn't live anywhere. But I can tell you, when Cecilia left and I was . . . when I had my accident, he was the one who came running, man, and took care of the hospital, got the best doctors, looked after Lolo. So don't bad-mouth Tomás to me."

"My judgments are political," says Felipe, "not personal. Person X works well for a few years, and one fine day he doesn't want any more to do with Chile, no more solidarity, no more anything. One fine day, he up and throws it all away, without even leaving so much as an address where we can reach him, with no explanation, nothing. That's why we take so long to throw these bastards out. What if everybody's into this self-exploration bit, just into his own pleasure? This is a war. It's not on one day and off the next, and later, well, maybe. It's a lifetime commitment, David."

"People," says David, "can't always know what they want. While he was working, nobody could've accomplished what Tomás did. From the moment he left Chile, he committed himself body and soul."

"So why did he leave? Why didn't he stay? Who was looking for him? They were after Enrique, sure, but not Tomás."

"A lot of years have gone by, Felipe. Don't you think it's time to forget why people left? Or are we going to talk about that? Do you want to talk about that?"

"Why shouldn't I want to talk about that?"

"OK. So let's talk about it. But I want you to know it was lucky for a lot of people that Tomás did leave. Because of his help Cecilia got special care when Nicola was born. And it was the same with lots of others, too."

"How did he do it?"

"We never found out for a long time," says David. "Contacts he made. People that were impressed with him or with the cause, with Chile. But little by little, we started to realize, indirectly and very discreetly, that they were always women. Women older than Tomás. He told me later, one of the times I went to see him in London. I'm going to use you, he would tell the old dolls; I'm going to squeeze you. And they thought that anybody who talked like that, so openly, had to be legit. He was, how can I explain it? So defenseless. There was something so clear and urgent and youthful in him."

"My, my," says Felipe. "I can see you're one of his conquests."

"I don't think he laid them all," says David. "Besides, he wasn't one to go around bragging about his exploits in bed. Back then, Felipe, it was sheer necessity, nothing more. We had no means at our disposal, no infrastructure, no contacts. You had to publish, to send people undercover to Chile, to house new arrivals, to get psychiatric treatment for recently released prisoners, to get residency permits, to falsify documents, to make contacts with government ministers. Most of those things were accomplished by solidarity groups, churches, political parties, by any number of people. Good people, you know. People who understood that our tragedy touched them. Unions, university professors, groups of lawyers. I could never list them all. But there were limits to what they could do. And what was needed was always much, much more. In Santiago they always wanted more; for the political leaders, it was never enough. That's where somebody like Tomás came in, somebody who really delivered."

"He must've had a whopping big guilt complex."

"That's possible. But the fact is he got nothing but praise. Well done, *compañero*. I wish everybody was that efficient."

"Nothing but a pimp. I can't believe it."

"It's not that clear-cut. Lots of people who wanted to help joined around solidarity. So they had their own problems, Felipe. So they wanted to solve their personal problems by helping out. What are you going to do? Reject them? People, Felipe, who are broken in some way, hurt, people who need love, some channel to express themselves. Most of those people, Felipe, at least in this society, are women. Gringa's a little like that, you know."

"I don't want to believe what you're telling me, David."

"You'd better believe me, Felipe. Tomás was successful with those people, the solitary types, lost, past their prime, people who'd lived through lots of disillusionment but who were still leftists. Good, generous people. Tomás built special relationships with those women. He offered them affection, attention; he gave purpose to their lives."

"And he took their money."

"Not just money. Not always. But they all ended up giving something. You're going to have to do something for Chile, he'd tell them; you're going to have to do something for the revolution. And they were happy. Tomás discovered that he had that talent, almost magical, and he played it to the hilt."

"That's really sick, awful," Felipe says. "I can't see how you can build anything worthwhile on that kind of foundation."

"Nothing you can say," says David, "could be any worse than his own judgment. That's why he couldn't go on like that forever."

"Fortunately. How long did it last?"

"Until Tomás fell in love. An English widow with three kids. A really fine actress. A woman with a little money. It was like a conversion. He said to hell with militancy. He swore he'd never take advantage of anybody again in his life, that it was all the same, whether it was exploiting the masses or exploiting individuals and that he was through with it."

"An irresponsible guy," says Felipe. "What happened to the rest of his lady friends? What about all his contacts? A real disaster."

"Really irresponsible," says David. "But you said yourself that what he was doing was sick, awful. He thought the same thing. So he decided not to do it any more. But what you don't forgive Tomás for is something else. He asked himself a question that makes political activism impossible. He asked himself, why not be happy? It's a hard question, isn't it? Why the hell not be happy?"

"Oh sure, I know. In the meantime, screw the peasants and the workers, the Indians and the laborers. While Tomás searches for his way to inner perfection."

"Tomás isn't so different from Christians, Felipe. I suppose you can't complain about how they're behaving. He said the only problem each one of us can solve is the problem of his own soul. That revolutions have failed because they hadn't taken into account that the ones who made them were the old men. That exploitation starts in everyday life, in the family, in sexual relationships, in emotional unhappiness, in the authority of the father over the child and the husband over the wife. That while that wasn't changed, revolutions would go on reproducing the same old structures of domination."

"So do you agree with him, David? Tell me the truth. Do you agree with him or not?"

"No," says David, slowly. "Unfortunately I don't agree with him. Unfortunately, because it would make my life one hell of a lot simpler. But his solution . . . I don't know . . . It seems cowardly to me. Monastic, if you will. It doesn't take real human beings into account, the power brokers, the ones really responsible for what's happening, the Foilbacks and the Marrases."

"Do you know why he could make all those experiments? Go through all that therapy? Because his new catch had money."

"Of course she had money. I already said that. It's all artificial, Tomás, I told him. You're getting involved in something that's not open to everybody."

"How did he answer that?"

"That you had to get rid of any preconceived ideas, to go back to the primitive state, to be like a newborn child. Everybody can do it, he said. You have to start sometime. That kind of thing."

"I wish a coal miner had that kind of choice," says Felipe. "I'm off. Ciao. Bound for India."

"But isn't it just possible," says David, "that it's all the same battle, yours and Tomás's? Has that ever occurred to you?"

Brusquely, Felipe brakes the car and parks.

"Hindu philosophy, pacifism, ecology, antinuclear demonstrations, life in communes, gay liberation, drugs . . . Hey, is that son of a bitch Tomás into drugs?"

"I suppose so."

". . . drugs, the motherfuckin' gonad liberation, and you want to tell me that all that has anything to do with my country's liberation? You mean to tell me that it has anything at all to do with my damned country, David?"

"Not much, Felipe."

"So, where's the limit, David? You start to entertain these ideas. You start to play around with this, that, and the other thing, and you end up doubting everything. Tell me, where does it all end? Where does our effectiveness go? What happens to the people who just want a house, bread, a roof over their heads, a little education? Where do we draw the line?"

"I don't know, Felipe."

"Decency," says Felipe. "That's the word. I'm going to tell you something that not even Juana knows. There were times in there when I was sure they were going to kill me. Mock firing squads, you know, that sort of thing. What they tell you about your whole life passing before your eyes at a time like that is true. Not that it's anything concrete, like a film running from birth to death. No. Your eye focuses on any old insignificant detail. For example, the fact that one of the soldiers' shoestrings is untied and you feel like tying it for him and you know you'll never be able to do it. And your mind remembers trivial incidents. I remembered my mom climbing a staircase and I was little and was upstairs. But it's true that your whole life's inside you. And you ask yourself, I swear it's true, if what's about to happen is the result of what's best in you, if what's about to happen is justified. In the end the only thing that matters, David, is the answer to that question."

For a while David doesn't say anything. Then, "What if the answer wasn't so easy? Or at least, was more complicated for some people than for others? Or rather, some people have to rediscover it again, because they're not satisfied with the old answer. They're afraid of repeating their mistakes. I'm not justifying Tomás. Don't misunderstand me. But it's a symptom of a greater crisis that you have to face, the need to withdraw from the picture in order to look at things with distance, perspective. To renew yourself."

"Some novelty Tomás offers us. His solutions have failed a thousand times over. He ought to join the Christian Democrats. Then he can go up to Pinochet and tell him not to be a bad boy, to behave himself, and the good General is going to experience a divine illumination. Shit, this discussion is making me sick. At least people like him aren't coming back. One less fool to worry about."

"He tried to go back to Chile, Felipe. But he couldn't."

"Couldn't? The Junta would've received him with open arms. An extremist who finds peace. Imagine how *El Mercurio* would've handled that one. The latest fad. The Chilean guru of Trafalgar Square."

"His old lady was dying, Felipe."

With a violent gesture, Felipe starts the motor.

"His mom? Enrique's mom? I'm really sorry. But, why didn't he go then?"

"Did I tell you I'd gone to see him once, alone? Two years after all this, you know. A little while before I decided to leave the Party . . . It was a delicate situation. One *compañero* had gone back to Chile and they grabbed him at the border. He had to blame somebody for being his contact in Chile. He said it was Tomás. He had to do it. Since Tomás had been very active abroad during those first years and had then disappeared from public view, well, the idea that he had come back undercover wasn't a bad one, right? We had already told that story to some of his women who were asking about him."

"It's a good idea," Felipe admits.

"But a fuckin' bad one for him, right? With his old lady dying, to have to explain to Tomás that he couldn't go back to Chile and that he couldn't even publish a clarification or anything like that."

"So what did he say?"

"Tomás came through. After all, with his new philosophy he could've told us to go to hell. He looked me in the eye and said it was all right. The fact that I warned him he might put his brother, might put Enrique, in danger may have had something to do with it."

"Was it true that Enrique was in danger?"

"How do I know? The important thing was to get Tomás to take the blame, to use the most convincing arguments at hand . . . what do you have to say about that? I'm going back, you're going back, and he's still going to be outside. The intelligence guys will wait for him at the border till Judgment Day."

"So a lot of people owe him their lives."

"You do too. One of his ladies was Giscard's female Minister of Health in France. Her intervention was instrumental in your release . . ."

"Thank him for me, when you see him," says Felipe. "But he's still a renegade."

"It's really easy for you, isn't it, Felipe, to define who is and who isn't a renegade?'

"Let's go home, once and for all," says Felipe, starting the motor. But he shows no sign of moving. A car passes, blowing its horn loudly. "You're so quiet," says Felipe all of a sudden. "Is something the matter?"

"Nothing," says David. "Nothing's the matter."

"Are you thinking about how to define a renegade?" asks Felipe. "I can see in your face that's what's bothering you."

"I'm thinking about how people end up being trapped," says David. "About Parks. I was thinking about that old bastard, Carl Parks."

FIRST FRAME: The Laboratory is quiet that morning. Dr. Garay in a white jacket. Two gigantic TV screens. On one, a faceless man, naked, stretched out on a table. On the other, the multicolor interior of a human chest.

SECOND FRAME: The chest: a bright little light is turned on in the heart.

THIRD FRAME: Dr. Garay's face.
Dr. Garay: "Aha! Now we've got you, damn you!"

"Don't you think that's a little strong," Paula would say. "Do we have to imitate American horror films?"

"It's what people have in their heads," answers David.

FOURTH FRAME: The door opens. Carl Parks enters in a wheelchair pushed by the interpreter.

FIFTH FRAME: The screens go wild. They show the inside of the brain, the lungs, the stomach, the genital organs.

SIXTH FRAME: Eyes and mouth of Dr. Garay.
Dr. Garay: "Mr. Parks. We're following the tracks of the X-Factor. The volunteer on the screen has swallowed a red dye. Now he must repent of past mistakes and violent acts. This meditation forces the X-Factor to seek refuge. See. It camouflages itself,

hides, resists ordering and education. But however fluctuating it may be, we've got it cornered. There's no escape. See. You see."

"I woke up," says David, "one night. It was late. The voices of two clowns in my dreams. They were torturing somebody. They were making him say terrible things, treacherous things, really twisted. Things against Allende, against the people. With clown laughs, jokes, real vaudeville. They were telling jokes while they were beating him, beating me. I think I was the one they were beating after a while."

"Did you tell them what they wanted to hear?"

"I woke up," says David.

After a while, Felipe says: "So, what happens next?"

"We see Parks as if he were on somebody's screen—his wheelchair and his useless hands. Before Parks can ask Garay for help, Garay asks him for a favor: the doctor thinks that Parks might be able to draw the contours, the colors of the X-Factor—because it has, up till now, been like a chameleon, inapprehensible. He explains that the only way to get it to reveal its true form is to provoke extreme, incurable situations in the patient. The only problem is that once a specimen has been isolated, the X-Factor turns to ashes, dissolves, unable to live apart from its original body, which, in turn, shows an unfortunate tendency toward devitalization."

FOURTEENTH FRAME: The screen showing the naked body. Dr. Garay's words in a bubble: "The X-Factor is something like life's shadow, its twin, its auxiliary, its consequence perhaps. But they should never be confused. They're not the same, as the subversives insist. Plants, protozoa, and chimpanzees have no X-Factor. It already potentially exists in the fetus."

FIFTEENTH FRAME: Consternation in Carl Parks's face.

Carl Parks: "In the fetus?"

Dr. Garay turns toward Parks, his hands out of view.

Dr. Garay: "Signs of rebellion, indications of rage, even nostalgia."

SIXTEENTH FRAME: Dr. Garay's hands, a hypodermic needle in them.
Dr. Garay: "So science marches on . . . But maybe it's time to help you, Mr. Parks. We'll have you fixed up in no time."

"The mad scientist," says Felipe. "That's all we needed."

"What we need," says David, "is a more comfortable car. If we're going to be stuck here all night . . ."

"What's wrong with my car?" asks Felipe, in a good mood, taking off and moving out into the traffic. "I bet it's better than yours."

"Much better than mine," says David. "We don't even have one. In Holland all you need is a couple of bikes and you're set."

"So what do you do when it rains?"

"You get wet."

"Can't you afford a car?"

"Can you afford it?"

"I can," says Felipe. "We're going to buy a new one. Without two cars in Mexico City . . ."

"I'd rather own nothing, Felipe. When you have to leave, you sell the three or four things you have, you return what's borrowed or give things to a friend, and ciao, you've gone. In March we have to move again. The whole world in a suitcase."

"You get tired of living like that, David."

"You get tired. No work. No medical insurance. No furniture. I must be getting old, because before it didn't bother me. Lately I feel like staying in one place. The answer would be for them to let me go back."

"What do you expect to live on in Chile?"

"Don't have the slightest idea," says David.

"It'd be good to have one, before you go back," says Felipe. "If they let you."

"Let's see. Nothing in journalism. Not the university. Not television either. And they haven't made a film in years. A tourist guide maybe. Or German classes. Everybody's giving German classes."

"David wasn't going to tell you, Felipe," Paula would say. "They were paying some old debts with Gringa's salary. This comic strip was a great opportunity. They were broke. That's why he didn't phone Chile."

"And what about you, Paula?" says Felipe. "How are you?"

"Me?" Paula would say. "Oh, I can't complain."

"You're going to have to get into advertising, David," says Felipe. "You don't have any choice."

"No way," says David. "Selling things. Writing slogans. Making poems about toothpaste, dog food campaigns. Commercializing everything. That's not for me."

"So what do you expect?" Paula will ask. "Over here everybody ends up buried in the marketplace, buying and selling. Consumerism. You adjust or you leave."

"I'll have just gotten back. How am I going to leave?"

"So get to work on a marvelous formula for dehydrated milk. And don't think you can play tricks. If you don't give the best you have, they'll throw you out. It's not a question of saving your talent for your art."

"And don't they screw you?" asks Felipe. "When they came to arrest Gonzalo. Didn't it start then?"

"I give them pretty colors, designs, psychedelic diagrams," Paula will say. "And that sells. The rest is my business. They've behaved well with me, if you can believe that."

"And what about this strip? How will they take that?"

"As long as it doesn't make any direct references to the country, nothing will happen."

"You don't have to sign it," says David.

"I sign my work," Paula will say.

"I'd been thinking, Felipe," says David. "that maybe I could take over a book-importing company, you know. I don't think they're buying many books in Chile, but there'll be a few pesos in it. You must know people who'd be interested in that sort of thing, here in Mexico, right?"

"There's a possibility," says Felipe, "but we're using that for a friend in the Party who's about to go back."

"Oh," says David. "Well, he probably needs it too."

"That's the way the system operates," says Felipe.

"I can't get used to it," says David. "I just can't."

"You'll adjust," Paula will say. "That's the worst of it. You end up getting used to everything."

"Not everything," says Felipe.

"Not everything," Paula will say. "Agreed."

"That's what you go back for," says Felipe. "To get screwed . . . It's not a paid vacation . . . going back."

"I thought I could keep on collaborating from Santiago with a strip every few months. Is that possible?"

"It depends on what Ceballos thinks of this one."

"What do you think?"

"If I were you, I wouldn't put all my eggs in that basket. You have to separate your art from the way you make your living. You can't make a living with your art. That's that."

"You don't like the strip."

"I'd have to hear the whole thing before I gave my opinion. But up to this point, I'm not sure it's what our magazine is looking for. This kind of satire is too topical. You read them one day and forget them the next. We wanted something more permanent."

"You don't like it."

"Let me explain it to you; it's not that I don't like it. I feel that the whole thing . . . how can I put it? The whole thing is forced. As if you just couldn't get the necessary distance. Like being locked into an obsession, with a country that no one except you would recognize. A metaphor of a country. A madness. I don't know if our Mexican readers are going to understand it. Or even other exiles. Maybe even the Chileans for that matter."

"So what should I add to satisfy you?"

"That's your business. But what about the people, David? And the resistance? The struggle? Why not put those things in the strip?"

"I'd rather not talk about those things," says David.

"So," Paula would ask, "what are you going back for?"

Felipe waits for David to add something. Several minutes of silence pass in which only the slow movement of the traffic can be heard. Then he says:

"Tell me the next episode. Maybe I'll end up liking it better."

Sarah Barks didn't realize how late it was getting to be until she was alone with the little girl in the park. As always, she had allowed herself to become absorbed in the children's games, the back-and-forth of voices, and balls and dogs, the little ones begging for just one more, just one more swing, one more slide, until the only one remaining had been Susana's solitary voice, because all the brothers and aunts, grandparents and mothers, had grown tired, and, one by one, had gone off with their children, leaving behind a dirty confusion of candy wrappers and burst balloons. She didn't look at her watch right away, she was still confused by the warm memory of echoes, when what she was really hearing was Susana, who now wasn't begging for one more of anything, but instead was just humming a song . . . But the arrival of darkness convinced her that something serious was going on. It was now dark.

Until then Becky had never been late. At the end of each meeting, with religious regularity, the reporter indicated a time, a day, a place. Always a different playground, where the little girl, Susana, would be waiting for her with open arms, where a few hours later, Becky would arrive, supposedly to pick up her daughter, but really to talk to Sarah about the progress of the investigation. The reporter hadn't wanted to give her either her telephone number or her address, a decision that Sarah Barks respected. Whenever Susana wasn't there, it was an unfailing indication that the appointment had been postponed until the next day. But the mere presence of the little girl, or so it had been up until then, guaranteed that in a little while Becky herself would come, punctually, as fresh as a daisy, not at all nervous. That's how it had been. Until now.

Because now that the reporter wasn't keeping her part of the arrangement, Sarah had no way of contacting her. Just today, when the news promised to be dramatic, revelations of singular importance. Her first chill coincided with the last ray of the sun through the trees. She felt around in her purse and with her fingers touched the wrinkled picture of the woman who Carl evoked in his dreams with the whispered and dazzling name Agueda.

The last time Sarah had spoken with Becky, they had connected with such intimacy that the old woman felt that next time she would be able to ask the journalist the history of her family, about her mother and her grandmother. Sarah had discovered that picture by chance decades ago, without mentioning it to Carl, who had a right, after all, to his secrets. But even when Sarah closed her eyes, like someone who happens to stumble upon her neighbor's curtainless window, those dark eyes and that splendor of a complexion were still burning in her memory the day she talked with Becky, and then with little Susana, identical to her mother, probably a replica of female ancestors who hardly varied from generation to generation. The recognition had been conclusive. And now she had stolen that picture to show it to the reporter—to see if she could account for that strange resemblance.

Maybe that's why God had arranged things so Becky wouldn't show up for this rendezvous. So that Sarah would not have to answer the unavoidable question: Did my husband know some woman in your family previously? Could he have fathered a daughter with her and then that daughter another daughter?

But what if Becky didn't come at all, and her address remained forever inaccessible? Then Sarah would have no choice but to take charge of the little girl, taking her back to California. She immediately repented of having considered such a perverse eventuality, but the fantasy didn't go away, because Susana was still in the sandbox and Becky was not arriving and Sarah knew with ferocity and something of disgust that if Providence had not been willing to grant her a male born from her own womb, it may have at least been kind enough to offer her someone like this sweet, singing little flower . . . someone who might also be a product of Carl, the only man from whom she would have accepted procreation.

Then, in the distance, while in the twilight, like a photographic image, with both relief and sadness, she saw the woman approaching. Running.

"In the first frames," David reads, "Sarah is waiting for Becky, who is late. When Becky finally arrives, she tells Sarah breathlessly that they're going to have to drop the whole investigation. José Suárez has just disappeared. Sarah tries to calm her down, tells her she will get Suárez released. But Becky answers: 'You don't know them. They're watching me.' She takes Susana in her arms, asking Sarah: 'Promise me that if anything happens to me, you'll take care of my little girl.' Sarah promises."

"What a dialogue!" says Felipe.

"People swallow anything," says David. "Anyway, Sarah takes a taxi out to the airport and—hold it, first she gets Becky's phone number, right? Sarah watches, through binoculars, the arrival of a new plane—people coming out, masks of hatred and death just like the ones she saw that first time they tried to strangle her. When they get into a car, she follows it in her own taxi. They don't realize they're being tailed."

"Absurd," says Felipe. "It's clear you were never clandestine. A professional would never let that happen."

"No," says David, "I was never clandestine. But you're not going to deny me the right to tell this story just the way I want to, are you? And I say the old lady follows them to an enormous apartment building, then she calls Becky on the phone."

NEXT TO THE LAST FRAME: Sarah, inside a phone booth, dialing. *Sarah:* "Hello, Becky? We found them, Becky. We found them."

LAST FRAME: The receiver in Sarah Barks's hand. Voice from the receiver: "We're very sorry. The number you dialed is not in service. Please consult the directory."

TO BE CONTINUED

"Speaking of cars," says David, "why don't you buy the new one right away? We're never going to get there at this rate."

"And why don't you go to hell?" says Felipe.

"Speed up and we'll get there soon enough. OK?"

"Exactly what I'm doing," says Felipe. "Something's wrong. I press the accelerator all the way down and nothing happens."

The car slows downs until it comes to a complete stop. Felipe turns on the emergency flashers.

"Park over there," says David. "There's a space."

"You'd better get out and push. We don't fit there."

David opens the car door. "For this you bring me all the way over here, damn it. Just to push your car. This must be the victory wagon, Felipe. It was about time for me to get a ride in the victory wagon."

"Shut up and start pushing!"

"This is what I get for being an exile."

"Go ahead and blame it on the exile, you shithead . . . Look, the pedal must be broken, this little thing, the accelerator cable. That must be it. The same thing happened to a friend of mine's VW."

"I told you you'd be better off with a bicycle."

"Keep your advice to yourself and use your muscles."

"Son of a bitch, Pinochet!" says David, getting out of the car.

"It's always Pinochet's fault," says Felipe. "Just push."

"Happy New Year," says David, starting to push.[20]

[20] And so, with these three lines (fragment 6A) we reach the end of our analysis: it is the last fragment that we have. As is clear, it does not help us much in clarifying the dilemmas that we have opened up in preceding notes. The obsession with the Dragon Pinchot continues, as the protagonists continue to blame it for all their problems. But several critics have inferred here, in this farewell of sorts, a new and different atmosphere, as if another author were involved, a more optimistic and energetic feeling. Perhaps it is that we are informed that David is beginning to forge ahead, perhaps it is the idea of a new year, or perhaps simply the dynamism with which the insults are pronounced. Be that as it may, there are those who affirm that David and Felipe are lost from our view in order to enter into the *Legend,* from there to break the cycle of their own doubts and disharmony. Can that be the case? Can it be possible that two men who throughout the *Dialogue* (what we have of the *Dialogue*) have dedicated themselves to arguing about visas and comic strips, permits and Dutch asparagus, could find within themselves the strength to become heroes? This is something that history decided thirty thousand years ago and that we, in any case, would not know how to discover. Perhaps someday, and this must be the dream of every student who has ever studied Prehistoric Amerspanish III, another fragment of the lost literary work will be discovered and will enable us to answer this and so many other questions. Thank you for your attention.

PART III

Pangs

INSIDE

That was when the dead joined up with us, when Pamela and the others left. No, kids, I'm not referring to our immortal uncle. The recently-dead really don't deserve the title dead; they still hold out in our immediate memory. They're really tireless pilgrims who refuse to leave the bellies of the living in peace. The long-dead. The ones who don't even have a grandchild of a grandchild to remember them. The ones who supposedly disappear one spring morning, when we have to clean out some ancestor's trunk, and we find an old daguerreotype and recognize no one in it, not even the furniture, and we then proceed to burn up all those people who once frolicked in bed, paid medical bills, got up at four in the morning to warm milk and added the loving milk of their own glances. We burn them up as if they were foreigners or heretics. Do you think they go up in smoke just like that? They come to visit us, well, visit in a manner of speaking. To occupy the space left by the children who have flown the coop.

It can't have been by chance. It happened almost as soon as the failure of the first rebellion had been confirmed, when the majority of the rebels and strikers chose the one-way path of birth, not having anticipated in their enthusiasm perhaps that this path would someday lead them to the same annihilation that the definitively perpetual-dead were trying to overcome. Unlike the recently-dead or the babies, the long-dead did not aspire to an identity of their own: like salmon trying to get back to their place of origin high in the mountains just to lay an egg, the long-dead were swimming toward the elevator where I was bound to my father and my mother. Let the fetuses escape toward land, toward life. The legendary mass of the dead had no other escape, other than being totally extinguished, no choice but to come and live among us.

I say us, so you won't think I was alone. A few stubborn souls had stayed, the twins to begin with, who still kept me company for a while, just to teach the novices the techniques and methodology of fetal power, but you could hear that they were disheartened and the new recruits weren't learning much, so I told them myself that they could go. We'll help you from out there, they said, we're not going to forget you. Grandfather had heard that kind of spurious promise before and he thanked them. You can go, he said. The last one of his generation to leave was the blind girl, who, against all Grandfather's expectations, kept on telling a thousand and one fragments over on the other side for years, until one day she also faded away.

Grandfather went on building there in the darkness for the ones yet to come, the ones who will feel pain, and it didn't matter to him that the majority of human beings need something more substantial, the desire for children, some concrete heritage or some chain of murmurings that offers a delusion of immortality; he didn't realize that most people need something real and nourishing to hold on to.

Even the dead need something to munch on—those who have just died can subsist for a while on their memories of who they were or who they might have been, but the long-dead always try to hold on to something more concrete, even if it is just a word, a piece of fruit to pass to the living, a whisper of hope. They may have been the ones who taught the son of Manuel Sendero that nothing in this world, or in the one of prebirth, is done alone. It's true that everything is done from solitude, but without all the other solitudes it would be impossible, my dear Pamela's children, absolutely impossible. It may have been the tenacity of those dead that inspired him to plan for the future, to scheme even then a second and final insurrection. It wasn't, at any rate, easy to go on persuading and training the recently conceived babies of the new wave just when those who made up the old guard were graduating into life.

If we find it hard to believe what Grandfather tells about that period, imagine what the little cells that were just awakening in a million wombs must have thought. The chronology of what happened is hard to follow. This may have been because of the state of shock in which he was drifting, abandoned by his beloved and surrounded by ignorant, sleepy, and inexperienced companions. Or it may have been that he did not know how to tell the difference between the voices of the dead and the underground voices which came from the cellars of the vast apartment building where his father's elevator made the rounds. He gets confused when he talks about that time—and you all know how Grandfather was; he never admitted to any contradictions in his sprawling sack of stories. He rejected those efforts to be orderly as being too much like Eduardo—and therefore never would clarify whether he was talking about the voices that reached Manuel Sendero from the building's crumbling cellar, or if it was the blind girl's fairy tales woven from the other world, or if those were messages he received from the dead, particles and legends that they insisted on pouring into his ears and that had remained up till then scattered in the air of the past. Not to mention our very own selves, his own grandchildren, his faithful servants who were sending him messages about how you can be conceived if you only try hard enough from this something, that, for lack of a better name, we usually call the future. And if that were not confusion enough, those were the days in which he managed to find, aboard his three caravels, the intrauterine channel that led to the sweet sea of Doralisa's dreams.

So to ask for order and coherence in his stories at this point, to examine every one of his statements from Skinny's or Eduardo's perspective, is like killing the poor man. Surely others could tell it, person by person, incident by incident, like chroniclers or historians, couple by couple, a slow, realistic, and documented reconstruction of the period. Eduardo would've searched for other ways of making it more explicit, for example, taking two prototypical characters and dissecting their mistakes, directions, and disagreements, until he'd investigated the last secret wall of dignity that in spite of everything refused to be demolished, and Eduardo would've brought out the fact that like those people, those two, three, or four people, so exhaustively observed, raked over, swallowed up in their own misery and in their own morality, that like those, there were thousands, millions more, and that that's the way it had been done, one plus one, people completely secondary and of no particular interest, chaotic and boring, like objects stolen from hither and yon in a thieves' market. That's how Eduardo would've chosen to tell the story. But Eduardo chose to be born, I said, all of a sudden. He was the first one who made that decision, so long, he said, all aboard for reality, he said, doubting we could do or even see anything from here and he must've known that Pamela, in the long run, was going to feel the pull of life, the wonder of life, and would follow him, that both nature and history, quite an alliance, were in his favor. And if Manuel Sendero sang—and Eduardo didn't consider that to be anything so extraordinary—he was just one more in a long line of troubadours and rock singers; if he sang, it was the result of having actively participated in an almost choral movement, one more piece in a collective bond or hymn. That he descended into Hell? That Pamela's parents, among others, whispered in his ear? That the elevator descended into the earth? That the song came from Doralisa's dreams in her here-and-now delirium?

False, Eduardo would have said, drawing pentagrams and instruments of acoustic measurement.

But Manuel did go down, kids, grandkids, all my little seeds. He did go down there and they did whisper to him, and Doralisa was like a marsupial of inexhaustible dreams, and the elevator did exist.

Although many years later even the son of Manuel Sendero couldn't find a single vestige of that place.

"Here," he said, in front of a café, even though nothing could be seen that corresponded to his previous description. No hundreds of buildings. No main post office. No pair of statues. No enormous square. And especially no elevators like the ones he had expected, the ones he arrived at carrying his parents, as if he had to give birth to them and not vice versa. "Let's go in," he said, and they sat down beside the window. It hadn't been washed for a long time.

"Look." Grandfather's finger pointed. On the other side of the avenue, between a repaired factory and a wholesale warehouse, there was a hopelessly run-down apartment building, which the municipal authorities had marked for demolition. "Over there. There is something left."

"Of course there had to be some apartment building," Eduardo explained. "He might just as well have chosen any other place. It was the only one that more or less approached what he had predicted they would find."

"If we get separated sometime," said the son of Manuel Sendero, knowing that sometime would be in just a few brief minutes, "I want you to meet me there inside."

"Inside?" asked Pamela. "It's dangerous. That building's falling down."

"You'll find an elevator," said the son of Manuel Sendero, "a huge giant of an elevator on the first floor. Wait for me there."

"What time is all this going to happen?" she inquired mockingly.

"At dusk," he answered. "If you have to have a specific time for everything, it'll be when the sun's going down." He turned around, pointed in the direction of the rear wall of the café, informed her that that's where the square had been and that crossing it you came to the post office, in front of which were the two statues.

"So you really swallowed that story about the two statues?" said Eduardo.

"Why was that neighborhood called 'The Messengers' then?" asked Pamela.

"Because the government," explained Eduardo, "had decided to give the names of professions to every neighborhood. Since the workers didn't participate in the nation's political destiny, they were at least allowed to have a small part through the names of their guilds. A typical demagogic act."

That wasn't the reason—the son of Manuel Sendero turned down a cup of coffee because tonight he was going to need his rest, and, even more than rest, he was going to need to get in touch with his dreams and caffeine would wreak havoc on his young organism—that wasn't the reason it was called "The Messengers." Before you entered the post office you had to pass under the shadow of two statues, a man and a woman, facing each other; their gender was indistinguishable, but that's what they were, their fingers almost touching. Back then, kids, post offices were more like reading centers than places to expedite correspondence. Just the way you buy stamps now, back then everybody had to wait for his words to be read and approved before he could mail them. Words became coded, perverted, sterile; they beat around the bush in order to make contact. Tremendous contraband operations. Nothing could be said just like that. And if they caught you, punishment was immediate. If the guards found a forbidden word, a verse or an unauthorized message, don't think it took so long. The letter would speed along inside, toward a long, incisive fingernail, belonging to a reading machine. It tore open the envelope, as cleanly as a surgeon, always in the same methodical way, then it purred, kids, impatiently, sure that its Eyes were too benevolent. Besides, the nail was contemptuous, because it never made a mistake; it had already identified the transgressing letter. Then it prepared to mark the face of the one who wrote it, the one awaiting permission to leave. That's the way things were done back then, kids. Somebody was always reading over your shoulder. We became ramblers, used indirect references, turned into guessers, and by dint of stammering things halfway, we sometimes forgot how to say them with precision. The guards' fingernails—you *all* saw them in action when you arrived at the post office. That's the reason for the statues. Right at the moment you were going in, they were being tortured.

"The statues?" asked Pamela, astonished. "But what had they done?"

The Messengers, that was their name, were the first to discover there was a different way of communicating, a direct way. They dared to break the rule. Bare, formal communication wasn't enough for them. Not even the secret code of bedspreads and masks. Because theirs was a love like a naked sun that couldn't be translated into crosswords, allusions, and ashtrays. Since both of them worked for the post office—they were almost guards—it was easy at first to exchange uncensored letters, to take advantage of the situation for their own purposes. They could've kept on like that and no one would've ever been the wiser. But it was natural that later they did the same thing for those less fortunate, and they became lovers' messengers, infiltrating among the piles of approved letters others that had not been approved, letters full of sincerity, intimacy, and even obscene words. The problem was that bands of illegitimate children, as well as the illegal words, the fruits of those clandestine affairs, started to circulate about the city. The investigation was speedy and efficient, and the punishment was exemplary. They were submitted to a slow flame, leaving them alive inside the lime and rock, immobile and without the use of any sense except that of touch, of pain. The two statues were placed facing each other, the fingers of their hands almost touching, just a millimeter from each other to make the distance separating them for the rest of eternity more total. Besides the smallpox of those fingernails, always on them, a chorus of vagabonds made fun of the couple, surrounding them with pornographic gestures and grimaces, showing them pictures of kids who could never be born, their own children, waiting for them and unable to be born. The expression on the faces of the statues is frozen on the edge of a sound: something unarticulated, more like a bellow than a word. As if garbage could talk, what it would say while it was burning, while it was being scattered to the winds.

"Thank God they've taken those statues away from here," said Pamela. "What a horrible story!"

"You still haven't heard the ending," said the son of Manuel Sendero. "You shouldn't judge a story until you've heard the ending."

"Horrible!" Pamela reiterated, convinced. "Who told it to you?"

"A little girl," said the son of Manuel Sendero.

"A little girl?" asked Pamela, using the same tone that Grandfather used in repeating Eduardo's name on the way to the public cemetery, something very close to jealousy.

"You met her. Don't you remember? She was going to be born blind. The last one of the old group to leave. The last one to leave me."

"Why not?" said Pamela. "If you're going to be born blind, who wants to be born at all?"

"That wasn't the reason," said the son of Manuel Sendero, who didn't know how to lie. Even if it was to spare someone pain. "It was for love."

"And who, might I ask, told her the story?"

"You wouldn't believe me," he said.

"I wouldn't believe you? Is there anything left that I wouldn't believe?"

Grandfather had a lot more. The story of the Messengers was already stretching the limits of what she could tolerate, but he'd wanted, maybe because he sensed that the moment for a second farewell was drawing near, to leave her that love story as a kind of offering or as an excuse or a riddle to be solved later. Sitting there in that café, watching cars and trucks and buses pass by along the hard avenue, looking at the condemned apartment building in front of them, weighing the absence of another specific landmark, he decided he could tell her no more than that. It wasn't the fault of either one of them. She had gone that far with him out of a fierce sense of loyalty. But no farther. After all, it wasn't for nothing that years and years before, when they were approaching this site, she had started to be born. She had accompanied him no farther than the threshold of the elevator, and that was how it was going to be now. It would be impossible for her to follow him. Once again he was going to be alone. Grandfather had been illuminated by the intuition that it was dangerous to her health for her to participate in the search for the Caballero. Now he understood that in addition it was dangerous for their relationship. In a little while the sarcastic tone would have come, disbelief would have taken possession of her sunken cheekbones. She would have ended up leaving him yet again. Women are capable of following their men up to a certain point and no farther, the twins said, and the blind girl insisted, that is, except for a few women. Crippled women, Grandfather had thought, prophesying those lagoonlike eyes in which indeed the whole world was reflected, Pamela's eyes, which would be clearing at that moment. He wanted that woman and no one else to be the one and only mother of all his descendants.

Maybe because she was so healthy, and that had to be protected too. Maybe that's why she'd gone, to protect herself, to protect her future children, from what we saw below the elevator, when the elevator descended. The story of the statues, she had said, was horrible. Even worse things awaited us. Health, Grandfather said, doesn't come from the inability to live through certain things, but rather from the inability to imagine them. She refused to imagine them. She refused to listen to what would soon happen to her own parents there in the darkness. Perhaps the dead arrived before the rebellion failed, arrived quietly and simply pressured her with their silence to leave. There was no room for someone like her in that boneyard of voices. Everything he'd told her up to then awakened in that woman a hidden, mutual resonance. What's been forgotten can be recovered, kids. What was never lived, can never be. While he and the others, he and then no one else, he and then one or another who joined him in complete deliberateness to prepare the second and final insurrection, while he was lost in thought in the elevator and was collecting gardens of the dead, Papa Ramón and Mama Teresa were teaching Pamela not to spit on the ground and to distinguish between sleigh bells and oranges and not to hit her adoptive brothers and sisters. She was as far from him as the sky is from the earth, above it, face downward, breathless. At the moment when Doralisa's body, getting out of a cart, penetrated the elevator, Pamela's simultaneous body was turning blue in the light, denying the existence of tunnels, betting on apocryphal immortality.

And the move to the elevator, kids, was impossible to avoid.

Because Papa's job as poll taker had not lasted very long. Just act foolish, Skinny had instructed him. Lie just enough, beat around the bush with the questions, just so their calculations come out a little bit skewed.

Papa didn't act foolish. He was foolish. Doralisa knew he wasn't capable of tricking anybody, and she would have suggested prudence. But she was asleep, and, from within his moderation, the kid lavished advice, happy with the new game. Easy to answer, automatic. The pollster had hardly phrased the question when he would urge his father to tap out exactly the opposite of his real opinion. That method, in addition to being reversely transparent, had another slight drawback: they canceled his contract the next day. A shame that we weren't in the elevator at that point, because the dead, with their usual generosity, could have passed on to us some of their shrewdness. After all, they had to fool the guards of the subworld in order to get some message back into the world of the living, to murmur a word or two of hope to the babies in their moment of conception, keep the torch lit so to speak. They could have given Manuel lessons in survival. What a shame they weren't around—or hadn't made themselves felt yet. What a shame for Manuel.

"What a shame," entoned the Caballero with ice in his voice, like an ironic echo. "We have proof that you've been lying." Behind him appeared the powerful arms of a crew of carpenters, who chastely asked permission to come in and then proceeded to violently break down the walls of the house. Papa made no move to stop them.

"What a shame," the Caballero repeated, raising his voice above the din of hammers and screwdrivers and counterorders, opening and closing a door that was the only thing left between Manuel and the street, like a phony set where they were about to film a farewell scene, showing Manuel the computer evidence that he'd been screwing things up, a shame, but it was a forgivable sin, because a project of even greater scope was now in progress. At the instance of an illustrious foreign delegation, which had requested information on the personality of the Fatherland, the Geopsychological Military Institute had decided to trace the map of the country's internal geography, the permanent idiosyncrasy of our country. So I calmed those who were asking for an exemplary punishment for you. They shouldn't worry about a few lies here and there, when I was sure Mr. Sendero would be able to collaborate with his irreplaceable talents in that search for the national soul or in even more ambitious plans. The fundamental thing was to save that voice for the Fatherland. That's what I told them. I hope I wasn't wrong in my diagnosis . . . But one final question. One they didn't ask you because then you had the job of poll taker but now you've got your idler's card back again. The Caballero went to the door, but precisely at that moment a couple of carpenters were carting it off, leaving it open to the night outside, where a few stars were shining dirtily. It's of tremendous interest to me, said the Caballero. Would you perchance be among that ninety-five percent who are prepared to move to an elevator? Eh? Is that an affirmative? One tap?

It was an affirmative. As so often happens in this life, Papa had no choice.

You really shouldn't consider it a job, Manuel. It's more like a recuperation center, where citizens who aren't in full control of their faculties, but who aren't totally incapacitated for physical work, can be gradually reincorporated into the labor force. Besides, it also helps overcome the temporary housing shortage: your family would fit into the elevator.

The Caballero pointed outside, or rather to what once must've been outside the house, when there'd been windows and walls and rooms. Now that everything was outside, everything was inclemency and clouds and wasteland. Now that the only thing really inside was Doralisa and in here I and we were sticking it out, and Papa had no way of reaching this place of delights, unless he died and crossed over to Mama's warm, sheltering resort by that extreme act. Now that nothing was inside and everything was outside, Manuel could see the street directly, and in the street a cart, parked as if it had always been part of the scenery. For an instant Manuel thought he saw a horse in front of it, stamping its feet, shaking its ragged, filthy mane like a shroud.

"Shall we go?" asked the Caballero.

He took a step toward Doralisa, as if he wanted to help Papa move her. Something in Manuel Sendero's eyes must've reminded that envoy from the Arctic what Papa had once been, perhaps what he could still be. As though they were responding to that sunny and sheltered spot, as if we were calling to them, one by one, Manuel's friends arrived at what had been the place reserved for my birth. As if they just happened to be dropping by, to have a glass of wine, to see how the family was doing. For hours they'd been watching the whole scene from the fringes, seeing the Caballero with Manuel in the bare, crude circle that remained as the money-lenders carted off every board and ivy leaf from the house. Skinny, Don Ramón, Mama Teresa, Luis, Dr. Arismendi, Gringo's wife, and many more, landed like waves on that cliff, surrounded it. Like the movements of a ballet, they surrounded the slow and sleeping body of Doralisa, Mama's gently breathing form, and when they touched her, it was as if the earth were shouting here inside me, as if a root could shout when fingers were strangling it and pulling at it. They lifted her with loving care, but more like the loving care taken with a coffin than with a sick person. They carried her, horizontal and bent, and at that moment Pamela cried for help. In some part of the city the waters were pushing her gracefully and speedily into a worse life, and I couldn't do anything, disoriented as I was by the sudden, initiating movement. And the flood tide of friends flowed toward the cart, carrying Mama.

Nothing's free in this life, Manuel, said the Caballero, ignoring the presence of the others, indicating to him that he should get in the front seat of the cart, as if he were courteously inviting him to the dedication of a mausoleum. You have to work. Because you're going to be required—and this is the essence of the most prestigious of modern therapies—to pay for your treatment and the period of recuperation.

Manuel looked at his friends, placed both hands on the shafts of the cart, and started to pull.

The Caballero escorted him all the way. And talked to him all the way.

Yes, sir. He should produce the energy required to move the elevator in which he lived. During hours he had freely chosen, of course. Producing energy and storing it. If his arm was maimed, well, that's what legs were for. If his legs were damaged, his arms would do the work just as well. Nobody was totally useless, and especially now, when the human metabolism was much cheaper as a means of converting energy than were the forces hidden in combustible fuels. It was true, we were a long way from achieving absolute autonomy in this regard. But the important thing, according to the doctors, was to persuade the sick to be rehabilitated, and if that happened, it was possible that, pedaling day and night, Manuel would find his voice, would find an authentic destiny for his voice. And if Manuel recovered from his illness, not to worry. No one would take his elevator away. That would be like punishing him for improving. He would simply pass to the category of normal person with an elevator. Everyone had now decided that it was indispensable to count on your own elevator, your very own elevator boy. No building, no house without an elevator, and no elevator without its family. That was the goal. That was the way you exercised—what's the word you all like so much? Solidarity? That's the word. Pedaling, you get to heaven, Manuel.

We had reached our new home.

I should've paid more attention to the itinerary, even if it was just to follow the trail several decades later. I should've tried to guess, with my friends' help, the rows of buildings, like enormous tombstones, the tormented shadow of the statues, the porticoes of monstrous, false lions through which we had to pass. It was, after all, my first trip. Physically, I mean. I, who would be the freest of embryos, the most prone to wander, up until then had lived closed up in the still sweetness of a woman who didn't aspire even to sleepwalking.

But my mistakes don't need to be explained by the slight seasickness caused by the motion of the maternal barcarole. That wasn't the case at all. No, I was confused by Pamela's greater seasickness, the emptiness that was being verified in my mother's belly and in her lover's heart when those friendly arms lifted Doralisa, with Cancer rising, and forced along an endless birth. As the first rebellion fizzled out like a dying cat, the universe was gradually cut off from me. One by one, someone put out the candles in a house that had rung with so many voices in so many strangers' wombs, leaving me here in the dark of this land of elevators. And there were other voices, the long-dead and the not-yet-conceived babies gradually filling the emptiness of the ventilation ducts' infected air. It was hard to hear Pamela whispering as she grew more distant. I repeated my last message like a drunken telegraph operator sending condolences to his own funeral. I'll camp for six weeks on the border; it'll take me till I come of age to arrive. Wait for me. Wait for me. And suddenly in the middle of my answerless calls, calls that bounced off no wall and failed to beat the drums of my archipelago of Pamelas, suddenly the sound of others going, a flood of lieutenants going down without coming up, fleeing from the cause, following my beloved toward the false light. I witnessed the argument with them as if it were an academic debate, a television forum, a fight between alien animals. They had been so enthusiastic, they'd sworn commitment until life did us part and—now you see, they said to me, now you see how it is, even your beloved is leaving you, somebody always dominates somebody else, somebody always gets the upper hand, it's part of nature, even in love somebody ends up hurting somebody else, so why should we remain? We're going. Total inequality is impossible. Stay, the twins told the fugitives. Stay, the blind girl told them. Stay with us, came a pale echo from a group of old faithful who still had not absconded. A utopia, the flood of departing babies said, rationalizing their decision, but in reality already hearing the noise of the midwife on the other side of their mamas, the nervous pacing of their fathers, nothing but a dream that no longer inspires or convinces anyone.

Why couldn't I open my mouth, this mouth that was still mine, after all? Even if it was barely mine, in the interior of my mountain that all of a sudden started to pedal, to move up and down, to turn into an elevator. Why couldn't I tie my arguments to their umbilical cords? Why didn't I tell them that without the utopia, without nourishing, dreaming it, we would betray everyone who ever lived? Why didn't I pile scorn upon them, shame them into remaining, warn them that there would be a second rebellion and they would be on the wrong side, they would be our enemies? Why didn't I tell them that dreams are the hardest thing to exile?

I didn't find, for once, the words inside me to proclaim anything and, behind them, two and two are four, four and two are six, as if they were already rehearsing the addition tables in the school that was waiting for them, now the one who was leaving was Croupy, bound for his lack of medicine and his shack in a shantytown and his early grave, everybody would leave, two and two and two are everybody. I didn't say anything and I was left brotherless in this land where it is always night.

But I was wrong.

It was not always night in that land.

Even though my Pamela must have thought so, in order to fight the despair she felt when her eyes opened on that cruel light on the other side, telling herself that back there it had always been dark. Even though I made myself think so, when the light that was Pamela left me. Even though it was Papa who felt that darkness like a plague as he contemplated the back of the Caballero, who was walking away, leaving him in the elevator's nocturnal hole.

Night? Always?

They answered. They were the ones. The invalids who shouted from floor to floor, hidden in the closets of the building. The whispers that had stayed there, stuck beneath the ground floor, where no elevator can reach. The grandchildren who in their cobweb existence were getting organized to make known their right to be born, their right to aspire to the status of procreated fossils someday. The mass of murdered victims of civilizations whose names no one knows how to pronounce any longer.

Pamela had left so she would not have to listen to them.

Night? They murmured to me that it was not true, not even when they were buried deep in burnt earth. At first it was only a flash of lightning, sir, lasting a few seconds beyond itself—and those of us with eye sockets could at least catch the glimmer of the face of the guards and the stairway that leads from this almost eternal cellar where we have been banished, where someday your Pamela will also have to come. No wonder she does not want to listen to us. But it is not always night: think of how it is when my eyes come to visit me, these warm grapes of my love, crossing centuries to bring me reminiscences of dunes, silhouettes that might have been, and then my eyes melt, saying farewell, faltering between my lids, and I have not yet seen if this violence of crabs scuttling at the end of my body could possibly be my hands coming back to me. The guards of this country threw my hands, our hands, into the sea, thinking they would be like bottles without messages. But my hands whisper back to me: we miss you. When are you coming for us? my hands ask. They will be the first thing that we rescue. Slowly, of course. Because nothing grows in this country, sir. The seeds we managed to bring here, secretly, rot waiting for the sun to appear. When we cried out, protesting, they told us to sleep, to remember the past only as a nightmare. Behave, they said—or do you want to go back to the way it was when you'd just arrived? At first they hung us out, sir, like birds on the windows of an insane asylum, not carrying a sound, just a string of birds with their wings torn and backward, until we sank into the waters of the gulf, going nowhere, like a sex so sterile it's no longer distinguishable from stone.

"You wouldn't believe me," I simply repeated to Pamela in the café. She would have gone off again, would have feared the leprosy moon in my voice, would have been disgusted by the stench of those nomad voices burning their garbage inside me.

Because the dead use the remains and the ruins of words, the recent arrivals to that world always manage to smuggle something in. Even if the guards search each new visitor thoroughly. They weigh him, demolish him, spray the cemetery of his vocabulary with pesticides. They know their mission only too well: that we must never return, not even by filtration, by chlorophyll, not even in the taste of an apple, the fleeting color of an insect inflamed with pollen, that no Pamela should be able to listen and understand. "These aren't bringing anything," the guards said that time, scrubbing the newest arrivals clean. But they were bringing, we were bringing, the scorpion of a slow, cradled, censored alphabet. It had survived the passage from life, it had survived this dead sun that burns the skin but doesn't illuminate, that evaporates all memory. You had to care for each word as if nursing it or it would fly away, falling like a shattered dove, never to come back. That's the way things were at first, sir. We were so afraid of having those crumbs of words taken away that we often did not talk to each other, reciting to ourselves a phrase of stone in order not to forget it. That is how we survived. That is how our message now comes to you, something more than a ground swell of ashes.

"Maybe someday," Grandfather told Pamela.

Maybe someday she would have to pronounce similar words, thousands of years after they buried the slender towers of her legs beside our immortal uncle in the graveyard. Perhaps the very grandchildren who hadn't believed Grandfather either had lived in that way in the land of the unliving, organizing a skim of words to help themselves crawl toward the seed, swimming out of the mire and the nothingness where the long-dead had taken up residence.

But if the cell that had been Pamela had refused to pay the price earlier, by listening to those voices, had been afraid that if she heard them she would risk never being born, there was no reason why she would have believed him now. Not the adult Pamela. Not the grandchildren and not anyone else.

Not that.

On the other hand, that I was involved in something so incredible, so impossible and pointless, so unreal and fortuitous as a television program, that they believe of me. With that there are no problems. To them it's the most natural thing in the world that television programs like the one I participated in that night exist. It doesn't bother them that one person can accumulate all the words in the world and other people have to listen to him and are left with none of their own. OK, you kids. Answer this one for me. What good does it do to run away from death, to run away from birth, to run away from the dreams your mother told you the day before they conceived you, so you would arrive gentle, if, after a few years, we're going to have to face a TV set as Pamela did that same night, separated from the person we love by the infinite space of a television screen?

It wasn't hard for Grandfather to get in, after all. He'd left the most improbable places, had crossed a mountain range without being noticed by anyone, had gotten through immigration without having his passport stamped; so it was child's play to get on the most popular program on television.

"What's the program everybody watches?" Grandfather asked in the café. "What program would the Caballero be likely to watch?"

"Does he watch television?" Pamela asked, finally scenting a real fact, one of those trails based on honest-to-goodness clues.

"A screen, a transmitter, a commercial—what difference does it make?" the son of Manuel Sendero said enigmatically and bitterly. "Just tell me the name of the program, please."

" 'Search, Search,' " Pamela says that the master of ceremonies said, as he opened the program that night. "Search, search and you shall find. The program that's at your service and for your entertainment pleasure. Are you looking for something? For someone? Do you have a dream? Some unrealizable wish? An impossible personal desire that you wouldn't confess to a living soul? Every decent, reasonable, and clean wish can be fulfilled on this program. Search, search . . . and together we'll solve your problems. Search, search and . . . you shall find."

The camera focused on the deliriously happy audience and Pamela was able suddenly and without surprise to pick out the flash of Grandfather's face in the front row, perfectly impassive, as if he were thinking about something else, about her whom he could not see or touch or smell; about her, watching him there in the middle of a crowd of gesturing and applauding strangers.

"Last month," the emcee said, once again filling almost the entire screen—and Pamela resented that usurpation—"if you remember well, we had a participant who was searching for something that seemed so difficult that many people felt that his desire was unreasonable. A quick telephone poll, a survey of our spectators happily gathered here, letters sent in afterward, all indicated that that was the majority opinion. Don Andrés Achurras. You remember him. A rather plump gentleman. Well, Mr. Achurras expressed his desire, which of course became ours and everybody else's, because we're all here together to solve our problems, his desire to lose half his weight. But . . . and here was the complication. He wanted to lose weight and keep on eating as much as always. And what Mr. Achurras always had eaten was no small amount. This program's illustrious jury, in spite of your opinions, decided—it was a surprise to everyone and even to Mr. Achurras, I believe—decided, I say, to accept his wish. Today, ladies and gentlemen out there in television land, we have him back with us. I warn you. You're not going to recognize him. Let's give a welcoming round of applause to . . . Andrés Achurras!"

Pamela had seen that earlier program and she remembered a whale of a man, a veritable colossus, stubborn and gluttonous. And all of a sudden she remembered another detail. On the lower part of his Buddha body, his pants were drooping, at about the level of his thighs, which were overflowing and bursting through, so that a kind of crack, a crease, a little bit of bun was bursting through. Laughing at that overflowing creature, along with Eduardo and some other friends; they had commented that the program, for once, had made a mistake in going along with that brainless whim.

The man who walked into the studio was tall and rather slim, almost athletic, you might say.

Instead of the applause that the emcee had asked for, there was a moment of silent stupor.

"Andrés Achurras?"

"In person."

"Are you sure you're not somebody else?"

"Here are my fingerprints, Don Gastón."

"And how many kilos have you lost, Andrés?"

"One hundred kilos, more or less, Don Gastón."

"More or less, eh? One hundred kilos . . . Are you hungry? More or less too, eh? You've been on a diet of bread and water, right?"

"Don Gastón, actually I'm eating more than ever."

"More than ever! And, might I ask, how was this miracle, this dream of all lovers of fine cuisine, accomplished?"

"Well, you gave me some pills, Don Gastón. I take two before each meal and instead of gaining weight, I lose it."

"I see expressions of consternation . . . I'm going to tell you, Andrés, what our problem is. Nobody really believes this. They're going to think it's all a fraud. Unless, unless . . ."

To underscore the emcee's words, the camera had begun to rapidly scan the astonished audience. Suddenly Pamela managed to capture, just for the amount of time required for an ax to fall, the blurred face of the son of Manuel Sendero, lost in the crowd. That fleeting apparition, like a play in which one curtain is raised only to show another one fall behind it without our being able to glimpse the actors for more than a second, that momentary presence, distressed Pamela. An absurd feeling was born in her, almost a certainty, that she would never see him again, that she was seeing him for the last or the next to the last time, that someone was stealing him from her, stealing him forever, and within that feeling there was another, even more absurd feeling, telling her that in the end she had only met that tender and extraordinary man in passing, the way whores meet up with sailors, and that if the camera didn't show him again, it would be hard for her to fix his features in her mind, that if her grandchildren should ask her about that man, she wouldn't know how to describe him, he was like a lamp that someone blew out from far away.

"Unless," the emcee went on in the center and axis and axiom of the screen, "unless we test you right here, live and direct, right now. I'll tell you what we're going to do. First we're going to weigh our Andrés right now and write down his exact weight in kilos and grams and then we're going to place your stomach, which, despite its reduced size, we can still qualify as legendary, if you don't mind our saying so, yes, we're going to place it in front of one of the most limitless feasts that it's been our privilege to offer anyone, and then, while you exercise your jaws, our faithful camera will be following you, with the audience as witnesses, and at the end of the show, we're going to weigh you again, and if your epic reduction in weight continues, then, Andrés Achurras searched and searched . . . and found what he wished for."

While the camera came to rest on the panorama of a table lavishly laden with food at which the guest of honor sat down in ecstasy, Pamela tried to shake off her unsettling feeling. She would have wished—and nobody asked her what she was searching for, nobody helped her find it—that the camera could be an extension of her eyes and she could orient its curiosity toward her beloved, could trace the itinerary of his body and could feast on it, make it materialize here at her side and eat it piece by piece, could grow fat from him and with him and toward him, digest him in her opulent belly, pass him through her gut the way he had passed through her sex. She promised to explore with her tongue up to the last detail of what she had lost by being on the other side of the camera that night and on the other side of reality ever since she was born.

Pamela promised herself that she would take his seed.

But she wouldn't even find out what happened that night. Not even we found out, because he never wanted to speak of that experience. I went to that place just as I might've gone to any other, he said, so the Caballero would see me, so he'd realize I'd arrived and was looking for him. The things adults do to entertain themselves don't concern me in the slightest. Feigning indifference, our grandfather. Feigning, because on other occasions, when we expressed the opinion that it seemed improbable, that there was no evidence that the dead could organize so as not to die completely, or that anyone who aspired to fetushood was already, even before the male had mounted the female, making his way and exercising the privileges of the born, every time we objected, Grandfather would come back with his obsession, as if his information about the world came from that brief program he had attended. Me you don't believe. OK, he would growl. But you believed everything that damned emcee said.

"And while our friend Mr. Achurras is trying to lose another crafty kilo," said the emcee whom everyone believed, "we're going to answer the question you're asking at this very moment. What kind of pills are these? What miracle drug is it? That's why we have with us and I'm honored to present him to you, yes, right in your living rooms or even your dining rooms, yes, our special guest, I want you to meet Mr. Amilcar Corona, general manager of Food Incorporated, producers of Apetitoma, patented product, which will soon be on the market throughout the country. A national product for the world's gourmets, Apetitoma, the drug responsible for the fact that Andrés Achurras, like all of you, searched and searched . . . and found. Good evening, Don Amilcar."

"Good evening, Don Gastón. Good evening to you all."

"Let's go straight to the point, Don Amilcar. Can this remedy really reduce his waistline without the patient having to go through the crucifixion, the Golgotha, of an endless diet?"

"With Apetitoma the more you eat, the more weight you lose."

"But what about toxic elements? Chemical additives?"

"Apetitoma is made," Pamela heard the general manager of Food Incorporated say, she heard it, the son of Manuel Sendero must've heard it too, "of exclusively human and natural by-products."

"And could you tell our millions of anxious televiewers who are searching and searching and don't know how to find, what the secret is?"

"We have nothing to hide. Lowering the consumption of calories, Don Gastón, is a painful method of combating the affliction of overweight. My company attacked the problem at its heart: some people can survive for long periods, even years, in an extreme state of malnutrition. Take those fanatics who go on hunger strikes; it may take them up to two months to die, you see. Something has to be keeping them going, right?"

"But what does malnutrition have to do with this matter?"

"Everything," Pamela says the manager answered, and once again she had the feeling she was on a train that was taking her away from the son of Manuel Sendero, that they'd passed like two ships in the night, and it was hard for her to piece together his image there in the audience. "There's a notion that the less you eat, the more you need to compensate later. Nothing's further from the truth. On the sixth day you're as hungry as on the fifth, but no hungrier. Our researchers discovered the reason for this phenomenon. From that day on the organism segregates a substance that helps it to subsist with fewer calories. Mother Nature wisely takes care of her own."

"And that substance . . ."

"The extract of that substance works miracles. If someone has been deprived of food for several days and takes these pills, his desire to nourish himself is reduced even more. But for someone who eats regularly, like yourself, like Mr. Achurras, the effect is reversed. You barely take a dose and your body is deceived, your digestive system starts to obey the orders of that alien substance as if it were your own."

"You mean," the emcee interrupted, "that it starts to lose weight the way any other organism that's undernourished would . . . ?"

"You eat however much you want," Pamela says the manager said, "and your metabolism believes, erroneously, that the food is insufficient. It then enters into a cycle of rapid weight loss."

"And what's the price of this, Don Amilcar? How much does this blessing cost? This blessing our long-suffering TV audience has been searching for and searching for and at last will find tomorrow in supermarkets and drugstores everywhere."

"Our motto at Apetitoma is 'A product worthy of a Roman emperor but within the reach of the contemporary pocketbook.' Live to eat, we always say, not eat to live . . ."

When we grandchildren heard this episode much later, we were amazed that Grandfather hadn't noticed the similarity between the language of the manager of Food Incorporated and the intonations typical of the Caballero. We asked Grandmother Pamela. Couldn't this man be the Caballero? He did meet all the requirements, after all. She answered us a little angrily that she didn't know much about the Caballero and even less about what the son of Manuel Sendero was thinking about on that occasion and that we'd been swallowing too many adventure stories about masked heroes and confused identities. Besides, that man couldn't have been the Caballero, because, if he was, what happened almost immediately afterward and Grandfather's attitude were incomprehensible.

The emcee had ended the conversation with his special guest, had gone over to ascertain the impressive progress on the feast, and had then approached the studio audience.

"And now," Pamela says the emcee said, "and now, while we wait for the voracious appetite of Andrés Achurras to calm down, we're going to search and search and we're going to find a new contestant, a new participant in our great game of life, someone who's nurturing a decent and reasonable wish, a clean wish that together, united, and with no ill will, we can fulfill on the program where your dreams . . . come true. Who volunteers?"

A thousand souls fitted into those studios. Nine hundred and ninety-nine souls roared, offering themselves, searching, wishing, wanting to find. Only the son of Manuel Sendero remained quietly in his seat, not saying a word, determined in his solitude to raise one obedient hand with dignity and serenity, like a child who knows the answer to the question the teacher has been asking for weeks and is sure that this time will be his turn.

But the emcee didn't choose him.

He pointed with the lottery of his finger at a woman not far from

Grandfather and she, jumping for joy, hurriedly left her seat to join the emcee. The rest of the audience, dispirited but expectant, sat down again, but Pamela could see the discordant and serene hand of the son of Manuel Sendero still patiently raised in the expectation of being called upon.

"Good evening, Mrs.? Miss?"

"I'm married, Don Gastón, and the mother of two children."

"And are they here with you tonight, madam?"

Like all normal, everyday inhabitants of this planet, all those who are born once and who from that moment on follow the route of least resistance in this world as they find it, Pamela had often asked herself what would happen if all at once, at the climactic moment of a concert, a pledge to the flag, a mass, a presentation of medals, a speech at the opening of the judicial year, what would happen if somebody chose that moment to erupt into the proceedings with a cavalry charge; she had felt within her an irrepressible urge to scream, to throw a tomato, to shout a hallelujah, to take off her clothes and provoke a disturbance. She'd never done it. As if in the act of being born, she had used up her entire capacity for shocking the universe.

What would happen?

Pamela found out part of the answer that night.

"Just a minute," said the voice of the son of Manuel Sendero, offscreen, but filling the studio with the sonority of a second and definitive rebel. "Just a minute. I'm searching for someone."

The emcee's face showed no visible reaction. Maybe he'd always expected that kind of scandal, had anticipated it in his nightmares, not in his dreams certainly, like Pamela.

"There's a gentleman in the audience who's searching for someone," said the emcee, sweating bonhomie. "All of us are searching and searching, but only one per program may have the privilege of finding. Tonight's participant has already been chosen and we're going to go on with our program."

The son of Manuel Sendero must've seen the two policemen who were advancing from both sides of the studio, quickly but without ostentation. Pamela imagined him leaping over the barrier that separated the front row from the sacred precinct of the stage, because all of a sudden he stood directly in front of the emcee, appearing on the screen the way someone might enter the annals of history.

"I raised my hand first," he said. "Besides, everybody knows you arranged with this lady to choose her. Everybody knows that."

Pamela noticed that the camera vacillated. If it had not been for that last accusation, they could've cut for a commercial break, clearing the area of the intruder without the televiewers having to witness the scuffle. But someone no doubt thought that such an intervention might be interpreted now as an admission of guilt, and for the first time the camera seemed to become independent, acting on its own volition. All at once it focused on Andrés Achurras, who had suddenly stopped eating, paralyzed with knife in hand in front of an enormous cake. Then it returned to the audience, and ended up with a close-up shot of the emcee's face, which still maintained its toothpaste smile.

"Wishes, sir," said the emcee, "are infinite in number. And the world's resources, not to mention those of this program, are unfortunately limited. If we accepted your request, we'd have to do the same for everybody else here and for everybody out there across the land. Come back again, sir, and I'm sure your search will be rewarded."

"I'm searching," said the son of Manuel Sendero in front of millions of bewildered spectators, "for a man, the Caballero. Show us that you're not a fraud by finding him and bringing him here."

"Sir," responded the emcee, "we're opposed to the use of force on this program. We abhor violence of any kind, sir. In over fifteen years of transmission, we've never had a problem. We beg you, sir, go back to your seat, and allow us to go on with the show that everyone enjoys, the show that's at your service and for your entertainment pleasure."

The camera scanned the audience. Pamela could almost touch the wave of hatred that emanated from each person there, the mounting rush of insults and obscenities.

The son of Manuel Sendero waited for the camera to come back to him. Without raising the tone of his voice, so that everyone would hear him in the innermost part of his being, just as had happened years before with his father's last song.

"If all of you," he said, "would follow me, life wouldn't be a search, my friends. Life would be an endless encounter."

In a flash, the camera left him.

"Very well, ma'am," said the emcee. "After this unpleasant but understandable interruption, we can go on with our show. Because it's natural that everybody wants to find. But it's not natural to use violence to get your own way. What is it you're looking for, reasonably, cleanly, and decently? How can we help you?"

It was irritating to note how the camera was depriving her of knowledge of what was really happening. Pamela decided that the emcee's calmness could only stem from the fact that the policemen, without the televiewers seeing it, but in full view of the studio audience, had finally carried off the son of Manuel Sendero. She felt the lonely impotence of one who cannot step into the machine and strangle the villain, as if someone had condemned her ever since her first appearance in the world to see things always from afar, never taking part, always through a dark screen. But the son of Manuel Sendero went on refusing to accept those rules he had not written himself. Possibly the rebel had managed to get away, because the lady who had been chosen, instead of answering that friendly question, had gone from a blush to a state of real agitation and now was at the point of a nervous crisis, watching out of the corner of her eye a scene that must've been going on nearby, out of Pamela's view as well as that of the camera, a chase of some kind, a hunt that had turned into a game of tag, of hide-and-seek, with loud shouting, falling glasses, breaking dishes, and an audience that, all of a sudden, like a change in the wind, had taken sides with the troublemaker.

"They're going to break for a commercial," Pamela said to herself, as if what they were going to break was her existence, her jugular, rather than the TV image. "They're going to break right now."

As if the director of the program were listening, a dog appeared on the screen at that moment, a pleasant enough animal, sniffing at its favorite food.

So Pamela was unable to see, nor could those other millions who had been born years before and who, because of that fact, were forced to watch that program and those dogs, the immense cake that Don Andrés Achurras never managed to eat, dripping from the emcee's face, neck, and suit.

Nor did she hear the words of the son of Manuel Sendero.

"I'll have to find the Caballero on my own," he said.

But Pamela knew—she didn't need the cameras, she knew it without need of screens, she knew it almost without need of her own body, which had accepted the defeat of being cornered into a single body and now had glimpsed the possibility of being two bodies, three, four, infinite bodies—that the Caballero had been watching the program that night, that the Caballero too had been searching and searching ever since the son of Manuel Sendero had escaped him, and that in a little while he would find him, would find him in the jail where they carried me, kids, just as they had my father. That night they returned me to a place like the one from which my father went out on that same day when spring had a false start. I waited for that man there, while Pamela made the rounds of barracks and regiments and commissaries, a replica of the old woman and of Doralisa, decades earlier. I waited for the Caballero, grandchildren of my roots, as if I had made a date with him.

OUTSIDE

I have news for you, Sarah. I asked Marras. I asked him what they could be doing with all those people. The people without the X-Factor.

said Carl Parks.

I spoke with Marras too, Carl. What a coincidence! He was looking for me. I wanted to see him. Last night I couldn't sleep. I didn't want to tell you, Carl, but Becky . . . I can't find her. Marras has always said he was at our beck and call. I wanted to see if he really was.

said Sarah.

Genetics, Mr. Parks, Marras answered me. Life planning. Some people say the decisive influence in our existence is the environment and others say heredity, biological factors are more important. A pointless controversy, Marras explained to me. One with no future. Till now.

said Carl Parks.

Till now, Carl. And Mr. Marras didn't wait for me to explain the reason for my visit. Till now we haven't been able to discover a way for older women to have children. He laid it out for me, direct. If that wasn't what interested me most in the world.

said Sarah.

Because it's the only science, Sarah, the only one, according to Marras, in which you can't experiment. Because every man is irreplaceable. With a rat, fine. You dissect it. You lock it in a maze. If we could take one child, and Marras emphasized that, that child and no other, and have it pass through various educational experiences, varying a single factor in each of its lives. An insignificant one, like using sheets or not. Or a big one, like varying the type of mother it has.

said Carl Parks.

That's the news, Carl. A mother! I could be a mother! Me, Carl.

said Sarah.

Then, yes, Marras told me. We would have real proof in our hands. We could determine all the variables of human existence. We'd repeat a person's life again and again and again until we had used up all the possibilities. You'd know—but, imagine! Imagine it, Sarah!—If it's good to discipline children. Or what harm you might do them.

said Carl Parks.

I'll never beat my son.

said Sarah.

But there's more, Sarah. Don't interrupt me. If afterward you could take the same child—and Marras repeated, the same child—and modify some genetic feature. Just one. And then have that child go through the same variable experiences, we'd measure the influence of heredity down to the centimeter. Marras asked me what that would mean for humanity. Do you know, Sarah? The total solution, Mr. Parks. The total solution, Sarah. A scientific model for conduct, finally, for the improvement of the human race. There'd be no reason to fear some genetic catastrophe. Everything would already have been tested in a laboratory.

said Carl Parks.

Yes, I told him, you're right. He'd discovered the thing that interested me most. I don't know how you guessed it, I told him. But in fact, that's it. I came down here with the certainty that my problem would be solved in this country. And now you see, Carl. Now you see.

said Sarah.

But before there wasn't the necessary raw material. Millions of identical twins were needed. How could you find the same subject for several experiments, Sarah? How do you do it?

said Carl Parks.

I told him: Look at me. I'm old. At my age, you wouldn't deceive a lady, would you? I felt that he was so kind. I talked to him as if he were a midwife. That's how I talked to him. Don't worry, said that persuasive voice. The treatment will be explained to you soon.

said Sarah.

The children of a man and a woman who don't have the X-Factor. Those children. Yes, they're the ones. Yes. they'll all be alike. A series. We make up a thousand particular situations for them. You, Mr. Parks. Me, Sarah, he was talking to me. I would make up experiences for them. Like in a Hollywood studio. A story in which only one element changes each time. A story of happiness that we try out again and again, Mr. Parks.

said Carl Parks.

Treatment? The word sounded sudden. I suddenly remembered what I had intended to speak to him about. I asked him if that treatment might have something to do with a process of rejuvenation.

said Sarah.

"Rejuvenation?" asked Marras.

I asked him about the children, Sarah. Of course I asked him about that. Are the little ones well treated? That's what I asked him, Sarah. Why did I open my big mouth? Education, said Marras, nutrition, he said, housing, clothing, love. Only in this country, Mr. Parks, do the authorities and private enterprise care about childhood like this. And on a massive scale, Sarah. Thousands and thousands of children. In order for the experiment to have real scientific value.

said Carl Parks.

Rejuvenation, Carl. I had to tell him. My voice was shaking. It changed a little when I told him. But after all, they take years off those people. Maybe they want to do the same thing to me so I can start to bear children. I won't allow it. Not in that company. Never. So I told him. Someone, I said, not specifying their sex. Someone has told me the following. Nothing about Suárez's disappearance or Becky's. Just the business of the house.

said Sarah.

"What did you say?" asked Marras. "An apartment house?"

I didn't answer him. I told him: Before starting my treatment, Mr. Marras, I must, for the sake of my conscience, visit that place.

said Sarah.

"Visit it?" asked Marras.

Only if he had the authority, Carl. Yes. To be sure that treatment had nothing to do with mine. Marras was unruffled. Did I realize those people that I was so interested in were sick, that they'd been guaranteed rest and complete discretion? By contract? Did I realize that? Of course. How could I not realize it? I'd seen them, those people. And they were frightening, frankly. It was like running into a bunch of monsters.

said Sarah.

"Seen them?" asked Marras. "You've seen them?"

The whole affair on the plane, Carl. You remember. I told you about it. Not mentioning that one of them had dared to . . . Well, why go into all the disagreeable details.

said Sarah.

"And if I swear to you, madam," said Marras, "that both treatments are completely different? Isn't the word of a gentleman enough?"

It was enough, and I thanked him, but for ethical reasons I believed it was essential to visit that sanatorium. Because I still don't know where Becky is. Or the child. Although I didn't tell him that.

said Sarah.

"What you're asking me, madam," said Marras, "is a very delicate matter. Extraordinarily delicate."

Old Sarah's counteroffensive. I asked him if perhaps he didn't have confidence in Carl's wife. How could I fail to have? Marras said. When her husband's imagination was the key to the new country. But there were other matters of an intimate nature . . . Would I like it if someone, a complete stranger, were present during my treatment for having a child? Would I accept that without protest?

said Sarah.

I would be the father of all those children, Sarah. Papa Parks. That's what they'll call me, Marras told me. They'll look at you as though you were their father. Millions of children. You deciding on their smiles, all their happy lives. What do you say, Mr. Parks? What do you say?

said Carl Parks.

It was a powerful argument, Carl. Because I would never allow it. But at the same time, I have the assurance that what I'm doing and what is being done to me is safe and legal. Do those people who come for the other treatment, with those hands, have the same assurance? So I said to Marras: Your obstinacy proves that something's amiss, that there's something rotten in Denmark. I have no alternative, I told him, but to leave this country along with my husband. They must be very interested in your staying, Carl. They must need your imagination very much.

said Sarah.

"Very well," said Marras. "As you wish, madam. We'll arrange your visit. Tomorrow."

Tomorrow, Carl. Carl? Carl? Are you listening?

said Sarah.

And one more thing, Mr. Parks, Marras told me. Something more . . . Remember what we said about El Dorado? The Fountain of Youth? Do you remember?

said Carl Parks.

Carl? It's Becky. Becky's disappeared. I can't find her. Carl? It's Becky. The woman in the picture in your billfold. Carl? Becky's disappeared. Are you listening?

said Sarah.

"Well, Mr. Parks," said Marras. "I want to advise you that the Spaniards were not wrong. They were not at all wrong."

Sarah brought her mouth close to Carl's ear.

"We're going to have a baby, Carl," she said. "Just like in the Bible."

Carl Parks went on talking and talking, paying no attention to her, talking about a city covered entirely with gold, about a land of eternal springtime.

Then Sarah realized that her husband had gone deaf. She called Dr. Garay. And, with sadness, she checked the plane schedule for a return flight to Los Angeles.

But none of this was ever to be known. Because, as will be seen, David was not able to tell either Felipe or Paula the final episodes of the comic strip. David had other problems.

"What is to be done?" asks Felipe, sitting down suddenly, reaching his hand out to see if, in fact, his beer has lost even that little bit of coolness it had barely had before he stood up to talk endlessly on the telephone. What to do? A question Felipe Cuadra has formulated on other occasions.

David doesn't answer him. Ever since they entered the bar, lugging the two suitcases, David hasn't opened his mouth. Without saying a word, he sat down, pushing the suitcases with his foot until they disappeared from view under the table, comfortable in his spectator's role, while Felipe orders the beers, asks for the phone, walks to the back of the bar to make the calls. Felipe can feel his glare, as if he were seeing him through the dirty glass of an aquarium; David, observing him above the clatter and through the smoke of the men in the bar, his eyes fixed on Felipe's distant mouth as it moves.

"What is to be done?" Felipe repeats. "Go home or wait for a mechanic?"

David raises his hands, then touches one of the suitcases, as if the answer were in there, looking around him with very little interest. Felipe waits for David to intervene, to ask something: How long? What did the mechanic say? What did Juana say? For David to make a comment. But no response.

"An hour," says Felipe. "He promised to be here in an hour. But in this traffic, he'll give up before he gets here. The new year is two and a half hours away. If he sees he might miss his party, he'll turn around and go back home . . . That's the way it is."

For the first time since they came into the bar, David speaks.

"Let's go then," he says.

"Let's go. Fine. But how? In a cab? Forget it. I called and they can't promise me anything for at least a couple of hours . . . And we need the car anyway. If we don't get it fixed now, it'll be out of commission for who knows how long, what with the weekend and the holiday . . ."

"So we stay then," says David.

For a while neither of them moves or expresses an opinion. They just sit there, savoring the noise of male voices commenting on a television film or on the beer or on both at the same time. David shuts his eyes as if he were about to fall asleep with that intense ability that only a drunk possesses.

"Juana told me to call somebody," says Felipe. "But you have to be really close to drag a man out of his house on New Year's Eve, don't you? It's not like it would be with Elías or Enrique or you if you lived here, right?"

David keeps his eyes closed.

Felipe waits a moment, then goes on: "Juana doesn't understand. There's got to be somebody, she says. Somebody who owes you a favor. She doesn't realize it's just the opposite. I'm the one who owes the favors. Ever since we got here, I've been asking people to help us out with this, that, or the other thing. Until one fine day I told Juana, I said, about a year ago: Juana, we're not going to ask any more favors of anybody. I was getting to be dependent on other people. That's a dangerous business. Dangerous because all those favors end up being collected on. It's easy for a woman to keep on asking."

"I'm fine here," says David, not opening his eyes. "I could stay here until tomorrow."

"You probably will," says Felipe. "We can't even find out if Agustín's going to come. I couldn't even put a time limit. If I tell him, for example, that we'll wait till eleven, and then we'll leave, you know what'll happen? . . . He won't come at all. He won't even leave the house. Only if he thinks we might be waiting for him, then there's a possibility he'll come."

David opens his eyes and looks at the image on the TV screen. A blind woman is waiting in a lonely house for them to come looking for her, perhaps to kill her. She breaks one lamp, then another. The bartender changes the channel. Now it's a comedy. A Mexican one.

"Let's leave the suitcases then," says David, "if they're such a problem. To hell with the suitcases."

"I don't think that's a very good idea," says Felipe. He lights up a cigarette, taking his time, inhaling deeply, with a certain indifferent greed. "Want another drink?"

David nods.

At that moment four or five men burst into the bar. Laughing, pushing each other, obviously celebrating something. They lean on the bar and shout orders for tequila. All of them have flowers in their lapels.

"Eight years," says Felipe, signaling for the young man who's waiting on the tables to bring them two more. "Doesn't that seem incredible?"

"Everything seems incredible to me," says David.

"You're melodramatic," says Felipe.

"This place does that to me," says David. "Doesn't it have that effect on you?"

"No."

"Doesn't it remind you of something?"

"The Nicaragua Bar," says Felipe. "Lecumberri Street. I've never been here before."

"Or these people? Don't they remind you of anything?"

Felipe doesn't answer because they bring the beers at that point. Two new bottles.

"Don't you have any ice cold?" asks Felipe.

"Don't serve ice cream," says the young man.

"Cold, I said. Don't you have any colder beer?"

"Try them, sir," the young man suggests. "These are really cold."

The bottles are lukewarm. David pours for Felipe, then for himself.

"What are they celebrating?" David asks the young man, pointing to the group of friends who just came in.

"The new year, sir."

"Naturally," says David. "The new year."

Felipe opens his address book and starts to leaf through it, page by page, letter by letter. He doesn't hurry. Between pages he stops to smoke, to take another drag, to look at David.

David points to the group of friends. They're getting happier by the minute, hugging each other, very excited, offering one toast after another. "I'd like to go talk to them. I'd like to know what the devil they're celebrating."

"Don't do it," says Felipe. "They're celebrating the new year."

"I don't think so," says David.

Felipe turns his attention back to the address book.

"What're you doing?"

"Seeing if there's somebody in this book that could help, somebody that could come to get us," says Felipe. "You never know."

"Want to look in mine?"

"I don't think there are many Mexicans in yours, David."

"Are there many in yours?"

"A few."

"What about Chileans?"

"People change out here, David. They get used to things. Besides, on holidays they go out. They try to get away from this city. We stayed because of you and Paula."

"There must be at least one person you can call."

"Now you're starting to sound like Juana." Felipe turns a page, then another and another. "Look," he says, "look who we've got here."

"The cavalry to the rescue," says David. "Finally."

"Not exactly," says Felipe. "It's someone who doesn't live here. He passed through Mexico City a couple of months ago. He remembered you a lot."

"Me?"

"He said he'd look you up in Holland. He had your address. You must've seen him. Right?"

"Who're you talking about, Felipe?"

"Pepe Jérez. Did you see him?"

There's a slight hesitation in David's voice, but he answers: "Yes."

"I was really surprised. He was gathering material for the *Revista del Domingo*, a report on Chileans abroad. Said *El Mercurio** was interested in the series. I was frankly amazed. He's free-lance, but I didn't give him the interview. I don't want anything to do with *El Mercurio*, I told him. Did he find you?"

"Yeah," says David.

"I asked him if he could guarantee me that everything I said

* *El Mercurio* is Chile's main newspaper. It opposed Allende with CIA backing and has been the primary supporter of General Pinochet.—TRANS.

would come out in the paper, just the way I said it. I asked him just for the hell of it, because I had no intention of giving him the interview anyway. Besides, I already knew the answer. He looked at me like I was nuts. You know how it is in Chile, he said. It's a real victory if your name just appears in a newspaper. A real victory. The hell it is, I said. They won't get a word out of me until I can tell it all, the prison, the torture, what I think of the Junta, everything, and naming names besides. It doesn't matter, Pepe told me, laughing. Anyway, it's not for sure they'll publish yours. They're going to select the material that interests them most. He was going to talk to a lot of people living abroad, and he'd convinced the fellow from *Revista del Domingo* that it was only fair to include one or two from the exiled left. Tokens, shall we say. If you get my drift. No, sir, I told him. We represent 44.5 percent of the electorate in the last free elections, and we refuse to be stuck in like a sample in a show window."

"I've got to take a leak," says David all of a sudden, standing up.

"Wait," says Felipe. "Let me finish. Can you believe those sons of bitches . . ."

"I've got to take a leak," says David. "It can't wait."

"I'll go with you," says Felipe, standing up. "Naturally the sons of . . ."

"You'd better stay with the suitcases," says David.

"Hell no. Nothing'll happen to them. Let me tell you about Jérez or I'll forget it. Pepe didn't want to admit it to me, but I squeezed it out of him. The sons of bitches want to show how the folks are making out overseas," Felipe goes on, while he and David walk toward the back of the bar, in the direction of the toilet. "The main point wasn't going to be the political exile, man. People who left ages ago, who knows how long, something like 'The Globe-trotting Chilean.' An old lady who makes *empanadas* in Lisbon, an educator with the OAS in Washington, workers in the Argentine Patagonia, a dockworker in Auckland. And there among them all, Felipe Cuadra. Censored, and, to top it all off, with no guarantee they'll publish it. No, sir, I told him . . ."

But Felipe doesn't finish.

Through the door of the toilet the smell of disinfectant, the acrid scent of a thousand years of urine, the stained dampness of cigarette butts on the floor, almost knocks him over. It's just a toilet like any other, like so many others all over the world. At that moment, under the dim light of a yellowish bulb, surrounded by indecipherable obscenities, David's shadow struggles to unzip his fly. The zipper sticks halfway down. It won't budge.

"Shit," says David with a half-angry, half-desperate movement of his right hand there in the semidarkness, a gesture that falls somewhere between weak and aggressive, and he slowly lifts his gaze toward the mirror, meeting Felipe's eyes there, watching and looking at him from another mirror, another sink, another bar, from a dimension that both of them finally remember and recognize as the past.

Felipe now knows, as David has known ever since they entered the bar, that this mirror was waiting there for them, that in some toilet, somewhere on the planet, a mirror like this one, that gesture, that word, this smell, were waiting for them. The whiplash of that same word, the gesture in the darkness, the smell, David's barely visible profile, the eyes that meet and stand still in the no-man's-land of the stained mirror, the zipper that won't go down, and that clumsy hand of David's that will never learn to manage anything right. It's not the first time. As if the two of them were buried in a mutual memory that needs both of them to be liberated, to be smelled, touched, tasted, to live again. Eight years before, in the toilet of a Santiago bar, the two of them, Felipe and David, just like now, speaking to each other wordlessly into a mirror.

The last time they had seen each other.

"Shit," says David and said David eight years earlier and Felipe didn't know what to say then either. "I've got to take a leak." It was Felipe who announced it that time in a similar bar in Santiago, walking toward a room like this one and like so many others in which similar words are spit out and in which pals piss side by side beneath an opaque light in a sign of eternal friendship. "So they're going to screw me," said David. "So you're going to screw me," he'd said. "I won't leave," David had said eight years ago in Santiago, while Felipe gazed at him, knowing, as David also knew, that it was the last time they would see each other for many years. Both of us knew he was going to leave, that he'd accept the decision, because, once again, he had no choice.

We'd finally made connections the morning before, after numerous calls back and forth, always finding the other party out. David's body seemed to shift between home with Cecilia and passion with Patricia. Cecilia had told him she'd give him the message in the tone used by a woman who has no idea if her husband will come home to sleep or not, or even if she could call him by that title. Patricia answered that if she happened to bump into David, she'd be glad to tell him about my call, as if there was nothing special between them. One of the two, or both of them, had kept her promise, because David returned my call, and I, of course, had gone to Valparaiso that day to re-establish contact with the old propaganda team that operated in that zone, or, rather, with what was left of it. In those days, everything happened that way. Nothing was easy.

I didn't try to locate him. I waited for him to do it. Maybe, unconsciously, I had no desire to speak to him, preferred to avoid that conversation. Because when his voice finally woke me up that morning, I felt apprehension and fatigue rather than relief. How good that you called. We've got to get together, urgently, today, I told him. But it was as though he wasn't listening to me. Something had him all excited. Almost bubbling over.

"Not today," he said. "Tomorrow we have to have dinner together anyhow."

"What's going on tomorrow?"

"I've been trying to see you all week. Tomorrow we have dinner together."

"Without our wives?" I asked. That would give me a clue as to what he was cooking up.

"Definitely without our wives," and he laughed.

He refused to tell me what was going on, and, of course, I wasn't about to ask him, especially on the phone. It amazed me that he should mention right away that it was a surprise—a surprise, he said, and, to my even greater amazement, he added, please don't tell anyone, absolutely no one.

I confess I was fed up with him. That failure to observe the norms of security was typical of David, who went on living as if we still had the government in our hands, as if the coup hadn't happened, not to mention the terror that followed it. It was improbable that anyone was recording our conversation, but you had to get used to not giving any motive for suspicion and not even hinting at secrecy. But David adduced that we were wrong. According to him, what really attracted attention was our overeagerness to play spies when it really wasn't necessary, the long, elliptical, and coded exchanges we had put into effect five days after the coup as the means of communicating in public and of thinking in private, where you chatted on about your dead grandmother, your sick father, your kid's excellent health, the university where you had to register, the car that was screaming for repairs, the pool table that was still in good shape, in order to inform ourselves about unspeakable activities and illicit organizations and people. David tended—it was one of the things we had gone over during the meeting in which we'd decided on the order or rather the recommendation that I was now going to have to communicate to him—to forget about that code, to make fun of it, to ridicule it. Now you don't know if Grandmother is or is not dead, joked David. If you're inviting me to a barbecue or if they've killed a *compañero*.

He was partly right. Because in this case, when he insisted on the dinner, I couldn't discern whether David wanted a political appointment with me to talk about some problem with the assigned duties and to propose some new plan that was even more impracticable than the previous one, or whether it was just a personal rendezvous. It made no difference. Because I did have something essential to discuss with him. So I acceded to his summons.

But I felt enraged once again that they had given me this work with David, that I was his contact with the central propaganda structure. I recognized in that first meeting, in which we studied the whole question after David announced he intended to stay in the country, that the advantages of my having undertaken the matter were self-evident. We could see each other without arousing suspicion. Our wives were cousins, a fact that could easily be proven. We'd been close friends since before Popular Unity, and it would've been odd had we stopped seeing each other after the coup. But the most important thing: even if we'd crossed paths at the state publishing house, we had never been militant in the same Party structure. And in that initial period when everybody had to change places in the internal organization for security reasons, and nobody could continue working with the people associated with his prior political activity, that argument had proven to be decisive. Besides, in the task of preparing the Party's underground bulletin, who better than David to help me? Or so we'd thought. Who better than he to train a clandestine network of editors and people's reporters, giving rapid courses of instruction? Who better than he to centralize data and anecdotes and to give them an agreeable and interesting form, to produce concise satirical attacks on the new authorities from time to time? But David wouldn't settle for that. He was in a hurry. He kept on marching to the beat of past drums, with an energy level that just had to pour out projects, actions, extraordinary machinations. His imagination knew no bounds: he proposed an anthology of the jokes that were circulating; he himself, with more foolhardiness than daring, collected testimonials of the hellhole that was the Chile Stadium and El Nacional, to be distributed in book form; he decided it was necessary to develop a mural brigade to denounce the regime by means of comic strips painted on walls. Everything in him was spectacular, paradoxical, fantastic. It was hard to make him understand that, at that moment, the means didn't exist to carry out even one of his projects, that we had hardly reached the much more primitive phase, building a network of contacts that would allow an elementary distribution of news, a minimal reception of popular experiences. It was refreshing that he was so full of ideas and goals, and I was confident that the moment would come when his talents could be utilized to the fullest. But it was also wearing to censor each and every synopsis of his films that would never be made. Let's send up two thousand balloons with the words

PINOCHET MURDERER on them, right in the middle of the city. Sad to burst his balloons, one by one, like a child. All the virtues that made him an incomparable and hustling worker, everything that made him a phenomenal machine for the production of happiness throughout the Allende years, all of that public virtue wasn't worth a shit now that the only thing that counts is discretion, is that when I tell Juana I won't be home for dinner, she never asks me when, where, with whom, she only asks me, with her eyes, to try to get back before curfew, to let her know if I am going to be late. OK?

But that wasn't what I had to talk to David about that afternoon in the bar. It was another, more serious, and probably insoluble problem.

I arrived punctually. As always.

"Great, brother," he told me. "We still have an hour before dinner . . ."

"What dinner?" I asked him. "What are you up to?"

"It's a surprise," said David. "But you can't spoil it now . . . It's for Elías. His bachelor party."

I hadn't seen Elías since the weekend after the coup. We'd met once in the street, that was all. We'd kept on walking as if we were strangers.

"Elías is getting married?"

"You didn't know?"

"Look, it makes no sense for us to be discussing what I know or don't know . . . Does Elías know about this dinner?"

"In a way."

"What exactly does that mean? In a way."

"In a way, he knows about it. He knows he's going to have dinner with me."

"But he doesn't know I'm coming?"

"No, of course not. That's the surprise."

I sighed.

"David," I said to him, "who else did you invite, David?"

"Just some friends," said David. "Friends of Elías."

"The whole family," I said. "Right?"

"What family?"

I didn't lower my voice, because that would've indicated something surreptitious in my words. But my impatience must've been evident in my tone:

"Our family, you motherfucker, ours. What other family do you think I'd be talking about?"

"Oh, yeah. The family. Of course, the family. Felipe, Elías's friends are all part of the family, naturally."

I'd been asking myself how I was going to break the news to him, what subtle means I was going to use to present our decision to him, and he was handing me a blank bigger than an elephant to fire away at him.

I said to him:

"Look, I can't go to this dinner. I'm not going. I came to talk to you about something else."

"You're not going? But, hell, all your friends you haven't seen in . . . months are coming. Bernardo, Enrique, Carlitos, Fat Sánchez."

"I don't want to know who's coming. Call them and tell them I won't be showing up. Go on."

"It's late. They're probably already on their way. It'll be a surprise for everybody."

"Call them."

"I can't do that, Felipe. I already paid for the dinner."

"You paid for the dinner? With what?"

"What difference does that make? I got some money."

"You're crazy, David. How did you pay for the dinner?"

"Don't look at me like I got a loan from the Yankee Embassy. Listen . . . I just got it. That's the main thing."

That was the way David was. Later I found out he'd sold his set of encyclopedias. He thought he wouldn't need them—and he wasn't wrong—in the years ahead, and someone had to pay half the money in advance, and Elías wasn't going to go without a bachelor party. But the fact is that for David it was something more: a wild party where everyone could bid farewell not only to Elías, but also to each other. He sensed that it would be years, maybe a decade or maybe never, before we'd be able to get together again the way we used to. He had put that rash party together out of the goodness of his heart, out of sheer feelings of solidarity, and out of the most blatant irresponsibility. I could already imagine the demented scene: each person entering the Hong Kong Restaurant, not suspecting that he wasn't the only guest, finding himself face to face with all the others, as if he were falling into an extraordinary telephone booth occupied by Groucho and Company. At first, they would make a move toward the door; they'd shake their heads in disapproval. But they'd stay to drink a toast to the bridegroom, to down the first pisco sour, and then they'd go along inventing all kinds of plausible excuses for not leaving. Not admitting the real reason: the wonder of pretending that the coup was imaginary and that the risks were nonexistent.

Nevertheless, the risks were extremely existent. David had gathered all his closest friends there. People from his local cell and from regional commands. My people and Elías's people. He'd even persuaded Enrique to come with who knows what unspeakable trick, what sweet words. People who possessed among themselves as their only bond and justification having belonged to the same party that today had no right to exist, that should be erasing its own past. With his foolhardiness David had undone the planning of months of division, checking, counterchecking, experimentation, bringing together around a banquet table beneath the flashes of wandering unemployed photographers all those militants we had painfully scattered to the four winds.

I hadn't seen them for months. The Saturday after the coup we had gotten together for the last time on a soccer field, talking in low voices in the middle of the struggle for the ball, passing along more rumors than information, and passing more information than balls, romping up and down the playing field without placing a single goal. Afterward we said good-bye trying not to show our despair, above all asking each other about Jerónimo that early September spring. Jerónimo, who had not come to give final instructions. Enrique took over. We all slipped away. To neighbors and relatives we announced our complete disenchantment with

Allende and the previous regime and our desire to collaborate in the task of national reconstruction. The regional command had changed from top to bottom and everyone would be advised of his new job by the chain of contacts. In a final aside, Enrique told me: "In case something happened to Jerónimo, I'm your contact. Me and nobody else," and he made a date with me at a bus stop for the next Monday.

The rest of them ceased to exist.

So I had run into Elías along the street without even blinking an eye. Not even the smallest sign of recognition should appear on our faces. As if we'd been making love with an amnesiac. It was that coldness that was so painful and it was also that same coldness that said they were doing something, something they didn't want to admit. That silence was the only message, the only confession that we were still united underneath it all. That we still belonged to the same tribe. It was nonetheless impossible to snuff out that strange sense that we were growing apart, accumulating a backlog of too many things to tell each other, when the time came. How great that last, victorious meeting would be! That full theater. That packed boulevard. And suddenly to know, as if you were dealing with a dispatch from Alpha Centauri, that that moment would never materialize, because they'd taken you prisoner outside a movie theater or at the entrance to your house, and at the bus stop where you should have been there is no one, and we're glad we didn't talk with you; we're sad not to have said "See you soon," to have whispered, "Dear friend, see you never," even if it was just another squeeze of the hands. We're happy and sad to be still breathing.

David didn't want to admit it. Before it was too late, like the ringmaster in a circus that's been closed down and is giving one last show, without a single spectator, he was going to stop the calendar for one eternal instant, to return us to the past, to advance us twenty, thirty years, until the moment when once again we'd be able to freely reunite beneath our banners. David must've sensed, besides, that that future moment, in terms in which we imagined it, would never really take place, that time would take charge of absences, that even tonight there would already be empty seats, where the ones we hadn't been able to say good-bye to, whether as bachelors or as retirees, should have been sitting, that still others would become disheartened or change their minds, that David himself would be taking a leak and saying "Shit" in a Mexico City bar just as he might have done in Frankfurt or in Los Angeles or in Caracas, eight years later. That they would come to look for Gonzalo at dawn one day just as they had come for Jerónimo. Perhaps David knew it was tonight or never, this pretext or none.

And I knew if someone didn't muzzle David, didn't rein in his irresponsibility, they'd come for all of us that morning or the next, four men getting out of an unmarked car, then a soundproof basement and another name added to a list.

"I came to talk to you about something else," I told David.

"So, out with it. Overcome your fears," he said, adding in a histrionic whisper and looking out of the corner of his eye at the other customers in the bar: "At least we can overcome something someday!"

"Do you remember, David, the first time we spoke after the . . . takeover"—it was hard for me to pronounce that word, disguise the coup and the massacre that followed in the gift wrapping of that word. The noise in the bar was deafening and no one was paying the least attention to us, but I preferred to talk to David in private using the same vocabulary we had to use in public. You had to train yourself in the lie, to make it a habit, a matter of routine. It was the only way to survive.

"Sure, I remember."

He answered lackadaisically, absently. He was already seeing himself at the party, tossing dishes around, passing the succulent morsels that the Chinese chef Vladimir had prepared, inviting Carlitos to tell his latest jokes, exchanging crude, private jokes with Elías, betting Bernardo that he couldn't lift the bridegroom up on his benign butcher's shoulders.

"I told you we thought you should leave the country. Remember? That it was for the best."

"Sure, man. I remember. But we already discussed that. And I already told you no. I've already run away from too many places.

Me, my old lady, my grandparents. Nobody's going to push me out of here. Are you going to drag up the same old subject?"

"Yes," I told him. "I have something to say to you." He was hardly listening to what I was saying. He was saying good-bye to Elías, giving a final hug to Gonzalo, proposing a toast for the ones who had fallen by the wayside. "We've got to cut you off," I told him. "That's what I have to tell you. This time it's really serious."

The party drained, started to drain, from David's face.

"For this?" he asked. "Because of this business with Elías?"

"Of course not," I told him, impatient, too quickly. "This just confirms to me that we're doing the right thing. But the decision was made a week ago."

"A week ago? Enrique didn't say anything."

"What do you mean, Enrique? He doesn't have anything to do with this."

"Enrique's higher up than you. He had to know it."

I felt like pulling my hair out, in a gesture from the old silent films. David had no reason to know that. No reason to know anything, except that I was his contact. How had he found out, guessed, deduced, that Enrique . . . That's how it had been all those months. One day I went into David's study, and he had written everything down. All the ideas, instructions, the latest political information. He just couldn't get used to secrecy. I won't do it again, he'd told me then, when confronted with the evidence. It's just a question of learning. Which ended up really irritating me: his happy-go-lucky naive air, like that of an innocent who nothing's going to happen to, someone who's always going to be saved by the bell, as if luck were going to stick with us all our lives. Just like kids who promise not to do it the next time. Except this time there wasn't going to be a next time.

That was the terrible thing. At a time when you were already noticing that some people were withdrawing to their homes, were going abroad even though they were not being threatened, or were suddenly discovering new vocations, David was faithful to the cause. He was no traitor, and he certainly wasn't ineffective or cowardly.

Just plain useless. He was brilliant. And that was the word that both defined and buried him: brilliance, splendor, high noon in Technicolor and stereophonic sound. He had nothing to do with where we all were at this stage.

"The decision's irrevocable," I told him.

"They have to give me another chance," said David, still not taking me entirely seriously. "What did I do now?"

"What did you do? You really want to know?"

"Yeah. What did I do?"

"Shit. You told Paula. You told her what you were doing. That's all you did."

"But we can trust Paula."

"We can trust her more than we can you. But how do you know that? Huh?"

"I've known her for years, so how am I going to pretend now that she's just anybody? She or Gonzalo? Listen, you know I invited Gonzalo tonight too? He doesn't know Elías very well, but I thought . . ."

"When are you going to stop treating life like a game, David?" I interrupted him. "When are you going to start thinking about other people a little?"

It really hurt to say that to him, my voice severe and cutting. It had to have hurt me more than it did him.

"It's a problem of love," said David. Out of the blue. Absurdly. "If I loved the people more, I could change. The people would change me . . ."

He could call it whatever he wanted. I thought, and still think, that it had nothing to do with love. It was a matter of character. He had a basic need for the esteem of others. He fed on being able to amaze and to stupefy them. But the time for exhibitionism had ended. Maybe abroad there'd be room for that kind of extroversion, that lunatic niceness of his. It would do wonders for solidarity. In five or ten years it could be that there'd be a place for people like him here again. But for a good many years we were going to have to be camouflaged, mute, nonexistent, like insignificant ants. So nobody would know we were still active. Little by little, we'd stick our noses out. The ones who'd survived in public positions would begin showing their true colors, as we managed to drag a greater margin for maneuvering out of the dictatorship, to create a certain space for freedom. But none of that would be possible without years of going underground, years of caution, and, far from being heroic or spectacular, it would be a gray, frustrating, almost neutral advance. Someone who demanded to always be the center of attention, who could not exercise self-control, someone who would spill the beans that he was still "involved" in something mysterious whenever he was approached in a halfway friendly manner, whenever his self-love was even pricked, somebody like that was a danger to himself and to everybody else.

David had just recognized it. He had just wished that the people, or their love, would change him. But behind that anxiety was hidden a self-hatred that took me by surprise, as though he'd always considered his personality an obstacle and saw the coup as a chance to change himself, to finally become someone else: taciturn, reserved, introverted, trustworthy. He wanted to kill his old personality, to start over again, from scratch. In a word: to be reborn. That fantasy must not have lasted for long.

"I just wanted to get our friends together," said David.

"Tell me something, David. Do you think you can change?"

"I don't know . . . Of course I can. Sure I can change. If I . . . No, Felipe. The truth is I don't think I can. I am what I am. There's nothing wrong with that."

To top it all off, he was incapable of lying. You could tell it a mile away. You gave him a little smile and out poured what he really thought. The mess with Cecilia stemmed precisely from that chronic ineptitude when it came to deceiving her.

"It was a unanimous decision, David."

"Unanimous! Unanimous! Three guys who don't even know me get together and agree and now you call that unanimous! What gives them the right to decide on my life? Huh? What right?"

The thing was heating up. I tried to control my voice.

"We're not forcing you into anything, David. All we've done is cut you off. We recommend that you leave. Just a recommendation. That's all. What you do is your own business."

"Other guys," David goes on. "It's always somebody else deciding. Making the decisions. But I'm the one who pays. Did you know that? My kids, man. They're the ones who'll suffer the consequences."

"What the family wants," I answered calmly, "is precisely that nobody have to suffer the consequences. The family knows what it's doing."

"The family. The family. Three guys who send me off to rot overseas. I'd like to tell them exactly what I think of their reasoning."

"I'm one of the three," I told him. "So tell me what you think."

"I'm not going, man. That's what I think," said David. "My dad left Austria. And nobody else from my family, *my* family, is going to leave anyplace! Do you understand?"

He wouldn't stay. He knew it and I knew it. He needed to find an elegant and comfortable way of accepting it, before me and before himself. He wouldn't be able to stand the years of loneliness here inside, isolated, not able to make any contribution while the Fascists were destroying the country. Without the hand guiding him in the darkness, without the company of others in sniffing out the direction the wind would take, without people with whom to argue and to program and to advance, it'd be hard to keep on going. And David needed a structure in which to move. Without the Party, he'd be screwed.

"When?" David demanded suddenly.

"As soon as possible."

"I need time."

"Time for what?"

"Just time."

I suddenly asked myself if, with all my psychological analysis, I hadn't overlooked an even more important factor. Cecilia. Patricia. Time to decide. Time for that to be worked out, for him to find out if he wanted to separate from Cecilia for good. If Patricia was anything more than one of his momentary passions. Because if he left without having made a commitment, still tied to both of them—and David was perfectly capable of that kind of madness—both of them would follow him abroad, and that's where the shit would hit the fan. I wanted desperately to be far away when the explosion came. I couldn't, didn't want to, be there to take command of that ship. I wasn't about to assume the role of nursemaid.

"Time," I said to him. "What is it exactly that you want to do, David?"

The rage contained in his next words caught me by surprise.

"There was supposed to be a civil war, Felipe. Remember? We were ready for the armed forces to be divided. Remember? So what happened, Felipe? We were on the peaceful road to Socialism. That wasn't just some old mistake."

My lowered voice came out like the hiss of a snake: "This is neither the time nor the place to talk about that."

"So when is the time? Huh? Tell me when."

"Later." I tried to lower my voice even more, but it would've looked suspicious. I leaned across the table, as if I'd been drinking too much and was trying to get my balance and was looking for support. "The first thing is to regroup. To salvage what can be salvaged."

"Later, when?"

And David was really asking me about his return, how long he'd be abroad. That's what he was asking.

"I'm no prophet," I told him. "But this can't last long."

"You were all wrong before," said David. "You were wrong about the big things. So why should you be right now about little things? About me for instance."

"And how do you expect us to get rid of these sons of bitches, if everybody does his own thing?" I asked him.

"I'm not going to leave." He was talking too loud. "There's no reason for me to leave. No reason at all."

I stood up brusquely. What more could I say? So stay? Stay with Cecilia and Patricia? Go ahead and screw us? Just what could I say to him?

"I've got to take a leak," I said to him.

"Just tell me one thing," said David. "Do you think it's fair for them to punish me for putting this party together? We need to breathe a little, to have a little fun. What's the harm in getting together for dinner? What's the harm?"

"No harm till it happens."

"You've always got an answer. Right, Felipe? Always."

"Not always. So let me take a leak, man. Let go of my arm."

He let me go.

I heard him following me. The smell of disinfectant, that sinister dampness, the yellow light; we could've been in Mexico City eight years later. We still didn't know that mirror existed, that it was waiting for us eight years down the road.

I let the stream flow with relief.

"They're going to screw me, Felipe. So you're going to screw me?"

I didn't say anything.

"I'll never get back, Felipe. Do you understand, man? I'll leave and I'll never get back. I'll die out there."

I buttoned my fly. I moved away so he could occupy the space in front of the urinal, as if we had to make confession one by one.

"How about if I think about it, Felipe? If I give you my answer next time?"

"There's no next time, David. It's decided. Ratified by the people upstairs. I won't be seeing you again."

He just stood there, not moving, not even a gesture.

"Why, Felipe? Just explain it to me. That's all."

I looked at him and used my last argument. The only one he wouldn't be able to answer.

"Do you want them to pick me up, man? Do you want them to kill me? Is that what you want?"

His zipper had stuck. He tried to unfasten it with a wild, sudden movement.

"Shit!" said David, like an echo of his own voice eight years later. "God damn it!"

He raised his eyes to mine, watching him from the mirror.

"Let's go, man," I said to him, then, in Santiago, Chile. "Let's go finish those beers."

Not knowing that in Mexico City, in that miserable bar, he'd be telling me, while he finally released that stream of honey-colored piss:

"Pepe Jérez," says David. "Right. I gave him an interview. Did you know that? Did you know I gave him an interview?"

INSIDE

We would never have known it. If the blind woman hadn't come to see Pamela the next day. If she hadn't kept her promise, we'd never have known what happened to Grandfather in jail the night before he finally met with the Caballero.

"Who sent you?" the one who'd be our grandmother asked her without turning on the hall light. That is, the one who'd be our grandmother provided she could find out the whereabouts of the son of Manuel Sendero and rescue him just in the nick of time. She asked her in spite of the fact that the woman came preceded by the suspicious scent of a little Sendero, by a suspicious senderious sweat, in spite of the fact that she came with a Sendero-style celestial massage that Pamela had believed was reserved for her own muscles and hers alone.

"He did," said the blind woman, as if there were no other "he" in the universe.

Pamela opened the door a little wider and saw that, besides the fluttering erotic atmosphere which the son of Manuel Sendero had spread over her body, nothing and no one accompanied the woman. She'd heard the stumbling, zigzagging footsteps of someone unknown and unknowing on the staircase, and they were so lonely she'd thought maybe it was a drunk. Then that puff of his love reached her, our grandfather's presence in the alien sky of the other woman, his innocent lips that had explored her female back, amen, and she didn't want her to come in. She thought about slamming the door and leaving her there—as if it would matter to a blind woman—in the same darkness in which they had carried out their infidelity.

"How do I know that's true?" demanded Pamela, trying to repeat to herself her credo that we're all free, that everybody can do what he wants with his own body.

"Proof. Proof," the blind woman answered. And to Pamela it seemed like an imitation of Grandfather's impatience. "You always ask for proof. He warned me. She'll require proof, he said. As if I really wanted to deliver this message. But I came prepared. Don't worry."

Pamela tried to think of some proof she could've given if someone had asked for it. A photograph. A lock of hair. A birth certificate. A description maybe. And she couldn't come up with a single one. The pleasures of this life, kids, last about as long as it takes a tree to fall, and Grandfather had passed through her life like a comet on a screen, without leaving so much as a trace.

"I need evidence," said Pamela roughly. "That's the way we are."

"The two statues," the blind woman said then, tired and indifferent. "Do you remember that story? You weren't told the end, right? He got up from the café table and promised you that some other time. Someday. Well, I'm going to finish it. The story, I mean. So you'll believe me."

"He told you the end?" asked Pamela, envious.

"He didn't need to," the blind woman said, making her even more envious. "I was the one who told it to him in the first place. A long time ago, according to him. That couple, you remember, well, there'll come a time when their fingers will touch. That's what he told me to tell you. Every time a word crosses the bridge. Every time two people tell each other the uncensored truth. Those fingers get imperceptibly closer. They're always an abyss, a millimeter, from touching, but it'll be enough if the whole country'll communicate the way those two lovers learned to do it. That'll be enough for one hand to entwine with the other. On that day all the persecution will come to an end and they'll be moved to a lovers' park. OK?"

She'd recited that ending in a monotone, as if she were bored or were being forced to take medicine.

"A happy ending," said Pamela. "He promised me the ending would be happy."

"If that's the way you want to interpret it."

"I do want to," said Pamela. "Where is he? Have you . . . ? Do you know where he is?"

Instead of speaking to her the way a woman speaks to her rival, the blind woman used the kind of indifferent tone a legitimate wife uses with her mother-in-law, the day after the wedding.

"I know everything," she answered. "Are you going to ask me in? Or would you rather that I give you the message out here in the hall?"

The blind woman was putting on airs, because she knew less than she implied. Although she would have believed the son of Manuel Sendero if he had told her he was God Himself, if he had whispered in her ear that he was her own father, or that he was she herself. Anything at all. But Grandfather only told her what was absolutely indispensable.

The blind woman knew, for example, because the sergeant had told her with great detail, that when they'd put the son of Manuel Sendero into the police van, he'd been surprised to see another prisoner there. "Welcome. Welcome one and all," said a voice in the darkness and a hand took his and moved it up and down in the sweet motion of a pump, up and down, just as at that same instant years before Manuel Sendero had pedaled his elevator. "Why'd they pick you up?" But what was going on in Grandfather's head the blind woman could never have guessed, even if she'd applied all her prophetic gifts to the task. Grandfather noted the familiarity of that voice, the warmth of that familiarity, but it was hard for him to trace it back to its origin. It was as if something was missing from that man to make him complete, as if he needed something added or some appendix to be complete, fulfilled, total. At some time, part of that voice had grazed his pilgrimage on the road toward life. Maybe they'd even been accomplices, but Grandfather couldn't remember when. He had the momentary anguish of thinking his fetal memories might be escaping him. Maybe he'd been contaminated by the television cameras that had crushed his brain and his double heart, and, in order not to end up wandering directionless, just like any adult, he closed his eyes the way he would do so many times in subsequent hours, in order to return himself to the powers of the imaginary, to a real darkness within the artificial darkness of that van. Nevertheless, the anesthetic of forgetfulness wasn't cleared away until much later, when they got out in the police station and another voice fell upon him like a serpent and then he was to repent, for the first time in his existence, of not being an amnesiac like everybody else born on earth.

"They aren't going to keep me here for long," the other prisoner went on. He banged on the metal grill that separated them from the driver's seat. "Hey, did you tell my family? Did you tell them?"

One of the policemen turned around and smiled.

"Calm down. You'll get out soon enough. It's a good thing we grabbed you before you got into that show, right?"

The prisoner ignored him.

"The next time I'll get in," he confided to Grandfather. "Even if it's disguised as a military officer. I'm going to win the 'Search, Search' . . . What about you? What happened? Did they steal your prize too?"

The blind woman well knew the one they called crazy. He came in and went out of jail the way some people go to the market to buy eggs. He was a man pursued not by an evil star, but by a rotten one. Everything he touched turned into a disaster. He had started lots of careers without ever finishing one of them. Nevertheless, among his defects was not to be found a poor memory, and through the years he accumulated an encyclopedic knowledge. Which only helped him the day he decided to go on a television quiz show, where week after week he collected correct answers and the corresponding money, until he was on the point of breaking the all-time record and could aspire to the grand prize, which was a lifetime pension. The night before, however, the blind woman explained to the son of Manuel Sendero, his unlucky star ended up overtaking him. His brother called him to give him the tremendous news. The show's emcee had been arrested for fraud. In an exclusive and sensational interview a previous contestant, long ago defeated, made the accusation: the emcee gave him the questions beforehand, in exchange for getting a slice of the winnings later. The accused admitted to the judge that it was true. He wasn't helped by the argument, which is always a tearjerker, that those infrequent practices were meant to pay for an operation needed by his paralyzed wife. And, in the middle of the scandal, it didn't help the current champion and also the current prisonmate of the son of Manuel Sendero to insist upon his absolute innocence. The justifiable though unjust suspicion fell upon him that he too was involved in the little game, and, if not, how had he known the name of an Australian worm that lives in the toenails of kangaroos? How had he been able to recite from memory the final verses of the Upanishads in Sanskrit? Was it really possible to know every one of Brenda Lee's songs down to the last note? Then, not only suspicion but the hand of the law fell upon him and his brother had to rescue him for the first but not the last time, because the next day he was released from jail completely transformed by that night's insomnia and now determined to prosper in delinquency.

"Life's a lottery," the ex-contestant proclaimed, according to the blind woman. "All you have to do is win once and then retire."

He sold tickets for the first trip to the stars. He sent a group of emigrants to a municipality in Sweden where supposedly jobs, medical attention, and little wooden houses awaited them. He promised a group of North American tourists, advanced in age, that a method existed in this country to become young again or even to conceive children. He got funds to investigate a telephone that would speak directly with fetuses before they were born, so their parents could have everything arranged to order for them.

"He offered that to me there in the police van," said the son of Manuel Sendero to the blind woman. "Can you imagine that! To me!"

He also dedicated himself to crimes of lesser degree, stealing merchandise like crazy, trying on eight shirts and walking out of the store with all of them on, offering to break windows just to collect the insurance, disguising himself as a little old lady to collect, his false ID in hand, the pension of a general who was killed in the wars of the last century. His brother saved him with equal zeal, paying the fines, convincing litigants not to press charges or prosecuting attorneys to mitigate sentences, to the point of hiring a corps of lawyers and detectives to protect him. Because his brother was as much a success in life as he was a disaster, and, having made a brilliant career in social security, banking, insurance, and mortgages, he always refused to accept the obvious solution of committing his mother's other son to an asylum where he could have won all the contests and could have amazed all the patients and nurses; rather he seemed to have to compensate the black sheep of the family for the fact that Dame Fortune had showered all the luck upon him, leaving nothing for the other one who had shared the better part of nine months in his mama's internal savings and loan.

"I'm not going to lock him up," he would say. "I'm never going to let them lock him up again."

It didn't matter that his brother made fun of him, saying that they both practiced the same profession. Only that he makes the laws first, the ex-contestant laughed, talking with the blind woman, and then he earns the money, while I don't wait to have the law in my favor. Can you imagine? He gets money for forty years from poor, unfortunate people, millions of them, people who are young and could enjoy it when they start giving it to him and by the time they finish giving it are old and worn out, and all that for him to offer them a miserable pension or some hypothetical medical assistance later on—and we'll see if he really does keep his promise. And he has the whole world calculating whether it's a good idea for them or not. Just minor participants, very minor ones, in a business where the only real winner is him.

The other one didn't care.

"I'm not going to let them lock him up," he said. "Not ever again."

The son of Manuel Sendero knew why. He'd known it before the blind woman explained all the details of that asymmetrical tale. He'd known it when they'd hardly gotten out of the van at police headquarters and there waiting for them, like a garden without trees or flowers, was the brother of the man they were holding prisoner along with him. There waiting for them like a landless garden was the complement, the other side of the coin and of the personality. There waiting for them was the other twin, like a garden surrounded by an iron fence. And then Grandfather had to accept, with a sadness almost as immeasurable as the one he'd felt the day they departed from paradise, expelled by the angel of their mother's vagina, that he had finally found his beloved twins.

That's how much life can corrupt us, kids, Grandfather told us. So much that you can't even recognize your best friends. My one and only two-voiced lieutenant, my joint chiefs of staff, my committee of joy and liaison. I heard the voice, kids, and can you imagine that for just an instant I confused it with the Caballero's?

"My company," said that voice from inside headquarters, "is financing this program, Sergeant. So release my brother right away. Tonight. We'll drop the charges against him. Is there a fine? We'll pay it. Bail? Simón, pay the bail."

It wasn't the Caballero. Experience was lacking in that voice, and some affection was still there. He still loved someone else in that funereal universe. He still loved his womb companion.

"Sir, your brother," said another voice that must have belonged to a policeman, "was selling seats for the program 'Search, Search.' He personally guaranteed 333 people that he was going to get them in and, on top of that, he told them that they'd all be rewarded, that they'd be chosen to search and to find. Later, not content with abandoning all those people, who had started a riot in the street, he even tried to use a counterfeit ticket and to bribe one of the guards to . . ."

At that moment Grandfather and the arrested twin came in, and the owner of that voice that still wasn't the Caballero's turned around, as if he'd been stabbed in the back.

The one he looked at was the son of Manuel Sendero, stared at him from the vacant lot of his eyes, out of those swindler's eyes of his that looked as if they'd never bid farewell to a mother or to a granddaughter.

"That man," he said. "What's that man doing with my brother? Sergeant, that's the man who interrupted the program. What's he doing with my brother?"

The son of Manuel Sendero said nothing. He stood contemplating him as if they were still planning the first rebellion, dreaming up the conditions of the second and final rebellion, whispering to each other that the dead would come to our rescue this time.

"Don't be angry with him, brother," said the contestant and star-crossed twin. "He didn't do anything I wouldn't have done."

"You stay out of it," the other one told him, although his words were harsher than his face, which, for an instant, seemed to soften. Grandfather remembered the way one of the brothers had tried to calm the other's fears, telling him the world really wasn't so scary, that he'd take care of him. I'll take care of you; we can go out. "This one," and now his face corresponded to the machete of his voice. "We want to make an example of this one. Fifteen years of clean, reasonable programs and along comes this . . . this clown, and spoils our reputation."

"That it should end like this," said the son of Manuel Sendero. "That you should end up like this."

He made a gesture toward his jail companion, as if to come to his aid, like a mother hen.

"Don't you touch my brother," said the banker-twin. "Don't you dare touch him. That's how you people contaminate other people; you infect them. Somebody like you probably filled his head with all these weird ideas. I warn you, Sergeant, we're going to be very upset, if this man touches my brother."

One of the policemen separated them, lightly pushing Grandfather toward the sergeant's desk.

"What's your name?"

Grandfather had no name. He'd had no baptism, religious or pagan. Nobody had received him with a couple of syllables so he'd know when to answer, when to obey commands, or when to declare himself guilty.

"Your name and address?"

He didn't intend to be rude, but the anguish that was gnawing away at him after observing the twins for the first time in his existence with the eyes of his body, his heart couldn't contain so much anguish, let alone his tongue. For decades he'd blamed the Caballero for everything that was happening, systematically tracing all the evils of the universe back to that extraordinary coldness. But it was impossible for the Caballero to be responsible for the path his friends had taken. He didn't want to do it. He really didn't. But for a moment he was forced to ask himself if the system wasn't unbeatable after all. If he wasn't witnessing here the conclusive proof of its efficiency, since these two had ended up, one of them a businessman, the other a delinquent, adapting to the world just the way they'd found it. Both of them were convinced that the very society they'd sworn to destroy from the placenta could now bring them happiness, success, satisfaction. Contemplating this sad fact was so painful for the son of Manuel Sendero that, when the idea finally died of itself, he even felt a passing joy. But it would've been better if it hadn't died, because another even more painful and almost opposite idea replaced it. It wouldn't be enough to kill the Caballero. He'd have to kill the twin and his brother, and after that, who knows who else, who knows how many bullies would still lie in his path. Eduardo had said that they had to abolish capital punishment, because once you started it, it was impossible for that kind of process of justice to have any limits. Where was the dividing line? And he, they, the ones who had dreamed of one day abolishing not only the death penalty but also death itself . . .

"For the last time, sir. What's your name and address?"

"Tell him," said the son of Manuel Sendero to the twin who was now a banker and who once had operated a love bank, a bank full of emotions, hanging like garlands, where the only thing lent out was hope. "Tell your brother he's not going to get rich that way."

The other one spoke directly to the sergeant. It was as if by ignoring Grandfather he could return him to the common grave from which he had escaped.

"This man," he said, "clearly intends to attack me, Sergeant. You're a witness."

"Do you want him to get better?" asked the son of Manuel Sendero. But what he was really looking for was to get better himself. He was asking for medicine for himself, using the only bond that still tied him to that stranger, his love for his brother, the fact that he'd agreed to be both mother and father to his brother. "Don't you want that? Didn't you swear to take care of him? Didn't you convince him you should both go out? Didn't you tell me dreams cost a lot, but you'd be waiting for me with the price and the payment, you'd protect our dreams? There's still time. Don't feed him any more lies. Go on and tell him. Tell him the system doesn't work for him. Tell him maybe it works for you and for a few others. But for the majority it just doesn't work. Go ahead and tell him."

But what he was trying to do was to save the second and final rebellion, trying not to admit his own defeat. But even if they won, if the Caballero accepted the three irreversible and irreverent conditions, how many fetuses would end up following the bubbling path of the twins once they were born? If he went back to the scattered Council of the Unborn right now, how could he really trust all their promises? How could he pick out the traitors among them?

Don't be too hard on Grandfather. He was very young and he was an extremist, and we young people tend to see every obstacle on the runway as another proof that we're never going to fly. Night falls once and we think the sun's gone forever. On the other hand, if he'd seen Pamela right then, with a little glimpse of eternity in her belly, if he'd seen Pamela, who, without being able to describe him or even to stammer out his name, had searched all night in police station after police station, undoubtedly Grandfather would have declared that humanity is a festival and always will be and that we're invincible.

"Do you know where he is?" Pamela asked again.

"He's made a date with you. Today at sunset in the place he told you."

"Today at sunset in the place he told me." Besides being loyal, our Pamela is obedient.

"But you aren't statues," added the blind woman on her own. "You're not going to touch. Believe me!"

"Touch isn't the word," said Pamela, thinking about what she'd do to him and he to her.

"Touch," said the blind woman bitterly, "is the only word."

Pamela wasn't prepared to reveal to her rival all the intimate details that would have belied that affirmation. "Is he in danger?" she asked. "Do you think he's in danger?"

"I asked him," said the blind woman. "He was going to see an old enemy, one he calls the Caballero. I don't know if you know it, but it's not the first time they're meeting. I asked him. The other time. About how it had gone the other time."

"And how did he answer?"

"He wouldn't tell me," said the blind woman. "I'm going to tell you a story. That'll be better, he said. One you don't know. One they told me after you'd already left, he said. About the human mannequins in the Grand Department Store, he told me. About how hard it is to be born, but also how hard it is to die. About an apple, he told me."

"He wouldn't tell me either," said Pamela, all of a sudden feeling like an old woman facing another old woman, knitting in front of a fireplace. "I asked him, but he wouldn't answer."

"If she doubts that I'll come," their little Sendero had said to the blind woman, "cheer her up with that story. Tell her the Devil himself couldn't keep me away."

But the son of Manuel Sendero had said that the way a child sings in the dark to keep his mind off his own fear until his parents arrive. I'd always thought, kids, that death is something that exists the night before your mother's born. Try to go back to that night. Try it. Then you'll know what death is like. I had said that. But that's not what death is. Death was in front of me. And I searched those wolf-eyes to see if I sensed the least hesitation, the ashes of a loyalty that might be able to revive me. Nothing. The other one looked through me as if he were weighing a piece of meat before selling it. If they'd kept on that way, staring at each other as if across a corpse, Grandfather would've had no other alternative but to wipe him out right then and there. He could've found no other means of turning those merchant-eyes off.

To avoid it, to never have to speak to him again, to put a no-return situation between them, so that the other one would knowingly betray him with the fallen seraph of his own tongue, Grandfather finally answered the sergeant.

"I won't talk," said the son of Manuel Sendero, loudly, as though taunting him, so the twin would hear, so he could repeat every syllable in someone else's presence, "to anybody but the Caballero."

According to the blind woman, the sergeant had scratched his head, had considered the possibility of resorting to one of his superiors, but had decided to go on with the interrogation.

"Who is this Caballero you're so interested in?"

"I don't know his real name. But I can describe his voice."

"So you don't know his name. But you can describe his voice. That's lucky. So what's his voice like?"

"It sounds like a refrigerator running."

Pamela should've burst in at that moment, just to be near her man. She would've explained to the sergeant that this child's, excuse me, this man's mental faculties were a bit unbalanced. So they should release him into her custody at once.

"That's what I would've done," Pamela told the blind woman. "I'd have defended him."

"A shame," said the blind woman. "You weren't there."

"And if I should bump into this Caballero," asked the sergeant, winking a benevolent eye at the policeman, at the twins, and at a drunk who staggered as he waited his turn, "what should I tell him?"

The voice of the banker-twin wasn't like a refrigerator, but it soon would be. "Sergeant, either this fellow's acting crazy just to get out of all this or he really is off his rocker. In either case there's no competent authority to determine how dangerous he is at the moment. He seems to have turned on me. I'm begging you to take care of my brother's problem first, so I can leave."

"Off my rocker?" asked Grandfather, turning his back on him. "My rocker?"

And he started to recite women's names: Abeliuk, María; Aguilar, Gloria; Aranda, Sylvia Gertrude. He went on like that for a good while, just with the first letter of the alphabet, as though he were reading a list from a directory.

"Well, what's this all about?" the sergeant burst out. "What new kind of craziness is this, for God's sake? How much longer are you going to make a mockery of authority and of the law?"

Brusquely, the son of Manuel Sendero interrupted his litany.

"Do you know what all these women have in common, Sergeant?" he asked him. "Do you know what it is? All of them have been expecting babies for ten months or more. In spite of induced labor . . .

Every one of them. Do you want to hear the Bs and the Cs and the Ds?"

For an instant a profound silence reigned in the headquarters, as if even the drunks in their cells had realized that something extraordinary was happening.

"My daughter," said the sergeant, "my youngest daughter has been expecting a child, our first grandchild, for almost eleven months."

"What letter?" asked the son of Manuel Sendero.

"González," said the sergeant. "G."

"There are four Gonzálezes," said the son of Manuel Sendero. "It's a popular name. Carola, Guillermina, Petronila, Rosa."

"Rosa," said the sergeant. "Rosa González. That's my daughter."

"Rosita," said Grandfather, as if they were bosom friends. "If you find the Caballero, Sergeant, tell him an old acquaintance of his is around here. Tell him I've come to negotiate the conditions."

What wasn't to be negotiated, on the other hand, was a modification in the sergeant's attitude.

"This Caballero," he said obsequiously, "the truth is I don't know who he could be, sir. But if I do find him, I'm at your service."

"He'll find me on his own soon enough," said the son of Manuel Sendero, and he said it because it was true. Because he knew the twin had recorded every sentence on his brain's magnetic tape. He knew the twin had all the information on the whereabouts of someone who corresponded to that description, that he'd wait for them to free his brother and then he'd go home. He'd dial a telephone number; at the other end another voice, temperature absolute zero, would answer.

"It's not the first time it's happened to us, sir," said the sergeant. "I'd like to ask you something. Do you think the child'll be born defective?"

"Why should it be born defective?" asked the prisoner, now speaking as one grandfather to another.

"Because another daughter we had," said the sergeant, and the son of Manuel Sendero didn't pay much attention because once again he realized he had underestimated the adversary. The twin was in too big a hurry to wait for his brother. Faced with the dilemma of choosing between the Caballero who was his future and his maternal companion who, in spite of himself, connected him to the past, he was leaving, striding firmly toward the door, going to inform his own self, that entity he would be in thirty years' time, when we, the grandchildren, would exist, to be trained and tempted by him, going to meet the Caballero, his father, his real or adoptive father. "Our other daughter was late," the sergeant went on. "She was late, you know, and she was born blind."

It's strange, kids. His former friends were always turning up around Grandfather. Companions of long ago. Rivals like Eduardo. And he was the one who recognized them, gave them a genealogy and a prebirth lineage. With the blind woman it was the opposite. He didn't realize who she was; didn't even suspect it. She was the one who felt—when her father came home to dinner very upset that night—the presence of a cataclysm in her existence, the certainty that that prisoner who possessed the secrets of life and of death was someone she'd been waiting for since time immemorial, someone who finally, even though he had sight, didn't describe people by the features of their faces but rather by the evil in their voices, someone who didn't need people's names to make his way through the world. It wasn't hard for her to convince her father to open the cell of the son of Manuel Sendero, under the pretext of getting information from him that might rescue the child who was kicking around inside her younger sister Rosa from the fate of plundered eyes and too fertile an imagination, which, according to the sergeant, who, like all intelligent men, was superstitious, would befall any sprout who burst untimely into this world. Because that's the way it had been with his firstborn. She compensated for the curse of not being able to see by the barely tolerable blessing of being able to recount and to remember dimensions that others neither knew of nor saw. Ever since she was little she had run around her father's jail, handing out to the prisoners delirious stories whose prenatal provenance she would only discover that night when Grandfather paid homage to a vagina with nothing blind about it, and led her to understand that all of them, bodies, stories, words, came from the same place, that one and this one, all from the same act. Because the blind woman had paid with her loneliness more than with her twisted optic nerve—and also with her body's barrenness—for the fact that she hadn't been able to completely forget the months of the first rebellion. Such was the no-man's-land into which she had stumbled. The memories were so meager and so intermittent she didn't identify their origin, and they didn't help her to orient herself in the darkness either. But, like a patchwork dream that we can't shake off during our waking hours, they were persistent enough to make her miserable and to keep her from fitting into everyday life.

Those hours with the son of Manuel Sendero were going to save her, because just as he had opened up the present between her thighs, he was also opening up the floodgates of her memory. She'd spend the rest of her life wandering through hospitals and schools, not to mention prisons, searching from street to street for the vestiges of her memories, restoring to people the words that birth and their parents had made them forget. But nothing in this life, as the twin or the Caballero would say, is free. Not even love.

Grandfather—Was he growing up? Turning into a consummate manipulator?—would insist that she deliver a message to Pamela, and that later she go to speak with Eduardo, knowing that she'd keep her promise, because her word was all she had as a legacy. The business with Pamela would be long and painful. He was sorry, but that was the deal. With Eduardo, on the other hand, it ought to be different, and it wouldn't take long. Just a ten-word sentence, first telling him where he'd find Pamela and then the ten words.

"Why Eduardo?" asked the blind woman; with her tentacular eighth sense she mus[illegible] uessed from Grandfather's recalcitrant attitude that Eduardo wasn't, after all, the person he most loved or admired.

No one could say that our grandfather was one of those people who leave their childhood behind them easily. Maybe in all his existence the words he now had to murmur to the blind woman were the only ones that could be brandished as proof that that was the case, that, in fact, he had learned something during his brief span in the land of his ancestors.

"Eduardo," said the son of Manuel Sendero, "because there's nobody else that can do it."

She could've refused to be his messenger. Because he needed her anyway. He could not have survived that night without the tenderness of someone with half a memory at her disposal. But that's the way women are, kids. She didn't ask for anything and she gave him everything; she was his shower. Just as others bathe to get rid of the day's grime, he tried to wash away the worst memories of that day, to blot out the twin who had been his disciple and who had just now measured him like a bank account or an IOU. He tried to extract him like extracting a child from a dead, pregnant mother who doesn't want to let him be born.

He had asked them to turn off the light in his cell so the darkness would distract him from recent memories and he'd have the impression he was still living, and they along with him, in that nook where stories passed from mouth to mouth, the expanded and twisted stories those same twins had joined in, or ones that had been filled in by the blind girl, the twins exhibiting those voices as proof they were not alone, that we'd rise again, the four survivors, listening to whispers from the basement of the building, or from the land of the invaded dead, the voices that, had they arrived, would've once again made the son of Manuel Sendero's wait bearable so many years later.

But the time of crystal, of sweetness, was over. It was almost impossible for those voices to filter into his cell. Years before, they'd barely been able to reach the elevator. We'd warned him when he was camping out in the neighboring country, and when the blind woman repeated it to him in a voice from the past, when she came close to lodge a whisper in his ear, he tried to believe it wasn't true, that his grandchildren and his dead were answering his first confidential report just as they had answered his grief when the Caballero came with the cart to carry Doralisa away.

It's hard to get this far, the blind woman told him. They make you forget everything. Before being born, after dying, before and after dreaming. They put you on your knees at the border of death or of birth for hours. Just to hold on to a word you have to stick it inside your sex like a leech; you hide it like a mollusk in the warm and stirring water while they sink the bayonet into you. You go to customs and then the worst begins: you have to be searched, to hand in your old ID. That is the border where those who are about to be conceived meet those who are already dead, where their identity is taken away from them systematically, our faces and our names shuffled and melted, changing them around until nobody knows anymore who they are, who they were.

The son of Manuel Sendero hadn't gone through that experience, said the blind woman, as she, the twins, and everyone who was going to die or to be born had done. But he remembered the replica of her voice twenty years earlier, the twins about to leave thirty years earlier, the other voices, recounting what that cancerous itinerary was like. For an instant, he didn't know where he was, whether perhaps he was caught in the stalled time of the first and failed rebellion, whether he was squirming in Doralisa's womb, waiting for the Caballero to tell his father, it's time now, Manuel, let's go to the Laboratory, or if this was the prison cell with the blind woman who was still not offering him the nakedness of her body because first she would offer him the more elemental nakedness of her memory.

They deported them, remember, said the blind woman. They subdivided them, scattering them in basements, on islands, like light bulbs of constantly diminishing voltage, blinking on and off whenever anybody touches a switch, until each one of us wandered off inside a new name and with unknown parents and with memories ascribed to us that we did not recognize, and only then can you be born or can you transit toward definitive death. The trip there, the trip back, going toward oblivion, coming from it, what difference does it make? Twice, said the blind woman, we have to go through it twice. So your original name gets erased. You don't join anybody. It's impossible. Who do you look for? What bond? After that, said the blind woman, said the invalids in the next elevator or in Doralisa's daydreams, no one ever finds anybody.

Manuel Sendero wondered if those voices could be telling the truth. He managed to ask himself if Doralisa, sleeping so far away and yet so nearby, had not kept his real name there inside her, the name with which they'd met, the one with which she'd called him when they crossed their first threshold of fire together. Was he still live inside her? The Manuel who insisted we couldn't lose because we were too beautiful? Manuel the whirlwind, who insisted that each child who was saved from poverty, each illiterate peasant who learned how to spell "This land is my land" was giving insomnia to the Devil? Or was that Manuel gone forever and only this Manuel existed, curled up like a ball of yarn, his matches wet, a footnote, a yellow card, a piece of statistical data? Only this Manuel who was illegal in the country that had seen him born, while the legs that had warmed his heart dancing and heartening the dances of so many lovers until they threatened to awaken the very dead, those legs were now pedaling a dirty coffin between floors? Our solitary, wounded sentry, our Manuel Sendero.

Because there was no refuge in that womb, just as there was none in the past. Manuel Sendero searched for himself. Believe me, kids, he really searched. And if he could have found himself . . . But that's not the way it was. He must have known, as his son did in that jail cell slowly mounting the blind woman some twenty years later so she would keep him company through the night, they, father and son, must have realized that memories are never enough to find yourself. Even if the child landed with some. Even if he came to the surface bringing them with him out of Doralisa's Pacific Ocean. Even if the blind woman had been able to repeat the songs of death and of birth one by one. Even then it wouldn't be enough.

He was going to have to grow up in the school of hard knocks. Even if it takes you a thousand years, Manuel Sendero, you're going to have to grow up.

But no one, not even our father of miracles, Manuel Sendero, has a thousand years in which to grow up. Decisions have to be made when it's convenient for others and never when it's convenient for ourselves. We have to grow up, while the floor is moving under us, while the apple tree still doesn't dare send out its blossoms. We have to do it from an elevator that seems only to go down, to go down. We have to do it with the hope that something, perhaps the building where the elevator is located, is going up, but you can never be sure. We can never really know until later, when it's already too late, whether we've made a mistake, whether you've made a mistake, Manuel Sendero. And Doralisa couldn't tell you, because she was becoming more and more unreal, like a never-shifting floor which the same elevator always passes by without ever stopping, and the child couldn't tell him, because he was becoming more and more distant, just as he would disappear from Pamela's view in front of that same building now without statues and without a square, just as his image would fade out on Pamela's television screen, just as he would become blurred for Pamela in the blind woman's words and legends.

Because at that moment a frigid figure was advancing along the street, crossing the square of the two statues that would never touch, bringing in his hand a proposition that Papa could no longer avoid.

Manuel Sendero would have to grow up in one moment, in an hour, in a day, more than he had grown in all the rest of his life.

Some decisions, I whispered to Papa, are forever. Be careful, the blind woman told Pamela, forever. While my father, Manuel Sendero, tried to believe that an angel was passing through that territory of his. An angel? Or a demon?

The Caballero entered the elevator.

He came to take away his last possessions, his only defense. He came to take away his silence.

"I tell you, my breezy Manuel," that glacial voice advised him, "maybe I can get you another job. Because we're about to go into the silence-packaging business. Yes, indeed. We think we can put it in boxes and export it. Genuine silence. Homemade. What you find at the bottom of the ocean or up on the plateau—no use at all, any old microbe can break it. But human silence, the really pampered kind, that forms a protective layer around the customer's ears, really soothing the nerves. It's a silent presence, not an absence. If you only knew all the industrial, military, and medical uses for that, Manuel. Professors, strict parents, traditional churches, manufacturers of nuclear arms. Even the hippies want a little salt of silence for their transcendental meditations. Of course it was easier before, when people were not so rebellious, when they were calmer. And it's true it is a business that can be sabotaged. One little kid's shout, a mischievous peal of laughter, one love poem, and the whole shipment's ruined and has to be thrown out. We've already caught them telling jokes, grumbling about the rising cost of bread, ruminating poetry, just about anything to impede the production of silence and to undermine the national economy. There really are vile people in this world of ours. But we have enough deposits to last for years, and we'll keep on advancing. I can't promise you anything. But you were a pioneer in the whole endeavor, and even though it's not at all certain you'll get either a percentage of the profits or an award, you'd certainly occupy an important place in this productive process, because the air of a mute is doubly soothing, even more than the air of a whisper, the air of a cold, the air of a sleeping person. Yes, the air of a mute with no physical cause, the air of purest defeat. We'll use it for official funerals. For soldiers suffering from insomnia. For a campaign urging respect for superiors. Yes, Manuel, your silence is the best kind. Of course, your song's even more important, Manuel. Your silence will be even more valuable when you start to sing again."

When he started to sing.

The next day the Caballero came looking for Mama; he came looking for me, who was blowing for all I was worth in the opposite direction, so he couldn't carry me away. He invited Papa to go with him.

In the middle of the filthy, exterminating emptiness, I said nothing. It wasn't that I was already learning, so many years later, the limits that words and promises can have. I just kept quiet because I knew how to recognize, humbly, when two adults agree on an action, coming to it from different and even opposite directions. Yes. When two enemies agree, it's wise to stand aside.

Because Manuel and his persecutor had, in fact, reached the same conclusion: the pursuit was coming to an end. Now was the moment to settle that up-and-down destiny; now was the time to burn not only his bridges but even the rivers themselves.

"It's me," said those icy teeth. "So you can stop pedaling."

A woman came in.

"Fourteen," she said, smoothing her hair.

Manuel pedaled. I put in my share from my immobile tricycle there in Mama's belly. They waited for the woman to get off and then the Caballero spoke: "It's about time. I think you've reached the age of reason," and then, right after that: "We're going to take Doralisa away now, Manuel. It's time for you to sing. Would you be so kind as to come along with us?"

So, did Manuel Sendero sing, Grandfather? Is it really true?

Of course he sang. How many times have I told you that, you little doubting Thomases, you ruffians?

But we don't understand, Grandfather. It doesn't make sense. Things had gotten worse. Not even Esmeralda had been able to rescue him. Even the kid was fading out, wasn't such a live wire anymore. As if he were already anticipating the defeat of the second and final insurrection. As if he were realizing that the only allies he had left in the world were a blind woman who would act as messenger and a woman he would never seed or make a mother. Where did Manuel Sendero get the strength? How was it possible?

The son of Manuel Sendero never wanted to answer that question directly—it was his elliptical period, his period of mysterious orbits. Some ways of life, he said, disappear forever. Whole civilizations fade, leaving nothing behind them except some stones, a few drawings, and a couple of cooking utensils. When some bit of humanity, some tribe, knows it's going to disappear, knows it'll be conquered, knows nothing's going to be left, those are the moments. The valuable moments when something tries to stay behind. I knew it there in the darkness, caressing the blind woman, denying to her what I'd also denied to Pamela, the satisfaction of a child or of a torch. Papa knew it. He must have known it, like a third eye opening up in his throat, when they put Doralisa in the ambulance and put him in another car. And the others, the dead, the candidates for life, the little fragments of dreams, the survivors of cities whose names no one can pronounce, the illiterate on their islands since forever, the invalids in the other elevators, the insane, inside and outside of asylums, the exploited who are already dead when they're born, the farm workers who inhale pesticides, Pamela's parents, they all knew it too. How could they help but know it, when they had walked along those same corridors, the same ones Mama moved down, while I uselessly pushed against the wind, like a cat somebody has by the scruff of the neck, with nothing but air to push against; they'd heard the corridor swallow the footsteps of the suffering just the way Papa heard them before they took Doralisa into the operating room. They examined them one by one, like counterfeit bills. Papa and I and them and us, hoping that instead of a hospital it was a greenhouse, that it was a greenhouse instead of a basement. How could we ignore it? At some point in his existence everybody has to realize fully, to realize that in a few years, centuries, millennia, in some space of time, we'll cease to exist absolutely and that for that reason we don't really exist now either; right now doesn't exist either; we're all a lie between two equally false shores. I knew it when I saw the twins, when I understood that that world was so strong and all-devouring that it could overcome any of us, that if I'd been born right then instead of hanging on stubbornly in my mother's womb, it would have happened to me too. They'd have me filling out papers, asking for or granting bank loans. They'd have me appearing on or financing TV programs for the mentally defective. They'd have me saving money for a third car when there were families who hadn't had a first breakfast. They'd have me searching and searching without ever finding anything or anybody that was worth a plugged nickel.

Never leave anybody alone at those times, kids. Talk to him from out there, even if he can't hear you.

Because they didn't leave me, us, alone to confront that moment. I told the blind woman, before dawn, told that one who thought she'd heard all the stories: "I'm going to tell you one you don't know, one they told me when you went away; while you were going. I want you to tell it to Pamela the way they whispered it to me, so I wouldn't despair. The way they accompanied Papa, when the Caballero came to look for us."

Another story, Grandfather? Another one? We want to know what happened in the Laboratory. We want to know where Doralisa is.

What you did to the Caballero when your paths finally crossed. How you got this far. We want some action, Grandfather. We're tired of all these people who have no names, who have no memories, who have no country, who pass censors and borders and are shuffled like cards and whose shadows are captured and whose hands are cut off and who come out of basements into an underground land where it never rains and where nothing bears fruit. Why don't you tell us the end of the story once and for all, Grandfather? Why are you so afraid to remember the end?

You impatient little rascals! It's perfectly clear you have Eduardo's blood, Pamela's coltish blood, in your veins. Or that someday you will have.

But did those people really exist, Grandfather? Did they? Did they do some kind of work?

If they didn't exist, said the son of Manuel Sendero, you aren't going to exist either. Your own forefathers wouldn't exist nor will your descendants. You can't ever tell anybody's story without telling everybody's story, the story of all the rest.

No one ever finds anyone, the blind woman had told him, even the blind woman had told him that, when he asked her to go and talk to Pamela, to exchange ten words with Eduardo, to be his messenger for the last time, and she couldn't refuse him. No one ever finds anyone, but I'll go. Not anyone. Ever.

It's not true, Grandfather told the blind woman, and the blind woman told Pamela the next day, and Pamela told her own grandchildren years later. The long-dead whispered it to Grandfather so he could whisper it to his own dead if ever they needed that message: sometimes it is not true that no one ever finds anyone.

We looked for something to give him when he heard the smell of the ambulance stopping in front of the building, when they opened the doors of the ambulance and took out a stretcher for Doralisa. For your trip, Senderito. Here's an apple for your trip. It took centuries for it to get to your hands.

An apple? asked the blind woman. What on earth are you talking about?

Not the earth, said the son of Manuel Sendero. I am not talking about the earth but a place under the earth. You have forgotten, but before some of the dead are sent off to the islands or the basements, before they are snuffed out forever, they are given one last chance to be in contact with life. The owners of a Great Department Store have contracted their services. They are offered a job there, as mannequins. Because they were once alive, because the recent-dead still keep some embers from the land of the living, there is in them a realism, an intensity, which contrasts with the vacant eyes of dolls of wax or wood. And in order to keep up the illusion of health, so they won't look starved and scare the shoppers off, those mannequins are fed, believe it or not, they are fed apples. But it's a terrible job, even for someone who is dead. By the third month, by the fourth, by the end of the year, or the first century, they're already starting to stiffen. The rules are that they can never move or sigh or even smile. The symptoms of stiffness start in the legs and then climb like cold lava through the rest of the body until a day comes when all memory has disappeared, they become total mannequins. Then they are shipped off.

But not before we have done our job, the recent-dead told Manuel Sendero directly, as he was leaving the elevator, as he watched that icy mountain range overshadow Doralisa's body. We have come up with ways to secretly channel that food, those apples, to the children about to be born, passing the food from hand to stiff hand. In the total silence of the Great Department Store, any movement, any whisper, can be picked up at a distance and is immediately punished. But we have found ways of moving all together so they do not know who moved, or imperceptibly so the guards will not notice. You don't know what it's like, hours and hours with the urge to shout growing inside you, days trying not to stiffen, they told the son of Manuel Sendero on the way to the Laboratory, hours and hours trying to ignore the itch on your right forearm and the way the vertebrae start to press against each other like lines of dead soldiers, they told Manuel Sendero when he couldn't hold on to Doralisa's sleeping hand any longer, we can hardly stand to listen to the comments of the shoppers who come to buy relics of the past or styles from the future, picking up whatever they can use from all civilizations that passed away. But we manage to move. Just a little. Real slow. Like somebody who really isn't moving his thumb, but signaling to the mannequin nearby that there is no guard in sight. And waiting for that mannequin to pass you an apple, the son of Manuel Sendero told the blind woman. A shriveled, ugly apple, maybe even with a bite out of it. But an apple all the same. One that will be useful for something, that will be passed down to even our children, to yours and mine, Pamela told Eduardo. Then waiting another hour or another millennium, the apple sweating secretly in the palm of your hand, until that other mannequin over there signals with her almost motionless thumb that there's no guard to see us now, that I'm passing the apple along to her and in my turn I'm receiving a lump of sticky, half-melted sugar, and understanding with something approaching happiness—

Happiness, Grandfather? Can such a word really exist for a child who is not going to be born and for a father who can't wake up his wife and for a crowd of dead people whose names are no longer remembered? Can such a word exist for a blind woman who can only hear this story because she can't see the world, for a Pamela who can hear it only because she lost her lover's trail?

—something approaching happiness, when the next mannequin hands that sad and glorious apple to a child who was innocently passing by at the agreed-upon hour. And she passes it on to another child one century later, who is clearing customs in the Great Department Store without being searched, and then skipping and jumping toward the vast soup kitchen of the world of the womb to deposit the apple as if she were a sort of mother, and the voices, kids, were fading out more and more, as we went farther from the corridor. Now it was hard to hear what they were saying to me, what they were filtering through to Papa. I was the last one and there wasn't a single witness to share that farewell, and they closed the ambulance doors and I still tried to maintain contact; the Caballero's men were coming for me along that jail corridor twenty years later to cart me off to the same Laboratory; they were coming for me because my favorite twin had betrayed me, and I speeded up the rhythm. I made the blind woman swear she'd speak with Pamela, that she'd tell her about the date and the place and that later she'd take my last message to Eduardo and she accepted while I finally whispered what I'd managed to hear above the ambulance siren and Papa in the car behind us and no longer here beside me, the children of sterile women talking to me, the grandchildren of the apocalypse, the parents of my Pamela, the brothers who ended up in the gutters when their future progenitors died in an accident, telling her and them that someone managed to pass me something, someone was slipping something between my fingers as stiff as a dead man's, and the Caballero put his hand on Doralisa's skin and Papa who's in the other car couldn't prevent it, and I couldn't enter from the other world, and it's the apple that enters the soup kitchen of all wombs and all futures and it's divided up for children I don't know, children I may not get to know, if I harden, if I die a second and then a third time when the company takes me away, and we've finally reached the Laboratory, this must be the Laboratory, and I can barely hear the voices, one last word, they whispered it to me, I whispered it to the blind woman who had gotten up because she too became aware of the footsteps of the Caballero's men, one last word, Pamela got up, glancing at her watch, for all the children I'll never know, and who are, could be, and who would bite, just as the son of Manuel Sendero bit, that apple that was stolen so it can accompany you on your long journey, child, grandfather, and who could be my children, will you be my messenger, my blind love? Will you?

"Did he make you a baby?" asked the blind woman all of a sudden, addressing her with fresh familiarity that morning.

Pamela shook her head, but it seemed that the other woman, in spite of her affliction, interpreted her silence correctly, almost as if she had seen her.

"No baby for me either," said the blind woman. "So go to meet him. Let's see how you do. But I don't think you'll do very well."

Again Pamela asked her why with her eyes. And again the blind woman understood.

Because they had carried him away. That's why. Didn't you want to see the Caballero? they told him, when he asked those men where they were taking him and why. And then the car speeded up and the blind woman didn't know, none of us could ever find out, anything else.

Grandfather couldn't either.

Everything happened too fast, as if it were not happening at all.

He recognized him immediately. He recognized him because of the darkness. That voice came from beyond the giant floodlights that were dazzling my vision and it was impossible and unnecessary to see his face, the thousand faces, the thousand terminals of his unique voice, all the more reason for it to be him; we were face to face at last, with no Doralisa between us as it had been the last time. Without Papa as a hostage like he had been the last time.

"What do you want?" the Caballero asked me, and he, at least, had no doubts as to my identity. "Let's see if your terms are reasonable."

Grandfather had sworn that the first word his enemy heard from his lips would be plural and far-reaching and multiple.

"We," I told him. That was the word. "We've always been reasonable. They're not my terms. They're ours."

"We?"

"All the children who refuse to be born," I said. Grandfather was talking as if from far off and inside. "I'm here as their representative. They've declared their unilateral independence from the human race. They won't change their attitude until their conditions are accepted."

I didn't recognize my own voice. It sounded ridiculous to me. Flat. Pompous. If the twin had been nearby to help me, if together we could have stuck our tongues out at the Caballero the way we had so many times in the past, if I could have held on to his warm puppy voice inside my own. But my encounter with him had poisoned my throat, leaving me alone with the biting ridicule in the Caballero's voice, the same voice that had managed to convince Doralisa to take the pills, that had convinced Papa to accompany him to the Laboratory. The same voice that would try to prove to me that the second and final rebellion had already failed. The twin had deserted to the enemy. Who knows how many others might have done the same thing? And it was as if the two of us, the Caballero and I, the twin and I, were in the same womb, arguing before coming into the world, arguing about which one of the two of us would have the right to come into the world.

"Your conditions?" the Caballero repeated. "And they are . . . ?"

I was silent and tried to avoid the crippling beams of the spotlights.

"The government must declare its own immediate dissolution. As proof that it will do that, there are three prior measures that must be taken."

"Only three?"

Pamela would have known how to announce them. Or even Eduardo. Anybody but me. "First," I said, "it must destroy its stock of weapons."

"Even stones and slingshots? Everything?"

I tried to think about the apple they had given me as a present some thirty years earlier. I tried to think that somebody was still putting it into my thousand-year-old hand for this journey.

"Get rid of the big arms. The ones that eat up the budget," I answered him. "And we'll take care of the rest, when the time comes."

"That's number one."

"Second. Instead of freedom of prices, freedom of food must be declared."

"Anything else?"

I felt cornered. Like my father. The sentences I had rehearsed for decades in wombs scattered by the wind, all the solemn and altruistic declarations, took on a certain irreality in that atmosphere, facing that iciness and that irony, as if it'd be hard even for me—and not just for Pamela, Eduardo, and Skinny—to believe them. As if I were examining them with the same caustic and crafty eye as any adult.

"Yes," I told him. "There's a third . . . Everybody has to take off his clothes."

"Take off his clothes." The Caballero seemed to be jotting the phrase down. "And, might I ask, with what practical purpose in mind?"

It seemed obvious to me. Neither he nor anyone else deserved any explanation if they didn't understand it on their own. So I told him:

"Those are our conditions."

"Easy enough," said the Caballero. "Nothing to it. We'll have them carried out at once. Right away . . . What else? Something just for you perhaps? Some little favor I can do for you? You're going to be in power, right? I've always had good relations with the government in power. So just any little thing at all . . ."

"I don't want power," I answered him, trying not to penetrate the darkness that was hiding him. Trying to keep from turning to stone if I saw his face.

"Come now. We all have some unfulfilled wish. Come on. Tell me yours. Maybe I can do something."

I could've killed him right then, kids. Why didn't I do it? Why didn't I raise my fist with my apple in it and break his life to bits?

Because, yes, there was something, something he could give me, he and he alone. That Devil still possessed the faculty of reading his enemies' thoughts.

As long as he made the offer, I told him, and I noticed that his feet, his thighs, his waist, were starting to inch forward. In a little while his face would come into the light. I'd have to see that face when I killed him—"There's something I'd like to know. What happened that night my father came here with Mama? I have all the other information. But that, I don't remember."

That's the way it is, kids. Now you know. Now he knew. That's why I haven't been able to tell you the ending. Because I never knew what had happened in that room, in that Laboratory.

"Don't you remember that night?" asked the Caballero. "That's strange. With a memory like yours. Well, why not? There's nothing simpler. It'll really be a pleasure to tell you everything. Yes, sir. Every last detail."

"So, frankly, I don't believe he'll return," said the blind woman at that same moment on the other side of the city. And Pamela had the feeling that only that woman whose eyes the dead had eaten still linked her to the other shore of the son of Manuel Sendero. That he was going, going. "That's the way things are. No one ever finds anyone. It seems that with me he lost his last chance. He could've left us a baby to remember him by, couldn't he?"

And Pamela didn't see, either in her eyes or in her hand, even the seed of a seed of an apple.

O U T S I D E

So David won't be able to tell Felipe about the last episodes of the comic strip. He won't be able to tell Paula either.

But some plots just seem to unfold beyond anything their author desires or plans. And nothing that David could say, nothing he could do, can prevent Dr. Garay from visiting Sarah Barks's husband, or Marras, with his gloved hands, from coming to pick her up.

"I'm going to tell you, ma'am," Dr. Garay stated, "your husband is a lucky man."

"Lucky?" Sarah Barks bit at the word.

The doctor disentangled a couple of mechanisms that appeared to be headsets from his briefcase. "Illness is never lucky for anybody, and especially for somebody Mr. Barks's age." He started to polish the end of each one of those mechanisms with his handkerchief until they shone. "The lucky thing was that he got sick here in a country like this one where there's a cure for everything."

"What have you done to Carl? Tell me right now."

"Madam, please. Calm down. Your husband was already a weakened man when he got here. But if I'd told you his illness was worse when you got off the plane, if I'd said it just like that, the way it was, you'd have taken him back home. Right?"

"Naturally," said Sarah Barks. "And it was my understanding that doctors are pledged to tell their patients the truth."

Dr. Garay went on unrolling multicolored plastic wires. "I fulfilled my obligation. I said there was no cause for worry. I say it again. Because even though the state of his health is getting worse every day, we're also making advances. We're going to save every one of his vital functions. And I mean every one. We'll go even further. You'll see. He'll be as good as new."

"All I've heard up to now are promises," said Sarah Barks.

"Trust, my dear lady. Just a little trust. You could prove our ability in your own case. A matter I hadn't made reference to out of a sense of delicacy."

"All I can see right now," said Sarah Barks, "is that my husband is in a wheelchair, without the use of both hands, and deaf, on top of everything else."

"Have you ever heard our 'radar of the mind' mentioned, madam?"

"What?"

Dr. Garay plugged each one of the wires into the huge television set beside the bed.

"Just imagine that dreams could be sucked up, as if in a vacuum cleaner, that they could be read and projected onto a screen. Television programs are recorded to be watched later. So why not do the same thing with thoughts and mental images? Why not explore the regions of the brain like a scuba diver? That would be a kind of immortality, madam. You do agree with me there, don't you?"

"And is that what you propose to do with that headset, Doctor?"

Garay laughed. "Of course not. These are to cure your husband's deafness. We'll take care of that in an instant. A matter of seconds really."

So David, no matter how much Paula might beg him, will not be able to prevent those two knocks of a gloved hand that announce Marras's presence. Nor can he be prevented from sticking his head in the door.

"Are you ready, madam?" he asked.

"I'm going to put this mechanism that you confused with a headset into Mr. Parks's ears. That is, one on this side, one on the other. How nice. And you're going to hear Rev. Rex. He can explain this business of health and salvation better than I can."

Marras advanced.

"We must leave, Mrs. Parks," he said.

"Fine, right away," said Sarah Barks. Then, to the doctor: "Will Carl be able to hear? Is he cured then?"

"Only what comes from that screen," Garay answered. "If you'd like to communicate with him you'll have to make a broadcast. With a camera in your room . . ."

"I really would like to talk with him," said Sarah Barks.

"When we get back," said Marras. "Right now we're late."

"If you don't mind, Mr. Marras, I'd like to be sure my husband really can hear."

"We're going to be late," said Marras. "But if that would make you feel better . . ."

"It's a shame you have to go," said Garay, "because Rev. Rex would answer all your doubts, madam. Let's see."

The doctor pushed a button and the television screen lit up, showing a colossal figure standing behind a pulpit. "From God's point of view," said the voice that was undoubtedly that of Rev. Rex, "from the point of view of the most exalted values, every man and every woman has one outstanding quality, something special that distinguishes him from everybody else. Anything else is extra, just window dressing, nothing but clay."

At the very first words Carl Parks moved his head, incredulous, as if they'd awakened him. He looked at Sarah. "I can hear," he said, hoarse from lack of practice. "I can hear again."

"It's what's down deep, the stuff that makes a man function like clockwork, like an alarm clock, what makes him learn a career and surpass everyone else. That's what's important for eternity." The Rev. Rex went on with his homily in his melodious baritone. "What good does it do to waste an eternal life in woes, meanness, and imperfection? Do you think God wants to resurrect a lame man's leg or a nearsighted man's eyes or an impotent man's sex?"

"Are you satisfied now, madam?" asked Marras impatiently.

"We'll see," said Sarah Barks, "what we'll see. Can Carl carry on a dialogue with this machine? Or does he just receive what it says?"

In answer, Dr. Garay stood in front of the screen. He paid no attention to Carl Barks's howls of protest.

"What kind of question would you like your husband to ask, madam?"

Sarah scribbled some brief, nervous words on a piece of paper. Carl Parks read them in silence and at once made a gesture: indicating the doctor should get out of the way. Rev. Rex's face reappeared.

"I'd like to know," said Carl Parks, spelling out the words the way a child learning the alphabet would do, "if I should stay in this country or leave."

"Mr. Parks," said Rev. Rex from the screen as if he were participating in a contest. "That's a fine question. I'm going to give you an answer right away."

"All right," said Sarah Barks. "We can leave, Mr. Marras." She said good-bye to Carl with a peck on the cheek. He paid no attention to her, his eyes glued to the screen.

"In this country," said the voice of Rev. Rex, "that privileged instrument of yours, your fantasy, can be given the place it deserves in eternity."

All of a sudden, in the doorway, Sarah Barks turned around, as if she'd been bitten by an emotion. But Paula will be unable to convince David to let her go back and take Carl's hand and say farewell. Paula won't find the means to do even that. Sarah Barks stood watching her husband for another moment. Then closed the door.

"That's what God wants," Rev. Rex went on. "To recover that divine spark he put in each of us. To exalt and glorify Himself in each one of us. You, Mr. Parks, will be alive. It doesn't matter that your body will be functioning by artificial means. Your body never belonged to you. It was always just an accident. Our organs are like machines. They can be substituted. The fundamental thing is that your soul, that part of your spirit where your capacity to dream, to create, to imagine landscapes and animals, resides, the recorder will be there, inside, the radar of the mind, and here on the outside, what you dream, create, imagine, will be projected, like a cinematographic production in which it's enough to think something for it to exist for the spectator. And on the Day of Final Judgment the Lord will find you there, with your primary faculty intact, ready to be glorified in His name, en route to the Great Beyond."

"The Great Beyond," said Carl Parks.

"Haven't you ever wondered what Heaven will be like? How the angels will amuse themselves? What they will do to avoid boredom? Haven't you ever wondered about that?"

"Yes," said Carl Parks. "I have. Occasionally."

"God," announced Rev. Rex, "is like a giant computer, a screen filling infinity, a videocassette recording every one of our thoughts, retaining in its Memory everything we did or tried to do. The faithful have to facilitate God's labor, so that His work will be advanced. That's why His ideal man is being fashioned in this exceptional country. One who will not kiss with pornographically tainted lips. One who will not contemplate his Creator with myopic or Communist eyes. And you ask me if you should stay. You who are to participate in the creation of that perfect being. What better imagination for that man than your own? What greater contribution could you hope to make, Mr. Parks? To live forever, Mr. Parks, is an assurance that your dreams will enrich paradise, will bring smiles to the lips of the archangels, will move the saints to compassion. To live forever, my dear friend, is to colonize the Great Beyond. Hadn't you ever thought of that?"

"Yes," said Carl Parks, "colonizing the Great Beyond. To tell you the truth, I had thought of that."

"So you will stay here with us. How nice!"

"I'll stay," said Carl Parks. "Provided I can consult Sarah about it."

But he won't be able to consult Sarah about it. Because David will never tell Paula that at that very minute Marras's gloved hand is pressing the button of an elevator on the other side of the city. Because Paula can't prevent Sarah Barks from saying:

"Those sick people," said Sarah Barks, "I hope they're not here."

"Those people are absolutely normal," Marras corrected her. "They're not sick at all. Far from it. What is happening to them can be summed up in two words. Traffic signals."

"Traffic signals?"

"Traffic signals in the head. Red one minute. Green the next. Braking, accelerating, braking again to keep from running over a child who's crossing. Traffic signals. An excessive self-repression. But sick? Not at all. They're all very respectable people, even people of public importance in their own country."

Sarah Barks contemplated the elevator doors that were opening soundlessly.

"Is that why they didn't need to go through the usual procedures? I mean customs, the police? And there aren't ever any reporters present when they arrive?"

Marras registered a certain surprise, and with a slight bow signaled for the woman to precede him.

"You're very well informed, madam. In fact, someone in whom we have complete trust waits for them at the airport and brings them here. Because this is the building, as I understand it, into which you saw them enter. Is that correct?"

"But now they aren't going to be here. Correct?" Sarah Barks asked again.

"They've left for a while," said Marras. "They'd be very upset if they knew we were visiting their private reserve. It so happens that contemporary life, with all its virtues, imposes some intolerable limits on human beings. Limitations, ties, absurd legalisms which don't allow us to develop our personalities spontaneously. Traffic signals. An impression is generated, an erroneous one of course, that other people are manipulating us or spying on us. The therapy they go through in our country has as its goal to eliminate that unfounded anxiety, to offer our distinguished visitors certain liberties that the laws and constraints of their own countries deny them."

The elevator came imperceptibly to a halt. Marras invited Sarah Barks to enter the softly lighted and Muzak-filled corridor, at the end of which was a door. An opaque key opened it. "No comfort has been spared, madam."

"They can enjoy the same comforts in their own homes," said Sarah Barks, austerely. "I see no reason why this should improve their state of mind."

Marras helped her off with her coat, then took off his own. Nevertheless, he kept his gloves on, as always.

"But I don't think they have this in their homes," said Marras, tiptoeing toward another room. "Or do they?"

Paula could have suggested to David that Sarah not enter that room, that Marras not show it to her, that she go back later to investigate what really went on in that place.

But Sarah Barks went in. The room resembled the control room of a television studio: twelve screens, all off at that moment, lined one wall, with knobs and buttons to monitor the transmission. The furniture, on the other hand, was different, and belied that first impression: a couple of beds, two or three armchairs, a round mahogany table on which there was a basket of fruit, a combination bar and refrigerator, some pleasant watercolors, everything to suggest that there was life in this place. And a good life. On the table Sarah Barks noticed pencils, file cards, and some opened file boxes scattered about.

"Each one of these audiovisual machines," said Marras, "is connected to the home of a family that resides in the neighborhood. The cameras hidden in their homes make it possible to follow their every move, meticulously, day and night. These files, very complete, contain all the biographical information about those families, as well as some other data. The first phase of the treatment, the preliminary phase, what might be called the synopsis phase, takes a week. The visitors, very carefully and without haste, take time to examine the conduct of the various members of each family in circumstances which are, after all, completely private. They measure their reactions and study all their problems and habits. Then, on the last day, they're asked to concentrate on two of those families. Of course there's a wide social spectrum from which to choose."

Sarah Barks found herself staring at Marras's gloved hands. He returned her stare calmly and she felt obliged to sit down in one of the armchairs and to direct her attention to the screens.

"Could I see?"

"That's impossible, madam," said Marras. "We'd be committing an unspeakable indiscretion."

"The patients do it," argued Sarah Barks.

"It's not just out of idle curiosity, madam. It's part of a medical treatment. Then comes the second step. The two families have been chosen. In technical terms, it's a therapy group. The patient now must elaborate a plan of action, a kind of docudrama, establishing directions he or she would like the chosen subjects to move in during the subsequent weeks. It's like a film script or a libretto. All that's left from that moment on is to find the most subtle means of directing them toward that final objective."

"What kind of means?"

"Government cooperation is indispensable in order to bring certain forces to bear whenever the patient decides it."

Sarah Barks could not keep a mounting hostility out of her voice. "And after that, what happens?"

Paula, had she been present, would have whispered to her not to talk like that, would have advised her to pretend. But Paula isn't there.

"My, but you're in a hurry, madam," said Marras. "Please, let's calm down. It's only an innocent little plan for tourists. Nothing more than that. Don't look at me as though we were doing something improper here . . . What happens then? There are two ways to proceed, according to the psychiatrists. Two ways: on the one hand, the families can be benefited, compensating them, and, on the other hand, they can be treated in, shall we say, a less benevolent manner, by using other methods of intervention."

"I'd be interested in hearing them," said Sarah Barks.

"You are insatiable, dear lady. I beg you to remember that the purpose of this visit was to give you assurance that this treatment would not be applied to you. But perhaps you're becoming more excited, more interested, now that you've seen it firsthand, and would like to adopt a similar plan . . ."

This was the moment for Sarah Barks to smile, to accept Marras's explanations, and to leave. That's what Paula would have done, or what any other woman who had lived through what Paula had would have done.

"And these people," asked Sarah Barks, instead of smiling, "these families know nothing about what is going on, I suppose?"

Marras settled down in front of her, leaning a bit against the edge of the control table. He crossed his arms.

"What do you think, madam?"

"Frankly, Mr. Marras, I don't know what to think."

"It makes very little difference what the people who appear on these screens know or don't know, madam. What does matter, as is always the case in the practice of medicine, is the health of the patients and that they believe they have complete power over the fate of another person. Traffic signals, madam, red lights in front of every human being who crosses our path. Being able to observe another person without being observed in turn, what a sense of relief! To finally know how a person acts when he's alone, beyond mere appearances. To learn to move others like pieces on a chessboard. It's not easy. One must be skillful, tying and untying the threads of the plot, planning a goal for each one, weaving a tapestry that doesn't ignore even the least detail. If he saw some of the episodes that have been programmed and carried out, even Shakespeare himself would be jealous. There's nothing to prevent the tourist from intervening personally, appearing directly in the home of the family he's chosen, making a visit. While his spouse watches the whole thing on the screen. Or he may prefer never to appear in their presence, always working from a position of anonymity. There are no rules, no interdictions. An adventure beyond all morality. So what do you think, madam?"

"There are some things that should be done, sir," said Sarah Barks, "and others that are best left undone. That's the way I was brought up."

"I gather you don't approve then. Nevertheless, it's an excellent treatment. The results are truly astonishing. At the end of three weeks all depression, guilt complexes, nightmares, and paranoia have disappeared. The patient has practiced his vices and his virtues to the limit, that is, up to the limit he himself, and not society, imposes. Once he comes to know himself, he experiences a sense of well-being, a catharsis, like no other in the history of mental health treatment."

"And you want me to believe that that's the way they're rejuvenated?"

"That's only one of our methods. There are others. For Mr. Parks, for example. But this is one of the best, because the means employed are entirely natural. No drugs, nothing artificial."

Sarah Barks got up from the chair, walked toward the back of the room, and ended up approaching the control table. Avoiding Marras's gloved hands, almost as if she had heard the suggestion that Paula never made.

"And all this is done without the knowledge of the families?"

"I would have preferred your not asking me that kind of question, madam. What would you like me to answer?"

"Just the truth, Mr. Marras, the truth will be enough."

"Do you sincerely believe, madam, that we could carry out experiments which would endanger the stability of our fellow citizens? Could you think that of us?"

"What I believe is of no importance," said Sarah Barks.

"Look, madam. Your husband is an artist. You're familiar with the spiritual liberation that comes to Mr. Parks through the creative process. It's the peak of happiness, of euphoria, is it not? That, in spite of the fact that the artist sublimates his passion in the imaginary, in sheer fantasy. Our treatment goes a step beyond that: the patient carries out the art of life itself. A staging with real people stimulates all the hormones of youth, making us into deities. Don't you sometimes feel like letting yourself go? Like plunging headlong into the world of your obsessions, opening up the background of other human beings? Don't you ever dream of controlling them?"

"Sir, it is my belief that God made us civilized and that it's our duty to remain so."

"But that's exactly what we are doing, my dear lady. If this therapy rejuvenates and performs miracles, it is precisely because it draws the patients closer to God. They sit down behind their windows or protective screens and take all the mud baths they want, without getting dirty. They return from our country completely at peace with themselves, thus going back to a responsible social life. In a word, totally humanized."

"I have asked you repeatedly, sir, if this treatment implies a risk to the families. You invariably answer me that it's excellent for the patients. I don't wish to offend you, but I need an answer. For the last time: do these people know what is being done to them or not?"

Marras bit his lip.

"If I answer that question, Miss Sarah, you could never receive the benefits of this treatment."

"It's not my intention, Mr. Marras, to have anything to do with it."

Marras sighed.

"All right, madam, very well. I've tried to protect you, but since you insist . . . Look. In order for this treatment to succeed, there is, was, only one basic condition. The patients must believe that they are really and truly intervening in real lives. Without that assurance, without that faith, there's no improvement. They are sure that there are no more traffic signals here. Just green lights. Not a single cross street. What would they say if they knew the families aren't real? That they're made up of actors who are playing roles, that they offer the illusion of an absolute power which, in fact, doesn't exist? What would they say?"

For an instant that seemed an eternity Sarah Barks saw herself in a hospital bed, saw her legs powerfully and infinitely extended, saw a child slipping out from the open eclipse of her legs. She collapsed into a chair.

"Is that the way it is, Mr. Marras? They're actors? Just actors?"

"A live TV serial, prefabricated for our patients. But if they should find that out, Mrs. Barks? If they should come to believe that a show is being put on for them, that they're being deceived? Do you know what deplorable effects that kind of revelation would have on their lives?"

"That's why you didn't explain it to me from the beginning. That's the reason."

"And why I had hoped, madam, that you'd be able to accept this treatment. We thought that after you had your child, you might need greater energy, some vitamins of youth, in order to bring him up and to play with him. I understand you want a boy, isn't that right?"

Sarah Barks's voice sparkled like a sword.

"Yes. I'm going to have a little boy."

"I understand why you want to have children, madam. And grandchildren. I understand it very well. I'm going to tell you a secret. How old do you think I am, Mrs. Barks?"

"Forty. Perhaps forty-five."

Marras smiled.

"Would you like to know how old I am? A little older than you yourself. I was eighty-two a few months ago."

"You?"

"I'm a great-grandfather. I went through this therapy too. I was also rejuvenated, traveling to the depths of my own heart. If you don't believe me, look at my hands." With great energy Marras pulled off his gloves, as if he were performing a violent striptease with his hands. There they were, in front of Sarah Barks, naked.

"His hands, Paula," David would have said. "His hands."

"Look at them. There are some things no treatment can repair. My hands will reveal my true age to you, madam. That's why I understand your passion for children. And I thought it would be good for you to knock off a couple of decades. I tried to warn you. I begged you—you do remember—not to force me to tell you the truth. Now the treatment is useless for you. Completely impossible."

"Because I now know they're actors and not real people?"

"Actors," Marras repeated.

"And what happens," asked Sarah Barks, "afterward? What happens to them?" She nodded her head in the direction of the screens with apparent indifference.

"To the families? After the first year the patient has the opportunity, every four months, for a reasonable sum, to suggest measures that he thinks should be taken for his adoptive families. They are told that the authorities tend to look upon these recommendations with deference."

"And they never return?"

"Some become attached to the whole thing, the taste lingers with them. But it's expensive. Even for people so well off . . ."

"Yes, really. Hiring so many actors," said Sarah Barks. "Undoubtedly it'd be more economical to use real people."

"In any case, I'm counting on your discretion in this matter. I have passed all limits in order to satisfy your curiosity, and if it were discovered that the families are not authentic, this whole business would come to an end. And with so many tourists signed up. The patients must never find out, never, that it's all a fiction."

Without giving the matter any further thought, not a shred of tension showing in her voice, Sarah Barks brought her old body, her suddenly tired and defeated body, closer to the control table.

"It shouldn't ever be discovered, Mr. Marras?"

"Never, madam."

"Well then, how do you know it? You were a patient, weren't you? How did you find out?"

At this moment Paula would have tried to convince David. To convince him that Sarah Barks should not approach one of the camera controls. To convince him that she shouldn't stumble and lose her balance, that she shouldn't pretend to slip. To convince David that she shouldn't bend over the control table in order to catch herself, that she shouldn't touch one of those buttons, that one of the screens shouldn't light up.

But David has his own problems and won't be able to tell Paula this episode, won't have the chance to hear her recommendations. And Sarah Barks begged Marras's pardon anxiously. Begged his pardon, but turned around nevertheless to see what was being transmitted on the screen. Paula would have told her not to look.

Because Sarah Barks couldn't repress or even identify the cry of rage and desperation that rose in her throat; the cry of a woman who sees a stillborn child. Or who sees a faceless rag doll instead of a child. But she managed to smother, she thought she could smother, the words that were reverberating like fingernails inside her head, pushing to get out. She heard them, there inside, hysterical and silent, the words that for days she had been preparing, whispering, not wanting to give them definitive form, not wanting to admit the defeat they represented: "I'm leaving. Tomorrow, if I can. Both of us are leaving, both of us are leaving tomorrow. We're leaving this monstrous country."

There, on the screen, resting on a sofa or perhaps a cot, was the unmistakable figure of Becky. Beside her could be seen the child. Susana was holding her hand; she wouldn't let it go for anything in the world. Off-camera, something or someone was coming closer, a shadow of one or maybe two heads was moving in while mother and daughter watched, watched and waited.

Marras's left hand was lifted in the air without haste and then proceeded to descend with the slowness of an eagle onto one of the buttons. Becky's last gesture, before her face was reduced to a brilliant white spot in the middle of the dark-green screen that was going off, was with her hands, that were slipping downward, from her face down toward her daughter's breasts, as if she were trying to hide them. Then Becky disappeared like a useless howl of light.

The world was a still photograph. From the soles of her feet that were nailed to the floor Sarah Barks felt that the world was a still photograph. Marras was the one descending on her, canceling out all the other objects in the room with his body. As if she were the fixed and unalterable lens of a movie camera that someone had forgotten to turn off, filming the only thing that was changing position in that kettledrum quietness, Marras, growing larger, blotting out the horizon.

Then Sarah Barks realized that she hadn't thought those final thoughts to herself, as she'd believed. She had pronounced them out loud.

"Marras's hands," David would have said, if he were present, narrating this next-to-the-last episode. "In close-up."

"I know. I know," Paula would answer, tiredly. "Marras's famous hands."

"A shame," David would have said, shutting his notebook. "I really did sympathize with her. But ever since I saw that nun that cold day, the nun that was singing, I knew there'd be no happy ending. Soon they'd kill that nun in a foreign country. And Sarah . . ."

And Paula would say: "Why don't we save her, David? We can save her if we want to. She's just a character."

And David would have said: "What do you suggest?"

And Paula: "That she pretend. That she get away. That she rescue Becky and the little girl, at least the little girl."

And David: "A happy ending, eh? And after that, then what? They flee the country? Overthrow tyranny with a press conference in New York that nobody attends? Adopt one of the Chilex children so it can be the baby she can't have? After that, then what?"

"Even if it's just one child," Paula would say. "Sure. Why not? Don't you think so?"

"I think so," David would have said. "I've always thought so. But you're forgetting one little detail. I'm not the one in control of this world of ours. Marras's famous hands do the commanding."

"We'll see," says Paula. "That remains to be seen."

But David doesn't answer her. David has his own problems.

"You gave it to him?" asks Felipe in the rest room of that Mexico City bar. "You gave him an interview?"

"He's a good guy, old Jérez is," says David.

"We're all good guys," says Felipe. "The world's full of good guys."

"He tried to do me a favor, Felipe. He's owed me a favor ever since school days."

"So now he owes you two. He's doing himself the favor. He's using you as a token so they'll praise him for his broad-mindedness."

"Using. Using. Somebody's always going to be using me. That's inevitable. What's important is whether it suits me or not."

"So you trust him."

"What he proposed is reasonable enough. Let's look for the humanitarian side, the human interest angle, he told me. We show you, among lots of others, peacefully earning your living abroad. No roughneck stuff. No terrorism. Nothing about dangerous men, just wrenching problems. Some of you hoping to go back. Others getting old here on the outside. We break with the image you have as extremists, he told me. That's the main thing. He was right. And yeah, I trusted him. It's as simple as that, Felipe."

"How can you trust those guys? One day they're denouncing the government and the next day they're in dialogue with them to get a change in direction. This one works for that Fascist newspaper *El Mercurio*, the paper that denied that Gonzalo had ever been arrested, and he whispers in your ear that he's on your side. Sometimes I can't believe how naive you are, David."

"But Jérez is really against the dictatorship, Felipe. He says really tremendous things."

"In Holland he says tremendous things. In Chile he probably doesn't talk so loud."

"I don't know what's being said in Chile. I'm not there. When I get back, I'll be sure to let you know, OK?"

"That's some way to get back in."

"What do you mean by that?"

"Let's see what you had to say in the interview. Do you tell him that the only way to get rid of a son of a bitch is with bullets and cannonballs and that's it? Do you tell him that the first thing you're going to do is to see your friend Gonzalo Jaramillo but that you can't because he's disappeared? Do you tell him that there can't be any peace until the torturers are brought to justice? Do you say the old men in the Supreme Court have got to be given a good swift kick in the ass and sent packing?"

"How could I say those things, Felipe?"

"When Jérez prints those things for you, then I'll trust him."

Behind them, at the door to the toilet, a Mexican voice erupts.

"The conversation's real interesting. Real interesting, fellows. That's for sure. Yeah, I'm completely, totally convinced you fellows could find some other place to . . . to . . . go on with it. If you'll excuse me, there are some things Mother Nature just can't put off."

He's a stocky man, and if he hasn't managed to get totally drunk, it's not for lack of effort and determination. He's circumnavigating, skirting, right on the edge of a state of drunkenness that announces itself good-naturedly, with no hostility toward anybody. His tie is hanging half untied. His cuffs are unbuttoned. He's sweating profusely. But there in his lapel, perhaps as a proof or a reminder of his usual soberness and balance, he still has, imperturbable, that marvelous flower which is the distinctive feature of the group of celebrants who just came into the bar.

Felipe smiles.

"Sorry, man. We didn't realize . . ."

"No problem. No problem at all," says the man, ushering them out with an exaggeratedly wide sweep of his arm. And then he adds, when they're already out in the hall: "The fact is I think this gentleman," pointing to Felipe, "is right in this argument, if you'll pardon me for saying so . . . The only way to get rid of any son of a bitch is with bullets. There's no use wasting time talking to them. You listen to him, sir," he says to David. "This man's your brother and he knows what he's talking about."

"You see, David," says Felipe.

"I see," says David.

Before sitting down at the table, Felipe asks for the check.

"This damn mechanic's not going to show up," says Felipe. "We may as well leave."

"It's your car."

"They're your suitcases."

"Safe and sound, fortunately." David kicks at them under the table, as if to guarantee they're still there.

"Let's go then," says Felipe. "Juana must be worried."

"You know something?" says David. "It really amazes me you're so tough on the Christian Democrats, Felipe. Have you forgotten how Hernández defended you? He was loyal and took lots of risks to get you out of the camp."

"I haven't forgotten anything, David. Not anything."

"Neither have I."

"So we're two of a kind. Look, the ones who took risks back then were few and far between. Most of them started to squeal only when they turned on them, when it was clear they weren't going to give them even this much power. Before that they were as quiet as could be. They even applauded. And tomorrow, if those Christian Democrats see a loophole to keep us out, and it's necessary to repress us, you can be sure they'll do it. Just like in El Salvador. Because the truth is, we're dangerous, David. They can dress you up with all that pacifist and altruistic clothing. But I'd rather they thought I was dangerous."

"They're never going to let you go back."

"To go back you have to become one of them. You have to wear a disguise. Pledge allegiance to the flag and kiss ass. Turn the other cheek. Like a Christian Democrat."

"You're nuts. The Christian Democrats are getting screwed just like we are."

"Just like us? How many of their people have disappeared? How many of them are prisoners? How many of them are living in exile? How many of them lost jobs?"

"We're not involved in some kind of competition here. They're being hit hard, Felipe."

"So they're being hit hard, are they?"

"Does that please you?"

"Yeah, as a matter of fact. I enjoy it. I don't say that publicly because we need them. But I think it's great they're socking it to them. They're the ones who put those bastards in power. And when the crisis comes, they never want to take the risks. So let them pay the consequences now. I'll tell you when I'm going to trust them. One: when they've been persecuted the way we have. Two: when they criticize the Yankees. Three: when Jérez tells what brand of champagne he opened the day of the coup. Meanwhile, I don't believe a word they say. I'll work with them, but I won't believe a thing they say."

"They say the same thing. That they don't trust us. That tomorrow we'll stab them in the back."

"Who broke with democracy in Chile? Them or us?"

"And they say we were all for democracy in Chile, but played a different tune when it came to Czechoslovakia."

"Is that what they say or is it what you say, David?"

"You're as sectarian as ever, Felipe. You haven't learned a thing in all these years."

"Answer me. Is it what they say or what you say?"

The man who had interrupted them in the rest room passes by

their table, greeting them effusively, as if he were the owner of the bar or the official host. He goes back to his group, where he is received with shouts. David follows his trajectory. The man leans on the bar, with one hand on the shoulder of one of his companions and the other reaching for a bottle. All of a sudden, he turns his head and looks at David. He winks at him and points with his thumb meaningfully at Felipe, while a wide accomplice's smile spreads across his face. The message is clear, the same as in the toilet: David should pay more attention to his brother. He should listen to Felipe.

"They're inconsistent. We're inconsistent. That's all I'm saying, Felipe. And until both of us change, nothing's going to happen to Chile. And I don't want to stay here on the outside waiting for other people to evolve."

"But you're inconsistent too. You're going to appear in a newspaper you hate, one you swore to destroy."

"A person swears a lot of things."

"But an interview for *El Mercurio*, David. That's impossible."

"For whatever newspaper is interested. It's a way to go back. To get down there again. Down there, Felipe. Down there and not up here. The people who read you look up and see Ahumada Street in Santiago. Shit, man. And not this damned bar. This bar. Hey, are you sure your so-called mechanic really exists?"

"Are you sure Ahumada Street really exists?"

"What do you mean?"

"There is no Ahumada Street now. It's a pedestrian mall."

"You see. I don't even know the city I'm talking to you about."

Felipe signals with one hand, trying to get the attention of the proprietor of the bar, who is seated behind the cash register. But no one is paying any attention to him. He turns to David: "And did he promise you they'd publish it?"

"He said it was almost certain. I think the business with Lolo, the medal and all that, you know. I think it made them especially interested in my case."

"So did he ask you about Lolo?"

"Not a word."

"Did you mention it?"

"Indirectly. Something about this not being a time for heroes. About it being time for the heroism of dialogue."

"The heroism of dialogue. You should get a prize for that phrase. With that definition of a hero, old Jérez must've felt like Lawrence of Arabia."

"It's an antimilitary expression, Felipe."

"So, did he impose any conditions? What you could say and what you couldn't?"

"It was more me imposing them on him. I told him not to publish anything until I gave him the go-ahead. He owes me a favor, like I told you."

"What kind of favor?"

"Just a favor."

"Boy, you really trust me, don't you?"

"I got him a doctor once. He'd gotten a girl pregnant and didn't know what to do. I went with him. Arranged the whole thing. That kind of thing."

"He fucked the maid. What do you want to bet it was the maid? Self-righteous hypocrites. They're always the same, whether it's in bed or in politics. Always the same. First they drop their pants, then they try to cover their trail."

"What would you want him to do? Marry the girl?"

"I don't want to talk about that son of a bitch anymore. He bores me. Those people just make me sick."

"You never arranged for an abortion? You never got in that kind of fix?"

"I don't go around proclaiming my morality and beating my breast." He looks at his watch. "OK. Enough waiting. It's quarter past eleven. Almost quarter past. Shit."

Felipe stands up abruptly.

"What are you going to do?"

"I'm going to call my man the mechanic. So we'll know what to expect."

This time, while Felipe's on the phone, David doesn't stay in his seat. He gets up, almost bumping into the boy who's waiting on tables, and orders a couple more beers. Then he goes up to the bar.

"Excuse me, man," he says to the man they'd talked to, as he taps him on the shoulder.

The man turns around, smiling openly.

"Great, great. Really nice. Antonio, here's the fellow I was talking about. So tell me. What can I do for you?"

"Can I be allowed to ask you a question?"

"Sure. If I can be allowed to answer it."

"I'd like to know what you guys are celebrating."

"Antonio, this gentleman wants to know what we're celebrating."

The man called Antonio doesn't turn around. Neither do the others. In the mirror behind the bar David sees Antonio's eyes looking him over from head to toe.

"So tell him we're celebrating the new year."

"You heard what Antonio said," explains the man.

"I see," says David. "I guess I was wrong. I thought maybe you were celebrating something else."

"You're really sharp," says the man. "Didn't I tell you, Antonio? They're really nice guys. So I'm going to tell you that you're right. Because our friend Antonio here is about to get married. I told him not to do it, but he's in love. So next weekend he'll be married."

"I had a friend who got married," says David.

"You had a friend who got married. What a coincidence! So is he happy?"

"I don't know. I haven't seen him since then."

The man explodes into guffaws of laughter, slapping his legs exaggeratedly.

"Didn't I tell you, Antonio? Didn't I tell you you'd never see us again?"

"Good luck," says David, raising his hand as if to wave goodbye and returning to his table.

Felipe is waiting for him.

"So what about the Party?" Felipe asks him, as if the conversation hadn't been interrupted. "Did you consult the Party there in Holland?"

"I'm no longer a member, Felipe."

"What's that got to do with it? You're not on bad terms either. You weren't expelled. It was your idea to pull out. Temporarily."

"I don't think it's so temporary."

"David, we're living through a time when everything's mixed up. Sometimes there are people who can understand what's going on better, because of the position they occupy or the information they get. It's hard for you to accept that. But there are people who know more than we do. People who have a wider view of things."

"I don't ask the Party anything, Felipe. This is a problem between David and his conscience. That's all. His petit bourgeois conscience. Because the one who's going to get screwed in this world is me. Not the sacrosanct Party. I already let the Party decide my life once. And it didn't go so well, Felipe."

"What do you mean?"

"I'm here because you people decided it, Felipe."

"Finally. We're really getting to the bottom of things."

"Yeah. The bottom of things."

"Ever since you got off the plane, you've been choking on something. You've been dying to say something. OK. Let's have it. Here I am."

The boy comes with the two beers.

"Who ordered these?" asks Felipe. "What I want is the check."

"I ordered them," says David.

"Let's go," says Felipe.

"I thought we were going to talk."

"We'll drink the beers and then go."

"It's your family and your new year. We can talk about it later."

"Right now, man."

"That's fine with me."

"David, your leaving Chile was the right decision."

"You really believe that, don't you?"

"It was more than right."

"More than right?"

"If you had stayed, you'd be dead or in prison right now."

"Maybe yes, maybe no. But that wasn't the argument you used back then."

"What argument did I use?"

"That they were going to arrest you. That I was a risk."

"Did I say that?"

"That or something like it. And two months later they grabbed you anyway, Felipe. And I had nothing to do with it. The one they were watching was you. I could have stayed."

"What you forget is that if you hadn't been working outside the country, you and so many others, who knows if they might have killed me back there. Or they wouldn't have released me. Don't underestimate the work you people did, are still doing."

"Thanks for reminding me. What a relief. Thanks."

"Don't talk like that, David."

"But that's not the reason I had to leave, Felipe. I left because you guys got it into your heads that I was a danger to you."

"The Party has to look out for itself. That's legitimate."

"If you only knew what a relief it is not to be connected to anybody. I don't know anything and I'm not interested in knowing anything. I'm going back and I can't do anybody any harm. If you only knew, Felipe. What happens to me depends on me and on nobody else."

"If everybody felt like that, we'd have Pinochet for a thousand years."

"Of course we're going to have him for a thousand years, Felipe. Didn't you know that?"

"I must be pretty stupid. But no, I never realized that."

"And you didn't realize that we're all alone either, I suppose."

"No, not that either."

"That's why people join parties. To hide their loneliness. To maintain the illusion that we have company and that the future's rosy."

"Maybe that's why you joined. I joined because I wanted to change the way things are. Because you have to be organized to fight an enemy that's superorganized. Parties aren't perfect. They're just like the men who make them up. They make the same mistakes.

Frankly I'm amazed at all this anger, all this resentment of yours."

"Anger? Resentment? Not true. The thing with me is I'm tired. Parties get involved in what's none of their business, man. And what they ought to be doing, the business of change and all that, of taking power, they're not involved enough in that. And when they do get involved in that, they just fuck it up. So if I have problems, that's what friends are for. Right? What does a party know about that? Is the Party going to solve my problems with Gringa? Is it going to help me work things out with Lolo? Is it going to get me back inside Chile? Let's see, man. Exactly who's going to take responsibility for my being out of Chile? You people made the decision and now you wash your hands of it. So who do I appeal to? To you?"

"You're a fine son of a bitch to be complaining, man. You could've stayed, David. If you really believe this business of everybody deciding for himself, don't be blaming other people all the time. We did what was best, what seemed to be best for the security of everybody. If you didn't agree, you could have stayed."

"That wasn't the way you laid the whole thing out then. But it doesn't really matter. Because you're right. The decision was mine. In the final analysis we all make our own decisions. That's why I gave the interview to Jérez. Because I'm the one who has to find my way back. Nobody else."

"He did lay down conditions, then, and you accepted them."

"I asked him up front what could be said. I told him if they were going to make a lot of cuts, I'd rather forget the whole thing. At that point, he said it all depended. Depends on what? I asked him. On my answers, he told me. He was grinning from ear to ear . . . But I said to myself, if I do go back to Chile that's the way it's going to be all day, every day, always measuring my words. Those are the rules of the game."

"So you gave in."

"So did you read it, man? Is that why you're making that kind of accusation? Did you? Do you know what else? Everything I said there is what I think, what I subscribe to, down to the last comma. I didn't lie once."

"So what did you say about the Socialist countries? About the parties?"

"Jérez asked me about writers in Socialist countries. I told it like I saw it."

"Did you tell him that in Socialist countries writers have social security, free health care, that they can make a living from their work because the editions are really massive, that there's no illiteracy?"

"Were you giving the interview or was I? I stressed the fact that I was against censorship in any country. Aren't we against censorship, Felipe?"

"What about the parties? What did you say about them?"

"The interview wasn't about politics, Felipe. That wasn't the main point."

"Did you tell him you weren't active anymore?"

Just then both of them realize that the Mexican, now drunker than before and with that ever-present smile, has stopped beside the table. He's listening to the last part of the dialogue with his head slightly inclined, as if he were recording every word and translating it into his very own confidential, internal language. He has a bottle of tequila in one hand and a glass in the other.

David tries not to look at him. Lowering his voice a little, he says:

"I said what I thought. I defended Allende. I said that one day his greatness would be recognized. His service to Chile. But I also said what I thought about Popular Unity."

"What did you say?"

"The same things I've been criticizing for years. That it was an outdated coalition, with no political initiative. That it looked backward without recognizing its mistakes. That we had to share the responsibility for the disaster we all lived through. Why should I keep quiet about what I think?"

"They won't publish what you said about Allende," says Felipe. "But you can be sure the business about Popular Unity will be there. In capital letters."

"You fellows are from Chile," the man says.

"Yeah," says David, not looking up at him. "Sometimes I'm not so sure. But yeah. We're from Chile."

Felipe draws closer to David, on the other side of the table, as if he were whispering a secret. But the man doesn't let him speak: "I always liked Salvador Allende," he says. "He knew how to die fighting, fuck it. Like a man."

"Excuse me," says Felipe, standing up. "We have to make a phone call. Are you coming?"

"Sure, let's go," says David. "Excuse us for leaving you . . ."

"I'll wait right here," the man says.

They cross the barroom. When they get to the telephone, far from their table, Felipe says: "That's all we needed. That guy parking himself there."

"He's one of your allies," says David. "You should be happy."

"Drunks get on my nerves."

"We're not in the greatest shape either, man."

Felipe dials, listening briefly, and hangs up. "That damned mechanic. He must've taken his phone off the hook."

"Look, Felipe, I want things to be perfectly clear. How long are we going to go along as if everything was perfect? We're floundering, man, and for my part, I'm not going to keep on with the same old song and dance that we're all good guys and geniuses. How long?"

"You know how long? Until we throw those criminals out. Or had you forgotten they're criminals?"

"Why should I forget?"

"When the tables are turned, then you can shout to the skies all the criticisms you want to against the parties and against Socialist countries. But if you're not going to help get rid of those guys, and that's OK, I can understand you're tired, that's your business, but if you've decided to throw in the towel, the least you can do is show a little bit of . . . responsibility. You're not Tomás, David. Even if you're not active, you know we're involved in a war and I demand a little responsibility from you. Even if it's just in honor of your fallen friends, and the ones who put their lives on the line every day. For those people your coming along and saying all those things, saying *anything* to *El Mercurio*, is like a . . . like a betrayal. It's as though all the sacrifices were for nothing, as though they had defeated us, David."

"They did defeat us, Felipe. You still don't realize how strong they are?"

"You're not going to do it, David. You can't do it. Write to Jérez and tell him you've changed your mind."

"Who do you think you're giving orders to?"

"It's just a suggestion."

"Not you and not anybody else is going to tell me, to suggest to me, what I have to do, Felipe. I'm not going to go around changing my mind, not in private and not in public, about things that I said and that I believe."

David turns around.

The man is still beside their table, rocking back and forth a little on his heels, like a pendulum.

"I hope I'm not bothering you," he says.

"Not at all," says David. "Two more beers," he tells the boy who's passing by at that moment. "And the check."

"You ought to drink something else," the man says. "That's no good."

Felipe returns and sits down. He moves his chair so that he doesn't have to look at the other man, who remains slightly behind him.

"How did it go?"

"The line's busy at home too. Who can Juana be talking to?"

"If the mechanic's line is busy and your home phone is too, they're probably talking to each other."

They bring the beers.

"No," says David. "Don't take the bottles away. I like for all the bottles to be on the table . . . Damn, it's good to be able to speak to a waiter in Spanish."

"David," says Felipe in a low voice, leaning forward, getting closer. "Do you really want to return so badly?"

"What does that mean?"

"Just what I said. Do you really want to go back so bad?"

"I didn't modify any opinion or make any accommodations for that interview, Felipe. Do you think I gave that interview just to get back in?"

"You don't understand . . ."

"You think . . ."

"It doesn't make the slightest difference what . . ."

The Mexican interrupts.

"Come on. Nobody gets mad on New Year's Eve. Nobody."

Felipe goes on, almost in a whisper: "It doesn't make the slightest difference why you gave it. Don't you understand that what's going on inside your head doesn't mean a fuckin' thing to anybody but you? What matters is what people will think. Jérez turns it in. *El Mercurio* publishes it. You go back to Chile. The whole arrangement is perfectly clear. Tell your mom she can stop petitioning, poor old woman. It won't be necessary . . ."

David's voice comes out like that of a man trying to, knowing how to, control himself.

"And what if I told you I couldn't care less what people think? What if I told you I've had it with making decisions about my life in terms of other people's prejudices and jealousies and small-mindedness? What if I told you that?"

"So go ahead. Tell me. Tell me you couldn't care less what people think."

David stares at Felipe for a long time. He empties the bottle of beer and waits for the foam to evaporate. Behind Felipe the Mexican lifts his glass, toasting them, a frown on his brow, and the same benevolent smile.

"What's the harm," says David, trying to pull his chair closer to the table, "in explaining in an interview how life is out here? It's clear I'm still with the opposition, Felipe. Don't think I kept that quiet. I made it clear I wasn't part of the consumer society."

"The limits, David. Those limits. If something's critical of the government, anything like that. There they draw the limit. There's where you have to be careful, to weigh every word. But if you want to shit on the parties, on Socialism, if you want to look defeated, there are no limits to that. And nobody can respond to you in Chile. Even if you wanted to rectify it yourself, they wouldn't publish it. Don't you see? It's a trap. They reduce you to playing whatever role they'll allow."

"So what's my role now? It's even more restricted. The young people don't even know I exist."

"That's just the way it is, man. Just grin and bear it. You were there in the good times. Nobody told you it was going to be easy. Now the hard times have come. And you have no right to undermine the people who won't abandon ship."

"But what gives you the right to represent them, Felipe? Who elected you? I'm Felipe Cuadra. I refuse to be interviewed because I represent 44.5 percent of the electorate. Myths. Falsehoods. We don't represent those people anymore. You represent yourself. And if you stay here a couple more years you'll end up staying forever and then you won't even represent yourself. That is, if Juana even wants to go back."

"I'll go back alone."

"Without your family you're not going anywhere, Felipe. Without your family, you're nothing. Because if worse comes to worse, you can count on the ones who gave birth to you, maybe on the mother of your kids, and maybe even on your kids. With luck, maybe even on a brother or a sister or a friend. And that's about it."

"Go ahead and send your fuckin' statement then. Send it if it's so damned important for you to see Lolo."

"That's what I'm going to do. You convinced me. First thing tomorrow I'll send Jérez a cable. We'll all go back with our tails between our legs and I'd rather go a little sooner."

"Not all of us."

"Yeah, all of us, man."

"You really believe that?"

"Yeah. I really do."

"I feel sorry for you, David. You know that? I really feel sorry for you."

Both of them have been raising their voices imperceptibly. David lifts his bottle to empty it, but there's nothing in it. He tips it over anyhow and watches a solitary drop slide down the side until it hangs on the rim and falls into the glass.

"At least I don't frighten you. Eight years ago I frightened you."

"They told me. They told me I wouldn't recognize you."

"Ah, so I'm being reported on. What do they say about me, Felipe? Do they say I'm a traitor? That I'm just like Tomás? What word do they use? Turncoat? Sellout? Fag? Traitor?"

"Don't flatter yourself. Nobody's going to write a report on you."

"Do me a favor, Felipe. I always wanted to know. What are they saying? Even I sent a report on my two conversations with Tomás. Did they tell you you shouldn't invite me? Is that what they recommend?"

"Do you want to know? Do you really want to know?"

The Mexican moves two steps closer. He pulls up a chair, but doesn't sit down.

"With your permission," he says, "I'd like to propose a toast. Boy, glasses please, bring me two clean glasses for these gentlemen. A toast to Don Salvador Allende. Who died like a hero. Who died like a man."

Neither Felipe nor David says anything. But Felipe stands up.

The man rests one foot on the chair and puts his own glass and the bottle of tequila on the table. His friends are paying no attention to him. They're still singing something alluding to Antonio's wedding, to woman's chronic infidelity. When the boy brings the glasses, the man pours the thick, colorless liquid from the bottle. His hand trembling, he pushes the full glasses across the table, one toward David, the other toward Felipe.

"To Salvador Allende," the man says. "To friendship between Chile and Mexico."

"To the people's victory," says Felipe, suddenly, lifting his glass. "To Salvador Allende."

The three of them drink.

The man staggers a little, but manages to regain his balance at once. "And now that we've toasted together, you might say we're something like buddies too. So . . . so," the man hesitates, as if he's forgotten what he was about to announce. "So, I'm going to take the liberty of giving you some advice. We're almost into the new year"—the man points toward the street, toward the television set, toward his own singing friends—"and you shouldn't start the new year as enemies. What happens later, that's up to you. But I've noticed that you've been wasting the last few minutes of the old year arguing. And that's just not right. I won't allow it. So shake hands."

A chorus of protests bursts from the group behind them. His friends are calling him. There are only ten more minutes until the new year begins.

"To show you how much we appreciate all the attention you, sir, have given our people and our president," says Felipe, "we're going to shake hands and follow your advice."

Beneath his attentive gaze David and Felipe shake hands.

"Good. That's the way I like it. Didn't I tell you"—and the man points a finger at David—"that this fellow is a real man? Pay attention to your brother here and you'll do fine. OK?"

"That's just what I'm trying to tell him," says Felipe. "But he's a good guy. He'll come around."

"Great," says the man. "So no more fighting. Until next year, no more fighting. OK?"

"OK," says Felipe. He picks up the tequila that's left. "To you, and to your friends and family."

"Thanks. Have a happy new year. And never get married. That's what I wish for you. Antonio won't listen to me, but you still have time to save yourselves."

"Thanks," says Felipe, sitting down.

David hasn't stood up in all that time, hasn't opened his mouth. He arranges the bottles in groups of three, then four, on the table, switching them around like rows of soldiers. In the bar there's an air of mounting excitement as midnight approaches. The man walks off toward the bar, toward his friends, backing away so as not to lose sight of them.

"Could I ask you a personal question?" asks Felipe.

David smiles tenuously. "As long as you don't publish my answer in *El Mercurio*."

"Do you want me to or not?"

"Fire away."

"It's about your dad. What would he think of all this?"

"My dad? What's he got to do with it? What do you know about my dad?"

"I just know what your mom told me. That he was something of a hero. That he gave his life for other people. He turned back at the Austrian border to help other people who were escaping. That's what I know. He sacrificed himself for other people. That's what I know about your father. That's enough. Now ask yourself: What would he tell you to do?"

"I have no father, Felipe. Don't ask me stupid questions."

"A man like that, David. What would he tell you to do?"

"So now you represent my dad too. Hell. All that's left now is for you to tell me to ask Lolo, my own son. If he can be proud of his father. Heroes, man. I'm surrounded by heroes. But I'm no hero, Felipe. I don't want Lolo to be a hero. Heroes end up dead. Like my old man. I didn't count for shit to him. Saving other people. And now Lolo goes on with the same old nonsense and the next time he won't be so lucky and the gas'll explode. What I want is for them to leave me alone. Let's see if they can leave me in peace to go on with my fuckin' life with nobody interfering. Just as if all those shitty years never happened. A blank slate and a new beginning. A blank slate and a new beginning, man."

"So send it. Go on and send the damned statement."

"I intend to. Of course I will. No question."

"If you're so anxious to go back, go ahead and send it."

Now David gets up from the table, turning over a bottle that shatters at his feet. He ignores it.

"Answer me. You are going to answer me now. You think I gave that interview just to get back in."

Felipe stands up too, more slowly. His voice comes out hoarse, low, impassioned.

"Yes, David. That's what I think. That's exactly what I think.

So tell me it's not true. Or is it? Is that why you did it? Is it true, man? Did you negotiate your return?"

Both of them look at each other for an instant, not saying anything else.

At that moment a chorus of voices bursts out from every corner of the bar, increasing, getting louder and louder. It's the customers and the owner and the waiters who are shouting, some of them standing on chairs, others on tables, watching the television screen, where a gigantic clock shows fifteen, fourteen, thirteen seconds until the new year.

The disorganized chorus, vibrant, rising and falling, sings out the numbers as if it were a rocket launch. Twelve, eleven, ten, nine, eight, seven. The whole bar shouts. The second hand of the clock moves spasmodically, resolutely forward. Six, five, four, three, two, one.

An indescribable babel explodes. Outside in the street horns, fireworks, an almost apocalyptic siren are heard.

It's as if Felipe and David are a pair of statues, completely motionless and dead in the middle of that defiant joy, contemplating each other's eyes, bodies, lips, without breathing.

David opens his arms and takes a step forward. He hears the crunch of broken glass beneath his feet.

"Brother," says Felipe and also opens his arms.

It's as if both of them are about to fall, to fall toward each other in the middle of an empty space.

They give each other a bear hug.

"Happy new year, brother."

"Let's hope this is the year, David."

Over David's shoulder Felipe can see the Mexican with the tequila and the flower embracing his friend Antonio, who's about to be married. All of a sudden their eyes meet, the Mexican smiles at him as if to say that's the way I like to see it, that's the way brothers should embrace.

"Is it true?" Felipe whispers in his ear. "Tell me, man. Before I let you go. Is that why you gave the interview?"

"Let me go."

"Is that why, David?"

David closes his eyes and hangs on to Felipe as if he is an anchor or a cradle in the middle of all that shouting.

"Yes, you son of a bitch," says David. "That's why."

"I never should've invited you," says Felipe.

But nothing would make him let go of him. Nothing.

INSIDE

The son of Manuel Sendero understood that something was going wrong, very wrong, when, a little after reaching the Laboratory, his shadow disappeared. He didn't have much of one because of the sparse light of his twilight landscape, and, besides, since we'd warned him that its loss could lead to irreparable consequences, he'd spent those six weeks while he camped out waiting for his authorization to come through looking for a good place to hide it, in some nook or cranny of his body, as if it were his immortal uncle in person.

His shadow disappeared, and in its place appeared something Grandfather would never have been able to give a name, it was so strange, if it hadn't been that we, his grandchildren from the future, had felt the same chill of the defenseless, and then helped him anonymously, whispering in his ear, it's fear, Grandfather. What you're feeling for the first time in your life is fear.

Five lights were turned on in the middle of the day, five artificial rays, each of them a billion watts, surrounding him. Five gray hands climbed toward their goal, and, with the fear, his shadow fell off like a bundle of wrinkled clothes, stretched out its limbs like someone who just woke up, and slipped away, miserably, to the tips of Grandfather's feet, where it stayed anchored in hope of better times, just a run-of-the-mill shadow, napping faithfully near its owner. Shadows aren't too bright, kids. That's a well-known fact. And Grandfather's had no reason to be the exception. It must have thought that all that light was a sign the danger was past, that we were coming out into the sunlight of victory, and that from now on it could devote itself to the relaxing exercises of ballet and hide-and-seek, which are a shadow's one and only form of happiness. In any case, it made no attempt to run away, even when the five hands yanked it out like a root, tied it up in a bundle with searchlights, tossed it into a sack full of other shadows, and closed the sack. It even managed to say good-bye.

Grandfather sensed a catastrophe in the fact that he could no longer count on it.

He remembered that every time the children were about to abandon their flagship mothers, their shadows were the first to be carried off into the other world, something like hostages. And when life was coming to an end, we whispered to the blind woman, and the blind woman whispered to the son of Manuel Sendero in the two dark places, the womb and the jail, which they had shared, from the double empty womb of her eyes, at the very moment the incinerator starts to burn, at the moment the top of the coffin comes down and the dead remain there with that unique pallor that comes from the memory of what they didn't do, the first thing they take away is your shadow. The blind woman had never seen hers, but she knew there was no better way to control a rebel, dead or alive, there was no better way for them to always know what you're doing, where you are, than to have your shadow in their power.

A captured shadow when it's released goes straight back to its owner, grieving like a dog who's lost his master, its fluid, black stain crossing every barrier, changing shape continuously, as if it were still joined to the one person who gives it life. And behind it, the horde of guards. You shouldn't reproach the shadow for its collaboration. Just imagine, kids, if instability were an everyday affair, being dissolved in water, becoming diffuse and multiple whenever light beams cross, depending on a mobile and human object for your very existence. A shadow knows it is mortal and transitory. Values, ideals, verses—it doesn't believe in them. Fiercely individualistic, with a kind of sick and parasitic love, it's the enemy of insubstantial things like soul and honor; nobody can convince it there's anything worse than disappearing, nobody can ask it to sacrifice itself for a cause. Just imagine, kids, that being the case, it's thrown into an incandescent cage with cold, white, flat bars, just imagine that it's amputated from the only thing that gives it life, the archangel of its own body, submerged in the promiscuous and starless membrane of other shadows. Because unlike the dead and the fetuses, shadows feel no affection for each other. Like castrated corpses in a railroad car, they stay there merging with each other, almost copulating, smoke blending and mixing, beginning to lose the sense of what their own shape is like. Just imagine. Scarcely are they released when they throw caution to the four winds and attach themselves to their original owners. They're linked to a fragile and impermanent god, joined to the body of a god who risks everything for a couple of promises, an imprudent god, clinging to his own offspring, a moralist, a dreamer.

It's easy for you to look down on your shadows, kids. Go ahead. Your shadow doesn't mind. But to the grandchild of a flesh-and-blood mother, when it's been taken from him, he feels like a man left alone, with no one and nothing to protect him. As if they'd taken away his instinct for self-preservation. Look what happened to the son of Manuel Sendero. For him, just as for his father, the world became quicksand, a swamp of filthy light, a place with no intermediary and no intercessor. All that was left to him were his dreams. And even they wouldn't last long.

Because from his father they took not his shadow but his Doralisa, shortly after they arrived at the Laboratory, and he discovered, as did his son, that something was going wrong. Very wrong. They put her on a stretcher. They pulled away the ringless hand with which Manuel was resting his sorrows on her belly, the hand he was using to talk to me. They took his wife and the son inside his wife and they placed us far away. And they started to undress Mama—my mama who did not need to undress to be naked, they began to take her clothes off.

When they take away your shadow, Papa, it won't be long before they come in to plunder your dreams.

"Do you know what these instruments are, Manuel Sendero? Do you know what they are? Don't look away, Manuel Sendero. There's no place to look. This is a hospital bed, Manuel. Do you know what it's for? There's an anesthetic in this bottle, Manuel. It's to make the patient more comfortable, to relax the entrance. You know where the entrance is, what entrance I'm talking about, don't you? So it will dilate and there won't be any laceration. So it won't be complicated by hemorrhaging. And, above all, so there won't be any perforation. It's really preferable to use a good dilator, Manuel. Do you see that? On the other hand, these are forceps. That's what they're called. They're about twenty centimeters long. But sometimes we need longer ones. The forceps can be turned, twisted, in general manipulated very easily. Do you know what they're for, Manuel Sendero? Or would you rather I show you this needle? It works this way: a saline solution is introduced into the cavity, the cavity in question, I mean. It's a more modern method. Do you want to know how it works?"

Papa didn't answer him. Years and years later I had to do it. I pronounced the same words that, way back then, bounced off Doralisa's walls, leaving no echoes or answers.

"And all this," I told him then, I'm telling him now, "all this just so my father would sing?"

"Your father?" I had the impression the Caballero was smiling, that something struck him as funny. "Yes. So he'd sing. As simple as that. We needed it."

"And all the threats, then and now, just for that. As though that would frighten us."

"Threats?" the Caballero asked from behind the lights of long ago. "Absolutely not. You asked me a favor. You wanted to know what happened that night. So I'm telling you. I showed him all the necessary instruments. That's all. Not a single threat."

We were there in Grandfather's voice, laboring like crazy.

"Yes, a threat," said Grandfather. "What you'll do to the babies, if they keep up their resistance."

"Babies?" said the Caballero. "You're obsessed with the baby business, just like Manuel Sendero was. But suction and scraping can be used for something besides the uterus. They can be used on other parts of the body. Did I say anything about a uterus? Have you heard me say anything about the method used to get rid of fetal tissues, then the placenta, and finally the calvarium and the spinal column, until the cavity is completely empty, until there's nothing that could lead to infection? Could that be the cavity I've been talking about? Have I mentioned dehydration by the use of a trans-abdominal saline solution? Have I suggested the modern technique of aspirotomy, where the forceps is called embryomatic and crushes or grinds, so that the extraction is facilitated? Have you heard me say a word about all that?"

But at that very moment, nevertheless, in the backlands of a thousand female mountains, they were stealing our shadows, Grandfather, they were blinding our bodies so there would be no shadows ever again. Five hands nailed us to a hospital bed, Grandfather. They're coming in to plunder our dreams. They believe that the last rebels and the last memories have taken refuge here inside, that certain names and hopes are shining here in that widows' fog. They're coming in to look for them. Grandfather saw how some wet boots were suddenly shining on the pavement of his dream, and they'd wait there, on a path or in front of an open window or with the motor running, for someone new to arrive, the carrier of a forbidden word, of some small flame, someone running from another dream or from another death, an emigrant in this timeless time. They'd wait in every womb till they heard the footsteps of the one who was coming with a message for the one who was going to be born. The hands that belonged to those solitary mouths became tense. They released the safeties on their weapons. Someone was on his way and they were ready. The Caballero, or someone identical to him—there were so many of them, so many of his twins in this universe—gave the order. Almost as if he were afraid that among all those children who had been in their mothers' wombs for more than ten months there would be one who in thirty or forty years, a thousand, ten thousand years, would return to settle accounts with him for what he and they had done to humanity. I know it. I was there. I witnessed it: The searchlights were being turned on all the innocents scattered around the world, and their sun was setting.

Among them, decades before, the last of the first rebellion, the first of the second and final rebellion, Grandfather. Grandfather, who now was beginning slowly to remember what happened that night. So slowly that it seemed as if the memory had preceded the experience. That first he ought to remember what happened and only then would he have to live through it. As if two mirrors, facing each other, could not decide which of the two is real.

The smell of anesthetic from that night revived his organism and in the middle of his shadowless terror he violently wished he were someplace else, walking toward Pamela in the sunset, entering Pamela's body at sunset, falling and rising like a sun toward Pamela's setting sun. He even wished he were facing Eduardo the way the blind woman would soon face Eduardo. He wished he were in Manuel Sendero's undesirable and impossible skin, having to decide between life and death, between life and life. He could even have wished he were facing Skinny, who had so triply denied him. He would even have settled for facing the Caballero thirty years later, dragging his combat gear toward the Caballero, his peaceful combat gear, step by step, toward the Caballero. Anywhere but there. Anywhere but in his memory. Anywhere but there inside Mama, who still wasn't waking up, who should have awakened so his memory would be different. Anywhere but here, listening to what the Caballero was saying to the other side of the wall of flesh, unable to hear the slight anthem of hope of the fetuses telling him that not all the apples that fall to the ground need to rot, anywhere but here.

The Caballero had started to show Manuel Sendero the accounts. Doralisa's pills, for example. How much did he think they had cost? Notice the food Manuel had consumed while in jail. When and how would they make up for all that? Or, to go no further, how about the air they had breathed ever since they were born, he and his parents, without ever having paid a tax? Next month the lawyers would appear, the accountants, the notaries, and they'd put their fingers in the wound of the bill of Sendero, Manuel. Where are our profits? they were going to ask. Where are the dividends in this case? And they had to be shown something. If they weren't shown the original voice, at least the pertinent working parts of Doralisa had to be given to them. Even then the initial investment wouldn't be recovered. It was a machine that could be dismantled and reassembled, and, given Doralisa's youth, could continue to be used for many, many years. But take note: it would never be worth as much as Manuel's voice. Because his voice was the first of its kind, a prototype, the essence, the main one of its kind, and she, on the other hand, however well she might have made love and her skin melted into the clothes and however excellent the condition of her womb might be, couldn't even think about first place, about being the foundation for the perfect new human beings they were projecting. But what they were talking about was to first recover their capital investment and then . . . Well, then a bonus for their stockholders. Just a little surprise. There was no reason to worry. Manuel would still have most of Doralisa. Of course he would. But they, for now, would keep the most income-producing part of her. He shouldn't regard it as such a tragedy. It would be like living with a nun . . . And if he didn't like this solution, the answer was simple enough: he should sing. We're waiting for you to sing.

In spite of himself Manuel Sendero must have felt his throat loosening up. To his sorrow, he must have felt the life of his son whispering in the depths of his lungs.

He could have sung.

But he didn't, kids. I remember now that he didn't. He begged his eyes to close rather than to watch the hands that were starting to come and go, undressing what had been that splendid knoll, golden and smooth and bronzed, which in better times had needed no clothing to express itself. He didn't see how the invading hands withdrew from the circle of light as if they didn't dare break the ring of moonlight that was surrounding that body like a halo. He didn't listen to the Caballero, who never left him and who was now offering him the last chance, because, Manuel Sendero, they were going to capitalize on those vocal cords, on that tongue, on that mouth, anyway; they would separate the voice from the brain that so stubbornly held back; everything was going to go along perfectly, and, in spite of himself, Manuel Sendero would achieve an eternal renown. Because his song would be injected into thousands of other men. Others who lacked musical talent. So why not cooperate a little? Just a little. A tiny little bit. You'll be an idol. You'll have overseas tours. We'll sell your records by the thousands. Papa paid no attention. He refused to pay attention. It's the only life you have,

Manuel Sendero. Don't throw it away. They're ready. I'm going to give the order, Manuel Sendero. Hearing in the distance and as though it were some other couple, some other Manuel, some other Doralisa, some other grandchild, wonder boy, not listening to the Caballero's voice that was saying, OK. You asked for it. You've really screwed yourself now, Manuel Sendero. Not even listening to my voice that was trying to come out, that like a crazed boxer inside me wanted to come out. Not even listening to me.

Because we had always expected this moment, he and I. A moment like this one can't be ignored. It separates a son from his father forever. She, Doralisa, would never have doubted what to do. She, pure shadow, tied to this bed that Papa had anticipated, that I, in my worst moments, also foresaw, she and the positive pole and the negative pole and the unshakable metal that was opening a way toward my voice that was trying to speak to him in the yellow darkness, in the persistent and thick and warm rain that was coming in from memory and from something worse and more bitter than memory. That's why I had decided not to be born, kids, never to be born. Because Manuel Sendero had decided for me long ago. And at the very moment he took his first breath, hanging upside down in the public soup that was coming out of his mother, he realized with the last flashes of memory that what was awaiting him at the end of this journey that was now beginning without even an apple in his hand was this decision, this beloved woman in a hospital bed, this man who was himself in the next bed, and he had spent the rest of his existence trying to trick that intuition, that initial scream. He had tried to change the world with his song, so that this foreseen outcome would be impossible, and when the world, far from changing, had gotten worse, Manuel Sendero had fallen back on that extreme recourse of muteness, in order not to have to collaborate. He had gotten rid of the only valuable thing he possessed, so they wouldn't have to ask him for it, kids. Such is life, kids. We think we will finally find a way to preserve our dignity and to save our lives and the lives of our families; Manuel Sendero tried to think that the day would never come when he would have to choose between his own song and the song that was taking shape inside Doralisa's body. That's the way the universe ought to be. But he picked the wrong universe, kids, and that day had finally arrived.

Once upon a time, kids, on the frontier of a fairy tale, there was a singer whose name was Manuel. Once upon a time there was we ourselves in that country that never was. Once upon a time there was a land of meanwhile, a time of between parentheses, a land of the back door, a land where they put women to sleep and take children prisoner. Once upon a time Manuel Sendero had dreamed that with his voice intact he could rescue his beloved from Hell and resurrect his son and move the beasts to pity. Once upon a time, in a word, Manuel Sendero believed he was immortal.

As we all do.

But Manuel Sendero discovered at last, facing the Caballero who was speaking, facing the body of the dying beauty, facing his son's words which were fading out, that that dream had been a lie, just one more lie, and that he, at least, was far from being immortal. Manuel Sendero would have to choose, kids. Once upon a time there was a man who was a hardly, a perhaps, a who knows, a therefore. But he was going to have to choose.

At that moment the sun was setting and in the land of forevernow Pamela was waiting for me, had to be waiting for me.

I have to see Pamela, Papa. I must see her.

Just an hour. If they'd just give me an hour in this world. What's one little hour in this world for someone who never asked for anything?

But the humanity of Manuel Sendero could no longer hear him. To keep from being tempted by the Caballero's proposition, to keep from imagining Doralisa's accusing eyes if she should awaken, Manuel Sendero had closed himself in and shut himself off so far inside himself that he had even lost the faculty of picking up Grandfather's voice demanding to be born. And anyhow that wouldn't have influenced him. Because he didn't decide then. He had decided earlier, much earlier, even before he was born. So often had we asked the blind woman and Pamela and the twins and Eduardo and every other child who is born with his coffin on his back, asked them to be loyal, not to put themselves in the Devil's service.

Papa had done just what we recommended.

If he couldn't do anything to save me, I would have to act on my own. I'd have to do something soon, kids, so this story would have a happy ending. Thirty-three years later, but still in time, I'd have to come to the rescue. Now do you understand why I camped for six weeks in that neighboring country? Why I had to find the Caballero? Why I came back by way of secret tunnels?

"Kill him, Grandfather."

The words of the son of Manuel Sendero, his first words to his father, now on our lips. We opened communication, the intrauterine direct line. We spoke to him from far and near and beside him and from the past and from the future and from any other-ultra place where we could connect with the fetal telegraph. He should kill him, before they broke into Doralisa's cave of the thousand and one days, before he gave them the signal to penetrate our dreams, the signal to hunt us down on the pavement, one by one, before even the memory of the second and final rebellion was extinguished.

"Kill me, kid."

As if the Caballero could hear us and was amused by us, he stood up and moved toward the light. Don't look at him, Grandfather, when he finally shows his face, don't look at it, Grandfather. Sing him your father's song, crush him with Sendero's song until he begs for pardon, until he disappears, Grandfather, but don't look at the exile of his light without a light.

"Kill me, kid," the Caballero tells him, stepping out from behind the spotlights, coming closer. "Go on, take this pistol. It's part of the arsenal you want to destroy. Go on."

Take it, Grandfather. Show him there's a grandfather in every mouth, a grandchild in every apple, tell him. Tell him your father sang, that he didn't give up his voice.

"Go on," said the Caballero, and I had to turn my head aside to keep from seeing him under the five dogs of light. "We're going to win anyhow. We always end up winning anyhow, whatever you do."

He took another step forward.

"Not always," I told him. "Not always. Every child is born new."

"Every child is born old," said the Caballero. "Fire."

I closed my eyes the way you told me to. All of a sudden, like a third, cold eye in the middle of my hand, a frigid throat in the middle of my hand, all of a sudden, I felt the cold metal of the gun in the center of my nothingness. Go on, Grandfather, corner him with your father's last song, go on.

"He didn't sing," said the Caballero, and his breath was so close, right on top of me, right on top, so it was like being inside that man and his gaze, kneeling on my knees and defenseless inside that man's breathing. "I have a voice too, kid. Are you sure he sang? Could you sing if you listened to the voices that he had to listen to, to my voices?"

He came another step closer until there was no one and nothing else left in the universe.

And then he came in to loot my dreams too.

Once upon a time there was a nest from which we fell, a nest from which I fell, and I had to witness the voices of the sons and the grandsons of the Caballero covering the face of the earth as if they were its only masters and would be its only heirs, entering us with their sound in that space we've reserved for the mothers of the world ever since the beginning of the waters, that place where every male being is an intruder if he's not a child. I had to listen to his voices, I had to hear them in my papa's dead mouth. Close your ears, kids. Close your ears. hey manuel they electrocuted me for raping ten little girls one of them was my sister do you still want to sing, hey manuel at the age of six they threw me into a reservoir and papa watched me fall like a floating feather and sink and mama didn't know and sink and afterward not a single word just papa's eyes and then not even his eyes do you still want to sing, hey manuel I told my son to go that you had to fight for your country the colonel convinced me that nothing would happen to him not one of them came back do you still want to sing, hey manuel I told my husband I didn't want to have another child every mouth to feed means more hunger and he stayed on top of me and I liked it and the next one I'll get rid of with pesticides and rat poison do you still want to sing, hey manuel my comrades killed me by mistake they put me on trial by mistake I was loyal I didn't even protest the place was like ice tell my brother to save my glasses too do you still want to sing, hey manuel I pulled the trigger when I was young the gas tablets I used a stick wrapped in barbed wire for the prisoners this seems to be a hospital at eighty-seven years cancer really isn't funny nobody ever knew what I squeezed in that little town the nurses bring me candy and I look at their legs do you still want to sing, hey manuel he was coming, she was coming with hands held out a peace offering fish and flower wreaths arms held out on the edge of the forests I picked up my stone and I killed my brother and his wife the she's expecting now my our do you still want to sing. hey manuel your son you're going to so that you'll be able to you're going to your own son him so you still want to sing, still still do you still want you still want to sing?

I fired at him, kids. I forgot that he had ever taken up residence in a womb that cannot be rented. I forgot he had ever had an infancy that nobody charged him a penny for. I forgot the new humanity we were proposing demands a beginning without bloodshed. I tried to forget the miraculous mechanism that joined us and made his muscles move and his blood pump and the millions of years of evolution it had taken the universe to produce a unique and irreplaceable specimen like that one. I broke all my promises, denied each and every one of my principles. I inaugurated the story and history with an execution instead of by sharing an apple. I assumed the burden of his refrigerator-soul to the end of my days. I accepted the fact that he'd never leave me and would be encrusted in my heart. It was in self-defense. It was so the universe would not die of a heart attack. It was so I wouldn't be born out of his mouth and so I'd never be his son's twin. I'd do it again. I have no justification and I'm not looking for any. I fired.

Too late, some will say. Too late? Too early really, Grandfather. It was like firing into the wind.

Or rather, kids, as if Grandfather were the wind, as though Grandfather had never had the privilege of having a father and was just passing through, without any certainty of having left a trace on the earth.

From the nest out of which I had fallen I listened to the voices that were still speaking to Manuel Sendero, dauntless, impregnating my refuge with a million years of voices, you still want you still want, I had to listen to the Caballero and to his grandchildren as if in a dream that we don't know how to interrupt.

"Not just anybody kills me," said the Caballero's voice in Papa's throat, stealing his song, deep inside the throat of the son of Manuel Sendero, swallowing the stars. "Do you want to know the secret? The only way to kill me?"

You should have been born, Grandfather. So what else is new? To kill another man, for the even harder task of engendering another man or a woman you have to be born first. For the children to be multiples of children and grandchildren and for them to be able to do it someday perhaps by the thousands, you first have to take the risk of entering the obscene and limited continent of a body, so what else is new, you have to adopt a country and a language and a woman, you have to make the trip. And then, Grandfather, understand that the hard thing isn't being born, the really hard thing is going on, going on being born.

"It doesn't make any difference," said the Caballero. "Because even if you knew the secret, it wouldn't do you any good. You can't kill me, because there's no such son of Manuel Sendero. You don't count, do you understand, you don't count for anything. Do you want to hear what else happened that night?"

Tell him, Grandfather. Tell him you're the only one who does count, Grandfather. Tell him. Go on. Don't let him have the last word. Tell him Pamela's waiting for you; we're waiting inside Pamela, now and always, then and always; we're going to come out; we'll come out on our steeds with our swords; we'll come out riding the wind. Tell him. We still haven't pronounced the last word. You hid, Grandfather. You'll hide. The world is full of wombs waiting for you. You'll hide in your father's song, Grandfather. We still haven't pronounced the last word. He'd better watch out; all of them had better watch out, Grandfather. They should die in advance, Grandfather, because the only thing that really counts is all those human beings who haven't been born yet. What counts is the fact that nine-tenths of our personality still hasn't emerged. Tell him,

Grandfather. Tell him who's going to have the last word in this story, when he's just a bad memory and we come out of Pamela and wake up in Doralisa's dawn, Grandfather. When the other half of Doralisa isn't sleeping anymore, when Manuel sings his other half, when the great-grandchildren of the sower of apples are born, Grandfather, when little men and pretty women are born who can't understand that there once was a time when such monsters were the only masters of the next to the last word. Tell him, Grandfather, don't be afraid, when we can come out into the peaceful night of the others without five men knocking at our door, without everybody thinking it's normal for five men to come knocking at our door, when they know it's an aberration and a scandal for such men who shouldn't even exist to come knocking at our door, when nobody will be born without a heart, Grandfather, it's guaranteed that you're born with a double heart, so that injustice will hurt us so much we'll have to do away with it once and for all, Grandfather, we still haven't pronounced the last word, tell him, Grandfather, proclaim it even if nobody listens to you, even if nobody pays any attention, even if nobody believes you, even if they tell you that the experience of history demonstrates that you're wrong, even if they call you an idealist and a romantic and a socialist and an anarchist and a stubborn dreamer, it's worth it just to say it, Grandfather, it's worth it to hear yourself saying it, Grandfather, it's worth it to be faithful to the joy that conception brings, it's worth it to love history the way other people have loved a woman or a man, it's worth it to strip naked and to take the risk of history, Grandfather, we still haven't pronounced the last word, Pamela, who's waiting for us up in the nest, and he she they we waiting for you, when the dead can be silent because life won't have been a lie, we still haven't pronounced the last word, Grandfather. Tell him he doesn't exist, Grandfather, that he has all the power and none of the love, tell him we're being born all the time, that nobody knows it but it's true all the same, that we won't leave him alone, that he'd have to be left all to himself on the planet in order to be successful, that every newborn baby comes with the last word that we still haven't pronounced and bet him that this time things are going to change and if you're wrong,

Grandfather, tell him, Grandfather, tell him it's better to be wrong the way we are than to be right the way he is, tell him that my father your father our father who art on the earth that is not yet ours will find us in a thousand years and will tell us again that he did not place himself at the service of lovelessness. Do anything but surrender, in order not to betray yourself, not to die, so we can climb up from Pamela with our your daily fire, now and then, then and always. Don't let him have the last word. Tell him we'll return. Tell him we'll camp for six weeks in a nearby country, Grandfather. Tell him we'll find him even if it takes the rest of eternity. Tell him that as far as we're concerned, Grandfather, we're going to find him and then we're going to tell him, Grandfather, we're going to tell him the last word then.

But he spoke first.

"Do you want to know what happened that night?" said the Caballero. "That's why you came, right? Do you want to hear it?"

There was nothing else to hear. It was true. I remember that it was true. Pamela was waiting for me, in spite of the skeptics and the embittered and the liars and the merchants; the temple of Pamela was waiting for me with my grandchildren's warm words inside; you were waiting for me like a torch in the sand, dear grandchildren of my only future. But it was also true that we went in, I went into the operating room. They closed the door. Papa, I said to him. Papa, without asking him to sing for them, not telling him. Although, yes, if you want to know the truth, yes, telling him to sing, to put himself at their service, to surrender his throat, his tonsils, his gums, his tongue, the square root of every tooth. What good were all his famous banners if they were going to kill me?

They're going to kill me, Papa.

He didn't answer me. It was as though he couldn't hear me, didn't want to hear me, was determined not to release the hurricane of his song for them, son. Son?

They closed the door. There was the smell of anesthetic. My shadow disappeared.

After that I remember nothing.

PART IV

Passages

FIRST EPILOGUE

When Carl awoke that last morning of his stay, he did not realize at once that he had gone blind. He thought the sun had not come up yet. He tried to move his head so he could look at the phosphorescent dial on the clock that Sarah had—where was Sarah? When would they bring her back from the treatment to help her bear a child? His head refused to obey the order. So all he could do was wait for daybreak—an almost endless time, immobile, images from the past parading by, images which he needed no eyes, open or closed, to examine.

It was the only time he could be with Agueda. Later, as soon as they'd realized he was awake, they'd plug that machine into his ears and he'd witness the voice of those people invading him like a sea reclaims dry land. He didn't want them to read and suck in his most intimate thoughts. He didn't want them to discover that in the semidarkness before dawn what Carl imagined was some other outcome for that cowardly episode from the remote past when a knock at the door had surprised him and he'd managed to ask himself why Sarah was returning so soon from the gynecologist, one more gynecologist. And there was Agueda in the doorway. Agueda, back after seven years, with a little girl holding on to her hand. Agueda, with not even a wrinkle, as though someone had painted a single face on her, a face that would never vary. And he, staring nervously in the direction of the bus stop where Sarah would get off the bus in a little while, didn't even ask her in, inside his mouth which suddenly felt old, he found the words that begged this woman to leave. This woman, who according to the memories in his own skin, he must have loved once. I've come to get you, she said as if it were out of a dream. And I won't go until I have your promise you'll follow me. If she would just leave, he'd promise anything. But she must disappear. If I go, she said, if she went, she'd travel through the desert to the south, to the ends of the world, until there was no more land, and if you don't come to find me, until you find me, your lawful wife will never be able to conceive a child.

Was that curse real? Could Agueda have said that? Did that woman really exist?

He still had doubts, over a half-century later. The words sounded false and melodramatic. In time he discovered it was easy to blot them out, as though they belonged to some gothic romance of the worst kind or had come out of one of those anonymous and false letters that you just throw in the trash. But at that moment he must have thought they weren't fictitious and that Agueda was no invention. Because he answered. He said yes, provided she left, provided Sarah would never see in that little girl the child she hadn't been able to feel growing inside her, the child her husband had fathered in another woman's womb, he told her, OK . . . Whatever she wanted. So long as the outcome could be postponed for a few hours, days, months, years. So long as she'd travel south and wait for him in some archipelago or other, that his great-grandchildren might ambush him if he were not telling the truth, that Heaven might wither his wife's womb. He'd follow her soon. She must go.

He had never heard from her again.

Sarah got off the bus that afternoon and it was as though the cameraman for the film had changed not only the roll of film but reality itself. It wasn't hard to convince himself that none of that had really happened.

But sixty years later, from the moment he had identified those eyes of holy serenity belonging to the reporter who asked if it was his first trip, who asked him what he thought about death, he started to wake up a little before dawn. He had gradually become accustomed to the special way the light exercised its dominion behind the slow mountains. He liked to think that it had been that way for centuries, and it would be that way a thousand years from now, and that perhaps that was the only thing that was permanent, the only true bridge with this land that had been promised to him, and that maybe it would belong to the children of the daughter he—once again the word was *perhaps*—had fathered with Agueda. It was an illusion, of course. The astounding resemblance to Becky, old age, a sense of guilt, the fact that the latitude was southern, everything had come together to make him think he'd come to that place to die, to see his grandchildren grow up. It was an illusion fostered by the darkness, but it was a happy and probable illusion and one that harmed no one. Some images that he didn't want the machine belonging to Marras and to Rev. Rex and to Milton FMI to capture, to suck up. His imagination for once working only for itself, for its own pleasure, not to entertain anybody else: a country where he could be young again, even be rejuvenated, and Agueda would come home and Sarah would welcome her and the little girl affectionately, and for a few marvelous moments it was Agueda's body and Sarah's face, they were both one, and Carl enjoying that unique body between the sheets. A country where one could choose again, this time making the right choice, inviting them in, the three of them waiting, he, Agueda, the little girl, waiting for his wife to come home, so they could all decide how to go on with life, so they could decide how to avoid the southern desert and Sarah's withered womb like a curse. A country where Sarah had a daughter with Agueda's face.

Anything was possible in those hours before dawn, before the guides and pulleys and doctors and factors and colonels and laboratories came for him. Those minutes which were the only thing in the world that truly belonged to him. The only thing he didn't reveal to anyone, that no comic strip artist would ever draw on a piece of paper.

Until he realized that the hospital was stirring, that a torrent of fresh sunlight should have come through the half-opened window, and he suddenly smelled toast and coffee passing by his door, and he understood that, during the night, the darkness—like a river—had overflowed the shores of his eyes. He was blind.

He tried out his voice, coughing out the first thing that crossed his mind.

"I'm dying," said Carl Parks, his voice strangely robust. "Bring Sarah." Each word came out like a black fly, standing out vividly against the whitest wall. He couldn't hear them. He couldn't see them. He had to taste them, chew them, to be sure they really existed. And he knew that a lot of people would be around him, that the guide or was it the Colonel or maybe Rev. Rex or Dr. Garay or Major General Soro or it might even be the inimitable and incomparable Foilback who had returned as promised, and Carl added, with something like a bark that no one had ever heard, that no one would ever hear again: "Right away."

He had spent, sighed, crossed every second of his existence with Sarah. But never, in all that time, had he found the courage to tell her of his predawn dreams. They had shared their bodies and their breakfasts without his ever daring to let her share that more fertile intimacy, that nakedness called fear, or was it called hope? As if by the act of revealing everything to her, of becoming a plate-glass window before her, of becoming transparent forever, he could at last find in that woman the refuge for his dreams that he'd always searched for, could see himself kneeling and breathing and renewed in the depths of the maternal space that she had reserved for their child.

Through all the omissions and silences everyone has some secret, some sacred or vulgar word he's never dared pronounce.

He was going to die, and he ought to drag that word out from inside like a woman who goes on suffering labor pains years after her child was stillborn, years after they tell her there was nothing and no one for her to bear. He was going to die, and if he was to move into forever like that dead child, it wasn't fair for Sarah to have to be that woman endlessly. He was going to die, and she deserved the truth, and he, for the first, last, the only time in his life had no reason to be afraid to tell her.

Die? But you can't, Mr. Parks, my son, Carl, my friend Barks, how could you think that? Don't you know how truly unpleasant the dead are? . . . This business of dying used to be an acceptable, a gentle, and even a Christian practice. But now. Our intelligence services tell us they're stirring up a rebellion. Yes, the dead themselves. In person. Just calculate, Mr. Barks, how many there must be. And in all that mob, the sheer weight of the ignorant, the shiftless, and the disabled. And the fanatics. If we could take out the X-Factor before they die. That's the way to go. Zip. They die and that's the end of it. But they carry a little bit with them and from the tomb they screw everything up, all of them, infectious, corrupt, virulent, still crawling with activity even centuries later, never giving up. Whispering rebellion to everybody who preceded them into the grave. Luckily they don't have much strength left. They're weakening. They're piling up, that's true, the sullen devils, so that one plus one plus one, you add it up, they'll manage to put out a warm little message. Dangerous. Because all the threats and punishments and sentences . . . What effect can they possibly have? Reason with them? Impossible. With all their rancor against the living. The living who are in the driver's seat and making progress. So don't you even think of crossing over to the other side, Mr. Parks. They'd give you a bad reception. They'd give all of us a bad reception. As if we had anything to do with what happened to them when they were slaves in Rome, serfs in the Middle Ages: just imagine, Carlie, how many there are. Russian peasants, Chinese, Hindus, Aymara. They didn't fare very well among the living. They're clearly in the minority, so off they go to stir up the corpses. What's our counterattack? We'll inject them. Yes, sir. A good fumigation with the anti-X-Factor. There won't be any stones left for them to hide behind. A summary purification of the earth and the game's over. Sleepy-time, kids. Self-determination for the living. Disinfectant for the dead. No demagoguery. No outside interference. So everybody's going to be equal in the other world, are they? Does it seem fair to you that death should level things out? The hard worker and the good-for-nothing, both equally dead? You and the garbage collector? A genius and a mental defective? You die? Whatever are you thinking about? No, instead, we're going to embalm your dreams. Save the best part of everybody. We're going to bandage you up completely, so well that your soul can't get away, wrapped up tight, so it can't slip away, right, Carl? As long as you keep on dreaming, you're alive. We'll find the X-Factor, you'll see. Just a matter of a few more days. Meanwhile we're not going to betray you, give us your mind, Mr. Parks, my son, give us your virtue. Let the others agonize. Like it was before when they were all peaceful and normal. Before this gang of atheists and blacks stirred them up, wallowing in egalitarianism, copulating shamelessly right there in the cemetery. Ten thousand, twenty thousand years and they're still fornicating and not able to have any kids. Echoes of X-Factor are interchanged, like venereal poison through the arteries, they're passionate and dogmatic to the bitter end, stirring up hatred in the very dust. We've tried persuasion, of course. We've sent emissaries, upstanding ladies, venerable churchmen, bank tellers, respectable people, mayors, captains, under secretaries, judges. But when they preach that it's better to die and get it over with once and for all, about its being a fine resting place and about leaving the living alone, the rabble-rousers shout them down. They stir up the natural resentment the dead feel for the living . . . How they'd love to get hold of your imagination, Mr. Parks, to suck it till it's dry. Because they don't have a single idea of their own. Why, these illiterates don't even have their own niche, they're buried in the same clothes they pretended to work in every day. Just imagine how they smell. They're going to steal your dreams, Charles, in order to do their brainwashing for them, to mortify the ears of the innocent dying, even stirring up the pebbles, making up for their earlier failures, lying in wait in the cemetery crossroads and wherever funeral processions form, putting more enthusiasm into the intoxication of our chlorophyll than they ever put into their daily work, popping up like subversive mushrooms. If you die, you'll hear that sound: a slight moss of music sticking like trichina and hunger to the grass beneath which they chew up and spit out weed-filled earth. All along the alleyways of dreams, they're lurking, lurking like infected semen in the early-morning cleanness of urinals, and nobody sees them. They were parasites when they were alive and they're still parasites. They're going to expropriate your imaginings, Carl, they need you, because they're incapable of carrying on an intelligent conversation. Instead of learning from death, like well-behaved schoolchildren, they sprout cancerous roots in the fetid air between their legs. Don't listen to their insults. How dare they say that we're the ones who are really dead and that they're really alive, straggly beards, long-nails, lice-ridden perverts, three-times-bedraggled, and beggaring? Singing in the dark, the impudent upstarts. Just as if they feared no one. They talk about plans to interrupt radio transmissions, regular programming. Words that've been blotted out turn up in the National Archives, in the official registries, in the history books. They have their allies among the living. That's the only explanation, Mr. Barks. They're the worst. Fraternizing with beggars who were drawn and quartered in an autopsy, skinned Jews, ill-mannered rabble. If you have to go, Mr. Parks, stay away from that rubbish. Because it's possible you could fall when we attack their rearguard. We cut off their supplies, we give them an injection, clean out a few drops of light. That's all. That's the operation we're involved in right now. But don't you worry. As they die off, that useless garbage, as more space is provided, we plan to bring our people back, all our loved ones: Papa, Granny, Wife, each one carries the memory of his own ancestors, so we'll gradually rescue and open up past generations until we gather together all those who merit resurrection. We know how to play at the ancestor game too. The whole family, together at last, from far and wide. And all the rest of them, left over there, the sick and the mad, left to practice their demographic subversion in death, good luck to them; but as for us, back here, alive. The way it always should have been. The Kingdom of Heaven. Our own preselection, to make God's work easier, my son. That's what's coming, Carl, you can believe me. But in your case I wouldn't risk it. Why? You go to sleep now, slowly, and the best part of you will stay here with us, immortalized, still creating for the great and for the small, for the fat and for the thin. And every dream with its own package, its number, its name, date, time. When you wake up, you can recover every image, just as if it were your birthday, Carlie baby, and you hadn't celebrated it for millennia. You're going to go well supplied, son, with your suitcases overflowing. What a trip that'll be, Mr. Parks. All your dreams, old friend, teacher, we'll preserve your dreams through the years, sleeping at your feet like puppy dogs, just outside the deep freeze, holding death at bay like a blue-fly. It won't hurt a bit. Can we count on your consent? OK?

At that last moment Carl Parks felt certain that no one was drawing him, no one was reading him, no one was following his actions in the day-to-day comic strip; he felt certain that for once the words *To be continued* would not appear at the end of his adventures. He managed to think, although barely, that the one who was dying was him. No one else.

He would have liked to have said something. He would have liked to have called out to some woman, to Sarah or to Agueda or to some other, to perpetuate a name so it would remain behind, a relic or an echo, son, daughter, grandson, children. He would have liked to have had a brother to keep him company or to go through what was coming.

Before the absolute darkness in which there were no animals and no happy laughter and not even the consolation of an easy pardon, he heard or thought he heard someone pressing a button.

After that, nothing at all. I mean *nada*. Nothing.

SECOND EPILOGUE

"They've been calling you, David," says Juana.

"Calling me?" says David.

"From Chile," says Juana. "The telephone's been ringing for hours."

Thirty thousand years later a voice says:

"I'm home."

And another voice answers: "Great. Just in time to tell the kids a story. They swore they wouldn't fall asleep until you got back."

"I'm so tired that . . ."

"Promises are promises."

"Who was it?" asks David. "Lolo?"

"Cecilia," says Juana.

"First a drink."

"A drink later. Right now I hear some children's voices calling for their quota of bedtime stories. Go tame the beasts before they tear our house apart."

"You convinced me, you convinced me. As long as I get my drink afterward."

"Tell them it's got to be short."

"As if they'd pay any attention to that."

"She didn't want to talk to me," says Juana. "It was for you, person to person."

"Something's happened to Lolo," says David.

"Cut it out," says Felipe. "Nothing could have happened to him."

"Something's happened to Lolo," David repeats.

"Tonight our story has to be short, kids."

"You promised a long one."

"When did I promise that?"

"You promised the other day."

"First let's see what you'd like me to tell you."

"David and Pinchot."

"I told you that one last week. Why not the one about Emiliano and the Magic Wheat?"

"The Dragon Pinchot. We want the Dragon Pinchot."

"It has to be the one about the Dragon Pinchot. That's a long one. After the day I've had . . . that's all I needed. How about a compromise? I'll just tell you part of it. Then the rest of it tomorrow."

"Whatever you say."

"Whatever I say. Right. Buyers. You kids are real bandits."

"Telephone," says Felipe.

"It's for you, David," says Juana. "Chile."

"Once upon a time, long ago, long long ago, thousands and thousands of years ago, when mankind was young and weak, there was a land called Tsil. We don't know much about that land. If you visit it now, you find sea and mountains and beautiful fields and people who love to laugh and dance. But back then they were very foolish. They fought among themselves, kicking up an infernal racket, or at least so the legend goes. Just let one of them say 'blue' and somebody else would say that yellow was the prettiest color. They didn't agree on anything. Just like you. Arguing all day long."

"But we're good."

"They were good too. They had some faults, like everybody, they made some mistakes, but nothing to make anybody think they'd be punished by such a terrible plague as the Dragon Pinchot."

"Who sent him, huh? Who sent the dragon?"

"David," says Felipe. "What's wrong, David? What happened?"

"Some people say he came from outside, from up north. Others say he was born right there, that he was up in the mountains, sleeping, and that the people's arguing woke him up. Some others say he was made by taking a little piece of heart from every inhabitant of the land and that's why he was so strong. Because he had an eye, an ear, or a claw in every man, woman, and child. In any case, what is for sure is that he had the power to see everything. There wasn't a corner anywhere that his gaze didn't reach and his voice was so powerful and persistent, so evil, that it invaded everybody's thoughts and forced all the people to sing the same chorus. And his claws. If you could have seen his claws! They shot out thunderbolts and lightning and bullets. He was so strong he could kill from a distance. Take David. He had run away to a foreign land, but the Dragon commanded that his hand be devoured and it was gobbled up just like that."

"And couldn't they kill him?"

"The people were all afraid, because they thought he was immortal. And because there was a rumor. A strange rumor. That whoever killed the Dragon Pinchot would first have to be dead himself."

"But that's impossible."

"That was the rumor, kids. Only a dead man could kill the Dragon. And to top it all off, do you think the men and women of Tsil had learned to agree and to speak in a single voice, all together? Not a chance. They kept right on arguing, getting angry at each other, saying it was the other people's fault the Dragon had come. One group would hardly have planned an attack when the others would say it was better not to take the risk, that soon they might convince him to go away of his own accord. Others thought he was about to die and that human beings would live thousands of years longer than dragons, so it was just a question of waiting. And there were even some who said the Dragon really wasn't so bad and that at least now the people were too afraid to fight and to kick up such an uncommon fuss all the time."

"That's so stupid."

"Of course, they seem stupid to us. But maybe they didn't know he was a dragon. Pinchot was an expert at disguise, at presenting himself as a benefactor."

"How did he disguise himself?"

"Sometimes as a grandmother, or as a king, or maybe as the sun, but always as good things. And he had his magic breath too. His breath."

"Magic breath?"

"Miss, could you tell us when the first connecting flight to Santiago is? . . . That's right, miss. Santiago, Chile."

"Anybody who breathed in the Dragon's breath for more than seven years joined his service forever. People in Tsil tried not to breathe, they tried breathing in air from the past, but that air was running out and there still wasn't any air coming from the future, so without their even realizing it, the Dragon was taking over their minds and their wills. When the Dragon finished hoarding all the air in the country, he was going to begin the conquest of other lands, other atmospheres, and other skies. That's why David had run away from his country. To keep from suffocating."

"David could kill the Dragon."

"Quite the contrary. Anybody would have said David was the last person to undertake that struggle. After all, he only had one hand and he was far away from the magical land of Tsil, far away from his family."

"You wouldn't go away without us, would you?"

"Of course not. Neither Mommy nor Daddy are going anywhere. But things were different then. They were strange. Look, I'm going to explain. Do you know what it means to be hungry?"

"You mean when we feel like eating."

"But what if there was nothing to eat when you felt like eating? For days and days? Back then children sat down to eat and there wasn't anything. That's real hunger."

"The Dragon ate all the food and drank all the air and there wasn't anything left for anybody else!"

"That's why David had left. He was hungry. And afraid to breathe the Dragon's breath. But he was just an ordinary man, nobody special. He only had one quality that could be called out of the ordinary. Do you know what it was?"

"We know, but tell us again."

"Did he fall asleep?" asks Juana.

"He has his eyes closed, but I don't think he's asleep," says Felipe.

"You shouldn't leave him alone," says Juana.

"He says he wants to be alone, that he wants to sleep," says Felipe.

"You shouldn't listen to him," says Juana.

"His love for his son Alejandro, that was it. He loved his son more than anything else in the world."

"Like a mommy? Like that?"

"Like a mommy and like a daddy. Just like that."

"He never punished his little boy?"

"Just a minute now. If his son misbehaved, of course he punished him. If he hadn't he wouldn't have really loved him . . . But David hadn't seen Alejandro for many years. David's greatest fear was that his son would end up breathing so much of the Dragon's breath he'd join his service and they'd end up being enemies when he went back, that he wouldn't even recognize his own son. David was so worried, he went to visit his friend Felipe, to convince him it was necessary to go back to the land of Tsil, taking along with them air from the future, that between them they should go into the future to look for new air."

"And was the land of the future far away?"

"It was really close, right there in fact, just around the corner, but it was hard to find the door. You would go in, and without your even knowing how it happened, just like that, you were back in the past, repeating the same old gestures. The future can turn into the past in the snap of a finger."

"And did Felipe know how to get there?"

"Felipe was a great warrior. Just imagine, he'd been Pinchot's prisoner and in all those years he hadn't taken a breath. Not one. To keep from being contaminated. And now he was planning an expedition against the Dragon. His plan was tremendous, really heroic. He was prepared to poison himself, to offer himself to the Dragon whole, hard and stiff, to slide down his throat and when he reached deep into his internal caverns to release the malevolent fluid, thus killing himself along with Pinchot. That's the way he planned to fulfill the prophecy. Felipe wasn't afraid of anybody. But, according to him, the moment had not yet come. The Dragon had to be weakened first, his rivers had to be dried up, his pastures withered, his food supply cut off, and then and only then could he be destroyed from within. Up to then David had been waiting patiently. But all of a sudden . . . when he was visiting Felipe and arguing with him, he was advised that something serious had happened to his son.

"What had happened to him?"

"And what if they turn him back at the border?" asks Juana.

"He won't have any problems," says Felipe.

"They're capable of refusing him entry," says Juana. "It's happened before."

"Believe me," says Felipe. "He won't have any problems."

"What had happened to him? Well, if I tell you, it'll spoil the story for you and you won't like that, right?"

"No it won't. We'll still love it."

"Tsil was a long way off in those days, so they weren't really sure what had happened. But what they told him was that Alejandro was dead, that he had run out of all the air from the past and, to keep from serving Pinchot, he had taken his own life. David refused to believe it. He pretended it was true, but down deep he didn't believe it. He believed Alejandro was wounded, wounded but still alive, inside the Dragon's guts. He believed that if he went back with a little air from the future, he'd be able to rescue him. That even if Alejandro was serving the Dragon, a little bit of air from the land of the future would be enough to save him. And so he left."

"With Felipe?"

"Felipe was sure David was going to breathe the Dragon's air, that he wouldn't be strong enough to hold enough air in his lungs to return him cleanly to Tsil. And then, he thought that when he, Felipe, returned for the final battle, he'd find David on the enemy's side too."

"So who was right? Who was right?"

"Did you tell him you're going back too?" asks Juana. "That you'll be back there in April?"

"I'm not going back with him," says Felipe. "I'm returning clandestinely. I'll be illegal there."

"Did you tell him?" Juana asks again.

"I can't tell him those things," Felipe says.

"OK. That's as far as the story goes today."

"You're not going to tell us the end?"

"It's too long. I'll go on tomorrow."

"We won't be able to sleep."

"Why not?"

"Because we don't know what happened. Whether they killed the Dragon or not. Whether David found the air from the future. Whether Felipe got there in time."

"All fairy tales have a happy ending. Right?"

"But sometimes you change the ending, so we won't know how it's really going to turn out . . ."

"Now who's not keeping promises? Huh? Enough of this. Off to sleep with you now."

"But what if the end's not pretty?"

"So you want the end to be pretty, do you?"

"Yeah."

"Well, you have to go to sleep then. And while you're sleeping, kids, breathe a lot in the direction of the past. Blow really hard, and let's see if a little bit of your air will reach David and Felipe. It's air from the future, after all. Isn't it?"

"But what if the Dragon comes?"

* * *

"Then you're not going to be able to see him back there?" says Juana.

"Impossible," says Felipe.

"It'd be good for him," says Juana, "to have a friend's support."

"Impossible," says Felipe. "It'd be too dangerous."

"I'm never able to sleep," says Juana, "whenever you're back there. You will be careful this time, won't you?"

"I can take care of myself," says Felipe.

"You men always say that," says Juana. "But I still won't sleep a wink."

"The Dragon knows you breathe air from the future too. So he won't come. He's afraid. And there's something else. If you dream sweet dreams, the air becomes fresh and so clean that it's sure to reach the land of Tsil. No doubt about it. Dreams go everywhere."

"That Dragon will really be afraid."

"Good night, kids. Sleep well."

And thirty thousand years later those voices say:

"Good night, Mommy."

The last scene of the first episode of the soap opera takes place in the same place as the first one: the Mexico City airport. But this time in the International Terminal. On camera, Felipe and David. They're standing very close to each other, so close they could be touching, almost embracing. But they don't touch and they don't embrace. Back view of Felipe. His face can't be seen. Raising his hand to wave good-bye. David, facing the camera. As the episode draws to an end the camera comes closer and closer, focusing in on David's face.

"David's face?" asks the actor. "What should his face show?"

"Sadness," says the director. "Sadness. But something else too. Something I can't get a handle on. I don't know what to call it."

"Defiance?" the actor will ask.

"No, that's not it either."

"Rage?"

"No, not that. Felipe would feel rage, but that's not the way I see David."

"Self-pity?"

"I don't think so. The guy tends to complain a lot, but not now."

"Hope?" the actor will ask. "Should there be something like hope in his eyes?"

"There's no reason for him to be hopeful," says the director. "But call it that, if you want."

"Hope?" the actor will ask again.

"I still don't know what to call it," says the director.

THIRD EPILOGUE

Pamela's grandsons and granddaughters often told us about their grandmother's long wait at the elevator in the old building where the son of Manuel Sendero had arranged their meeting. Outside, the city was swelling with soldiers and tanks, searching for something or someone, and even though she suspected it might be him, her beloved, they were looking for, she refused to accept the idea that those circumstances or any others might be enough to prevent his coming.

As if the very fact of harboring doubts about their meeting would be a sign that it would never take place, she went on suppressing any spark of the doubt that had been gnawing at her. Ever since she was a little girl she'd been nourished on the ever-changing story of the man who'd been her lover's father. She'd drunk it in at the feet of her own adoptive father, who, for better or worse, had been one of the few witnesses, along with Skinny, not of the last song itself, but of Manuel Sendero's proclaimed intention to produce it. If Manuel hadn't come to see him after the affair in the Laboratory, after what they did to Doralisa and to their child, everyone would certainly have listened—they had no choice—to the song. But very few would've attributed it to him, because it was a well-known fact that what was inside his throat was a desert and certainly not flowers. Don Ramón and Skinny could confirm—and what better guarantee than the word of two men of their stature—that that desert was blossoming, that he had announced the epic deed himself so it would be known.

The people accepted that version with a rush of excitement and went about the cantabile task of spreading it. The popular interpretation could not have been more biting or more melodramatic. They had murdered his son. They had violated his wife in an act more loathsome than rape, everybody said. But our Manuel Sendero who art in our dreams, instead of going off to die, had started to sing like a man who was finally on his rocker. Yes, that's right. And they searched for him and he kept on singing, fiercely pedaling his bicycle. Yes, sir. And then they disappeared him. Yes, sir. And he kept on singing, and he'll keep on, so they say, until all of us can sing it too and thus can give him back the son he lost serving our cause and until all of us come out of the nothingness to which they've relegated us. That's how it had been. Yes, sir. I saw him with my very own eyes, singing with his Doralisa along the streets as if to wake the dead.

Pamela had repeated that legend like any other child, to give her strength when things were going badly and nobody understood her, to be able to smile a little when the darkness was getting heavier and the monsters were lurking there, to invoke the saint of the Senderos, who was the saint of the pathways, to come to her aid in the midst of dangers, to keep the earth from swallowing her, and to cure her toothaches. She would've liked for Manuel to have sung and to have been able to save his little boy. That's the way kids are, so tender, or maybe it's cowardly and wise. But she vaguely understood, with a childish chill that wouldn't go away, that it was impossible to save both things, his throat and his offspring, and with the irresponsibility born of her age, she had managed to forget, as did Manuel Sendero himself in the course of his existence, that sometimes in our lives fate demands that we choose. What Pamela did not expect was that in her own joyful person she'd have to confront that legitimate thunderbolt that was the son of Manuel Sendero. She could only think that the mistake must stem from the confused transmission of the story and not in any way from that undeniable and glorious body that encompassed her nights and regaled her days, and she decided with that inborn optimism that her grandchildren would come to admire in her, that someday, when he'd lost the touchiness that his brutal reunion with Skinny had produced, when he'd gained enough in self-confidence to accept an invitation to plunge his exuberant tongue into Mama Teresa's cooking, the time would also come for them, together with Pamela's adoptive family, to explore the network of rumors and errors that had supposed the child to be dead when in fact he was very much alive and more than kicking, as Pamela knew in every magnolia of her being, right there beside her. With such overwhelming proof on her side, it wasn't hard for her to banish the contradictions between the story in which the son had to die and the very real streets and her own historic bed, in both of which that son had just been resurrected. Sometimes the people adorn and deform and re-form stories that way, superimposing and shifting and outlining until the singer is more heroic, the enemy more ruthless, the sacrifice more exemplary, and the reward, someday, the best in the world. Or something like that. And such a fantasy was not unusual among parentless children like Pamela. The one responsible for the confusion was that crafty Manuel Sendero who, in order to save his newborn son from the reprisals that his magnificent rebellion would bring down upon them, had himself spread the story of the little one's death, giving him into the care of some Papa Ramón with another name but identical generosity, or some Mama Teresa of less ample skirts but equally succulent hands, for them to raise until the time came when his return could be carried out with no fear of revenge from the Caballero. Pamela had even asked herself—as others imagine, who has not?, that they're the children of some emperor or the grandchildren of some queen—whether she herself or one of her orphaned brothers and sisters might not be the hidden fruit of the love of Manuel and Doralisa.

However it was, for one reason or another, whether it was from the decoration added in the mouth-to-mouth of folklore or from his own father's personal strategy, the son of Manuel Sendero had managed to escape the death assigned him in the fatalistic gossip and the chitchat of the people. It had to be that, said Grandmother Pamela, rubbing her hand across her wondrous belly. It had to be that or something even more marvelous: somehow Grandfather had been able to find a hideaway in the supposedly empty and in fact clean and hygienic womb of the Doralisa of his torments and had remained there all those years. Because the only thing for certain and sure is that the son of Manuel Sendero had come to her a first time and she would not accept the possibility that he would not come a second time, like Noah's ark laden with animals and seeds and fruits, until together they would found the hope of a third and final insurrection of bodies, which, if now they were adults, had once, they say, been children. Like the last song of his father, her Senderito would rise above the real live danger posed by the Caballero, would elude the patrols that were surrounding the building, and she would be there waiting in the prearranged body and in the prearranged place at the hour when the sun was going down.

Like the last song of his father.

Was that why she went to see her papa Ramón first? Was it to offer her lover and eventual father of the grandchildren who are now telling this tale, the story of the last song, like a trophy or a gift or a temptation, for him to impregnate her once and for all, for him to see that even the cruelest stories have happy endings? Or was it a kind of challenge, as though she wanted once again to compare her adoptive father's version with her own certainty and her own prophecies that the son had survived and was waiting for her in that elevator? Or was it, to take a more plausible and psychological line of explanation, because our Pamela needed the lagoon of some brief company at that moment of tribulation and there was nothing else to do but to hurry along that sun, which, in spite of everything, insisted on waiting until the accustomed hour to fade?

Again? asked Don Ramón. This business of the last song again? I don't believe it. Still interested in fairy tales at your age.

I told him, you little girls who now keep me company in weaving the tapestry of my old age, I told him it was so I could tell you, my grandsons and granddaughters.

Are you already so much in love? said Papa Ramón. So much so that you don't even have any kids and you already want to tell stories to your grandchildren? OK. He gave in and agreed to tell the story again. He interrupted the story from time to time to walk over to the window, watching the movements of the soldiers over the face of the city or listening to a military airplane flying low overhead or to a distant rattling of bullets. They're looking for somebody, he said. It's a lot like the night Manuel came to see us. I didn't expect him, Pamela. After what they'd done to Doralisa and to her prospective son or daughter, kids, Papa Ramón thought, after that, we would have bet it was all over. If he hadn't sung before, to save his family, why was he going to do it afterward? If he hadn't wanted or been able to give the world even one little syllable before, because the only thing whistling in his lungs was sadness and he wasn't about to add one more note of melancholy to a universe that already had it in abundance, what possible theme could he find now? Because how can you console a man who's been through all that? Do you tell him everything has or will have a meaning? Do you talk about paradise and brotherhood and the end of exploitation, about life going on in others? Do you show him a seed and a smile? Nothing. There's nothing you can say to a man who's lost what Manuel Sendero had lost.

"Doralisa," said Pamela, "could have said something. A woman could."

But Doralisa was sleeping. There, outside Papa Ramón's door, in the same old cart. There's nothing you can say to a man in that condition, to someone who's considering suicide. We already knew what had happened. One of our informants had a girlfriend who worked in the Laboratory kitchen; another one had gotten a job sweeping the hallways. We had people everywhere; and when they told us about the catastrophe, I thought right away: he'll kill himself. Just like his old friend, Eduardo's father. He's going to go the way of his old friend. One more. Suicide happens a lot in this country, Pamela. The best people end up taking their own lives. Maybe just to show that they control in their own bodies what they don't control in the universe. Their body, the only thing they have left, their last possession. The people's heroes are always martyrs, men and women who enter history by the back door instead of going in the front entrance, and who exercise a strange, posthumous fascination on the consciences of the future because of their act of self-elimination. Manuel Sendero wasn't one of them, no matter what people say. In spite of that, I told Teresa, the death wish must have really won the battle now. You'd better get ready for another funeral, I told her.

I was wrong, little Pamela. If he did destroy himself, it wasn't at all the way I had predicted it. He came to see me that night, as you know, and I heard the screech of brakes, like a bicycle in the street, and it never occurred to me that it could be him, and the door opened and the first thing I noticed was that he hadn't been crying. It was as if he had pulled his eyes out, ground them up, and put them back in the sockets. When I went to embrace him, to offer him the tears he hadn't been able to shed himself, he raised his hand, his fingers long and pale, as if he were showing me the X ray of a hand instead of the hand itself. He held it out, indicating I should come no closer. Maybe he was afraid that the contact of another human being would make him, well, afraid that he'd break down the way children do, who after there's been an accident don't really cry until they see their mothers. He told me to be still, with his hand I mean, to be still, lowering it little by little, as if I were an orchestra and he wanted me to play more softly. I didn't know what to say, what to do. I felt his helplessness as if it were my own. I didn't dare call Teresa, who was taking care of you kids, putting you to bed. The noise could be heard in the other part of the house. It would have been terrible if she had come in followed by a herd of small-fry and savages. Fortunately Skinny turned up at that moment. He must have been following him. He never let him out of his sight, as though Manuel were part of him. Skinny must have been waiting for him at the Laboratory entrance. He must have seen him go by his own building and come out with the bicycle and the cart. Skinny came in like a memory of the hunger we've felt forever, and, as if that were a signal, I started to cry like a baby, one more baby in that house full of kids. Silently, little Pamela. So you wouldn't hear me. So Teresa wouldn't come in. So Manuel wouldn't realize it. I let myself pour out a dry mountain of rage that I was carrying around inside me, asking God why He had abandoned us, knowing that neither I nor anybody else could do anything. That I couldn't even take his future children into my home, so they'd be your brothers. Because he wasn't going to have them.

Then Manuel Sendero spoke the first and only words we had heard from him since his imprisonment. They came out hoarsely, almost bronchially, like a crazy man's asthma or a cough. He didn't have any vocal cords left to say anything, so it was like a tape playing at a very low speed, hardly intelligible, every word fluttering about with a broken wing. Painful, really painful.

"I'm going to sing," said Manuel Sendero, slowly, like a dying man dictating his will. "Tonight."

Even under those circumstances, the truth is that I allowed myself a touch of skepticism. Those few words—he scarcely had the breath to pronounce them and the sound that came out was like the moan of a grieving primate. Every syllable was so long in coming out, so long in joining the next one, that it seemed like centuries, stretching themselves out above and beyond time itself, like a bell that somebody has forgotten to play for thousands of years and that is suddenly struck by a gust of wind, a hand, or a constellation.

But, Grandmother, we asked Pamela, why did Manuel go to the trouble of announcing what he would do? What did he care whether they knew the song was his or thought it was somebody else's?

Pamela had asked Papa Ramón the same thing.

He cared, child. He cared whether the rest of us believed he had sung. And he was right. There are so many people now starting to say he didn't sing, that all that never really happened, asking where the proof is, where all the records and the files are, insisting that Manuel Sendero left this world as defeated as he had been when he got here. So it was good that he still had that little bit of pride, that interest in what other people thought. It was good that he made that announcement.

So how come, then, our grandfather Eduardo says it doesn't really matter whether he sang or not? He says the people rescued and mythified the figure of their singer, that they refused to let the government have its victory, and that it's not bad that that's the way it was, because it would be intolerable for a popular story to end up with Manuel Sendero defeated and dispirited. But that he, at any rate, was not going to be bamboozled. Manuel Sendero sang, says Grandfather Eduardo, because you believe he did, because on that basis the first march against death was called.

Pamela's voice was shaking at that point in the narrative, as she confronted that question. She stood up to stare out into the street where so many years ago the soldiers had gone out to loot the night, and she went on:

"I'm very fond of your grandfather Eduardo. But I think he's wrong. You can't reduce everything to Manuel Sendero's political usefulness. It's not enough to say it's better for the people to think he sang, so we'll all sing a little more. The fact is he announced he was going to do it and there are two faithful witnesses to that fact. And he did do it."

He did it, daughter.

He left the house, and Doralisa's bundled-up figure was awaiting him there, still asleep, so quiet and pale that she seemed to be dead, in the same cart we put her in when Manuel moved, when he left his house. But unlike that night, when he put his muscles to work in the place of a nonexistent horse, this time he had managed to pick up—who knows where he could've gotten those wheels and pedals—something like a bicycle. He left so fast it was impossible to follow him, even though Skinny tried. Tell your grandchildren that, little Pamela. Don't let them ever doubt it.

Pamela did tell them. That very night she started to tell us the life and deeds of Manuel Sendero.

He pedaled that bicycle carrying the still-in-love ashes of the woman he loved so fast and so furiously it was as if he were driven by something more than his own star. He went so fast it must have been impossible for the soldiers to find them till much later that night, almost dawn. Perhaps that's why the song could last so long, kids.

How long did it last, Grandmother?

Hours and hours. Some people say it was days, weeks, months. As the years go by the people keep adding things from the storeroom of their own memories until in the next century they'll probably speak of decades. They'll say he descended into Hell. They'll say Manuel Sendero can still be heard. But Grandmother Pamela was there; she knows the truth: they killed him that same night. She woke up that night terrified and with her heart jumping wildly and she knew they had killed him. It wasn't easy. That song was as slippery as the bicycle, and, if he finally stopped, it must have been to make love to Doralisa and to look into that face that was awakening. And even then it was hard for them to find him because the dark refuge of a woman is the safest place in the world, kids. Impossible, you'll say. Of course it's impossible. A miracle. As impossible, as miraculous as it is for a woman to carry an entirely new and complete life in her womb. As impossible as you are, once not existing and here now listening to this old woman who once was young, to this young woman who is almost a great-grandmother. As impossible as you are, who tomorrow, in your turn, will have children and grandchildren and lovers who will listen when you tell them what Grandmother Pamela did to make sure that you would arrive skeptical and full of trust, glorious, majestic, real.

As impossible as the fact that at sunset I waited for your grandfather, the grandfather of all of us, listening for his footsteps in the hallway leading to that ancient elevator.

I already knew everything I was going to tell him.

"Come," I'd say to him. "One last time."

But, Grandmother, they'll be the footsteps of a man in a hurry, a man they're looking for, a man who has to stay in the doorway, still not crossing the line, his face submerged in the shadows. "How do you know it's the last time?" Grandfather will ask, would ask, if he really comes, Pamela. As if he had already gone far away from you forever. "How do you know?"

Kids, there are some things that women have to know, if they're going to survive in a world like this. I'll get up from the corner where I was waiting for him, and even though he may say, as you believe: "Don't look at me. Close your eyes." Even if he turns his face away, like a bridegroom with his face burned, and I, closing my eyes and drawing him toward my body there in the darkness the way my mother guided my father, in open defiance of those men who were searching for them at that very moment. Do you remember that other night of my parents, kids? Do you remember how she lay on her back, feeling the weight of the earth under her back, the weight of a man of earth between my legs that were her legs? Do you remember how she felt when Papa was on the point of climax, when that man was on the point of crying inside her, how she felt that it was the rain of the eighth day of creation?

He's going to try to withdraw as always, Grandmother.

"No." I'm going to tell you, Senderito, with my eyes closed to keep from hurting you, so you'll really be you in the middle of the nothingness. So you won't disappear. "I want you to stay inside me."

He'll quiet the trembling of his body. He'll take a deep breath. Once. Twice. "They're killing all the others," he'll say. "They're killing them and nobody cares. What would they say?"

What would you say, grandchildren, waiting with me there in the darkness, grandchildren my parents never saw, even though they molded you the way they molded one another, grandchildren who have to create yourselves as you create the world?

"It's worth it," I'm going to tell you, Senderito. I'm going to tell you that, speaking for all of them, "Mama told Papa; Doralisa told Manuel; I'll tell it to you."

"It's worth it?"

"Come," I'll tell him. "Leave me a souvenir," I'll say to him: "They're going to kill you," I'll say to him: "They've killed you once. Now they're going to kill you again and you'll never come back. They'll keep on killing you," I'll tell him, "no matter how many times you return," I'll tell him, with this voice of a woman on the threshold of being a grandmother, talking to him the way I spoke to my unborn grandchildren who refused to leave me alone. "Come," I'll say to him. "If you don't have a son, a daughter, grandchildren, there will be nothing left. Nothing."

He spoke to you with a sadness you'd never seen in him, Grandmother. That is, if he really did speak to you. If he even came. As if he saw a future that was just a replica of the past, some day when he'd have to sacrifice his son too, when he'd also abandon him, leaving us alone to face a Caballero with cold hands. A voice that swore he'd never see the Promised Land. "Nothing will be left of you anyhow," he'll say to you. If the son of Manuel Sendero ever says anything over your blossoming body.

"We'll see about that."

Because Manuel Sendero did sing, and they could also have sworn that there'd be nothing left of him. That's what Papa Ramón thought, watching him disappear toward the horizon of narrow streets with his Doralisa in tow. That's what Skinny thought, smoking a cigarette on his way home. That's what even Pamela must have thought when she went to bed that night early, the way everybody went to bed in a city with a curfew and with truckloads of soldiers intoxicating every street corner.

The next morning she woke up. Everybody woke up. And apparently the world had not been changed by Manuel Sendero's song, his last song. Everything was in its usual place. Just as they had left it the night before, when they went to bed. Pamela watched Mama Teresa open the curtains. A sunbeam curled about a book that was opened to a picture of a panda bear. It was late and there was no time for a pillow fight with her brothers and sisters. Not one speck of the dust of reality had changed. Outside the traffic went on at its usual rhythm beneath the same old billboards and in the presence of the same policemen who had left their houses with clear consciences. Pamela yawned. In the bathroom next door to her room Papa Ramón looked at himself in the mirror, while he was brushing his teeth, and thought: And if only we could change it, if we just had the courage to shout at the top of our lungs that we're wasting our fucking lives, the only goddamned life they gave me. That's what Papa Ramón thought. Along with every other inhabitant in the country. It's what Mama Teresa thought as she prepared the aroma of coffee and cream in the kitchen and yelled at the cat for having messed on the floor. That's what every child in that house thought, along with those in every other house, each in his own way, in his own words. That's what was almost unanimously thought. But far from saying it to anyone else, they were silent. As if they had guessed that the cards were stacked against them ever since the beginning of time. Because in some strange way they had predicted, not only Skinny and Papa Ramón, who knew about Manuel Sendero's warning, but every other decent human being, upon opening his eyes that morning as usual, had found in himself the courage to hope they would find the universe transfigured, like a beach at dawn.

And here it was. Everything the same as usual. As if some dirty divinity had played a trick on them. But that sense of radical dissatisfaction must have kept them company in the hours ahead, because even though the day had gone along with the usual monotony, at some surprising moment—it was brief, passing before they even realized it—they witnessed how their own bodies, acting almost autonomously, dug in for an act of rebellion. It was nothing, if we're talking about sacrilege. Just a slight blasphemy. Something no newspaper would pick up, either in its columns or in its obituaries. Something that only they would have noticed. One of those things we've wanted to do for a long time. That we always promise ourselves we'll do and that we never dare to do. The sort of naked truth you only mutter to the dead or, perhaps, the truth the dead themselves gnaw at you from beyond the barrier. As simple as that. You know what I mean, kids. Everybody has some secret wish, some little unconfessable truth he'd really like to declare, some rule we despise but are too timid or fearful to break, some remote prohibition or some person close to us that makes our lives miserable. So you want me to be more specific, you little rascals? You want me to tell you what I did, who I stuck my tongue out at? That's just the problem. Nobody knows. Because coming back home later, all of a sudden the memory of that incident started to burn my lips. Each one of us was suddenly attacked by the irrepressible need to tell someone else, someone close to us, about his little profanation. And feeling somewhat absurdly a little like warriors or maybe bards returning home to their country after an odyssey of many years, they opened their mouths to speak of their tiny deeds. I opened my mouth to tell Mama Teresa that I had finally, and she opened hers to tell Papa Ramón that she had finally dared to, and Papa Ramón and Skinny and Grandfather Eduardo and all of a sudden, at that instant, yes, at that very instant when they were trying, when I was trying, to communicate that small gesture of courage, just at that moment of anguish, I awoke.

Yes, kids, I awoke. We all awoke at the same mathematical instant. As if somebody had slapped us all in the face. We all woke up, and it was, it was still the night before. Kids, please understand.

That day hadn't really existed in the annals of history. We all looked at our watches in astonishment and we had barely moved ahead a few nocturnal hours. Dawn hadn't even come yet. Among us all we had dreamed and simultaneously created that ordinary day. We woke up to what is called truth and in that world what was really happening wasn't our rebellion or our desire to communicate it. What had obliged us to interrupt our dream was that at that particular juncture of history a bullet had reached Manuel Sendero's song. It must have pierced Doralisa's singing womb in the cart where she was to awaken. It had paralyzed the wheels of the bicycle in some alleyway of the uninhabited city where all the inhabitants were dreaming the same identical everyday dream, where we opened our eyes and there was nothing we could do to save that pair of lovers.

Manuel Sendero's song had for a few hours broken into that private and particular theater with its single spectator, that foreign country we call our dreams. It had placed us like brothers and sisters inside Doralisa's womb, so that all the rivers of sleep would flow together while she was awakening—unborn children, children without secrets, prenuptial and rebellious fetuses. And when they killed her and Manuel and the bicycle, when their pills were scattered forever, we couldn't find the way back to that song. We were seduced, caught up in rememberings, entranced. The memory persisted, little Sendero, worse than if it had figured on calendars. It persisted the way your eyes follow me everywhere.

Each one got up the next day, a day with a date and with a number, the first day since the beginning of the universe where Manuel Sendero was no more, would never be again. Each one woke up and thought there was no reason why this real day shouldn't be their own once again, thought fleetingly that it was enough for one or two or three or more to start singing in a low voice the way Manuel Sendero had, one simultaneous opening of a window was enough, a single gesture from all of them in order to share the rebellion, just as they had dreamed about and shared the world's womb. They suddenly suspected, more than suspected, that the world could be changed, that the world deserved to be changed, that it depended on them and on each one of us to prepare a world where parents would never have to choose between their own dignity and the lives of their children, between those two forms of the future, and to keep that suspicion, that more than a suspicion, from ever leaving their memory, they invented the first march against death.

"And so what?" the son of Manuel Sendero said, would say. "I had to disappear for that?"

And so what, Grandmother? all of us in chorus said. We're not impressed, Grandmother. For that our grandfather had to disappear, had to be satisfied with half an existence, to live only for grumbling and bickering there in the darkness? The people dreamed. Great! Good for them! And when they woke up, what had changed? Tell us that, Grandmother Pamela. Wasn't everything the same as before?

"Nothing will be left," the son of Manuel Sendero would say. "Nothing."

We shall see if nothing is left of you, my little Sendero. We shall see. Come, my little Sendero. Come die here inside me, if you have to die. Come. Come on farther into the sea of motherhood. Come, my little Sendero. Come in. Come here into my secret place. For millions of years fish have been coming there, whales drift toward its warm depths and breed there, floating as if they were on the river of themselves, every living thing mating there, leaving its eggs and its offspring and its nests. Come on down into the sea's bridal bed where anyone can peacefully yield to his children. Come, my little Sendero. There'll be no way to make that child piece by piece, tonight a little nose, tomorrow morning a kidney, rehearsing a finger tomorrow afternoon, another finger in the evening, making him with every act of love so he'll be complete, giving him our love that he'll need to protect himself against the world that never seems to be ours. There's no time, my little Sendero. They're searching for you; they've been searching for you for a million years; we'll have to, him, her, you, you all, grandsons, granddaughters, once and for all, in a single exploration of my twilight there inside, my little Sendero, in the sunlight and the lagoonlike calm of my bed. They leave the little ones there to pasture, unpolluted rivers will flow into the sea of life, the plankton is reshaped as if it were a placenta, the waters carry the serenely and fiercely nourishing earth from the mountains. They leave the children there—you can do it too—knowing they can come back for them later, that no cold wind and no alien hands will enter there nor—and how can they know that? where did they learn it?—can industry's chemicals infect them. They leave them there to grow, a sea that lies blue between the coast and the peninsula as between the two legs of a woman, the little ones sheltered there beyond birth by the guardian waters, by the protective tide. They leave them there the way you hand children over to the extended godfather of an open window, a watery kindergarten, as if they knew—how, where, when did they learn it?—that if something happens to their parents, if something should happen, that sweet inner sea would know what to do with the little ones, would bring the scattered fruits of the sea together. That's how it had been, my little Sendero, before human feet had trod the sands. That's the way it was and still is. The whales come together and copulate like demons in paradise; the crustaceans hide in the shadows of rocks and . . . Come, my little Sendero. Come to my silent nursery and dance. They leave them there, babies, eggs, cells, so they will multiply as they did long ago, dreaming of the ocean that awaits with its waves and its nets and its dangers, out there, the faraway ancestor already dead perhaps, who is waiting for them beyond the bays. They'll depart toward the horizon, which, of course, they never see, because it's above them like a line of water in retreat. They'll depart, knowing—how, where, when, everything except why—they must return from far away with their mates. The fish know, my little Sendero, what we should never have forgotten or what we are perhaps just in the process of discovering, that there are places and there are places, that there are seas that take care of their own, that you must go back to those seas and if they don't exist, then you must create them, my little Sendero; come here and stay with me. You'll have to hide yourself here deep inside my sexual waters, so they won't find you and, from inside there, keep on making them, keep on birthing them, giving names to the fauna and colors to the fruit, wandering in pilgrimage from womb to womb until the end of time, helping us to be born, telling each one about your father's song, telling them that once upon a time there was a bicyclist who never stopped pedaling, telling about the lovers who recognized each other across a street crowded with marchers, about a woman who fed the world when her own little ones died, about a pair of statues who touch each other when a letter arrives, about an immortal uncle who always manages to get away, about my parents who found the way to give me to Ramón like a bitten apple that passes from hand to hand, about a mother who made a pact with her own violator so they wouldn't kill you before, about so many imperfect and incomplete and unfinished human beings who nevertheless are waiting for you in my sweet and infinite foliage. Come, my little Sendero, come, for the soldiers have the building surrounded again and again, come, because you'll have to blow into the unborn child's ear as it is being formed, don't leave him alone. Tell him what he should do so that you can finally be born, so that along with him you will be born a little. It doesn't matter if he forgets it in passage; it doesn't even matter if I forget it. Am I not receiving you? Aren't you entering your own woman? Tell them everything, my little Sendero, so that later it'll be hard for them to repeat a lie, so that the sight of poverty will chill their blood, so that they won't be afraid to die, so that the last thing they'll see before they come out into the world, my little Sendero, the last thing they'll see is you there in the bright darkness full of children.

And what happened, Grandmother? What happened then?

Don't you remember, kids? Don't you remember how he became so tiny no soldier could find him? How the soldiers came and were outside the building waiting for him, but it was impossible for them to find him? Don't you remember how he paid no attention to the generals' orders for him to stop, paid no attention to their orders for him to die, for him to disappear, and how he turned into the river that was his own body entering my body, became a cell, became the sun and refused to withdraw, stayed there inside, with all of you, there in the infinite garden inside me? Don't you remember, kids? Don't you remember the stories he told you? Don't you remember how he preached the third and the fourth and the twentieth rebellion to you? Don't you remember how he described the Caballero so you'd beware? Don't you remember that voice of the father of himself and of his own fire that never goes out? Not ever?

No, Grandmother. What we remember is that you heard footsteps in the hallway, footsteps that sounded familiar, probably an adult's footsteps. That's the way they told us this story.

You touched your belly, Pamela, like a woman about to become pregnant, you rubbed your hand across your still smooth belly, Grandmother. And when you spoke, it was your voice, Grandmother, the one we've always known, but also a nuptial voice that we'd never heard before, another woman's voice, a woman who awakes in the middle of the night without anyone ever knowing it or appreciating it, just to comfort her child, and it was your mother's voice, Pamela, when she told your father it was all worth it, in spite of those beings who were waiting for her in a car with the motor running on a nearby street, and it was the voice of a wombless Doralisa, still dreaming with her eyes open about the day when the men would be the ones who would have to give birth, and meanwhile, not to add to Manuel's pain, lying to him, saying yes, it was worth it, until an instant before the bullets silenced her she tried to believe her own lie and whispered softly and fully awake to Pamela, who was sleeping somewhere in the city like a lost child, that yes, it was worth it, it is worth it, it will be worth it, but more than anything and above everything else in this world the voice we heard was new and was the voice of our mother, who is rehearsing her first song for the grandfather who nine months later she will have to begin to bring into this world.

"Sendero?" said Pamela. "My little Sendero? Is that you?"

PART V

Bearings

LAST EPILOGUE AND FIRST PROLOGUE

"Now I heard the story," said Eduardo. "Now I know where Pamela is. And I'm going to get her. But there's something I don't understand. What does he expect me to do?"

"The only thing he asks of you," the blind woman said slowly, giving him his whole lifetime to understand, "is to care for his children as if they were your own."

"As if they were my own," said Eduardo, thinking that it takes more than nine months for countries to be born. And he added, without realizing that it's true for some human beings as well: "I make no promises."

But it seemed like a promise to us, from afar, and maybe something more than a promise, that our stepfather and father, Eduardo, was going to care for us. I dared believe that he'd care for Manuel Sendero's many grandchildren as if they were his own.

Let's wait and let's hope, we'll keep on hoping that that's the way it is.

Sue P—
Thurs AM
US air via Charlotte
to G'boro

Monday AM / Sun eve'g / flights from G'boro to Tampa

Bobbie — Fac. Ctr — Fri. night
Sept. 18th — 7:30 P.M.

{ meet at Green's Crossing at 5:00PM
Friday, Aug. 22 }